LARRY BOND'S
Red Dragon Rising

**Forge Books by
Larry Bond and Jim DeFelice**

Larry Bond's First Team

Larry Bond's First Team: Angels of Wrath

Larry Bond's First Team: Fires of War

Larry Bond's First Team: Soul of the Assassin

Larry Bond's Red Dragon Rising: Shadows of War

Larry Bond's Red Dragon Rising: Edge of War

Larry Bond's Red Dragon Rising: Shock of War

LARRY BOND'S
Red Dragon Rising

SHOCK OF WAR

LARRY BOND
AND JIM DeFELICE

A TOM DOHERTY ASSOCIATES BOOK

NEW YORK

LARRY BOND'S RED DRAGON RISING: SHOCK OF WAR

Copyright © 2011 by Larry Bond and Jim DeFelice

A Forge Book
Published by Tom Doherty Associates, LLC
175 Fifth Avenue
New York, NY 10010

www.tor-forge.com

Forge® is a registered trademark of Tom Doherty Associates, LLC.

Library of Congress Cataloging-in-Publication Data

Bond, Larry.
    Larry Bond's red dragon rising : shock of war / Larry Bond and Jim
DeFelice. — 1st ed.
        p. cm.—(Red dragon rising)
    "A Tom Doherty Associates book."
    ISBN 978-0-7653-2139-8
    1. Intelligence officers—Fiction.   2. International relations—Fiction.
I. DeFelice, Jim, 1956–   II. Title.   III. Title: Red dragon rising.   IV. Title:
Shock of war.
    PS3552.O59725S56 2012
    813'.54—dc23

                                                                    2011024950

First Edition: January 2012

Printed in the United States of America

0   9   8   7   6   5   4   3   2   1

The term "global warming" is as misleading as it is inaccurate. True, the overall temperature of the earth as measured by annual average readings will rise. But averages tell us next to nothing. A shortening of a rainy season by two weeks in a given area might be reflected by an increase in the average annual temperature of only a third of a degree. But the impact on the water supply—and thus the growing season—would be considerably higher.

Paradoxically, rapid climate change may bring much lower temperatures in many places. It should also be noted that some changes may well benefit people in the affected areas, at least temporarily, by extending growing seasons, negating weather extremes, or having some other unpredictable effect.

Unfortunately, the sensationalistic term, combined with the slow evolution of the effects prior to the crisis point, will make it hard to convince the general population of the true danger.

—Int. Soc. of Environmental Scientists report

Major Characters

United States

Josh MacArthur, scientist
Mara Duncan, CIA officer
Peter Lucas, CIA chief of station, Bangkok/Southeast Asia
Major Zeus Murphy, former SF captain, adviser to Vietnam People's Army
Lieutenant Ric Kerfer, SEAL Team platoon commander
President George Chester Greene
CIA Director Peter Frost
National Security Adviser Walter Jackson

China

Lieutenant Jing Yo, commander, First Commando Detachment
*Colonel Li Sun, Commando Regiment commander, executive officer Task
    Force #1*
Premier Cho Lai

Vietnam

Premier Lein Thap
General Minh Trung, head of the Vietnam People's Army

February 2014

Commodity Prices—Chicago Board of Trade

COMMODITY	PRICE	1 YEAR AGO	5 YEARS AGO (2009)
Crude Oil	$735.87	$700.13	$74.86
Corn	$1,573	$1,234	$723
Wheat	$3,723	$1,534	$812
Rough Rice	$896	$310	$20.20

Average February Temperatures—Major World Cities

	(Celsius)			
CITY	HIGH	LOW	2009 average high	2009 average low
Washington, D.C.	13.0	3.2	8.2	−1.2
Beijing	30.2	5.0	4.2	−7.0
Tokyo	12.3	3.0	9.2	0.1
Rome	16.5	5.2	13.5	4.7
Johannesburg	19.1	7.5	24.8	14.7

Personal Chronicle: Looking Back to 2014 . . .

Markus:

In the late winter of 2014, your uncle Josh had stunned the world by appearing at the United Nations in New York City, telling the world how he had seen Chinese soldiers slaughter his scientific team and dozens of Vietnamese peasants. He brought back video and pictures. They were horrible images—little children dead, a nursing mother . . . I feel sick when I think of them. The images are burned into my brain.

But even with this evidence, the people of the world were not convinced that the Chinese were a great threat that had to be stopped. Their leader, Premier Cho Lai, was an evil man, but he was very clever. He plotted to undermine the evidence that your uncle had brought back. And to kill him and the people who helped him escape.

But that was just our own personal tragedy.

The whole world teetered on the brink of war. Far away in Southeast Asia, Vietnam was about to be overrun. A few ships from the American Navy, and a handful of advisers from the Army, were all that stood in the way. . . .

Lies

1

Beijing

Premier Cho Lai watched the American on the video screen dispassionately, willing himself to study the man and what he said with the mind of a scientist and observer. The American's message was one of venom, directed at Cho and his people, the Chinese country, and especially the Chinese army. It made Cho boil with anger and lust for vengeance. He wanted with all his heart to punch his hand through the video screen, to smash it—or better, to punch through the screen and somehow take this Josh MacArthur by his skinny, blotchy neck and strangle him. Cho could almost feel the boy's thorax collapsing beneath his hands.

Boy.

That was what he was. Not a scientist, not a man—a boy. A rodent. Scum.

No one would take him seriously if not for the images he'd brought back. They flashed on the screen as the scum's voice continued to speak. The Chinese translation played across the bottom of the screen, but Cho had no need for it; he spoke English reasonably well, and in any event the images themselves told the story.

All of his careful planning to make the invasion look as if the Vietnamese had instigated the war was threatened by this scum. It mattered nothing to Vietnam—Vietnam would be crushed no matter what the world thought. China needed its rice and oil, and it would have it.

But this threatened the next step. For Cho knew that his country's appetite was insatiable. The people who thronged the streets of Beijing not far from his compound were desperately short of food. Keeping them satisfied was an impossible task.

Impossible for anyone but him. The last two governments had toppled in rapid succession, each lasting less then two short months thanks to food riots and dissension. Cho had used the unrest to maneuver himself to power, promising to end the disturbances. He would remain in power only as long as he could keep that promise. It was not that he had any enemies—the most prominent had met unfortunate accidents over the past few months, or else been exposed in corruption trials, or, in a few cases, bought off with timely appointments outside the country. But as his own rise had shown, it was not the prominent one who had to fear in the chaos of the moment; it was the obscure. Cho had risen from a job as lieutenant governor for agriculture in the parched western provinces. Two years before, no one in Beijing would even have known his name. Now they bowed to him.

As the world would.

But first, this danger must be dealt with. America, the world, must not be brought into the conflict. The giant must not be wakened, until it was too late for it to stop the inevitable momentum of Chinese conquest.

Cho snapped off the video. He had seen enough.

2

Hainan Island, China

Major Zeus Murphy tried not to look too conspicuous as he walked down the concourse toward his flight. In theory, he had nothing to fear: the United States and China were not at war, and while his U.S. passport had caused a few seconds of hesitation at the security gate, the check of his baggage had been perfunctory at best. But theory and reality did not always mesh, especially in this case: the war between China and Vietnam had greatly strained relations between the two countries, and even in the best times Chinese customs officials and local police were not exactly known for being evenhanded when dealing with citizens from other countries.

And in this case, Zeus had a little extra to fear: he had just led a guerilla operation against the Chinese naval fleet gathered in the harbor, hopefully preventing it from launching an attack against the Vietnamese.

He could see the red glow of distant flames reflecting in the dark glass of the passageway as he walked toward the gate. Too much time had passed for the fire to be on one of the boats they had blown up; Zeus suspected instead it was due to friendly fire, panic set off by the supposed attack of Vietnamese submarines on the landing ships that were gathered in the port.

All for the better.

A television screen hung on the wall near the gate ahead. Zeus slowed down to get a look. In the U.S., it would be set to a local or all-news station; by now it would be carrying live feeds from the attack, breathless correspondents warning of the coming apocalypse. Here it showed some sort of Chinese soap opera, or maybe a reality show; he couldn't quite tell and didn't want to make himself too conspicuous by stopping.

He passed two more screens as he walked. Both were set to Chinese financial news stations. Though it was night here, it was still daytime in the U.S., and tickers showed stock prices across the bottom.

A lot of red letters and down arrows, Zeus noticed. War wasn't good for anyone's economy.

"I thought you'd never get here," said Win Christian, who rose from a seat across from the television.

Christian was also a major, was also in the U.S. Army, and had also just helped blow up part of the invasion fleet. The two men had snuck ashore with the help of a Vietnamese agent, assumed identities as businessmen, and headed for the easiest way out—a Chinese flight to Hong Kong, and from there to Japan.

Zeus nodded. They'd gotten into different lines at the security checkpoint, splitting up in case they were stopped.

"Where's the girl?" Christian asked, referring to the Vietnamese agent, Solt Jan.

"I thought she was with you," answered Zeus.

Christian seemed even more nervous than he had earlier. Fidgeting, his eyes shifted continually, glancing in every direction. "I hope she didn't bail."

"We got our tickets. Relax."

Christian glanced around. There were about forty people at the gate, waiting for the 11 p.m. flight to Hong Kong. The destination was written in English as well as Chinese on a whiteboard that sat on an easel next to the podium in front of the door to the plane tunnel. The door was closed, and the podium itself was roped off by a velvet-covered chain. There were no attendants nearby.

Zeus glanced at his watch.

"Half hour before boarding," he told Christian. "Let's get something to eat."

"You think that's wise?"

Zeus started toward a kiosk about ten meters away in the center of the gate area. Maybe some food would calm Christian down.

"Guess it can't be any worse than Vietnamese food," said Christian, catching up.

Zeus closed his eyes at the word *Vietnamese*. He glanced at Christian, who'd turned beet red.

"I know," muttered Christian almost inaudibly. "Sorry."

Zeus didn't reply. At least Christian realized he'd been an idiot; they were making progress.

The vendor was a few years younger than Zeus, twenty-one or twenty-two at most. Zeus pointed at a bag of American-style potato chips.

"Ten yuan," said the young man in English.

Zeus dug into his pocket. Solt had given him some Chinese money on the way over. He had some American money in his wallet as well—fifty dollars, barely enough to bribe the passport control people in Hong Kong, which would be necessary to get to Tokyo since his passport lacked the proper visa stamps.

"Here are your crisps," said the man, using the British term for the snack as he handed them over.

"I'll have a bag, too," said Christian.

The man kept his eyes locked on Zeus's. It was a menacing stare, a dare.

Why?

"My change," said Zeus.

The man's mouth twisted into a smile. Zeus held out his hand. The man looked down at it, and for a moment Zeus thought he was going to spit. Instead, he reached into the cash register. He took a bill and some coins, then dropped them into Zeus's outstretched palm.

Zeus locked his eyes on the man, not even bothering to count the change.

"All of it," he said.

The clerk's smile broadened. He reached into the register and fished out the right change, placing it into Zeus's hand.

"What the hell was that about?" Christian asked as they walked back to the gate.

"Got me," said Zeus.

"He spoke English pretty well."

"Yeah," said Zeus. "Good enough."

An airline employee had appeared at the podium and was fiddling with a microphone. She began to speak as Zeus and Christian approached. A few passengers got up from their seats; the rest looked anxiously toward her as she continued.

"What's she saying?" Christian asked.

"I didn't learn to speak Chinese in the last twenty minutes," snapped Zeus. "Did you?"

He reached into his pocket for his ticket, expecting she was trying to organize the boarding—probably asking for people with small children first. But no one moved forward.

A short, balding man near the gate began speaking to the woman, haranguing her in slightly angry Chinese. Zeus turned around, looking for Solt. She should have met them by now.

Admittedly, she hadn't told him that she'd been on the flight; he'd just assumed that when she pressed the ticket into his hand in the lobby before disappearing in the crowd.

"They're not moving," said Christian. "What's going on?"

"Flight cancel," said a grim-faced man nearby. He added something in Chinese.

"Excuse me," said Zeus. "The flight's canceled? Why?"

The man shook his head.

Zeus tried repeating the question, phrasing it more simply and speaking slower. "Why is the flight canceled?"

"Flight cancel," said the man. "Problem at airport. All flight."

"Shit," said Christian.

"Is it temporary?" asked Zeus.

Again, the man shook his head, not understanding. The passengers at the podium moved closer to the woman, apparently asking questions.

"Do you know . . . the next flight? When?" asked Zeus, trying to simplify what he wanted to know. "Is there another flight?"

The man said something in Chinese. Zeus didn't understand the words, but the meaning itself was clear: He had no idea.

Most of the people at the gate remained in their seats. Zeus guessed that the airline was making other arrangements, and they had been told to wait.

Or maybe not. Maybe the entire airport was closed. Maybe they thought they were under attack.

He told himself to calm down, to relax and think it through. He was a businessman, not a saboteur—be aggravated, annoyed, not alarmed.

"What are we going to do?" Christian asked.

"I'll ask what the story is," said Zeus. "Maybe some of the airline people speak English. Come on."

"Right behind you," hissed Christian.

They joined the small knot of people near the attendant. Zeus stood patiently, hoping to hear someone speaking English. He didn't.

The people around him were mostly men, speaking quickly and not very politely. The woman fended them off with short bursts, giving as good as she got. It struck him that she was speaking the universal language of airline gate attendants: *Sorry, you're shit out of luck.*

"Excuse me," said Zeus as the cacophony around him hit a lull. "Do you speak English?"

"Flight cancel," said the woman.

"Why?"

She turned to another passenger, who was saying something else. By the time she turned back in Zeus's direction, it was obvious she had forgotten what he had said.

"Is there another flight?" asked Zeus. "Will there *be* another flight? To Hong Kong."

"Oh, yes."

"When is the flight?"

Again she started to turn away to answer a different passenger. Zeus reached forward and touched her arm. The woman jerked back.

"I'm sorry," said Zeus. "When is the flight?"

"No flight," said the woman. She added something in Chinese, then began answering a man to Zeus's right.

Deciding he wasn't going to get any more information from her, Zeus took a few steps back.

The first order of business was to look for Solt Jan. Zeus turned to his left and faced the large aisle at the center of the gate area. He began scanning the faces of the crowd, examining each one in turn. The Vietnamese agent was a small woman, thin and petite. *Pretty* and petite. Dark hair, exotic looks: Asian and something else as well, probably Western, French maybe, or even Scandinavian.

Zeus turned almost completely around without spotting her.

"What do you think?" Christian's voice trembled.

"She must have gone back into the city," said Zeus. "It's just as well; they might suspect her. Let's just play this through. We find an airline person who speaks English. We're businessmen, stranded because of our flight. Just play it through."

"What if we can't get to Hong Kong?"

Zeus shook his head. There were plenty of alternatives.

"I don't like this," said Christian.

"Here. Have some crisps."

Zeus held the top of the bag in his two hands and began pulling the sides apart slowly, trying to keep the bag intact as he ripped it. It required a certain amount of finesse, strength, and restraint at the same time.

The bag top separated cleanly. He held the chips out to Christian. "Here," he said. "Have one."

Someone tapped Zeus from behind. He spun around, surprised.

"You are Mr. Murphy," said a short man in a Chinese army uniform. It didn't sound like a question.

"Excuse me?"

"You are Murphy?"

Zeus hesitated. If he said no and the man asked for his passport, then what would he do? Run?

Zeus looked at his uniform. It was light tan. He was an officer, a captain.

What did the insignia mean? Air force?

Would the airline have sent him?

We're not at war. Relax.

The officer started to put out his hand; Zeus guessed that he was about to ask for his ID.

"I'm Murphy," he admitted.

The Chinese officer said nothing, turning instead to Christian.

"You are Christian," he said.

Christian had nearly crossed his eyes. He looked at Zeus, undoubtedly wondering why the hell he had agreed.

Play it through, Zeus thought. We're businessmen.

"Mr. Christian?" repeated the officer.

"Yes?" said Christian finally.

"You are to come with me."

The officer turned sharply. Two other men, these in blue uniforms, stood a short distance away, watching. Zeus noticed that they had unsnapped to the protective strap at the top of their holsters, allowing free access to their sidearms.

"What's going on?" asked Christian.

The officer stopped abruptly. He wore a deep frown.

"You will follow me," he said again, in a voice that brooked no argument.

3

UN building, New York City

Josh MacArthur reached into his pocket for a tissue to blow his nose before remembering that he had used the last one a few minutes ago. He closed his eyes as he sneezed, his whole body shaking with the force.

"Allergies," he mumbled, getting up from his seat. "I just . . . need . . . a . . . tish—"

He sneezed before he could finish the sentence.

Mumbling another apology, Josh made his way to the private restroom at the side of the office, pushing through the door as his body was wracked by a quick success of sneezes.

Damn allergies!

His allergies had saved his life in Vietnam. But on the whole, he would just as well do without them.

There were no more tissues in the box on the shelf above the sink. Josh grabbed a length of toilet paper and unfurled it, folding it over quickly and then trying to clear the mess from his nose. It was a lost cause, as were antihistamines, saline sprays, and all manner of remedies he'd tried over the years. Removing the allergen was the only *real* solution.

But what the hell was the allergen here, midway up the UN building, in the middle of a block of offices whose windows didn't even open?

Josh sneezed again. He cleared his nose, dumped some of the paper into the toilet, and flushed. He sneezed, blew his nose, then felt his sinuses clear a bit.

Sneezing fit finally over, he turned to the sink and ran the cold water, splashing on it on his face. He looked at himself in the mirror. He looked more than a little worse for wear.

Josh patted his face dry—rubbing his eyes would only make them hurt even more—then took a deep breath, trying to relax.

There was a tap on the door.

"You, uh, all right in there, Josh?" asked William Jablonski, a political consultant to the President who'd been pressed into service as his minder and media adviser. Jablonski slurred the "sh"; with his deep voice, it sounded as if he were hushing him.

"Yeah, yeah. Just getting my breath back."

"The reporters have a few more questions."

"Yup."

Josh sat on the closed seat of the toilet and unrolled some more toilet tissue. When he'd been stuck behind the lines in Vietnam, he'd dreamed of the chance to tell the world what he had seen. That goal had kept him going, kept him alive. But at this point he really could use a break. A little more of a rest.

The questions were the same, over and over. He repeated the answers practically word for word:

Where did this happen?
Vietnam, the jungles near the Chinese border.
You saw all of this with your own eyes?
Yes.
How did you escape?
I had a phone—some SEALs were sent. And I guess, uh, some Army guys.

The last answer was, if not quite a lie, certainly not the whole truth. CIA officer Mara Duncan had been the person who found him in the jungle and truly saved him—the CIA had tracked his phone signal, then sent Mara to find and rescue him. But mentioning her—mentioning the agency's involvement at all—would blow her cover, ending her usefulness in Southeast Asia, and probably ending or at least harming her career.

So he left her out of the answers.

"Josh?" asked Jablonski through the door.

"Yeah?"

"You sure you're all right?"

"I'm good."

"The people from WINS have, uh, a deadline thing that they are hoping to meet. They want to talk, uh, about the bridge."

"I'll be out in just a sec," Josh told him.

"Sure."

The bridge. Someone had tried to blow him up, to stop him from getting to the UN. Those questions were harder to answer, since he wasn't exactly sure who it was.

He *was* sure—he saw the man in his mind's eye: early twenties, thin face, shaved head. Chinese, definitely Chinese.

Determined expression. Cold, hollow eyes.

Can't they all just go away?

Suddenly he felt ashamed of himself. The people in Vietnam whose bodies he'd seen—they would gladly trade places with him. Ma, the little girl he'd rescued: What would she think?

Josh rose, blew his nose again, then opened the door.

"All right," he said to the reporters as he emerged. "Where were we?"

4

Aboard the USS *McLane*, South China Sea

Dirk "Hurricane" Silas strode onto the bridge of the *McLane*, his legs adjusting unconsciously to the gentle roll of the vessel as she plied northward across the South China Sea. No other job in the world could compare with being the master of a ship: no post in the Navy came close to that of captain of a warship. And few moments could compare with those when Commander Silas stepped onto the deck of his bridge. The melding of crew and vessel was never more perfect than that moment, when a glance at the helmsman's steady hand on the wheel told Silas that the world—that his world—was steady and shipshape.

Silas often thought that he had been born several generations too late; his lust for the sea belonged more properly to the age of sail, when the elements were more immediate and a captain might truly strain his muscles in rallying his crew. But a scan of the bridge of any of the U.S. Navy's Arleigh Burke–class destroyers would remind even a landlubber that this age had wonders of its own. For a man to stand on this bridge, to know that this ship was under his control, answered to his voice—it was a heady and humbling feeling, and one that Commander Silas had worked all his life to obtain.

"Captain."

Lieutenant Commander Dorothy Li, Silas's executive officer, had been taking her turn on the bridge while he grabbed a brief respite. She nodded at him now, and so the routine began: the exchange of data, the trivial and the critical details merging.

The actual give-and-take of commanding a vessel, of keeping her on her course, of making sure her sailors were nourished in mind and spirit and emotion—they were little chinks and dents that accreted against the real core of the thing, the clean sense of duty and honor and courage that informed the soul of a sea captain, of a warrior following a path set by the Norse and beyond. Silas put up with the chinks and dents, attended to the details, because he knew they were the dues he paid for that brief moment on the bridge. He adjusted things deftly, attending to the needs of his ship's various departments.

He consulted immediately with the chief petty officer who had discovered an unexplained deficiency in the food stores. Ordinarily the chief was the calmest of men, at least in dealing with his commander, but he had become high-strung of late. Tonight, he couldn't account for two steaks—they were the most important of the items allegedly missing. Silas was reminded of Humphrey Bogart in the *Caine Mutiny*, and not in a particularly good way.

Almost surely it was an error in the tracking system or someone's memory, Silas thought; he had no thieves aboard his ship.

It was the borderline hysteria that really bothered Silas. He dealt with it first by making a joke—perhaps the Chinese had somehow snuck aboard the ship—and when that failed to work, gave the chief a reassuring speech and a pat literally on the back. It was stress, he knew; they had been playing chicken with the Chinese now for several days, skirting the bastards' bullying while obeying orders that prevented them from firing—from even defending themselves properly, in his opinion.

But that was hardly an excuse, and it was rather unseemly in a chief, a man who should be and was in many ways, part of the backbone of Silas's command. The man would be eased out at Silas's earliest opportunity. But that opportunity would not come for some time, surely, and as Silas needed him to function to his best ability, he would carry him until then, propping him up as best he could. A pat on the back was easy enough; if it could ease the pressure for a few hours, then Silas was all for it.

He went on to handle a few other minor matters, incidental bits of sand in the smooth grease of his warship's gears. Internal matters squared away, he turned his attention to external—the real matter at hand.

For days now, they'd been shadowed by a Chinese cruiser and frigate. The Chinese spent most of the time sailing just over the horizon, ducking back and forth as he moved, sometimes across his course, more often dogging his stern. They had briefly attempted to block his path into Vietnam's coastal waters—a move that could have started a war. They had threatened to interfere with his mission to send a helicopter to pick up a small group of SEALs rescuing some civilians—spies, he assumed, though the group included a small girl.

Whatever. The specifics of their mission didn't interest him. More to the point was the principle that a U.S. warship went wherever it pleased.

He hadn't fired—doing so would have been against orders—but he had still managed to do his job and to prove the point.

Since then, the *McLane* had sailed northward toward the Gulf of Tonkin. She was back in international waters, about twenty miles off the Vietnamese coast. Silas's orders were rather vague—remain off the coast of Vietnam—giving him considerable leeway, though in the end the lack of an actual mission frustrated him. Demonstrating America's right to be there was hardly the sort of job one pined for.

And so, as he reviewed the evening intelligence briefing and saw the reports of the Chinese amphibious fleet at Hainan, it was not surprising that Silas concluded he did in fact have something to do, and that was to head farther north. For though he had been told not to seek a conflict with either of the two aircraft carriers the Chinese were operating near their home port of Zhenjiang, he had not been ordered away from the amphibious fleet. And in fact, a good naval man would certainly deem it advisable to investigate the whereabouts of that fleet. Certainly in the absence of orders *against* doing so.

After he had arranged it—and noted that there was no need to alert fleet to his intention, as they would be clear to any observant seaman, let alone to the admiral who was his commander—Silas left the bridge to feel the spray of the ocean. As he lifted the binoculars to his eyes, he thought there was no better feeling in the world than to be standing on the deck of a warship, making his way northward.

And if there *was* a better feeling, surely it would be his within a few days.

5

Hainan Island, China

Zeus felt his heart pound against his chest. He couldn't slow it; the best he could do was control his breathing, taking deep, long breaths as he followed the Chinese military officer down the hallway. Christian was a few strides behind; the two Chinese soldiers were a pace or so to the rear.

The worst thing to do was panic. The Chinese had no way of knowing that they were involved in the attack; as long as he kept his mouth shut, they would ultimately have to release him.

Unless the Vietnamese spy had given them away. Then what?

Zeus slowed down another half step. "Let me do the talking," he whispered to Christian.

"They'll split us up," said Christian. "And where's the girl?"

The tremble was more pronounced, his voice unusually high.

"We're here on business. Hong Kong. Then Tokyo. We're businessmen," said Zeus. "Stay with it."

"Right."

The cover story didn't go very deep. How long would it take to get enough information for inconsistencies? Fifteen minutes? A half hour?

If Solt or one of the Vietnamese marines who'd been on the mission with them had been captured, the Chinese would expect them to lie. But there was no other alternative.

"Stick to the story," Zeus whispered as the Chinese officer opened a steel door near the gate entrance hall.

"That bitch must've sold us out," said Christian under his breath.

The door opened into a claustrophobically small room flooded with neon-bright light from above. Two men stood at the opposite end of the room. They wore blue fatigues with no insignias. To the right was a large corkboard covered with squares of paper tacked into neat rows. The squares were covered with Chinese characters, all unintelligible to Zeus.

The two men who had followed them came inside and closed the door.

"Passports," said the officer.

As Zeus reached to his pocket, it occurred to him that it might just be a simple shakedown—not unheard of at small airports in China.

If so, he should slip some cash into the passport before he handed it over. But that was risky, too. The man might be insulted. Worse, it might be too little.

He gave him only the passport. Christian's hand shook as he handed his over.

Buck up. Don't go to pieces on me now.

"What's this about?" Zeus asked calmly.

The officer ignored him, examining the documents. Though the room was small, it had a pair of air-conditioning vents, and it actually seemed cool.

The man said something in Chinese. The two men near the door, barely a foot away from Zeus, stiffened.

"Go with them," the officer said to him.

"What is this about?" asked Zeus, a little harsher.

"Go."

"Our passports."

"Go."

The officer stared so hard Zeus thought he was going to go cross-eyed. The passports remained in his hand.

What would he do if Zeus grabbed them from his hand?

Fight.

Zeus could bowl him over with a swipe of his hand, a hard shot to his throat. Then push against the other two goons behind him, grab one of their guns. But that left the other two men for Christian.

The major had surprised him over the past few days, but he was worn down now, tired by everything they'd done.

And what would they do next? Even if they had their weapons?

One of the men opened the door and stepped back into the hallway. Zeus followed warily, trying to decide what to do next.

"What the hell are they up to?" asked Christian, walking alongside of him. "Are they arresting us? Or what?"

"I don't know."

"Maybe they're going to take us out and shoot us."

Maybe, thought Zeus.

The man leading them walked toward the main part of the terminal. He took long strides. Zeus quickened his own pace, closing the distance. He glanced over his shoulder; Christian lagged nearly five yards behind, with the other guard a short distance behind him.

This seemed too casual for an arrest. But maybe that was the idea: keep things calm so there was less chance of trouble.

Zeus closed the distance between him and the Chinese soldier. He reached his hand up, plotting what he would do—grab the man's shoulder, pull him around, hit him with his other fist. But before he was quite close enough, the soldier turned slightly and pushed against a glass door that led to a set of steel stairs outside the building.

Zeus followed. It took his eyes a moment to adjust to the harsh light; when they did, he saw an armored personnel carrier sitting about ten yards away. Light spilled from the interior. A half-dozen soldiers sat inside, assault guns between splayed legs, cigarette smoke wafting across the warm night air. There were more soldiers, and more vehicles, a short distance away.

"We are truly fucked," said Christian, coming down the steps.

The man behind them said something in Chinese; probably *Hurry up*. Their guide was approaching a large two-and-a-half-ton truck beyond the APC.

Zeus rubbed his face. He'd missed his chance inside. With all these guards around, what the hell was he going to do?

And where the hell was Solt?

6

UN building, New York City

Mara Duncan stared at Josh MacArthur on the video, watching as he answered the questions from the correspondents a few rooms away. There was no sound; the video was streaming from a security unit, wired to cover the conference room in case of emergencies. But the lack of sound was perfect: it made it easier for Mara to watch him for some answer to the riddle of why she had fallen for the guy.

Because she was definitely attracted to him. Which didn't make a lot of sense.

Mara swiveled in the chair. The small office was one of several back-ups scattered throughout the complex. Her UN security escort had ducked out to get them some lunch.

Josh was intellectual, a scientist. She was not. Not that she was dumb, by any means. Going by her grades in college, certainly, she was anything but a dope. But she preferred outdoor things like hiking and waterskiing and even parachute jumping to reading. And when she did read, it was more along the lines of a mystery or something, not a scientific treatise.

What she admired—what she loved—was the way he treated the little girl, Mạ. He'd been so tenderly attentive and fiercely protective at the same time.

He had a good smile as well. Boyish. And shoulders—she liked his shoulders, though he wasn't a bodybuilder type.

Mara thought of the army officer she'd met in Vietnam—Zeus. Now there was a physical type she went for: high school quarterback, super jock, and not a dumb one, either.

Making love to him would be . . . interesting.

Athletic.

But it's Josh I want, Mara thought, glancing back at the video screen.

Her sat phone buzzed. It was Peter Lucas.

Mara cringed as she answered.

"Boss?"

"Mara, excellent work up there. Those Chinese assassins—dead?"

"I don't know."

"Secret Service says they are. They're singing your praises. There'll be a commendation. Good work. Hell of a job."

So I guess I don't have to do any more penance for Malaysia, Mara thought.

"I watched the show. CNN, Fox, everybody's got it. Your boy is good. Very, very good. You coached him?"

"Some special troubleshooter came down," said Mara. "Jablonski. The president's guy. He's a political handler or something."

"Well, Josh was great. Very, very convincing."

"How's Mạ?"

"The little girl is fine, as far as I know."

"Can you send somebody to check on her?"

"Don't go maternal on me, Mara. The girl isn't my department."

"I'm not being maternal. She has no family. I'm just looking out for her."

"You did that in Vietnam, Mara. That part of your job is done."

"But—"

"Look, they kept her from having to go in front of the UN, right? She's in good hands."

"That sounds perverse.

Lucas didn't respond. Normally his sense of humor was just as black as hers, but certain things he didn't joke about.

"When am I going back?" she asked.

"Back?"

"Are you sending me to Vietnam, or back to Bangkok?"

"I don't know yet. I was thinking . . ."

His voice trailed off. That was never good. Mara instantly realized the reason.

"Peter, you're not thinking of pulling me back to Langley, are you?" she said. It was more an accusation than a question. "Putting me on the desk?"

"I've been thinking I need some help here," said Lucas.

"*No.*"

Mara's voice was so loud she startled herself. She glanced around the room, making sure it was empty.

No way she was going to get herself locked into an assignment at CIA headquarters as a desk sitter.

"It's not a death sentence, for cryin' out loud," Lucas told her. "And it wouldn't be permanent. Hell, a promotion would be involved. Part of your career path."

"Bull."

"I need someone I can trust to represent me back here. I have to get back to Bangkok. When the Chinese take Vietnam, Thailand's going to be next."

"*When* the Chinese take Vietnam?"

"We're talking days, Mara. At most. And Thailand's next. Cambodia. Laos. The only question is which one they go after first."

Mara thought there were a lot of questions besides that one.

"What do you think?" Lucas asked.

"I'm not going to be your secretary, Peter. That's not my skill set."

"I was thinking more my spear thrower."

"You can't put a good gloss on it."

She got up from the seat, anger stoking her adrenaline. Lucas might think of it as a promotion—maybe in some ways it was—but she deserved some consideration after everything. He ought to be asking her what she wanted to do. Dozens of people could carry water for him here. And better than she could.

Unless . . .

"Peter, is my cover blown?" Mara asked.

"No," he said, a little more slowly than she would have liked. "No. I don't think so. Listen to me. This would be a good career move."

"Staying in the field would be better."

"Well, think about it. You don't have to make a decision yet."

"It's already made up."

"Take your time."

"I'm ready to go back now, Peter. I should be in Saigon. Did you find out who ripped off the money that was supposed to be at the drop?"

"I can't talk about it."

"I'd like to cut his balls off."

"*Mara.*" Lucas's voice had an exasperated tone that Mara recognized as a warning: the next thing out of his mouth would be a long speech about how much she owed him.

"I'll see you tomorrow."

"Take a few days off. Three or four."

"I'll see you tomorrow."

"Take one day off at least." He hung up.

Mara sighed and turned her attention back to the screen. Josh was getting up. The interviews were finally over.

————

Josh followed wearily as Jablonski and the two bodyguards from the federal marshal's office squeezed him down the back hallway and hurried him into a stairwell.

"Where are we going now?" Josh asked as they started down.

"We're going to get you some rest," answered Jablonski. "At least a few hours. We're setting up something with Sky News, and a BBC interview. But you should be able to do those by phone. The important things are the morning shows, and we want you better rested for that."

"Where's Mara?" asked Josh.

"She'll be along."

"I wanted to talk to her."

Jablonski started to make a face. The BlackBerry in his suit jacket rang; he reached in and took it out, glanced at the face for the caller ID, then held it to his ear.

"This is William. Fred, how *are* you? Glad you could get back to me. . . ." Jablonski stopped and glanced at Josh. "We *might* be able to give the congressman a personal briefing. A short one."

Josh tensed. The earlier "personal briefing" had almost gotten him killed this morning.

"He doesn't have a lot of time," Jablonski said. He winked at Josh. "The congressman is? Well, maybe if they were seen walking together . . . ? Hold on."

Jablonski muted the phone.

"I wonder if you could do a favor," he told Josh. "There's a congressman from Long Island who's going to be in a pretty hard reelection campaign. He's a reliable vote. If we could help him . . ."

"Like how?"

"Have your picture taken talking to him."

"How will that help?"

"One hand washes the other," said Jablonski, slurping in the end of the sentence. "Don't worry. It does."

Josh hated all this political bull. But as Jablonski had explained the other night, Congress was opposed to helping the Vietnamese. It wasn't going to be easy to change that.

"If we can get out of here when it's done, then okay," said Josh.

Jablonski put the phone back to his ear.

"We'll be down in a few minutes."

Jablonski sent a text, then put the phone away.

"Okay, Josh, it's all arranged," said Jablonski. "Let's go."

"Where's Mara?"

"I'll tell her to meet us. Come on, let's go."

———

A member of the federal marshal's detail was waiting as Mara stepped off the elevator into the garage below the UN building.

"They just changed plans," he said. "Mr. Jablonski told the cars to meet them on the street at the back."

"On the street? That makes no sense."

The marshal shrugged.

"Somebody tried to kill him this morning," said Mara. "He has to be protected."

"The whole area's sealed off," said the marshal.

"You can't think this is a good idea."

"What do you want me to tell you? I'm just following orders. There's tons of security around, ma'am. Tons."

Mara hated when anyone called her ma'am.

"Just take me to wherever the hell they are."

The marshal turned and walked across the smooth concrete of the underground parking garage. A few hours before, the place had been swarming with Secret Service men, some of them armed with submachine guns. But that was mostly because the President was here. Now the only security people she could spot were a pair of New York City policemen standing at the far end of garage, near the ramp to street level.

But maybe that made sense. The Chinese wouldn't kill Josh now; that would just prove his point. They would create a martyr.

She followed the marshal back up the stairs to the first floor, then out into the main lobby. There were a dozen photographers and several video crews crowded near the door. They glanced in her direction, then realized she was nobody and went back to waiting, hoping to get a look at Josh as he left.

The marshal led her through the throng to a section of roped-off elevators. They went up a flight, then out and across the hall to a staircase at the back of the building. These led to the long hallway flanking the General Assembly Chamber. Television lights flooded the space, glaring off the art displayed along the temporary wall at Mara's left. Diplomats were clustered at the far end, listening to someone give an impromptu news interview.

It was Josh. His voice, soft, tired, echoed through the hall. He was talking about Vietnam, what he had seen there.

As Mara approached the back of the crowd, it began to move. A uniformed security guard glanced at her as she approached, then turned back, spotting the un vip identification tag hanging around her neck. Mara followed along, not wanting to draw any attention to herself.

The procession grew as they pushed outside, swelling as reporters who'd missed the impromptu interview inside realized from the commotion that they would have another chance. A few shouted questions from the side. Mara spotted Jablonski guiding Josh around the side of the building, toward a pair of Lincoln town cars. A line of NYPD officers blocked the cars from the rest of the lot; as the reporters realized they were about to be cut off, they swarmed around, temporarily blocking the way.

Josh stopped and raised his hands.

"All right, I'll take questions. Whatever you want." His voice was hoarse. It sounded as tired as the first night she'd found him in Vietnam.

"We only have a few minutes," said Jablonski. Mara couldn't quite see his head through the crowd. "Then Mr. MacArthur has to brief Congressman Joyce. I'm sure you understand."

The reporters started asking questions, the same ones Josh had been fielding for hours:

What were you doing in Vietnam?

How did you escape?

How did you get the images?

Was anyone left alive?

He answered wearily, but patiently. His answers were getting shorter and shorter.

Poor guy, thought Mara. He was exhausted. Couldn't they see that?

Mara sidled around the edge of the crowd, moving to position herself closer to the line of policemen, trying to catch Jablonski's eye. Her escort had disappeared.

The back door of the second town car opened. A tall, thin man with slicked-back gray hair unfolded himself from the interior, popping up like the inside of birthday card. He had his jacket off, white shirtsleeves rolled up, and tie fluttering in the wind as he strode forward.

He was a congressman or some other politician, Mara realized. One more episode in Jablonski's dog-and-pony show, designed to please friends and to influence enemies.

She slipped behind a cameraman, pushing gently toward Josh and Jablonski. But the policemen nearest her pivoted, forming a wedge as the congressman approached. They were in her way.

Deciding it would be easier to go around to the other side of the scrum, Mara backed out, squeezing between two latecomers. Walking along the edge of the crowd, she looked for the marshal who'd accompanied her earlier. There were a few people standing around, employees she guessed, watching the proceedings. One or two smoked cigarettes.

A silver Lexus LX 470 pulled up near the entrance. Someone got out—a young Asian woman. She was dressed in a flower-print pink skirt, knee-length, with a tightly tailored business jacket. Her long hair was tied at the back. She wore glasses, but these softened her features, making her look interested rather than studious.

She waved her credentials at one of the police officers, and gestured back toward the main security post by the street. Meanwhile a young man in jeans and a blue blazer got out of the other side of the car, from the front seat, and hustled after her, carrying a video camera. The policeman waved her past.

Mara looked at the car. The windows were blacked out. What television news service drove around in a Lexus?

————

Josh did his best not to grimace as the congressman talked about the heinous crimes to mankind, naked aggression, and the need for immediate congressional hearings to determine the proper course of action.

"We don't need hearings," muttered Josh.

Jablonski poked him gently in the ribs.

"What about hearings?" asked one of the reporters nearby.

"He said they need them," said another.

"We don't need them. The Chinese need to stop their attacks," said Josh in frustration.

The congressman turned to glare at him. For a just a moment his eyes narrowed into daggers. Josh wouldn't have been surprised if a laser beam shot from them and burned away his tongue. He didn't care.

"Our scientist friend is right," said the congressman, the glare replaced by a fresh smile. "Action. Hopefully my colleagues in Congress will see it that way. Now, come on, I know you have several appointments. We'll talk on the way."

Jablonski took hold of Josh's arm. Josh looked over the crowd and saw Mara twenty or thirty feet away.

"Mara!" he yelled, resisting Jablonski's soft pull. "Mara!"

He waved. Jablonski stopped.

"It's Mara," Josh told him.

Jablonski turned to one of the marshals. The marshal nodded, then went to get Mara. She was already walking toward them.

"You are a liar, Mr. MacArthur!" shouted a voice from the crowd. "I don't know how you sleep at night!"

Josh stopped short. The accusation felt like a physical blow to the back of his neck.

"What? What?"

"Those photos we see—aren't they made up?"

Josh couldn't see the woman who was making the accusation. Where was she?

"Why would I make that up?" said Josh. He wasn't even sure who he was answering.

The reporters nearest Josh stepped aside to reveal a young Asian-looking woman with glasses—the one Mara had seen getting out of the car. She had a pad in her hand; her videographer was filming over her shoulder.

"Where did you get the photos?" the woman asked.

"In Vietnam. Northern Vietnam."

"Where precisely?"

Her voice was sweet, not shrill. Now that she was close, she spoke almost softly. Her English had a slight accent—Chinese, Josh thought, though he couldn't really be sure.

"It was near the border," said Josh. "We had established a camp—"

"It's okay, Josh. She's trying to provoke you," whispered Jablonski in his ear. "She's probably some sort of spy. Let's go."

"I didn't make anything up," said Josh. "We were north of a place called Ba Sin Sui Ho. I may not be pronouncing it right. We were study-ing climate change, its effects on the jungle and the life there."

"It's all right, Josh," repeated Jablonski. "Come on. Mara's here. Let's go."

"I'm not lying," he told Jablonski.

"They're trying to provoke you. Don't let them." Jablonksi looked up at the reporters. "You have all the data on the images and the ap-proximate location of the massacre," he said loudly. "You can download all of the information off the State Department Web site."

———

Josh was trembling as he got into the car.

"She called me a liar," he said as Mara slipped in next to him.

"I wouldn't worry about it, son," said Congressman Joyce on the other side of Josh. "These reporters—they spout bull just to get your reaction."

"I doubt that was a reporter," said Jablonski, who'd gotten into the front. "Probably a Chinese spy."

He leaned over the seat.

"Can you check on it?" he asked Mara.

"Sure," she said, wishing he hadn't said anything.

"I think it went very well, all things considered," said the congressman. He slapped Josh on the knee, then looked across to Mara. "And you are . . . ?"

"Mara Duncan."

"I take it you're with the FBI?" He glanced at Jablonski.

"State Department," said Jablonski. "She's our liaison."

"Good, very good," said the congressman, sitting back.

Mara looked at Josh. He was sweating, and staring at her.

"I don't think it's a big deal," Mara told him. "Relax."

"I know what I saw. I was right there. We were right there."

"I know you did, Josh," said Mara. "Don't worry."

7

Hainan Island, China

Zeus emptied his mind as he walked, focusing entirely on his surroundings. The airport was a collection of bright lights and shadows, blinking beacons and looming buildings. The runway was a good distance away, more than a hundred yards. Beyond it were four black lumps—military hangars, he guessed, as the other half of the airport was used by the People's Liberation Army's air force.

So don't run that way when you make your break.

Light from the interior of the terminal building washed over the apron where the planes were parked, tinting everything yellow. The planes themselves were unlit, seemingly without power or crews. That killed any temptation he might have had to fantasize about boarding one and hijacking it.

And there were simply too many soldiers around to think about running, much less overpowering them. Another truck crossed ahead at the end of the terminal building; as it passed, a floodlight on the building illuminated the faces of five men hanging from the back, giving them a ghostly pallor.

"What, do they have the whole damn Chinese army here?" grumbled Christian, a little louder than Zeus would have liked.

"They're under attack, remember?"

"What the hell are we going to do?" Christian asked. "Where are they taking us?"

Zeus had no answers. Better to go along, say nothing, hope for the best.

Hope isn't a plan.

That was his tactical instructor's motto at West Point. Zeus wondered how he'd deal with this. That was one thing they didn't teach you at the Point: how to be a successful spy.

As they drew parallel to the end of the terminal gate building, the soldier leading them turned right about forty-five degrees, and began walking across a long, open area toward another building. A row of armored personnel carriers sat to his right, about thirty yards away, blocking off part of the apron area.

Zeus went into G-2 mode, assessing the vehicles as an intelligence officer would. They were short and squat, with turrets toward the rear of the hull: NVH-1s, very old vehicles, with 30 mm or 25 mm guns in the turret. They'd hold nine soldiers, plus two crewmen.

You'd expect older gear on Hainan, so that fit.

Had they been upgraded? The Chinese got a lot of use out of their older vehicles by outfitting them with the latest technology.

A single radio whip off the turret. Not enough to go on.

So where had they come from?

Probably they were kept on the military side and just rushed over, assigned to take up positions in case the Vietnamese counterattacked. It would be standard procedure.

How many?

One company at least. How many had he passed now? How many were on the other side of the building?

Were they army or air force? How were the Chinese divisions organized—would these be attached to a regular division, or a separate unit?

There were two self-propelled antiaircraft guns in the distance, close to the runway; he could see the barrels rising above the hulls.

Two barrels. Which made them . . . what?

Russian ZSU-57s?

No way. Too old.

They weren't aligned very well for defense. The positioning was the sort of thing you would see if you were expecting some sort of civil disturbance.

They were still in that mode, not quite ready for the war they were actually fighting.

A vehicle moved from the shadows ahead. It had its running lights but not its headlights on. At first glance, Zeus thought it was a sedan, but as it approached he realized it was a crew cab pickup. There were soldiers standing in the back, leaning over the roof.

The man who had been leading them raised his hand as it pulled up. There were two soldiers sitting in the front seat. The man opened the rear passenger side door and gestured toward Zeus.

"We can't get in," whispered Christian. "Who the hell knows where they're taking us?"

"We don't really have much choice at this point," Zeus told him. "Just relax. We'll get through this."

"Fuck you, relax."

"Listen to me. Just play along—we're businessmen. Do not change your story."

"Businessmen get arrested by half the army?"

Zeus climbed in. The cab smelled funny—like roasted peanuts, he thought.

Neither of the two men in front said anything. The soldiers who had escorted them slammed the door shut after Christian got in.

"What the hell?" hissed Christian.

Zeus shook his head. The truck started forward in a gentle glide, barely moving at first, then gradually picking up speed. It moved toward the terminal building, on the opposite side from where they'd come out. The personnel carriers were on their right. Then the driver found a road marked with reflectors across the wide asphalt concourse and turned sharply. Their speed gradually increased as they moved away from the terminal building. They passed some maintenance vehicles, then slowed as they approached a hangar.

A two-engined Fokker 50 passenger plane sat out front. The truck stopped.

Zeus pulled the door handle next to him, only to find it was secured by a lock that allowed it to be opened only from the outside.

They sat in the dark for a moment. Zeus considered the odds of over-powering both men in the front. He could strangle the driver easily enough; could Christian take the other?

Push the man aside, flip over the seat—he'd probably be able to make it before anyone in the bed behind them or outside could react. Once in the driver's seat, he could simply back up, drive around to the front.

Desperation move.

Was it better than just doing nothing?

Yes.

He was just turning to Christian, intending on miming what he wanted to do, when the door next to him opened.

It was Solt Jan. "Out. On the plane. Let's go!" she ordered.

———

Zeus took a slow breath as he pushed out of the truck. Solt was already halfway to the plane.

"What the hell?" asked Christian under his breath.

Zeus followed Solt to the stairs leading to the aircraft. He walked deliberately, trying to observe the surroundings without being too obvious. There were some mechanics or maintenance personnel in the hangar, but no soldiers.

He glanced back at Christian, who was still back near the truck.

Was Christian thinking of making a break for it?

Don't, thought Zeus. Play this through.

Christian started walking. He was mumbling when he reached the steps.

"I'm hungry," he said.

"There's probably food on the plane."

"Right."

Zeus went up and found Solt waiting just inside the door.

"Take the seats in row six," she whispered. She handed him their passports. "Say nothing."

"Where are we going?"

"Say nothing," she hissed. "Good luck."

8

Beijing

Premier Cho Lai folded his arms as the defense minister continued. He was losing the struggle to keep his temper.

"The attack a few hours ago on our invasion fleet illustrates a capacity we had not realized the Vietnamese had," continued Lo Gong. He turned to the large display at the front of the war room. "There have been attacks on the harbor, and encounters all along the coast. We dare not move the fleet forward until we have cleared the waters."

"How many were true encounters, and how many were sailors having panic attacks?" said General Qingyun Pu sharply. It was not a question. Qingyun headed the air force, and was Cho Lai's most aggressive general.

"We have images of the attack and casualty reports," answered Lo Gong. "We've already lost two patrol boats and several landing craft. Perhaps the air force believes it can do a better job."

"We could flatten Vietnam in a day."

"You haven't even conquered Hanoi," answered Gong.

"Enough," said Cho Lai. The premier liked Qingyun Pu, but the defense minister had a point. "What is the impact on our plans?"

"We are shifting our resources," said the general. "We will be ready to launch a different attack along the coast within hours."

"Good."

"The next question is what the American Navy will do," said Lo Gong. He pointed to a spot near the southern Vietnamese coast. "The American destroyer sent to test the blockade has been moving north. We are continuing to shadow him. At the moment, it is the nearest vessel. Most of the American fleet is near Taiwan."

"How do we know the destroyer didn't launch the attack?" asked the premier.

"The destroyer was out of range, Your Excellency."

"What about an American submarine?"

The defense minister lowered his gaze. "As for an American submarine, I can assure you, the Americans would have made a much larger attack. We have our aircraft carrier to worry about. No, this was a surprise and beyond what we thought the Vietnamese could launch, but far less than the American capacity. They are still out of the war. They are afraid to attack."

Cho Lai kept his thoughts on that subject to himself.

The discussion continued. The main thrust of the Chinese army had been slowed by the destruction of the dams west of Hanoi. The floodwaters were gradually subsiding, and the attack could be resumed within a few days. Ho Chi Minh City would be theirs within a week.

"Assuming the political winds remain in our favor," said the defense minister.

"I will worry about the winds," said Cho Lai. "You push our generals to be more aggressive. They act like old women, afraid of their own shadows."

———

Cho Lai still pondered Lo Gung's assessment of the Americans a half hour later as he sat in his office, listening to the latest intelligence briefing on the UN speech. The American president was certainly doing his best to urge a confrontation.

The intelligence reports said American public opinion was against intervention. Cho Lai wasn't so sure.

Even with their well-documented decline, the Americans were a force that must be dealt with carefully. Militarily, they were still ahead of the Chinese in many areas—not all, however, and the gap was closing rapidly, but Cho Lai knew it was best to avoid direct conflict for at least another year, perhaps two or even three. He needed the time not so much to catch up with their weaponry—the estimate there was closer to a year and a half—but to get his people healthy again. The drought that had spread from western China had devastated much of the rural population. The impact could be measured in calories—the average peasant in Yunnan Province ate five hundred calories per day.

Five hundred. A quarter of what was needed to live. Those who had fled to the cities fared somewhat better, but even in the places where food was plentiful, wages were unable to keep up. He was not surprised that there had been food riots; the wonder was that there hadn't been more.

Just enough to bring him to power. But surely that wouldn't last. He needed Vietnam, its oil, but mostly its rice, its soil, and its climate. And he needed Cambodia and Thailand. The shifting of the weather patterns had favored them all at China's expense.

"Your Excellency?"

Cho Lai looked up. His intelligence minister, Ludi Yan, had returned to his office after taking a call outside.

"The agent we sent almost reached him on the bridge," said Ludi Yan. "But the plan fell short."

Cho Lai nodded.

"The man—we believe he died. We are looking for his body."

"Better that he is dead than captured."

Ludi nodded.

"We have already begun blunting the American propaganda," continued the intelligence minister. He handed Cho Lai a touchpad tablet. There was a video in the middle of the screen, poised to play. The premier touched the arrow. A scene outside the UN began to play, showing a press conference the scientist had held.

"I have no time for more of his lies," said Cho Lai.

"Wait for a moment, Your Excellency. It will pause."

The camera moved to the right, looking over the crowd. Then the image stopped on a young American woman. Her face zoomed to fill half the screen. Next to it, a black presentation-type slide came up.

"She was called the Dark Horse in Malaysia, we believe," said Ludi. "A very skilled operative."

"A woman."

"A CIA officer who has accompanied the scientist. Who is to say that she did not plant the information for him to discover?"

"His story is that he witnessed the massacre," said Cho Lai.

"He ran from the camp where the other scientists were, so he doesn't know what happened there. We have already begun to attack his credibility. Videos have been prepared. We have several operatives ready to contact media. It will be a subtle, but all-out campaign."

Cho Lai frowned.

"If you do not wish us to proceed, Your Excellency—"

"Do what you can to discredit him," said Cho Lai. "Do not harm the scientist. That will only make it look as if we are guilty. As for this girl—kill her if it is convenient. That would bring some measure of satisfaction for our agent's demise."

"It will be done." Ludi bowed deeply, then left the room.

9

Aboard Air Force One

For the briefest of moments, George Chester Greene thought he was going to get everything he wanted: a near unanimous censure of China in the UN, a vote in the Senate and House to provide troops to enforce a cease-fire in Vietnam, and a ten-point boost in his approval rating.

The last was always a pipe dream, but with Josh MacArthur's dramatic appearance before the UN, the first two seemed well within his grasp. Yet within hours, everything began to disintegrate. The UN vote was postponed by Iran, either as a payback for oil deals between it and China, or as the latest in a campaign to tweak America's nose—or very likely both. Senator Phillip Grasso, who had been among Greene's biggest critics since the start of his presidency, had fallen into line, thanks largely to a thwarted attempt by the Chinese to kill him and Josh MacArthur as they traveled together in New York. But Grasso's influence in the Senate only went so far, and as soon as he came out in favor of intervention, the antis began mounting an offensive.

Then there were the lies from China itself. Greene knew the Chinese would attempt to pass off the American information as so much propaganda. What he hadn't quite expected was how much the news media would play up that angle. Every story he saw seemed to focus on the Chinese counterarguments, rather than the clear evidence Josh MacArthur had brought back.

Greene had seen a confrontation coming with China for a long, long time. But the one thing he hadn't seen was that it would be over Vietnam.

It was a supreme irony. He'd spent several months at the end of the Vietnam War as a prisoner in Hanoi. And now he was trying to figure out a way to save the bastards.

Not for them. China, and more specifically its despotic premier, had to be stopped. Vietnam was clearly intended as just the first of Cho Lai's coveted prizes. The rest of Indo-China really would fall easily. The question was where would they go after that: Taiwan? Japan, perhaps?

Greene got off the exercise bike. The first time he had used it in Air Force One, he had thought it very strange indeed—he was literally pedaling at the just under the speed of sound. Now, like much he had experienced in his brief tenure as President, it felt like the most natural thing in the world.

He poked his head out the door of his private room. His national security director, Walter Jackson, was sitting on the couch of the executive office, talking to the National Security situation room for an update.

"Walter, I'm going to take a shower," said the President.

"Mr. President, a moment?"

"All right," said Greene, frowning.

Jackson hung up. "Can we get Lin in here?"

Linda Holmes was the legislative coordinator.

"It's your meeting, Walter."

Greene stooped down to the small beverage refrigerator. He paused over the selections—a beer would go down pretty well right now—then pulled out a bottle of water.

Linda Holmes came into the conference room holding a large binder in front of her chest. Now just past fifty, in younger years she was quite a beauty. Greene still found her attractive, though there wasn't a hint of flirtation between them. It would have gone nowhere in any event—she'd just celebrated her thirty-year marriage anniversary.

"Mr. President."

"Drink?" asked Greene, settling down on the couch.

"I just had coffee."

"How's it look?"

"Well." Holmes opened the binder. She had an iPad 3 in the pocket. She fired it up, then flipped about midway through her book. She tapped the iPad twice, coordinating whatever was on the screen with her documents. "You need eight more votes."

"In the House?" asked Greene.

"That's the Senate. The House is even tougher."

Greene cursed. Now he really wished he'd chosen the beer.

"It's because it's Vietnam that's being attacked," she added. "Anywhere else, even Taiwan—"

"I know," said Greene. "All right. Just tell me: Is there any hope?"

She made a face Greene had seen all too often in his short tenure as president. He called it the Bad News Grimace—*I don't want to be the one to tell you this, sir, but . . .*

"I wouldn't rule it out," said Holmes. "If you could make some calls, it might help."

"Give me a list," said Greene.

Holmes tapped her iPad. The printer at the far end of the room began humming.

"I'll let you know how I do," said Greene.

He got up. As Holmes left, he took a swig from the water bottle and turned toward the back to his private suite.

"George?"

"Yes, Walter?"

"Are you thinking of sending the troops without the authorization?" asked the national security director.

"Possibly."

"That's risky. Legally."

"Agreed."

"The worst thing would be to send them too late."

"I'm well aware of that, Walter. Do you mind if I take a shower now?"

"Couple of other things," said Jackson. "The operation against Hainan seems to have been successful. NSA has intercepts telling the fleet to look for Vietnamese submarines. The admiral who was supposed to lead the invasion force has been recalled to Beijing for consultation."

"Excellent."

"Yes and no. There's still a sizeable force on Hainan. They won't stay there forever. And the CIA thinks there's some sort of operation being planned against Hai Phong. The details are sketchy."

"What sort of operation?"

Jackson shrugged. "Details are sketchy."

"Get a hold of Frost and tell him to sharpen it up," snapped Greene. Peter Frost was the head of the CIA. "Tell him to stop sending me the latest fake YouTube and Twitter posts, and get real intelligence."

"One other thing you should know, George," added Jackson, his voice notably lower. "The two American Army officers involved in the Hainan operation as advisers? They're missing."

"Missing where?"

"Hainan."

Greene pursed his lips. Just what he needed—another public relations nightmare.

"Very possibly they're dead," added Jackson.

It was a horrible thought, yet in this circumstance their deaths would be far more desirable than their capture.

A terrible thought, especially for him. Would Nixon have thought that about his capture? And yet it was certainly true for the country.

Or at least for him.

Was that the same thing?

Absolutely not. He had to be clear about that.

"Keep me advised," Greene told Jackson, opening the door to his private suite.

10

Hainan Island, China

Zeus relaxed a little as the Fokker 50 lifted from the runway. They were off Hainan at least. The farther from the scene of the crime, the better.

The turboprops made a loud, droning noise that reminded him quite a lot of the turbocharger he'd installed in his old Firebird.

Odd to be thinking of the 'Bird now. She wasn't nearly as nice as the Corvette he'd kept, but she had been a pretty car in her own right, old-school muscle and gas guzzler. He'd done a good job with her, and she'd paid him back nicely, returning a decent premium over what he'd paid when he sold her to a millionaire over eBay. At least he assumed the guy was a millionaire; he didn't even bark about the price.

The Fokker banked sharply, pushing Zeus against Christian.

"Something's up," Christian told Zeus. "We're turning north."

"Solt's got it under control." She was sitting a few aisles away.

"I'll bet."

"You come up with a better plan, let me know."

Casually glancing to his right and then left, Zeus tried to get a read on the other passengers. He could only see a handful. They were all Asian, probably Chinese. They didn't seem particularly worried or thrilled to have escaped Hainan. He thought of striking up a conversation to see what they knew of the situation on the island, but decided it was too risky; there was no sense calling more attention to himself.

Zeus unbuckled his seatbelt.

"Where are you going?" asked Christian. There was panic in his eyes.

"Bathroom."

Zeus glanced at the faces of the passengers as he walked toward the back of the cabin.

No other Europeans. Mostly men, mostly in formal business clothes. His own clothes, a baggy pair of cotton pants and a Western-style sweatshirt with a pseudo designer name, were probably among the most casual on the plane.

The restrooms were occupied. Zeus turned back toward the cabin, hoping that Solt Jan had seen him and would follow. But she didn't.

The door to one of the commodes opened. Zeus stepped back to let a short, thin woman squeeze past. Then he went inside the restroom.

He needed to wash his face. The salt water from the ocean felt as if it had embedded itself into his pores. He rubbed the water from the faucet into his forehead and down across his cheekbones, to his jaw and chin. He filled his palms again and ran them over his face, trying to flush the salt and fatigue away.

He avoided looking in the mirror, knowing he looked terrible. He took a quick glance at his clothes—stolen from a gym locker, but reasonably close in size—then opened the door and went back out to his seat.

"We're going to Zhanjiang," whispered Christian as he sat down.

"How do you know?"

"Solt told me. She came by while you were in the restroom."

"Okay."

"She says there're flights from there to Beijing. From there we can go anywhere. I'm not crazy about going to Beijing."

"There's always Pyongyang," Zeus answered sarcastically, referring to the capital of North Korea.

"You're a real comedian."

"Did she say how long the flight was?"

"Didn't ask."

Zeus leaned over, trying to see through the window next to Christian. If they were going to Zhanjiang, it shouldn't take very long. They would fly directly over the island, cross a small strait, and then reach the mainland not far from the city.

"Not even anything to read," grumbled Christian.

"We'll be down soon."

"Yeah, I'm really looking forward to that."

The pilot began speaking over the loudspeaker in Chinese. There was some rustling in the seats as he went on.

Zeus waited for him to finish, hoping he would repeat the announcement in English, but he didn't. Finally, he leaned across the aisle.

"Excuse me," he said to the sleepy-eyed man sitting opposite him. "I don't speak Chinese. I wonder if you could tell me what he said."

The man simply stared at him.

Two rows ahead, Solt Jan heard him talking and turned her head back. She got up and came back, kneeling down next to his seat. She looked as if she were genuflecting.

"The plane is diverting because of the war emergency," she told him in a whisper.

"Uh-huh."

"Zhanjiang is closed," she added, her voice even softer. "The pilot didn't say, but we are most likely going to Beihai. We will be able to continue from there."

She shook her head, telling Zeus not to ask any more questions.

"Small airport," she whispered. "But adequate."

"We're in your hands."

She nodded, then went back to her seat. The aircraft had begun banking gently westward.

"Why do you think they closed Zhanjiang?" Christian asked.

"Need it for military operations," said Zeus. "Has to be." Probably in response to our fake attack, he thought. Zeus guessed there would be extra patrol flights now, the Chinese military in high paranoid mode.

Good. Though not necessarily for them.

The airplane leveled off. The harsh drone of its engines eased. Zeus wondered about the Vietnamese air force. They still had some flyable

MiGs, but he doubted they'd risk them this far from their base. In fact, he tended to doubt that they'd risk them at all.

"We're over the water," said Christian a few minutes later.

"What can you see?"

"Lights. I think I can see a boat. A ship, I mean. There's the coast."

Obviously, the Chinese didn't think the Vietnamese air force was much of a threat, or there'd be a blackout.

The airplane suddenly dipped down. Something flew past Christian's window.

"Shit," said Christian.

"Sshhh," said Zeus. But everyone else was talking, and pushing toward the windows near them.

"Fighters," said Christian.

"What are they doing?"

Christian didn't answer as the Fokker suddenly dipped down again. Zeus felt his stomach rising in his chest, and fought back a gag response.

Christian reached for the barf bag. So did several other passengers as the Fokker turned sharply eastward, tucking its left wing down and then pivoting even harder onto its right.

Zeus strained against the seatbelt, then felt himself pushed back as they leveled off. He wanted to look out the window, but Christian was in the way, getting sick. Zeus turned toward the aisle, trying to keep his own stomach from feeling too queasy.

The pilot came on with another announcement. His words seemed to come more quickly than before, though Zeus could only guess at what he was saying.

Don't worry. All is routine.

The plane leveled off. After a few moments, Zeus braved a glance at Christian.

"Maybe we should change seats," he suggested.

"Yeah. Okay."

"You all right?"

"No."

Zeus stepped into the aisle, then slipped in as Christian got out of the way.

A set of lights blinked beyond the wing. One of the planes that had buzzed them earlier was now flying parallel to the Fokker. Zeus guessed it was a fighter, and that they had inadvertently strayed into a military area.

That didn't seem to make much sense, though—they were still out over the water.

Then he saw lights in the distance. At first, he thought he had spotted a city; then he realized he was looking at one of the Chinese aircraft carriers.

Zeus pushed against the glass, trying to get a better view. The Chinese had two carriers. The last he had heard was that they were operating together. But he could see only one.

Something was landing on it. From this distance it was impossible to tell what kind of plane.

Zeus turned his attention to the dots of light near the larger ship. They were escorts. The Navy probably already knew exactly which ships they were, how they were equipped, even who their captains were. Very possibly an unmanned spy plane was watching them at this very moment. Still, this was a real intelligence opportunity: Zeus studied the dots, trying to memorize the pattern. Two small ships flanking the carrier, with a larger ship to the south. Three other vessels behind, to the north. Two seemed relatively large and wide; he guessed they were supply vessels of some sort, with their own escort.

When they were past the last of the ships, the aircraft on the wing veered away. A cone of orange appeared at the back of the gray fuselage, changing from a circle to an ellipse as it made its turn. Zeus stared after it. When he finally turned his attention back to the cabin, he saw that the stewardesses were handing out towels. They were landing soon.

"You okay?" he asked Christian.

"Better. Sorry."

"It's all right."

"Funny thing is, I feel hungry now."

"Yeah, well, I wouldn't push that."

Zeus went back to looking out the window. He couldn't see any more lights, just a dull, orange-brown glow ahead to his left. He glanced at his watch: fifteen past three.

Where had the time gone? And yet it had seemed to pass so slowly.

Ten minutes later, the plane began to bank in the direction of the glow. By now, it looked like a pale yellow foam rising from the crust of the blackness below. Zeus guessed it was Beihai, where they were headed.

The pilot confirmed it with an announcement a few seconds later. The only word Zeus recognized was the name of the city.

He tightened his seatbelt and waited patiently as the plane put down, the engines growing into a loud roar as the wheels hit the tarmac. The passengers applauded as the pilot feathered the engines and gently nudged the brakes.

The plane stopped a good distance from the terminal. A pair of buses waited nearby. Zeus watched a moveable stairway being pushed close to the fuselage.

The passengers got their things together, then filed out slowly, silently, no doubt wondering like Zeus and Christian what they were going to do next.

Solt was a few passengers ahead of them. Zeus angled to the left as he neared the bottom of the steps, intending to catch up. But as he reached the bottom of the stairs, the attendant standing there tapped his shoulder.

"This bus," she said in English. "That one is full."

Zeus turned dutifully and led the rest of the passengers to the second vehicle. The driver smiled and nodded as he boarded, greeting him in Chinese. Zeus found a seat a few rows back.

Christian slid in next to him silently. Zeus guessed that he was embarrassed that he'd gotten sick, though he had plenty of company.

The bus was quiet. When the last passenger had found a seat, the driver closed the door and put the vehicle into motion, gliding across the blacktop toward a two-story building about two hundred and fifty yards away. He stopped behind the first bus, which had already discharged its passengers.

Humming to himself, he opened the door, said something to the passengers in the front row, then hopped down the steps and trotted over to the building. No one moved; apparently he had told everyone to wait.

Zeus watched as the driver spoke to a pair of policemen standing next to a glass door, then ran back, hopped up the steps, and then said something in Chinese that Zeus assumed meant, "Everyone off the bus." The passengers rose slowly and began filing out.

Zeus rubbed his temples as he joined the small herd walking toward the door. He hadn't slept now for more than a day, not counting as-

sorted fitful turning in a cot aboard one of the boats they'd commandeered. He hadn't slept all that well for a few days before that, either.

The glass door opened on a narrow hallway, with rooms on the left
and right. The passengers were directed to the room at the right, which
was well lit by overhead fluorescents. It was a medium-sized office, bereft
of furniture.

They organized themselves along the far wall. No one from the first
bus was here; Solt was nowhere to be seen.

"Damn," grumbled Christian, standing next to him. "I feel like I'm
back in beast barracks."

"A lot worse than this."

"I guess." Beast barracks was West Point slang for the freshman
orientation period, traditionally a test for newcomers. Outright hazing
by upperclassmen was no longer permitted, but the older students still
found a way to make things hard for the new arrivals.

Christian cupped his face with his hands. "I gotta get out of here
and get some rest."

"I know what you mean," answered Zeus. "We'll have a chance soon.
They're probably just figuring out hotels and stuff."

"Where's Solt?"

Zeus shook his head.

A man in a dark suit came into the room after the passengers. He
told them something in Chinese that didn't seem to please anyone. They
began murmuring and making clucking sounds with their tongues.
The man behind Zeus said something out loud that made the airline
official redden. The two men began arguing; other passengers joined
in. Finally, the airline official left.

"What the hell is going on?" Christian asked.

"Does anyone here speak English?" asked Zeus, deciding there was
no sense keeping quiet anymore.

A young woman—the only woman in their group—said something
in Chinese, which prompted one of the older men near them to begin
speaking to them. It was clear he was trying to explain the predica-
ment, but Zeus had no way of understanding the words. He listened as
carefully as he could, and nodded to encourage the man to continue,
but the sounds flowed over him like the ocean.

"Let's go find somebody that can help us," insisted Christian. "Or at least
get to Solt. Hell."

"She may not be using that name," said Zeus.

"I don't care anymore," said Christian. "I want to get the hell out of here. I feel claustrophobic."

"Relax."

"Don't tell me that anymore," said Christian, starting for the door. "My head's going to explode."

The airline official who'd been speaking inside was talking to another employee in the hallway. Christian strode up to him and in a loud voice demanded to know what was going on.

The airline official briefly glanced at him, then went back to his own intense discussion with his fellow employee.

Christian grabbed his shoulder. "What's going on?"

The airline official jumped away from Christian's grip.

"Easy, Win," Zeus told Christian. "You're not helping. He doesn't understand what you're saying."

"I don't give a shit."

The airline official stepped back, hands out in horror. His companion began backing up the hall.

"He didn't mean anything," Zeus told them. "He's just a little tired."

The airline officials exchanged a look, then retreated farther into the building.

"Let's go after them," said Christian. "There has to be somebody who works for the airline who speaks English."

"They'll get somebody. Wait," said Zeus. But Christian had already started after them.

Reluctantly, Zeus followed in the direction that the two men had taken. A pair of policemen stood in the hallway just around the corner, blocking the way.

"Excuse me," said Christian.

Neither man moved. Zeus saw that Christian's face was beet red again, and his voice was shaky.

"Do you speak English?" Zeus asked the policemen. "A little? We're trying to find out what's going on. No one seems to be able to help us."

The man on the right said something in a sharp tone, then pointed behind them, indicating they should return to the room.

"What if we don't want to go back?" snapped Christian.

The policeman began gesticulating, thrusting his finger toward Christian's chest as he spoke in a rapid and clearly angry Chinese staccato.

Zeus suddenly had a premonition of what was going to happen.

"No!" he yelled, reaching for Christian.

But it was too late.

"I'm not taking this shit anymore!" said Christian, launching a left hook that caught his antagonist square in the side of the head.

11

Eastern Pennsylvania

Once the interviews were finished, the Marshal Service took Mara and Josh to a motel in eastern Pennsylvania where they could rest and not be bothered for the rest of the night. But even though they had rented an entire floor of the motel, they were concerned enough about security to tell Mara that she couldn't go out for a walk by herself.

Josh went right to bed, and fell asleep as soon as he'd pulled the thin blanket over his chest. He slept soundly, and woke smoothly and quickly, rising in the unfamiliar room about a half hour before dawn.

The heat was on, but after Vietnam, it felt cold. He pulled on a sweatshirt, then went to take a walk.

"Hey now, where do you think you're going, son?" asked the marshal sitting in the hallway when he emerged from his room. He had a Texas accent, accentuated by a pair of scuffed boots that poked far out of his pant legs.

"Walk," said Josh.

"Uh, not a good idea."

"Why not?"

The Texan blinked at him.

Josh shrugged and went to the stairs. The marshal hesitated for a moment, then got up to follow.

The crisp air outside felt bracing. The motel was located at the end of the town's business district, a mix of nineteenth- and twentieth-century Victorian storefronts and 1960s-era highway development. The stylistic mishmash was comforting to Josh—it reminded him of the area where he'd grown up. A large Mobil sign lit the corner ahead. Josh walked to it, thinking he would find a cup of coffee there. But the station wasn't open yet. He continued through the lot, trailed by his bodyguard, who for some reason didn't seem inclined to get very close.

A light shone through the window of a cement block building across the street. Josh glanced both ways, then crossed toward it. The place turned out to be a bagel shop, and there were people inside—the baker and his helper, along with two customers who sat talking at a corner table as Josh came in. Coffee was served at a counter to the side. Josh helped himself to a cup, then went and got two bagels.

"I'll get it," said the Texan, coming into the shop.

"Thanks," said Josh. He stood back and waited while the marshal poured himself a coffee. The two customers were talking about a high school football game, apparently played years before.

"Feel like walking some more?" asked Josh when the marshal finished paying.

He nodded.

Josh started to go out the door when the headline on the local newspaper caught his eye.

QUESTIONS RAISED ON
CHINA INVASION CLAIM

Invasion? It was a massacre, not just an invasion.

He nearly bumped into the marshal as he turned back to look at the paper. It was a tabloid, and the headline, in large bold type, ran over an unrelated photo of a local house fire. It referred to a story inside the paper.

Josh went back and bought the paper. He stood back from the counter, folding the paper over so he could read it.

Chinese officials immediately questioned whether the footage was authentic.

"All along, the Vietnamese have been very adept at manipulating public opinion," said Xi Hing Lee, a Chinese representative to the UN. "They have posted things on YouTube that are clearly fake."

"And I guess the missile on the bridge was made up, too?" said Josh aloud.

"Not here," said the marshal, in a gruff, though barely audible voice.

Josh continued reading. The story basically called him a liar, reporting the Chinese claims that the talk of atrocities was propaganda initiated by the Vietnamese.

He folded the newspaper beneath his arm as calmly as he could, took a small sip of coffee, then left the shop. This time, the marshal stayed with him as he walked down the street.

"What the hell?" said Josh, turning toward him. "I mean, what the hell?"

"Ah. Never believe what you read in the papers."

"How can they think I made it up? I gave them a video for crap's sake."

His bodyguard shrugged.

Josh shook his head. He was walking back in the direction of the hotel, but he was too mad to go back to his room—he needed to burn off some energy. He reversed course, steaming back past the bagel shop practically at flank speed.

"You can't take shit like this personally, kid," said the marshal finally. He was taller than Josh, but he seemed to be having trouble keeping up.

"You like being called a liar?" Josh asked.

"Well—"

"Yeah. That's exactly my point."

12

Beihai Airport, China

Zeus saw in slow motion:

Christian punching the policeman, the policeman falling against his comrade, Christian launching another punch, this one catching the man full in the face and throwing him backward.

Bowled over by his comrade, the second policeman sprawled on the ground. Zeus's first instinct was to reach down and help him up, but as he did, the man began pushing himself backward to get away.

"It's all right," said Zeus. "This is all a mistake. It's just a mistake."

The frightened policeman had a whistle attached to a ring on one of his fingers. He put his hand to his mouth and began to blow.

"Damn you!" yelled Christian.

Zeus grabbed him before he could kick the policeman. He pushed Christian back against the wall.

"This is just a big misunderstanding," yelled Zeus, still thinking he could calm the situation.

But it had gone far beyond that—the other policeman reached to his holster for his gun.

"We gotta get out of here!" yelled Christian. He slipped from Zeus's grasp and ran down the hall toward the door.

Zeus saw the officer pulling the gun out. He took two steps and kicked it away. Then he started running. Shouts and whistles echoed through the hall. The passengers in the room crowded around the door, gaping as Zeus passed.

Christian flew through the door to the outside. Zeus followed. There was no other choice; running was the only option now.

Eventually, though, he was going to kick Christian's head in.

Zeus hit the door with his left shoulder, jolting it open. The two policemen who'd been outside were yelling at Christian to stop. The one on the right raised his pistol to fire. Zeus launched himself at the man. He hit him hard in the back, toppling him over. The gun fired, then flew from the cop's hand as he hit the pavement. Zeus scrambled after it, scooping it up in his right hand before jumping to his feet.

Where the hell is Christian?

Zeus saw someone beyond the circle of light running behind the dark shadow of the nearby bus. He threw himself forward, tripping, but then regaining his balance. He pumped his legs. They felt as if they were thigh-deep in mud, each stride an effort. His heart pumped hard in his chest, the beats thick in his throat as he ran for the bus.

"Christian! For crap's sake, where the hell are you!" he yelled. "Christian!"

There was no answer, or at least none that he could hear. But the second bus pulled out from around the first. Zeus veered toward it, still running at top speed. The bus lurched, then slowed, its door open.

Zeus heard a pair of gunshots just as he reached the vehicle. He grabbed the bar inside the door and pulled himself up, holding on as Christian stepped on the gas.

"What the hell are you doing?" Zeus yelled.

"Getting the hell out of here! You got any better ideas?"

They barreled down the apron area for a few hundred feet, lights off, then veered left as Christian ran out of pavement. The bus tipped hard on its wheels, squealing ferociously but remaining upright.

"Where are you going?" demanded Zeus.

"Out of here!"

"You're heading for the runway."

"Tell me something better."

A white light cut across their path. The bus began to shake. The white turned black, then flashed red. A plane passed overhead so close Zeus thought it was going through them.

By the time Christian reacted the plane had already passed. He braked hard, then overcorrected as the bus veered left. They fishtailed back and forth. Zeus flew to the floor, arms curled around his head. He was sure they were going to roll over. But somehow the bus remained on all four wheels, weaving a little less wildly as Christian fought to find something approaching a straight line. By the time Zeus got to his feet, Christian had found a service road. There was a fence ahead; beyond it, an open field.

Christian headed straight for the fence.

"What!" yelled Zeus.

Christian didn't answer.

"Stay on the road! Turn!" yelled Zeus.

Christian, eyes glazed, drove straight through the fence. The bus wheezed as it went down a short hill. Shaking and groaning, its front wheels sunk into the loose dirt as it hit the field, but the vehicle had enough momentum to keep going, plowing through a shallow irrigation ditch and then continuing into a field.

In better days there would have been wheat or soybeans here, but the land was dry and hard-packed by the lack of rain over the past two years. The bus plowed on, hurling dust in a whirlwind around them. They continued across for a good three or four hundred feet, until they drove into a second ditch. This one was deep enough for the front bumper of the bus to strike the embankment as it came to the bottom. The bumper ground into the earth like a spear and the back of the bus flew to the right. For a moment it seemed to Zeus that he was flying. Time stopped in midair, everything frozen. All of his thoughts were frozen before him, snippets and shards of ideas and sensations: the war, the U.S., his prize Corvette, Solt Jan—they were all there around him, like playing cards spread out on a table.

Then time went fast again. The bus crashed onto its side with a thud. Zeus sprawled against the glass, bashing his face as he fell. His knee hit the top of a seatback as he fell, and he felt his kneecap pop. He rolled through the bus, arms flailing as he tried to grab a handhold.

Zeus lost his breath, his side collapsing from a sharp blow against the side of something in the bus. He fell on his back, trying to will his diaphragm and lungs to work again. He squeezed and squeezed until realizing that was exactly the wrong thing to do. He relaxed and his breath came back.

His vision widened from the black dot it had fled to. He saw the bus's interior, dust filtering in a yellowish-red glow that came from the dash lights and the LEDs on the floor and ceiling.

Christian groaned behind him.

"We have to get the hell out of here," said Zeus, getting to his knees. He rose and moved tentatively down the row of windows to one marked with red LEDs. He put his hands on the bottom, and pushed. His left wrist hurt; he wedged his elbow against the frame instead and popped out the emergency window.

"You comin'?" he yelled, climbing halfway out.

Christian groaned in response. Zeus looked around. The airport was straight ahead, quiet in the distance, at least for the moment.

There was a highway not fifty yards away, up a slight hill.

"Come on," said Zeus, ducking back into the bus. "There's a road."

Christian groaned on his right, near the back of the bus.

"How the hell did you get back here?" Zeus said, crawling toward him. "Win, come on. We gotta get out of here. There's a road."

Christian raised his head and turned toward Zeus. He blinked his eyes.

It wasn't Christian—it was the bus driver.

Shit, thought Zeus, backing away.

"Christian?"

"I'm here." Christian rose from the stairwell near the driver's seat. "What the hell?"

"Yeah, what the hell. That's my feeling exactly."

"Where are we?" muttered Christian.

"In deep shit, and headed deeper," said Zeus. "Come on. We gotta get out before they find us."

"Where?"

"There's a road up there. We'll find someplace to hide or something."

Zeus waited by the open window as Christian clambered toward him.

"Here's your gun," said Christian, handing over the pistol. He'd found it on the way.

Zeus grabbed it. "You're lucky I don't shoot you with it."

———

Zeus left the driver—there was nothing he could tell the authorities that they wouldn't already know.

They crossed the highway, walking in the direction of lights about a mile farther north. Zeus had only the vaguest idea of where they were, and no real plan on what to do next. They had no equipment, no phones, no GPS, no secret decoder rings or Enterprise communicators that would beam them up to safety.

Beijing and the embassy was probably their best bet, but getting there would be next to impossible. They had their passports, but those would surely identify them as the criminals who had caused such havoc in Beihai. They had only American money, and not all that much of that. Neither Zeus nor Christian spoke Chinese, and from what he'd heard and had seen already, it was unlikely they'd find many people who spoke English, at least until they got to a large city.

"You think we can find a car or something at one of those houses?" asked Christian as they got closer to the lights.

"I dunno," said Zeus.

"Can you hot-wire a car?"

Zeus *could* hot-wire a car, as a matter of fact, bypassing the key sole-noid; it wasn't that hard on most cars. At least not on the older cars that he had worked on and restored since he was thirteen. But could he do it to whatever little econobox rice-burner they found? And could he do it in the dark, without anyone seeing them?

Those were the more pertinent questions, and Zeus had no answer to them.

Stealing a car made sense, or would have, if there had been cars near any of the three houses and two farm buildings clustered around a fork in the road. The only vehicles they could find were bicycles, parked neatly against the side of the smallest of the three houses. Christian complained about his ankle, wondering if it would be up to pedaling.

"Suck it up," said Zeus, whose entire body was covered with bruises and welts. He took one of the bikes and pushed it as quietly as possible from the house toward the road. Christian eventually followed.

They rode along the dirt road for a few miles, moving roughly north. After about fifteen minutes, Zeus spotted a long highway overpass ahead. The highway crossed over the local road, veering through the hills. He rode under and beyond it, vainly hoping there would be an access ramp. When he realized there wasn't, he turned and went back to the stone and rubble embankment below the overpass. There he got off the bike and began hauling it up the hill toward the highway.

The bicycle was a heavy Chinese model, built to withstand the rugged roads of the Chinese countryside and small cities; it was not light. Christian groaned as he slipped sideways up the hill.

A truck whizzed by as Zeus reached the top. The highway was a two-lane national road, recently repaved. There was a wide shoulder next to the guardrail, and at the moment at least no other cars or trucks in sight. Zeus put his bike on the pavement and began pedaling.

"Are we allowed to ride on this?" said Christian, huffing as he caught up.

Zeus didn't answer.

"Hey, are we going to get stopped?"

"Do I look like a traffic cop?" snapped Zeus.

"I'm just asking."

Zeus concentrated on pedaling, pushing down his legs in long strokes. His kneecap was feeling odd. Not hurt, exactly; it was more like someone had taken it off and put it back on wrong.

After they had been riding for about ten minutes, they saw the glow of lights in the distance. Zeus lowered his head and began pedaling in earnest, pumping his legs and ignoring as much as possible the stitch developing in his side. He focused only on the pavement immediately in front of him. The world narrowed to the rush of wind around his head. Finally, the pain at his side was too much. He eased his pace and looked up, gazing into the distance at his goal.

It wasn't a city as he had thought. It was a pulloff, a truck stop, similar to those in the States. A small, well-lit building sat on a slight rise to the right in front of a sea of cement. Brightly colored fuel pumps stood like buoys near the building.

Four semitrailers and six large, open, and canvas-covered trucks were idling at the side of the road.

Opportunity knocks, Zeus thought.

Zeus rode along the side of the road until just short of the rest stop. Gliding to a stop, he picked up the bike and dropped it over the rail into the scraggly grass on the other side of the shoulder. He glanced back and saw Christian, puffing with exertion, some thirty yards away.

There was no reason to wait. Half-crouching, half-trotting, Zeus went to the last truck in the line. He climbed up on the running board, and put his hand to the door. It was locked. And not only that: the driver was dozing behind the wheel.

Zeus dropped quickly to the ground, bumping into Christian and knocking him to the pavement.

"What the hell are you doing?"

"Sssshhh."

Zeus checked each of the trucks. The drivers were sleeping in all of them. Dejected, Zeus trotted went back to his bike.

"My leg is killing me," said Christian, trailing him. "I think my ankle's going to fall off."

"You'll live."

"No, look at it." He held his right leg up. Even in the dim light Zeus could tell the ankle was swollen. "I don't know how much farther I can go."

"Damn."

"I know. It sucks."

More than you'll admit, Zeus thought, considering this mess is all your fault. But he kept his mouth shut; the last thing they needed now was another outburst of insanity.

"We'll hitch a ride on one of the trucks," said Zeus.

"What about carjacking one?"

Zeus considered the possibility.

"I don't know," said Zeus. "If we keep the driver with us, he'll be a problem. If we kick him out, he'll be sure to call the police."

"Just shoot him."

"For Christ's sake."

"Fuck him. This is a war."

"We're not at war, Win."

"Like hell we're not! We just blew up some of their landing ships. And a patrol boat."

"He's a civilian."

"Crap. What do you want to do? We can't just walk to Beijing. Why don't we just turn ourselves in and let them shoot us as spies?"

"You're the one that screwed this all up," answered Zeus. He began to seethe. "You snapped. You're an asshole."

"Don't call me an asshole."

"You are. You've always been an asshole. At school. At the com—"

Zeus stopped midsentence, ducking back as Christian threw a haymaker in his direction. Failing to connect, Christian crumbled as his ankle gave way under the weight of his swing.

"Asshole," said Zeus. "Proves my point."

Christian began pounding the ground. Zeus, disgusted, shook his head. Then he realized his companion was crying.

"I *am* an asshole," Christian sobbed. "I screwed everything up. I'm a wimp. I'm no good. I'm useless."

All true, thought Zeus. But this was one hell of a time for such a revelation.

He squeezed his fingers against the corner of his temple. They were coming apart—Christian obviously, but he was, too. He already had. The fatigue of the last few days, the stress of the mission, and then the danger behind the lines: they'd reached their breaking point.

God, was it this easy to crack?

Zeus had heard dozens of lectures about battle stress and fatigue and posttraumatic stress, but in every story, the flash point had come after real duress: guys being shelled for hours on end, or marching through jungles for days, getting bombed by their own planes.

What the hell had he been through? One mission.

Actually, several. And getting to Hainan Island had been an ordeal in and of itself. But still, it shouldn't have been enough to break him.

It wasn't. He was a goddamn, well-trained soldier, for Christ's sake—a freakin' *major*, a MAY-JOR, not some skinny pimple-faced skateboarder tossed into his first firefight without a weapon or a radio.

Goddamn.

"Pull yourself together," he said, addressing himself as much as Christian. "We gotta get our butts out of here."

Christian didn't answer. But his back stopped heaving, and he slowly rose from the ground.

"We'll hide in one of the trucks, and go as far as he takes us," Zeus said. "Come on."

He walked back to the line of trucks. He decided it would be better to hide in one of the smaller vehicles, since they wouldn't have to worry about opening the rear door. But the cargo area of the first truck was jammed tight with canisters that appeared from the colors to be acetylene and oxygen, and there was no room except on the top of them. The second was only half full: some furniture and boxes were secured in the front, leaving a good space on the bed. The truck was a flatbed with sides made of wooden staves, covered by a canvas tarp. Lying on his belly, Zeus could see off the sides as well as the rear, while from the distance he figured he would look like one of the furled rugs poking between the cab and the boxes.

"Say nothing," he whispered to Christian as he slid into the back.

Christian, head hanging down, complied.

———

A week before, Zeus would have enjoyed seeing Win Christian crumble. The truth was, he hated the son of a bitch with a passion. He'd been an obnoxious, holier-than-thou type at West Point, and had gotten worse as time went on. Most recently, he had been Zeus's main antagonist at the Red Dragon computerized war simulations, cocky and full of himself before the simulations, brimming with unjustified overconfidence. Cutting him down in the sims—Zeus had won *every* confrontation—had been the highlight of his posting.

But now Zeus only felt disgust at himself, not Christian. Because, if the truth be told, he suddenly felt just as weak. He should have stopped Christian from going nuts back at the airport. That was his responsibility, wasn't it? He'd known Christian was getting edgy. He could make excuses, explanations—he was damned tired himself—but what did they matter? They were where they were because he hadn't done anything to fix it.

Kill a civilian?

That was murder, pure and simple. Even if they were at war, it was wrong. Wrong. He had been trained, taught, better than that.

Much better. Zeus had served as a captain in Special Forces. He'd seen combat, real combat; not as much as a lot of other guys, including most of the men he'd led, but enough to have been tested and survived. And now he was falling apart without anyone even firing at him.

The truck rocked on its springs. Zeus turned back to Christian, ready to punch him for moving. Then he realized it was the driver in the cab. He'd woken up.

Zeus put up his finger and held it to his lips. Christian nodded.

They waited for a minute or two, lying silently on the bed of the truck. Finally, Zeus realized that the man had gone back to sleep. He curled back and put his face close to Christian's ear.

"We have to just be patient," he said.

"Yeah."

"We'll get out of this."

One of the tractor-trailers ahead of them rumbled to life. The motor was loud, and the vibrations from the tailpipe so strong that the bottom of their truck rattled.

Zeus squirreled himself around, trying to make himself more comfortable. He also took the gun from his belt, keeping it ready in his hand.

He didn't want to kill civilians. But if it came down to it, if it was him or them, what would he do?

He'd always thought kill-or-be-killed was an easy question. But now he wasn't sure. Was survival more important, or surviving as a moral man?

If you believed in eternity, if you believed in God and heaven, then surely being a moral man was more important.

But hell, he was Catholic. He could always confess his sins.

The irreverence struck him as funny, and it was all he could do to keep himself from laughing.

There was more shifting in the cab. The truck started. Its muffler was shot, and the whole vehicle vibrated with the engine's loud, uneven rumble.

The truck backed up slightly, then eased out onto the highway.

Zeus tried to quiet his mind. The jumbled emotions were due mostly to fatigue. He could get out of this—he *would* get out of this. All he had to do was keep his head.

They had driven for about twenty minutes when the truck began to slow down, then pulled off to the side. Zeus pushed himself tight against the boxes, holding his breath. He felt the gun in his hand.

Zeus caught a glimpse of the driver as he got out and went around the back of the truck, continuing into the nearby field. He was taking a leak.

Now's our chance.

Zeus slipped quietly along the truck bed, and climbed down. Glancing back, he saw Christian's eyes open, watching him. He motioned with his hands: *Stay there. Quiet.* Then he ran around to the front of the truck.

Zeus still had the gun in his right hand. He took it in his left, then quietly opened the driver's side door. But as he started to climb up into the cab, he saw that the keys weren't in the ignition.

Cursing to himself, he slipped down and gently closed the cab door. He took a deep breath, then another.

Come on, he told himself. Get to it.

Zeus slipped along the front of the truck, hiding behind the hood. He couldn't see the driver. It made more sense to wait for him to come back, but Zeus's adrenaline was rising. The urge to go and grab him was irresistible. He started to rise—and was startled to see the driver just turning the corner of the truck, not three feet away.

Zeus threw himself forward, striking the man awkwardly with his left fist. Had the driver been less surprised than Zeus, or perhaps a larger man, he would have been able to easily parry the blow; it was delivered off-balance, and Zeus was wide open for an easy counterpunch. But the last thing the man expected was to be confronted by a thief, and his eyes widened as Zeus's blow landed. Zeus swung the pistol toward his head, catching him at the side of the temple. The man collapsed on the pavement, his eyes shut.

Zeus dropped to his knees, anxious. The man was still breathing, but he was unconscious.

The keys were on a long chain at his belt. Zeus unhooked them, then dragged the man off the side of the road.

"What are you going to do with him?" Christian asked, limping around from the back.

"Just get in the truck," said Zeus.

"You gonna kill him?"

"Get in the truck."

Christian blinked, then did as he was told.

Zeus dragged the man about twenty yards from the road. He bent down, making sure one last time that he was still breathing, then ran back to the cab.

————

There was a large map among the papers in the cab's glove compartment. Between the map and the large compass on the dashboard, they figured out that they were headed toward National Road 325, headed for Qinzhou.

The map could get them all the way to Beijing, but they'd need to stop for fuel several times; they had barely a half a tank. Zeus unfolded the map and held it over the steering wheel, thinking how he might get fuel without only American money. Fifty dollars might very well cover a full tank—he had no idea what the price would be, let alone whether a station out here would even accept American money.

Surely not.

Robbing a place would be even more foolish.

Christian sat pitched into the corner of the cab, quiet, sullen. Zeus thought he should say something to him, give him some sort of morale booster, but he didn't feel like talking to him, much less cheering him up, so they drove in silence.

As best he could figure, they were on G050, the expressway heading westward. Qinzhou would be off to the right, to the northeast. They were so far from Beijing that it wasn't even on the map. Zeus pulled the map away from the wheel, folding it before handing it to Christian. The major took it wordlessly, holding it in his hand as if it were a train ticket waiting to be collected.

The highway was not very much different than those in the States. There were few other vehicles; most were trucks, and the majority were going the other way. Every time Zeus saw a set of lights growing in his side mirror, he eased off the gas, hoping to let them slip by him with a minimum of fuss. As they approached, he felt a quick pinch of fear. He worried that the vehicle would turn out to be a police car.

None did. As each passed, he felt a small burst of relief, enough to cheer him and push him on for a few miles, until more headlights appeared. This rollercoaster of emotions made it harder for Zeus to concentrate on a plan, and it was not until he saw the glow of Qinzhou to the north that he finally formulated one.

"Give me that map again," Zeus told Christian.

Once again he spread it along the top of the steering wheel. Rather than going all the way to Beijing, the best thing to do was to turn south. Vietnam was relatively close—the border was perhaps fifty miles away. True, there would be troops and border guards, but the fighting was much farther west, and in the jungle it should be relatively easy to find a place to slip through.

Even better: they could steal a boat from the coast and sail south. He already knew from the briefing for the mission that the Chinese weren't able to patrol the entire coastline, and were concentrating their ships to the east and south. A few hours in a small fishing vessel would be far less risky than trying to drive to Beijing.

"Take this," he told Christian, handing him the map. "We want to stay on G050 to S221. Can you follow it?"

"I guess."

"Don't guess."

"Yeah."

"I don't know the road system. It looks like it'll be a lesser road. Like a state highway compared to an interstate. Something like that."

"Mmmmm," said Christian, studying the map.

Though the map included Western letters and numbers for the highways, the road signs they passed were exclusively in Chinese. Christian worked on correlating the Chinese highway designations with the Western figures, and found the turnoff for S221, which cut south. But as soon as they pulled around the access ramp off the expressway, Zeus realized they had another problem. There was a toll booth ahead.

"Shit," he muttered. "Do we have money?"

"What?" said Christian.

"Tolls. Look around—maybe there's change in the glove compartment."

Christian opened it and rifled through even though they'd already looked.

Zeus wasn't sure what to do. There was a small, thin gate barring the lane; he could roll through easily enough. But surely the toll collector would alert the local police. They'd be pulled over in minutes.

He could play dumb foreigner. But why would a dumb foreigner be driving a truck?

He eased into the toll lane, deciding he would hit the gas just as he drew even with the booth. That would take the collector by surprise, and he might not get out quickly enough to see the truck's plate.

A bare hope, but all he had.

"Money!" said Christian. He'd found a small change purse between the seats. "How much?"

Zeus tapped the brake, jerking the truck to a stop just even with the window of the booth. A woman who barely came up to the handle on the truck's door peered up quizzically.

"Give me the biggest bill," Zeus whispered to Christian.

Christian handed him a twenty yuan note. Zeus leaned his hand down to the toll taker, hoping that she wouldn't get a good glimpse of his face and realize he was Caucasian.

The woman began jabbering at him. He guessed she was asking if he had something smaller, since she hadn't taken the bill.

He shrugged, holding his hand out in an empty gesture.

"We should just go," said Christian under his breath.

The gate was down. He could break through it easily enough, but that would mean they'd have to ditch the truck.

Zeus glanced to his right, looking to make sure there wasn't a police car on the shoulder ahead. He was about to stomp on the gas when Christian tapped him across the chest.

He held out a toll card.

Zeus took it and handed it down. The tollkeeper said something in an exasperated tone, probably accusing him of being a dope. She kept talking, asking for something else. Maybe his license—were foreigners allowed to drive in China?

It didn't matter. He didn't have a Chinese license—or *any* license. And he certainly wasn't going to give her his passport.

The woman scolded him. Zeus realized finally that she wanted more money.

"Give me another bill," he told Christian, turning to him.

"What?"

"Just give me some more money."

"There are two tens."

Christian gave them to him. Zeus held them down. The woman took them.

The gate remained down.

All right, thought Zeus. That's it. He put his foot on the gas. But instead of revving, the engine stalled, flooded by the sudden surge of fuel.

His throat tightened in an instant.

Quickly, he reached for the key. Nothing happened. He slipped the truck into neutral. Before he could try again, the tollkeeper banged on the door. He glanced in the mirror, saw her holding her hand up.

Change.

He reached down, took it, and with his hand shaking, restarted the truck. The gate was open; he eased through.

"Here," he told Christian, handing him the money.

———

They drove in silence for another fifteen minutes. Zeus's eyelids started to droop. Despite the anxiety and adrenaline, he teetered on the edge of sleep. Sleep was what he really needed—sleep would erase much of the fear; sleep would restore his strength; sleep would help him think clearly. If he slept, he could sort everything out. He could figure out how to get back to Vietnam.

He could decide what he felt about killing civilians.

He knew how he felt about that: he should not kill civilians. He could not. Even if he were at war, it would not be right.

If they tried to kill him?

Then they weren't civilians.

What if they didn't try to kill him themselves, but told other people who would try to kill him? What if they were going to do that, but hadn't yet?

Where was the line?

"Hey—you fallin' asleep?" asked Christian.

Zeus shook himself back to full consciousness.

"I'm okay," he said.

"You got a plan?"

"We go south. We get close to the water. We get a boat."

"Right."

"So you gotta get us close to the water. But not a big town. A small one."

"If we're gonna steal a boat we gotta do it soon," said Christian. "It'll be light maybe in an hour. Less."

"Yeah."

"I'd like to sleep," added Christian.

"So would I," admitted Zeus. "But we can't."

Christian checked the map. They were driving in the direction of Fangchenggang, a large port city. Would they have an easier time getting a boat there, or just outside it?

Outside, Zeus thought.

"We have to find a good road to take us around the city, into the suburbs but near the water," he told Christian. "It would be better south—the closer we are to Vietnam, the better."

Christian studied the map.

Zeus spotted a truck off the side of the road ahead. He slowed, saw it was two trucks. Then he realized both were army trucks.

"We're getting the hell off this road right away," he told Christian. He spotted a turnoff ahead. "Figure out where we are."

13

Beijing

Cho Lai shook his head as his interior minister continued speaking. There had been more food riots overnight in Harbin. Meanwhile, the governor of Guangdong Province had sent police to "guard" a number of factories owned by party officials—a move meant as a threat to get more aid from the central government.

"All of this disruption when the country is at war," said Cho Lai finally. "It is treason."

The minister bowed his head.

"Criminals will be dealt with harshly," continued the premier. "Remind them of that. And note, too, that we will not be blackmailed."

"Yes, Premier."

"You're dismissed.

Cho Lai struggled to maintain his calm. On the one hand, he realized his people needed food—the shortages were severe, even here in Beijing: he had seen them himself on unannounced tours of the markets. On the other hand, he was solving the country's problems. All he needed was time.

The premier rose and walked around his large office, working off some of his frustration. Things in Vietnam were not going as planned. His generals were like frightened children, afraid to take even the smallest of losses.

And despite everything, they remained petrified of the Americans. The Americans, who were hiding in the shadows.

Why be afraid of them? China had succeeded in blocking any vote in the UN. Cho Lai was confident that there would be no vote of condemnation from the American Congress, either. He had spent enough money on lobbyists there to feed Harbin Province for a month—if only there were food to buy.

Still, one American remained beyond his reach: the President. He was a clever enemy, the dragon of many forms.

Why should Greene of all people help the Vietnamese? It was absurd and unfair. They had been Greene's tormentors.

Admittedly, this had been an error of Cho Lai. He had thought the President would secretly endorse the punishment of Vietnam. He had even fantasized about calling him and sharing a few boasts. In his imagination, his foolish imagination, Cho Lai had thought Greene would welcome the country's humiliation.

The intercom buzzed. Lo Gong, the defense minister, was waiting outside.

Cho Lai ordered him in.

"We are proceeding with a new plan to take Hai Phong," Lo Gong said. "We will move down the coast with our tanks. And then, a stealth attack—we have ships that are prepared to enter the port."

"Excellent," said Cho Lai.

"The storm is the only difficulty."

"What storm?"

"The typhoon, Your Excellency."

"Damn the weather! Move ahead. Always timid! Is every general in my army a coward?"

The minister's face reddened.

"Out!" thundered Cho Lai. "Out, before I lose my patience."

The defense minister left without saying another word.

14

Outside Fangchenggang, China

There was still another hour before dawn, but the city was already stirring, with a stream of trucks headed both toward and away from the harbor area. Traffic had already congealed on the major roads. Even the small byroads Zeus threaded through had a fair amount of vehicles.

Clusters of PLA trucks and soldiers were parked along the sides of several roads. Their mission, if any, seemed to be one of reassurance rather than actual security. In any event, they weren't stopping civilian vehicles.

"There's a line ahead," said Christian. "More traffic."

"Any way around it?"

"Not that I can see. Nothing on the map, either."

Zeus drew to a stop behind a late model Buick. The GM car was a status symbol here, a sign of wealth and probably political influence, which went hand in hand.

"There are some lights about a half mile ahead," said Christian, leaning out of the cab to look. "Must be a checkpoint."

"You see a place I can turn around?"

"Nothing."

Pulling a U-turn at this point would undoubtedly draw a lot of attention. He could do it anyway, find a side street, turn off.

"Look for a store with a parking lot," he told Christian. "We'll pull in there and leave the truck."

"Yeah."

A better solution presented itself as he crept ahead: a gas station sat ahead on the left. He'd have to cross traffic to get there. But it would be perfect.

Zeus waited for the Buick to move up a little farther, then began angling the truck in the direction of the service station. There was a stream of cars coming from the other direction, spaced just far enough apart to make it dangerous to cross.

Finally, he saw his chance. The truck bucked, nearly stalling as he gave it too much gas. This time he was able to back his foot off the pedal in time to keep the engine working, and they made it across into the service station without stalling or getting hit.

As they pulled alongside a pump an attendant came out of the nearby building.

"We're outta here now," Zeus told Christian, turning off the engine.

The attendant looked at him quizzically as Zeus jumped from the truck.

"Fill 'er up," said Zeus.

He tossed the man the keys, hitting him in the chest. With a quick stride, he walked around the back of the truck. Christian was already out.

"The ocean's in that direction," he told Zeus.

"Let's go."

———

It took them nearly two hours to get close to the water, walking down narrow streets that curled through mini-hamlets before opening into wet fields of salt marsh and muck. The area was crisscrossed by canals and bridges. Not many years before, rice fields had dotted the land, which had been partially reclaimed from the ocean centuries ago. But effluence from the nearby city and factories had poisoned the shallow bay waters. The ocean was rising gently, flooding into the muck, but it couldn't come fast enough to cleanse the ground.

Adding insult to injury, much of the land was now being filled in, legally and illegally, with garbage from the industrial north. Zeus and Christian wended their way past several massive dumping grounds. One was a mountain of old computers and other electronic gear. A trio of squatters huts sat at the edge of the dump near the road, as if standing guard. An old woman and two children watched them as they walked past, no doubt wondering what they were up to.

The sea smelled worse with every step closer. A thick, oily stench hung in the air, stinging their eyes.

"End of the road," said Christian, pointing toward the rocks ahead. "God, the smell is wretched."

Zeus remained silent as he walked toward the water. He was calmer than he had been before, but even more tired. His stomach felt like a marble rock, smooth and hard. His mouth was dry, his neck ached.

The sun, low on the horizon, pinched his eyes when he looked back at it. They'd come out on the western side of a peninsula opposite the city proper, which lay two or three miles across a shallow bay. Zeus stood at the water's edge, gazing across at the buildings in the distance. A jungle of red seaweed and algae floated nearby, giving the water a purplish cast. Barges were lined up to the right, a vast array bereft of cargo.

A navy vessel was anchored in the open water to his left, too far to be identified even if Zeus had been an expert on the Chinese navy. From here it looked rather large and ominous.

"Now what do we do?" asked Christian.

"We find a boat," said Zeus. "There should be plenty of fishing boats around somewhere."

"Let's try this way," he said, starting back. "We'll work our way along the coast and see if we see anything."

"I really need to rest."

"Soon."

———

About a half hour later, after zigging and zagging across a few marshy dunes and hills of grass that came nearly to their chests, Zeus spotted a pair of boats anchored together about twenty yards from land. They rocked gently with the light breeze.

There didn't seem to be anyone around. Zeus sat down in muddy sand, and took off his shoes.

"We're swimming?" Christian asked.

"Unless you got a better idea."

The oily film on the water made Zeus decide he'd keep his pants and shirt on. He put his shoes on a rock, thinking he'd come back for them, then he put the gun there, too.

The mud and weeds were soft, like a carpet thrown beneath the water. The first few yards were almost flat; the angle was very gradual after that.

Zeus got within arm's length of the nearest boat when the depth suddenly dropped off. He reached out with his arm and grabbed the side of the boat, kicking his feet free of the muck.

Long and narrow, the wooden-hulled craft looked more like a racing shell than a fisherman's boat. It was propelled by two long oars, one at the bow and one at the stern. A tiny, open-sided canvas tent sat just aft of the midway point, its stretched fabric bleached and brittle from the sun.

"Front or back?" said Christian, working through the water behind him.

"You take the bow."

Zeus pulled the long oar from the bottom of the boat and positioned it in the yoke.

The boat was tied to a stick that poked out of the water on the starboard side. Christian unleashed it, then moved up to the bow.

"We'll go back for our shoes," Zeus told him. "We may need them."

In water this shallow, the oars were better used as poles, and they were much easier to manipulate standing up. But it took Zeus several minutes to realize that, and several more to master the technique well enough to get them close to the shore. Finally Christian jumped off, waded through the muck, and came back with the shoes and gun.

"Who do you think owns the boat?" he asked as he plunked Zeus's shoes down.

"Somebody."

"Maybe we should leave some money in the other boat."

It wasn't a bad idea, but Zeus ended up vetoing it. They might still need Chinese money they had—eighteen yuan from the trucker's envelope. And leaving the American money might give anyone looking for them too much of a clue.

They headed toward the city's shore, trying to skirt the Chinese warship by the widest margin possible. The wind began picking up when they were roughly halfway across; Zeus found it harder and harder to steer them in a straight line. By the time they got across they had been pushed back almost to the barges.

"We're beat," said Christian. "We really need sleep."

"We gotta keep going," insisted Zeus.

He tugged harder on the oar, angry with Christian even though he was only stating the obvious. They started doing better, then caught a break as the wind died.

"Look for a motorboat," Zeus told Christian. "We'll trade."

"Yeah, anybody would take that deal."

Zeus laughed. It was the first time he'd laughed in quite a while. It surprised him.

It felt good, shaking his lungs and clearing his head. They made it past the city peninsula, then began crossing a wide expanse of water toward an area of beaches. In happier times—only two years earlier—the beaches were popular with regional tourists. Now they were abandoned, flooded about halfway up, and cluttered with debris and seaweed.

No motorboats.

They kept going. The sun was high enough now to hit Zeus in the corner of his eye, the sharp edge of a nail in the flesh between socket and lid. He squinted against it, angling his head away as much as he could while still keeping his gaze on the direction he wanted to go.

Except for the glare, the sun was welcome. It felt warm rather than hot. The day turned pleasant, with just enough breeze to scatter the flies and mosquitoes.

An idyllic day, except for where they were.

Zeus saw that Christian wasn't paddling anymore.

"Christian?" said Zeus. "Christian?"

He slid his oar against the side of the boat. He should go check on his companion.

Later . . .

———

With both men asleep, the boat drifted toward shore. Pushed by the current, it ran aground in a twisted maze of debris and muck on one of the small islands southeast of port. Zeus slept on, oblivious to everything around him—the seabirds, the stench, the two large but half-empty grain carriers passing up the channel a few miles away. The water lapping against the side of the boat entered his dreams as a gentle sound, its monotonous beat reassuring and adding to his ease.

But eventually his dreams took strange shapes, past mixing with present. He was back in the plane when the attack on the dam began. The flight morphed into part of the war simulation as they looked at the shape war in Asia would take. He was driving the truck. He was shooting the guard in the airport.

He hadn't shot the guard in real life. But he was powerless to prevent it from happening in the dream.

In the dream, he shot the man who came for them in the hallway, then stood over him, pistol pointing at his forehead, daring him to move, even though the man was already dead. Blood began to spurt from the dead man's right eye, then his left. It started to pour from his nose and his mouth and his ears.

The hallway filled with blood. It flooded, rising to his knees, his stomach, his elbow. Zeus's hand was wet with it.

Then finally he woke up.

———

He was hanging half out of the boat, his arm deep in the murky water. He pushed himself upright, nearly losing his balance and flipping the craft over.

Or so it seemed.

Christian was huddled in the front. A rasping noise came from his chest. He was snoring.

Zeus stretched his back muscles, turning left and right slowly, his joints cracking. Perhaps they'd be better off staying here until nightfall. They'd have more strength.

On the other hand, a moving fishing boat was a lot less conspicuous than one hung up in the weeds.

By his reckoning, the border with Vietnam was no more than forty miles away.

Zeus crawled forward in the boat to wake Christian. But when he reached him he decided to let him rest. Better that one of them would have full strength, or as much as a few fitful hours of sleep would get him.

He went back and took the oar, pushing the boat backward out of the weeds. For a moment, he lost his balance and the boat tipped hard to the side. Zeus just barely managed to stay upright. He knelt for a moment, hunkered over to catch his breath. Then he rose and began to make his way.

The current flowed gently southward, which made it much easier to paddle. Zeus concentrated on making perfect strokes—long, powerful, with a subtle movement at the very end to correct his course. Inevitably, he tired of this, finding perfection unachievable. He began to concentrate instead on everything around him: the open water to his left; the succession of ragged, battered beaches and flooded swamps on his right.

Farther inland, up in the inlets and on the other side of man-made dykes, were pens for fish farms. Given the horrible smell and the waste that he saw along the shoreline, he wondered what sort of poisons the fish would contain.

———

The sun was nearing the horizon on his left when he spotted a Chinese naval vessel about a mile south. This one was much closer to shore than the one they'd skirted early in the day. It was smaller, with machine guns fore and aft.

It was infinitely more dangerous than the other one, Zeus realized; this was the sort of craft that would take an interest in him. Its guns could easily chew through the wood of his purloined boat.

Zeus decided he would slip toward shore and wait a few hours until sunset. It would be easier to get by then, and in any event, he could use a rest.

But as he edged the oar forward to act as a rudder, he saw the bow of the patrol boat tuck down, as if swallowed by a sudden wave. The flag on the mast shot to the left. The boat was turning. They'd already spotted them.

15

The White House

The past few presidents had gotten away from using the Oval Office as an actual working office, preferring the nearby study and even space upstairs in the residence, part of a trend toward demystifying and relaxing the presidency. But Greene liked the Oval Office for precisely the reason the others didn't—he wanted the gravitas of the place to impress everyone on how important their work was.

And to emphasize the fact that *he*, George Chester Greene, was the president.

Not that it was working all that well this morning. Not that it *ever* worked all that well with the chairman of the Joint Chiefs of Staff, Admiral Matthews.

Matthews was enumerating, for perhaps the hundredth time since the crisis with China began, the dangers inherent in bringing a full carrier group into the Gulf of Tonkin.

The Army chief of staff, Renata Gold, shifted in her seat. The Army general—the first woman to hold the post—had been in favor of intervention early on, but lately had come under so much criticism that she seemed now cautiously opposed.

Caution being the watchword of the day.

"You've made your point about the aircraft carriers," Walter Jackson, the National Security director, told Matthews. "But let's cut to the quick: could they defeat the Chinese naval forces?"

"Absolutely," said the admiral.

Jackson glanced toward Greene. The NSC head had a triumphant smile on his face.

"Good," said Greene, reaching for his coffee.

"But that's not an argument to intervene," added Matthews hastily.

"Noted," said Greene. "Now, about General Harland Perry's plan. Two divisions—"

"Impossible," said Matthews sharply. "We can't commit ground troops. Congress won't back intervention."

"If I might continue, Admiral," said Greene. "Perry has suggested two American divisions could win back the gains the Chinese have made in the west. But he also notes that's unrealistic, and I concur."

That was a sop to Matthews. All Greene got from him was a tight frown.

"The goal, as I see it, should be simply to contain the Chinese," said Greene. "We bring the A-10As there to stop the Chinese armor. That would be a first step. Then, establish a no-fly zone over the peninsula. F-22s and F-35s."

Greene glanced at Tommy Stills, the Air Force chief of staff and the one solidly hawkish member of the joint chiefs. He was nodding vigorously.

"The thing I need to be assured of," added Greene, "is that this works. Is it doable? Do we stop the Chinese?"

"There can be no assurances," said Matthews. "You're asking for the impossible."

"I think it has a reasonable chance," said Stills.

Greene turned to Gold. "General?"

"Better than fifty-fifty," she said.

"We can't commit forces without congressional approval," insisted Matthews. "Not on this scale."

"I'll worry about Congress," said Greene.

There was a tap on the door. One of Greene's schedule keepers was prompting him for his next appointment: breakfast with a group of senators currently opposed to his measure to aid Vietnam.

"I know everyone is on a tight schedule," said Greene, rising. "Thank you for your input. I'll keep you updated."

The chiefs and their aides filed out. Greene was feeling optimistic about the meeting; it had gone better than he had imagined.

Until he spotted Walter Jackson's frown.

"You think you have an agreement, don't you?" said Jackson after the military people had gone.

"You heard them: they agreed Perry's plan will work."

"No, they said *if* it was politically feasible. *If.* You don't have the votes in Congress. Matthews won't stand by idly if you send the troops on your own authority. It'll be leaked within an hour of your giving the order. Probably within the minute. The admiral's probably setting up an anonymous Twitter account to take care of it right now."

Greene looked over at his chief of staff, Dickson Theodore. Theodore had said nothing during the session. "Walter's right. All the admiral's talk about aircraft carriers? It's code for keep us out of it."

"The Air Force is gung-ho," said Greene.

"The Air Force alone isn't enough," said Jackson. "And what do you think will happen the first time an airplane is shot down? It'll be broadcast on the cable networks immediately."

"Congress will have a fit," added Theodore. "Troops—even airplanes—violate the neutrality act."

"We're not violating it," said Greene. "We're working around it. Allies are exempted. If we have a pending treaty with Vietnam, then by executive order they're an ally."

"You're starting to sound like a lawyer," said Theodore.

"That's my degree over there," said Greene.

"We can't get Congress to approve intervention," said Jackson. "We took our best shot with Josh MacArthur."

"Maybe we should push for a vote," said Theodore. "We do have the child. We could have her talk to the Senate."

Theodore meant the Vietnamese refugee they had rescued, Mạ.

"No. I'm not going to use her," said Greene. "She's just a kid. Besides, if Josh's images don't do it, nothing will. Senator Grasso's hearing should swing some votes."

Theodore's eyes widened: *Don't count on too many.*

"We can't just let the Chinese roll over the country," said Greene.

"We can keep working covertly," said Jackson. "Until we can get public opinion on our side."

"Covertly isn't going win the war," said Greene.

The Chinese might be stopped temporarily by judicious strikes and against-all-odds operations, but eventually their superior firepower would win the day.

Still, what were his other options?

None.

"We can at least ship them some weapons," said Jackson.

"Granted," said Greene.

That, too, was a problem—the neutrality act passed a year before forbade any outright sale or gift of weapons to any country in Asia, including allies.

"Has to be Russian weapons," said Theodore. "Through another country."

"Russia has been unwilling," said Jackson. "The Vietnamese don't have the money. And the Chinese are already giving them some good business. State has already made some backdoor inquiries."

"They're just not talking to the right people," said Greene. He looked over at his appointment sheet for the next two days, then picked up his phone. "Marlene, that reception at the Polish embassy tomorrow night. Could you find out somehow if the Russian ambassador is expected to be there?"

"You're not going to ask the Russian ambassador to supply the Vietnamese, are you?" asked Jackson when Greene hung up.

"No," said Greene. "You are."

16

Off the south China coast, near Vietnam

"Christian! Christian! Wake the fuck up!"

Zeus pushed on the handle of the long oar, aiming the boat in the direction of the shore. There was no question that the patrol boat was coming in their direction—it seemed to have grown twice its size in just a few moments.

"Up, Win, up!"

Christian showed no sign of stirring. Zeus kept pushing with the oar, his muscles straining. Adrenaline flushed through his body. Everything went into the oar, every ounce of energy, every sensation. He could feel the ocean pushing back, trying to tackle him, but he wasn't giving in—he was a quarterback in high school again, pushing through the line, squeezing for the last inch to make the touchdown.

The patrol boat's bow was head-on in their direction. Any moment now, he expected the forward gun to fire.

Push, his body told him. *Push!*

"Win, get your ass up!" Zeus yelled. He pushed harder. The muck gave way as he paddled, dirt and seaweed parting then pushing back.

The vegetation was thick, but not enough to hide them. The thing to do was reach shore and run.

Run!

The word rumbled from his muscles, his legs twitching with it. Zeus pushed the oar until the boat hung up on a cluster of sand-encrusted rocks. Christian still hadn't stirred in the bow. Zeus leapt forward into the water. He pushed the boat deeper into the weeds, then grabbed Christian's shoulder. He didn't try to rouse him; instead, he curled him over his back, hoisted him up, and staggered onto firm land.

"You are damn heavy," he muttered.

He pumped his legs in the direction of a clump of low shrubs on his left. He ran past, chugging up a small incline to a larger cluster of trees.

Run!

Every muscle, every tendon and ligament in his body strained. But there was no question that he was reaching those trees. There was no question that he was moving away from the warship that was chasing them.

Zeus got about forty yards into the jungle before his legs gave way. Even then, it wasn't a total collapse or surrender; it was more like a gradual winding down, his strides shortening, his back bending, until he practically crawled. He sank to his knees, then fell flat forward, pushed down by Christian's weight.

Zeus lay on the ground for the length of one long, deep breath, then pushed up, rose, alert again, strength restored. He pushed Christian to the side and slipped back through the trees to the shore, looking out to sea.

He couldn't see the warship. He looked down at the ground, took a long breath, then a second—it was as if his eyes needed to be reloaded.

Zeus raised his head. He spotted the patrol boat to his right, maybe a half mile off shore, no more.

He turned back and went to Christian.

"Up, Christian. You're getting up now," he said, prodding him with his foot. "I'm not carrying you any farther."

"Uhhhh?"

"At least you're not dead," said Zeus. "Let's go. Come on."

"What the hell . . . what's going on?"

"There's a Chinese patrol boat. Come on—we must be really close to the border. We may even be over it. Come on."

"Shit."

Zeus took Christian's arm and pulled him up.

"How did I get here?" asked Christian.

"I carried you, you bastard. Let's go."

Zeus tugged, then let go and began trotting farther inland. The jungle was thick; most likely the sailors wouldn't follow too far inland.

It didn't matter. They would outrun them. And if they didn't outrun them, he would shoot them.

Zeus reached to his beltline. He'd forgotten the gun back in the boat.

You'll kill them with your bare hands if you have to.

It was an idea, rather than a voice, something he felt rather than heard. Something he knew immediately was true.

He would kill them—he would succeed, there was no question of it, no doubt, only dead certainty.

The questions, the doubt he'd felt just a few hours before had disintegrated somewhere in the afternoon sun, dissolving into the steam rising from the shallow water above the sand amid the dank debris.

Something rumbled in the distance.

"What the hell?" said Christian, huffing behind him. "There's not a cloud in the sky."

"It's gunfire, not thunder," said Zeus tightly. "Don't worry. They're still pretty far away. Run. Run."

They ran for almost a mile, weaving through the trees, gradually moving uphill. There was no sign that they were being followed, and in fact the single gunshot they'd heard was the only indication that there were any other humans in the world nearby. Still, Zeus kept running, his legs pushing onward. In a sense, his mind was no longer in control—his body was telling it what to do, or what would be done: They would run until their energy completely flagged, then they would rest for only a short minute, then they would begin again.

It was as if the rest of his body no longer entirely trusted his brain, as if the questions that had bothered it earlier had shown it to be unreliable, unfit for command in a military sense.

"Let's go," said Zeus, pushing through the thick weeds. "Come on."

"I'm here," grumbled Christian behind him.

"Faster," said Zeus.

"Shit."

Christian picked up his pace, pushing through the trees until he was only a few paces behind Zeus. The ground rose sharply ahead. Zeus took a breath, girding himself for the climb. Suddenly his foot slipped, and he found himself pirouetting to the side, falling into a small, narrow stream that ran in the crevice at the base of the hill. He landed flat on his back with a thud, his head smacking against a rock. He saw stars, or an approximation thereof; with a shout he twisted to his stomach and began up the hill, climbing first on his hands and knees, then pushing to his feet and trudging up. Christian grabbed the back of his shirt, pulling him to the summit of the hill. There they both collapsed, finally out of breath and energy.

"Are they still after us?" managed Christian after a few minutes of rest.

"Probably," said Zeus.

"I just want to stay here."

"Yeah," admitted Zeus.

But they both got up.

They walked at a good pace across level ground. The trees were thicker and closer together than before. Every so often, Zeus turned to see if they were being followed. But he found he couldn't look more than ten or twenty yards behind them.

He tried listening instead. But the jungle had too many noises for him to tell—birds in the distance, insects near and far, a frog somewhere.

"They can't possibly follow us through all this," said Christian after they'd been walking for about ten minutes. "Why would they bother?"

"Why would they fire at a fishing boat?" answered Zeus. "We'll keep going for a while. It's our best bet."

"You really think we're in Vietnam?"

"Maybe. More likely we're still a few miles from the border."

"How many's a few?"

"I don't know."

Zeus took the map from his pocket. It was wet, either from the ocean or the stream. He unfolded it as he walked, then refolded it so he could hold and look at a small portion in one hand.

It was fine for roads, but trying to extrapolate the physical details of the coastline where they'd landed against the broad strokes of the map were next to impossible. They were definitely somewhere between Fangchenggang and the Vietnamese border, much closer to the border he thought than the city, but given the fact that they'd fallen asleep and drifted for hours, who really could tell?

"I'm hungry," said Christian.

"Yeah, well, you see a McDonald's, let me know."

"Why are you such a jerk?"

"What?" Zeus stopped and turned around. Christian, a few feet away, glared at him but continued walking. "What do you mean, I'm a jerk?"

"You're always busting on me."

"You're the jerk," muttered Zeus, speeding his pace.

"I'm a jerk?"

"Yeah."

"You're just jealous."

"Oh yeah, right."

Neither man spoke for a few minutes. Zeus's anger gradually dissipated. It made no sense to get mad at Christian, especially now. And it served no purpose: The guy had been a jerk for his whole life; a sudden conversion wasn't likely.

"I mean it, Zeus." Christian didn't slow down. "You're always riding me. You and your sidekick Rosen."

"Steve wasn't my sidekick."

"Well I'm guessing he wasn't your gay lover."

"Ha-ha. Hill rises to the left," said Zeus, pointing.

Zeus angled toward the hill. A narrow stream of water cascaded diagonally from above; he walked along it, crossing and recrossing to take advantage of the path. The vegetation thinned as they moved upward. Glancing back, Zeus realized that they had cut an easy-to-see path through the jungle as they brushed aside the thick vegetation; they would be easy to follow.

"We're going to have to keep going," he said. "Up along this creek and a lot farther, some place where we can't be tracked. We left a pretty big trail through the brush back there."

"You're just figuring that out?" said Christian.

"Yeah, actually."

"I'm surprised you admit it."

The steeper the grade, the slower Zeus went, until finally he was moving in what seemed like baby steps. Christian was even slower, pausing every third or fourth step.

Zeus reached a clearing on the side of the hill. The ocean lay in glittery azure in the distance, sparkling with the setting of the sun.

Belatedly realizing he was in the open, he dropped to his knees. He could still see the water.

It was a breathtaking scene, barely a mile from the water. It was the stuff of postcards.

Or would have been, if not for the trio of warships three or four miles from shore.

There was no doubt that they were Chinese. They were big vessels, destroyers Zeus guessed, though he was not an expert.

He saw something else near them.

Probably a submarine on the surface, he thought, though from the distance it was hard to tell if it was even there.

"What?" huffed Christian, dragging himself over. He collapsed next to Zeus.

"You think the Chinese would keep their ships on their side of the border?" Zeus asked.

"I have no clue."

"Do you remember from the G-2 estimates?"

"No."

"I think they'd be near the border," said Zeus.

"So?"

"Which means we're near it. Maybe still in China, but near it."

Zeus stared southward. He couldn't see any ships in that direction. But the way the land curved and jutted, there could easily be something closer to shore there. Or farther out—his eyes were tired, and the sun, now starting to set behind him, threw both glare and shadows across the water.

"I think we should keep moving," said Zeus. "Put more distance between us and the sailors, if they're still following. Once it's dark, we can rest for a little while, then get over the border. Or go farther, if we're already over. Maybe we'll run into some Vietnamese army patrols."

He tried to force optimism into his voice. Christian didn't answer, but rose before Zeus did. They walked for twenty minutes, moving along a rocky ridge, then down the path of another creek bed. About halfway down, Zeus decided to set a false path for anyone following. He had Christian stay where he was, then went through some brush, making sure to break several branches to make it obvious someone had gone through. He came to a clearing after about a hundred yards. This was an unexpected break: anyone tracking them would think they had gone clear through it. He backed out, retracing his steps to Christian.

"I think I heard some noise in that direction," said Christian. He pointed southwest.

"What kind?"

Christian shrugged. "Trucks."

Zeus got the map out. It didn't show the border area in any detail.

"Let's cut west," he told Christian.

"Why?"

Zeus shrugged. He honestly had no answer.

————

About a half hour later, they came to a narrow, hard-packed dirt road that twisted in both directions north and south. Judging from the piles of gravel to the side, it had either recently been built or reconstructed.

"Doesn't look as if it's been used much," said Zeus, staring at the surface. There were some tire tracks, but not the deep ruts that moving an army would leave.

"How much longer are we going to walk?" asked Christian.

"If we're already in Vietnam, we should find a patrol soon."

"If they don't shoot us."

Zeus started walking along the edge of the road. The Chinese had invaded in the western area of the country, aiming at sweeping south past Hanoi. The fact that they had been planning an amphibious assault suggested that they were going to cut off the northern portion of the country, avoiding the difficult Quàng Ninh highlands as well as the government's center of power. They could then simply strangle what remained.

But even with their basic plan, they wouldn't leave the frontier completely devoid of troops.

To Zeus, that meant they were already past the border. Otherwise they'd have seen more evidence of the Chinese army by now.

He walked on, following the road. It was getting dark now, hard to see. The shadows took on odd, threatening shapes.

Zeus tried warding off the boogies of his imagination by considering different strategies, things he would do if he were the Chinese. Where would he land in an amphibious attack? What would he do about Hai Phong, the port to the south? Would it be worth taking Hanoi at all, since clearly what the Chinese wanted was Vietnam's rice and oil?

"There," said Christian, suddenly rushing up to him and grabbing his arm. "Hear?"

"Huh?"

"Sssh. Listen."

He could hear motor sounds, an engine. Not far away.

"Just for safety, let's get off the road," said Zeus.

"Which way?"

"Here." Zeus crossed to the west. He slipped through the trees, his heart suddenly pounding hard—they were going home soon, finally, which meant that they'd be able to sleep, and get something to eat. He was starving.

Not home, exactly. Vietnam was far from home. But it would do.

After he'd gone far enough that he couldn't see the road anymore, Zeus turned left and headed south. The brush was so thick that it cut at his shirt.

The noise had settled into a vague hum, a low buzz in the distance. Zeus wished he had gone farther along the road; they were farther away from the noise than he'd thought.

"What's that?" said Christian, pointing to their right.

Zeus stared through the trees.

"The posts? You see it?"

Zeus didn't at first. Finally he saw something a little greener than the rest.

"It's a bridge. There's another road there," he said. "Bigger than what we were on."

"Should we take it?" asked Christian. "It'll be easier to walk."

"Even more dangerous than the dirt road."

"Yeah. Okay. You think you can find it on your map?"

Almost certainly not, thought Zeus, but he tried anyway, unfolding the map and staring at it for a while. It was too dark to see it without putting it right up to his eyes. And even that was futile. The roads over the Chinese border were just narrow red squiggles.

"I don't know," said Zeus finally. "Come on."

They moved slowly toward the underbrush. The sound seemed to move away from them.

They stopped for a rest after a few minutes. Christian was wheezing.

"You all right?" Zeus asked.

"Let's just keep going."

A few minutes later, Zeus heard the sound of a truck approaching. Instinctively, he dropped to his knees and turned toward it. It was on the hard-paved road to the right.

It was moving slowly northward. A troop truck.

Maybe bringing dinner to pickets or sentries farther north. He could smell something, a fire, food.

Zeus took a half step toward it, thinking he would hail the driver, but then stopped. He had to be sure it was Vietnamese.

They waited until they couldn't hear the truck anymore. Then they started again, walking southward steadily. Finally Zeus saw something through the leaves—a building, and wire. He stopped, crouching next to a tree, as much for support as cover.

"That's either a Vietnamese," he told Christian, "or a Chinese border post."

"Well, which is it?"

"Which do you want?" Zeus sidled to his left, trying to get a better view.

"Whichever is closer to my bed."

The complex ran in both directions. Zeus reasoned that the portion near the highway would be the most heavily guarded. It was also the place where the sentries would be most jumpy. So he started moving to his left, pushing quietly through the brush.

What if the Vietnamese heard him and thought he was an infiltrator, testing the line?

Zeus moved back, aiming to circle across to the dirt road. Christian gave him a perplexed look, then joined him silently.

Before they'd gone more than thirty yards, Zeus spotted a sandbagged position in the jungle. There was open ground all around it, a clearing that would make any intruder easy to spot.

The camp was about twenty-five or thirty yards beyond. He could see the roofs of several buildings, and the sides of a few tents.

There were two men behind the sandbags.

Vietnamese? Or Chinese?

Impossible to tell.

"Let's circle around the other side and see if we can get a look at their uniforms," said Zeus.

They retreated, carefully treading their way through the vegetation.

Zeus held his breath as they came back around. A floodlight had turned on behind the sandbagged post, throwing long shadows toward them.

They must be beyond the line, Zeus reasoned.

He was feeling good about this, finally very positive. The long ordeal was finally over.

All right, he told himself. Almost home.

"What's the Vietnamese word for hello?" Zeus asked Christian as he crawled next to a tree.

Christian grabbed his shirt. "You're not going to need it. Those guys are Chinese. Look at the guns in the shadows. They're bullpups, not AKs."

17

Eastern Pennsylvania

Mara woke up feeling stiff but relaxed. If not completely restored to her old self, she had more energy than she'd had in days. She took a long shower—the water pressure was surprisingly good—then had a cup of the surprisingly not-bad complimentary coffee in the room. Dressed, she went out into the hall and found that the marshal service bodyguard they'd been assigned was gone from his post.

That must mean Josh was gone as well. She knocked on his door just in case; when there was no answer, she went downstairs and asked the clerk at the desk where the best place was for breakfast. He directed her to a small shop around a side street in the middle of town, a five-minute walk.

They were sitting in the far corner. The marshal's plate was scrubbed clean except for some egg stains and a few crumbs from his toast; Josh's looked as if he had hardly touched his.

"How'd you sleep?" she asked him, pulling out a chair.

"Read this," he said tersely, shoving a newspaper in front of her.

Mara saw the headline, then flipped the paper over to the back.

"I don't see why people think the Knicks are a legitimate basketball team," she said pointedly. "They never win."

"It's all bull," said Josh. "They're saying I'm a liar."

"They're going to do that." She tapped his forearm lightly, then looked at the marshal. "How are you?"

"Fine."

Mara looked up as the waitress brought a menu.

"Coffee to start, hon?" asked the waitress. She was younger than Mara, but already had the matronly waitress bit down pat.

"Please." Mara took the menu.

"Maybe I'll just go home," said Josh darkly.

"There's nothing wrong with that," answered Mara.

He curled his arms across his chest.

Mara looked at the marshal. "Beautiful day," she said to him. "Not even cold."

"Yup."

"Is there fishing around here?"

"Outta season."

"No hunting either, then, huh?"

"You hunt?"

"I've been known to."

"Yeah. Outta season," he said.

He sounded slightly skeptical, doubting that she did actually hunt. She was tempted to ask how bad he thought the breath of a Malaysian tiger stank, but didn't.

"Isn't there an amusement park or something around here?" she said instead.

"Sure. There's Hershey's out a ways," said the marshal, his Texas accent twanging. "It's like an amusement park."

"Want to do that, Josh? Better than sitting around all day."

He frowned.

The waitress brought her coffee. Mara ordered two eggs over easy with French toast, home fries, and bacon on the side.

"That's what I like," said the waitress. "A woman with an appetite."

When she left, Mara leaned over and whispered in Josh's ear. "Let's ditch the chaperone. What do you say?" She put her hand on his thigh.

Josh turned red.

"Maybe we should go to Hershey's," he said aloud. Then he put his hand on hers, and squeezed before letting go.

"Hershey's," said Mara, straightening. "How do we get there?"

The marshal was just about to explain when Josh's phone rang. It was Jablonski.

"Maybe you shouldn't answer it," said Mara.

But Josh did.

———

Jablonski was almost supernaturally calm.

"You really can't take this too seriously," said the political operative. "You have to expect the Chinese to fight back."

"But they're lying."

"It'll come out in the wash." He pronounced "wash" as if it were spelled *wha-sssshhhh*. "Now what you need to do is get on down to D.C. for your congressional hearing. It'll start promptly at one."

"What hearing?"

"Senator Grasso's. You'll testify before his committee. Don't worry, he's now your biggest fan."

"You didn't tell me about a hearing."

"It just came up. Don't worry. It'll go fine." Jablonski made a sucking noise from the side of his mouth. "Listen, Josh, I have to get going. I'll get someone to make hotel arrangements. You want to stay at the Watergate? Or you want a quiet place out of town?"

"Who gives a crap," said Josh, killing the line.

18

On the border of China and Vietnam

Neither Christian nor Zeus spoke as they backed away, once more retracing their route away from the lookout station. They crossed the dirt road well out of view, then began moving east. The moon had risen; they had more than enough light to see by.

"We gotta take a break," said Christian finally.

"Keep moving."

Zeus caught sight of a bridge spanning another road. Apparently the camp had been set up at the confluence of several roads heading south.

They sat in a clump of bushes, wordlessly staring at each other as they rested. Both men were tired, but there was no question of spending the night this close to the Chinese. They'd move farther west, find a place to cross.

"I wonder what happened to the girl," said Christian.

"Solt can take care of herself," said Zeus.

"I mean that little kid the spy rescued. With the scientist and the Delta guys? Remember?"

"They were SEALs," said Zeus.

"Whatever."

"Big difference."

Christian shrugged. "You liked SOCOM?"

SOCOM was Special Operations Command, where Zeus had been assigned prior to his promotion to major.

"It was good," he said.

"You thinking of going back?"

"I'd like to."

"This'll help," said Christian. "You got your career all mapped out?"

"Funny time to be talking about careers, Win."

"What else we got to talk about?"

"True," said Zeus. "No. You?"

"I used to. I had a line drawn straight through to chief of staff," continued Christian, his voice softening so that it was barely audible.

"Perry has his eye on you."

"You're his fair-haired boy."

"I thought he hated me because of Red Dragon."

"He liked the fact that you kicked our ass in the war game."

"Isn't helping too much now."

"All right," said Christian, rolling slightly to the side and getting up. "Let's go."

"Be careful near the road," said Zeus. "I'll go first."

Zeus slipped through the brush, slowly approaching the bridge. It had been built over a wide but shallow ravine, possibly a spot where water ran during the rainy season, or had run—the weather patterns were so hard to predict now. The Chinese hadn't bothered to post guards, either because it was so close to the camp or because they simply didn't expect the Vietnamese to be able to attack them from this direction.

They made their way to the bridge along the south side of the gully. Zeus paused under the bridge, noticing a set of wires overhead. The bridge had been wired with demolition charges.

The ravine narrowed into a deeper cut, slicing back to the north. They walked in the middle of it until they came to a pool of water. When they climbed up the side, Zeus saw a fence through the trees to his left.

He walked toward it, expecting that it was the border fence. But instead he saw green splotches and rectangles on the other side—they were still near the camp.

A field had been bulldozed from the jungle on the other side of the fence. It was filled with tanks—at least two dozen from what Zeus could see. There were other vehicles as well: personnel carriers, supply trucks. All were arranged in neat rows, as if they'd stumbled upon a used-car lot.

"Wow," said Christian. "Where the hell did these come from? There have to be two companies, at least. That wasn't in any of the briefings."

The engine noises they'd heard earlier were a little louder here, but didn't seem to be coming from the tanks. Zeus put his head against the fence to try and get a better view.

What was going on in there?

He dropped to the ground.

"What are you doing?" hissed Christian, dropping beside him.

"I'm going to go get a better look."

"Where?"

"Inside."

"Are you nuts?"

The fence was staked every six or eight feet. Zeus couldn't budge the first one, but the next one he tried came out easily.

"Zeus," hissed Christian as he slipped beneath the fence. *"Zeus! Stop!"*

19

Alexandria

They opted for a hotel in Alexandria, reaching it a little over an hour before Josh's committee meeting was supposed to start.

Mara was just checking into her room when her cell phone rang. She pulled it from her pocket and without checking the number, answered.

"This is Mara."

"Mara Duncan?"

"Yes?" she answered.

"This is Kyle O'Brien from CNN."

Mara felt her fingers clench against the plastic of the phone.

"Ms. Duncan?"

"What can I do for you?" she said.

"I saw the video on YouTube—"

"What video?"

"On YouTube."

"What are you talking about? Who are you looking for?"

"Mara Duncan. Listen, Ms. Duncan—do you want to talk off the record?"

"Off the record about what?"

"Malaysia."

"This conversation is over."

It was all she could do to keep herself from slamming the phone to the ground.

———

Ten minutes later, Mara sat in the hotel's tiny business center, watching a YouTube video that purported to be from a newscast on Malaysia television. It detailed a CIA operation that had killed twelve civilians, including two children. Her image was flashed on the screen several times.

According to the hit counter, the video had already been seen 3,289 times. It appeared to have been posted only an hour or two earlier.

Mara's phone rang again. This time she examined the number before answering. It was an agency number.

Peter Lucas.

"Mara."

"Mara, this is Peter—"

"What the hell is going on?" she asked. "I just got a call from a reporter on CNN. Have you seen this YouTube video?"

"Which one?" asked Lucas.

"There's more than one?"

"There's one on the incident in Malaysia."

"I saw that. I'm cut into a newscast. Where did it come from?"

"Where do you think?" said Lucas. "There's one that focuses on you at the UN. Do a name search and you'll find it."

She did. A snippet of video of Josh and some others walking through the hall appeared. She was alongside for about three seconds, then eighteen in the slow-motion portion that followed the main part. Her head was conveniently circled with a light halo. The video had been seen only by 876 people.

There were three comments, all in English.

CIA agent Mara Duncan
Paid liar helps Vietnamese propaganda.
For better sex, call 202-555-8900

The number was her home phone number, fortunately disconnected a year before.

"The Chinese did this, obviously," said Mara.

"That or you pissed off an old boyfriend."

"I'm really, really not laughing, Peter."

"Neither am I, Mara. Nor is the director."

"What are we going to do?"

"Come in and we'll talk about it. Where are you?"

"I'm in D.C."

"Oh? . . . Well, good. Get over here."

"Damn. *Damn*."

"It's not the end of the world."

"Not for you. My cover's totally blown."

"In a way, they're doing us a favor," said Lucas. "We weren't positive it was blown. Now we are."

"You thought it was blown and you didn't tell me? When?"

"When the money disappeared in Hanoi."

"Well, thanks for telling me."

"Yeah, I know. You'll get through it. Listen, in the meantime, stay away from Josh MacArthur."

"I'm hanging up, Peter."

And she did.

20

On the border of China and Vietnam

Zeus crawled across a carpet of weeds and jungle debris, skirting the area where the tanks were parked.

They were large ZTZ99s—main battle tanks, massive beasts designed to do battle with the best the West had to offer, including the U.S. Army's M1A1. The Vietnamese had nothing in their inventory that could match it.

Two dozen tanks, that he could see; undoubtedly more over the small hill to his right, just out of view. Where had they come from? They would surely have been spotted by American satellites on the way down, yet there hadn't been one word about them in any of the briefings he'd given the Vietnamese.

They'd be seen soon, if they hadn't been spotted already. At least one Global Hawk should be covering the area 24/7. All China and Southeast Asia now had the highest priority from the satellite surveillance program. The camo netting might throw off the count slightly, but something this large wasn't going to escape notice.

Had they just gotten here?

Zeus kept crawling in the direction of the motor hum. It seemed more muffled inside the fence perimeter.

Strange.

There were voices to his left. Zeus froze, staring in the direction of the buildings, trying to see who was coming and where they were.

All he could see in the moonlight were hacked tree trunks, a small grove of them, clustered on a gentle rise.

He decided they would be good cover. Still crawling, he made his way toward them.

He didn't realize they weren't tree trunks until he reached them. They were plastic tubes sticking from the ground, covered in material and screening so that they looked like tree trunks.

Vents.

Just as the enormity of his discovery dawned on him, Zeus heard a fresh rumble fifty yards to the south. He raised his head in time to see a dark cloud billowing from behind the small hillock. Something emerged from it, moving toward the tanks he'd just passed.

Another tank. There was a vast underground garage below. The Chinese had moved down their tanks well before the beginning of the conflict, storing them here in preparation for this moment.

Two more tanks appeared while Zeus watched. They drove over to the field where the others were parked. Men scurried back and forth.

Zeus retreated, working his way back to the fence. A bank of clouds moved in, covering the moon; by the time he reached Christian, he could barely see two feet in front of him.

"What's going on?" asked Christian.

"There're a whole tunnel of tanks down there," said Zeus. "I saw three more come out. God knows how many there are."

"A tunnel or a bunker?"

"I don't know. One way or the other, it's vast. For all I know, it's a tunnel that goes back to Beijing."

"We'd better get out of here," said Christian. "If they're taking the tanks out, then they're going to use them. Tonight."

"We have to stop them," said Zeus.

"Oh yeah, right. What do you suggest? Call in an air strike?"

"If I had a radio, I would."

"Well, we don't have a radio. And the Vietnamese couldn't get close enough to attack them. Their best hope would be artillery, and most of that is to the west."

"We can stop them," said Zeus.

"Maybe we should steal one of the tanks and go south in it," suggested Christian sarcastically.

He wasn't serious, but Zeus thought about the idea. The tanks had three-man crews: a driver, a gunner, and a commander. Two men could easily handle it, if they knew what they were doing.

Which they didn't. But Zeus wondered how hard it could be.

"You're not really thinking about it," said Christian.

"We could get into them. They don't have any guards posted on this side. At least not that I could see."

"It's that last sentence that spells trouble."

Zeus smiled. It *was* nuts.

"We have to get as far south as we can, as fast as we can," added Christian. "Maybe we can warn the Vietnamese. It's better than nothing."

Calmer now that he was rested, Christian was back to being the somewhat competent Army officer he'd known before cracking. Ironically, now it was the nut they needed—the wild man, as Rosen used to say—a game-changing commander who could do the unexpected.

"Maybe we can blow up the tunnel," said Zeus.

"How?"

"Those explosives back on the bridge."

"Zeus . . . you have to plant explosive in pretty strategic spots to blow up a tunnel," said Christian. "Or a garage or whatever the hell they have."

"Maybe we can block the door."

"You're crazy."

"We gotta do something," said Zeus, starting back for the bridge.

Love

戀愛

1

On the border of China and Vietnam

The jungle had turned into a mélange of grays, with the occasional splash of brown and black. Zeus couldn't see more than a few feet in front of him, and what he did see was jagged and chameleonlike, altering shape as he approached. He found the gully by accident, stumbling into it and sliding down into the water. That hadn't been his plan, but it worked just fine. The ankle-deep water swelled his shoes; he felt his way along the side of the crevice and worked his way slowly toward the bridge.

"Christian, where are you?" he asked when he cleared the water.

"Up here."

"We can walk through this channel and we'll be right under the bridge."

"Yeah. And get soaked at the same time."

Zeus kept going. The plan was still only vaguely formed, but it wasn't the logic of it that drove him—it was the feeling, the emotion, that he had to do it. He had to stop these tanks somehow. He was just going to, whatever it took. Because not doing anything felt like a sharp stab to his stomach.

The shallow ravine widened as he walked. Water squished from his shoes. Something shot overhead, close, in the trees—a bird? A monkey?

Just the wind?

Zeus forced his eyes to focus in front of him. He couldn't afford other thoughts or distractions.

The noise from the camp seemed louder. They'd be planning on moving out in a few hours. There must be a large infantry concentration somewhere; you couldn't move tanks through a jungle like this without infantry supporting them.

Maybe they were coming down the road, meeting with the tanks. The crews didn't seem to be there, either.

He had to stay alert. Apprehension stoked his adrenaline and pushed him on. The overpass loomed ahead.

It was dark underneath, extremely dark. Zeus found the first charge by feel, a blind man slowly groping along the steel. He began collecting them.

In the demolition course he'd taken—that was three, four years ago now?—the instructor had had them assemble and disassemble simple charges in the dark.

That was child's play compared to what he had to do now. He'd been in a room with dummy charges, his feet dry and stomach full. No one was going to die if he screwed up. There was tension, sure, but it was child's play.

After they were done, they'd hit a bar.

Two bars, as he recalled.

He followed the wires to the second, then to a third.

"Where are you?" called Christian in a stage whisper.

"Here. The north end. Go the south."

"All right."

"You know what you're doing?"

"I know how to wire them. It's the dark I have trouble with."

They had to find the detonators. Zeus suspected there would be at least two, one on each side of the bridge.

Of course, it was possible there would be only a receiver—or worse, bare wires, waiting to be hooked up to the controller or timer.

"I don't know how the Chinese arrange their demos," said Zeus.

"Yeah, me neither."

"Be careful with the wire."

"You think they booby-trapped it?"

"No," said Zeus, though in truth he had no idea. "There'd be no reason for that. It wouldn't be logical."

"I hope these guys are big on logic."

Zeus laughed.

He found two more charges, tracing the wire along. Whoever had set up the demolitions had used far too much explosive—a common failing.

"Hey, look at this," said Christian from the other side.

Zeus made his way over. Christian had found a small mechanical hand unit wired in as a back-up detonating device, a slightly more modern version of the old-fashioned plungers used to ignite TNT in thousands of old Western movies.

"They're making it easy for us," Zeus told Christian, feeling his way to the wire connections.

"Can you see what the hell you're doing?"

"No. You?"

"I can see the screws with the wires and your fingers are nowhere near them."

Zeus stared down at his hands.

"You can see that?" he said.

"Here," said Christian, putting Zeus's fingers on the contact.

"Thanks."

"You going blind?"

"I didn't have my carrots today."

"Always with a joke."

"I'm rubbing off on you," answered Zeus. "You're making them yourself."

They pulled eight more charges off the bridge. There were probably more, Zeus thought, but they couldn't carry them.

There were certainly enough explosives to blow a tank, perhaps two or even three, depending on how they were situated.

The moon poked back through the clouds as they walked, sending silver slivers through the trees.

"What's the plan?" asked Christian when they reached the fence.

"I'm not sure yet."

"That's not a plan," said Christian.

"I'm going to have to improvise something. We'll put the charges under a tank, come back, blow it. We don't need more of a plan than that."

"What good is blowing one tank?"

"We can get two."

It did seem like a pathetic gesture—where was the wild man who'd just inhabited Christian?

But it might delay the Chinese even so. They'd think they were under attack. Even a few hours might help the Vietnamese.

"We string the wire as far back as we can, we blow it, and move back here," said Zeus, sketching the route with his finger in the air. "We go that way. We get as far from the camp as we can, then cross over into Vietnam."

"That's a bullshit plan."

"You got something better?"

"I'm not going to be a martyr for Vietnam."

"Just wait here."

Zeus stuck his elbow under the fence, then pushed himself through.

He didn't bother looking back, crawling on his belly through the weeds.

Something was better than nothing.

What if he blew the entrance to the tunnel? Could he get close enough?

Doubtful.

He could string the explosives together, push them down the air tube.

That might work.

He started crawling in that direction.

"Where are you going?" hissed Christian in the darkness behind him.

Startled, Zeus stopped. "Where are you?"

"Jesus, I'm right here. Two feet away."

"I thought you were staying back," said Zeus.

"What's the plan?"

"I'm not sure yet. There are air vents—"

"I have an idea," said Christian.

"Okay."

"They won't get very far if we blow up their fuel."

"Their tanks must be underground."

"They have some trucks lined up near the personnel carriers. Didn't you see them before?"

It was a brilliant, logical, simple plan. But the most amazing thing was that it had come from Christian.

"Show me," said Zeus.

———

They didn't see the guard walking along the line of tanks until he was less than ten yards away. Fortunately, the man was looking toward the fence line, and Zeus was close enough to the armored personnel carriers to cut between them and hide. Christian followed.

"Guard," whispered Zeus as he squatted.

"Yeah."

Zeus waited, chest tight.

They'd take the guard if he came this way. Zeus put the charges down, ready to leap out.

The man didn't appear. Finally, Zeus leaned forward and looked around the end of the vehicle.

The soldier was gone.

"Stay here," Zeus told Christian. "I'm going to scout ahead. I want to make sure we won't be seen"

"Go."

There was no light in the compound, but the moon was strong enough for him to see fairly well. The row of APCs gave way to tanks. As Zeus reached the back of the second tank, he saw the fuel trucks off to the right. Two were parked next to a pile of bulldozed debris, dirt, tree trunks, and rocks in a long mound. The fence cut toward the mound, running along to the right as far as Zeus could see.

He made his way to the mound, crawling along the side nearest the fence. There were more fuel trucks—a half dozen. Another row behind that.

Blow up one with each charge. Shrapnel from the blast might damage others. In any event, it would slow their advance considerably—the tanks could only go so far without topping off.

How many trucks were there? He lay at the top of the hill, staring.

Two dozen.

What was the ratio the Chinese used? God, that he should know—that was a factor in the game somewhere.

Five tanks to one truck?

Six?

No. Three?

It had to be more than three, or there were more trucks.

He couldn't think. And what did it matter now? Just blow the damn things up and be done with it.

Voices came to him as the wind shifted. Belatedly, Zeus realized there were men on the far side of the trucks all the way to his right.

He slid closer, trying to see.

Gradually, he realized what they were up to—filling the tankers with fuel from an underground tank.

He slipped back to Christian.

"They're putting fuel in them now. Let's go."

"Where?"

"Come on." Zeus shoved the demo packs back into his pockets. "Come on."

"What do we do after we plant the charges?"

"Go back the same way we came."

Zeus leapt up, heart pounding in his chest. He was suddenly on an adrenaline high, feeling no pain, completely focused on his mission. He rounded the corner of the APC. The moist jungle air felt heavy in his chest, thick.

Zeus glanced up, trying to gauge how far he was from the pile of debris. As he did, he saw the soldier he'd spotted earlier come out from behind the truck, then look directly at him.

2

CIA headquarters, suburban Virginia

Mara was on her way upstairs to see Peter Lucas when she decided to take a detour to Starbucks. The coffee shop, located on the ground floor of the CIA's main building at Langley, was reputedly one of the busiest Starbucks in the country. Mara could agree with that—the place was always jammed. She took her place in line.

"Well, speak of the devil and she appears," said a voice behind her as she debated whether to go for a regular or a latte. She'd moved about two feet in five minutes. "Mara Duncan, I hope you are well."

Mara turned and saw Jimmy "Grease" Parnel standing with his arms folded in front of his chest. The ceiling lights glared off his bald head, and his round face sported a wide smile. Grease had earned his nickname long ago, when he'd been able to make things happen: "greasing the wheels of progress" as he put it when he deigned to explain where the name had come from.

"Grease," said Mara. "How are you? I thought you were retired."

"No kiss?" He offered his cheek. She snorted in derision. "You don't know what you're missing," he said.

"Ignorance is bliss."

"I can vouch for that."

The line shifted. Mara moved with it. Grease took a spot near the back.

Grease *was* retired—he'd been shot up badly a few years while helping the Philippines government. Grease had spent somewhere over thirty years working in various places in Asia. He'd even been in Malaysia, briefly, when Mara was there, which was how she knew him.

She got her coffee—just a regular—and moved around toward the end of the line. Grease was chatting up two young—and pretty—office workers. Add their ages together, and they'd still come up more than a few years shy of his.

"Ask this one," he told them, nodding toward Mara. "She'll tell you."

"Tell them what?"

"How good I am in bed."

"He's good, all right," said Mara. "Loudest snorer in the bunch."

"Only after a full meal and extra dessert," said Grease. "And I don't mean ice cream."

The two women exchanged a glance, then did their best to ignore them.

"You're going to get written up for sexual harassment," said Mara.

"That's the beauty of being a contract worker," said Grease. "I can't be fired."

"They can terminate your contract."

"For flirting? If I knew it was that easy, I would have tried it years ago."

"I wouldn't elevate what you do to the status of flirting," countered Mara.

"Be kind." Grease winked at her. "Hang on for a minute, will you? I have to get my caffeine fix."

Grease ordered an Americano—a shot of espresso in water, so that it had the flavor of a very strong coffee.

"Reminds me of the coffee machine in the Bangkok office," he said, putting a top on the cup.

"I doubt that," said Mara.

"How is Bangkok?"

"Still there, last I saw."

Grease smiled. They walked out into the hall. "You coming in to see Peter?"

"Something like that."

"I'm working for him," said Grease. "Come on."

They walked past the glassed-in courtyard and across to a staircase, taking it down three flights. That was Grease—pushing seventy, with more replacement parts in him than a used car, and he still preferred what he called "the juice of the dance" to being carried.

He told Mara that he had been called back "to take a look at things" in Vietnam and China.

"A lot going on," he said as they cleared the second landing and headed for the third. "This Cho Lai—he's some piece of work."

"The Chinese were desperate for a strong leader," said Mara.

"They got that in spades," said Grease. Downstairs, they passed a security point, then entered a part of the building strongly shielded against eavesdropping equipment. Grease buzzed them through a door into a secure hallway with a series of small offices. These were temporary workplaces, where temporary assignees like Grease could hold conversations and work with sensitive material. He paused in front of an office door.

"You left your cell phone upstairs, right?" asked Grease. "No electronics."

"I know that."

"Just checking."

He smiled, punching the combination into the lock.

"I heard somebody blew your cover," Grease told Mara inside.

"You know who?"

"Obviously it was the Chinese. Question is how long they've known."

Mara had been wondering that herself. It could very well have been back in Malaysia, given all that had gone down there. But there were also problems with the Hanoi station, and Mara strongly suspected a double agent there had passed along the information.

"You think this kills me?" she asked.

"Hell no. You know how many times the Russians figured out who I was? Five or six different incarnations. Nothing stops the Peter Principle," Grease said. "You'll rise to your appropriate level of incompetence, I guarantee. You have a long way to go."

Mara smiled.

"Speaking of Peter," added Grease. "Before you go up to see him, there's a company I wanted to ask you about: Maccu Shang Shipping. A Philippine company. Sorry about the cramped space."

The room was tiny, with a bare desk, a pair of computer terminals, and two steel-and-vinyl chairs. Mara and Grease were sitting almost knee to knee.

"I know Shang," she told him. "The Philippines is a front. They're Chinese."

"You're positive? The evidence looks a little ambiguous."

"They're definitely Chinese."

"Five ships leased to the company left Macau last night and headed for Zhanjiang. Southern China. Big navy port."

"See?"

"Turns out some of our friends at the agency that doesn't exist happened to be tracking an army unit that was just sent there, real fast. Seems like they're in the port, waiting for something."

The agency that doesn't exist was Grease's quaint way of referring to the NSA, or National Security Agency, which specialized in eavesdropping. His pseudonym came from a popular nickname for the agency, formed from its initials: No Such Agency.

"They're getting on the ships?" asked Mara.

"Don't know. I have to check back in. They may be there already. A lot of things to keep tabs on. That one just happened to catch my interest."

"Shang Shipping brought all sorts of stuff into Malaysia," said Mara. "A lot of different things."

"Troops?"

Mara wasn't sure about that. The Chinese had smuggled some paramilitary and guerillas into the country as advisers, but most of their help to the rebels had been in the form of equipment. The ships had filed manifests that said they were shipping food to Burma—as unlikely an arrangement as Mara had ever heard of.

The Chinese unit's identity interested Grease—they were commandos, not regular army, and apparently not assigned to the amphibious assault that was to have been launched from Hainan.

"My question is where would they go?" said Grease.

"Could be anywhere," said Mara. "Vietnam has a long coast."

"The NSA suggested Hai Phong. Someone attached to the unit apparently gathered some sort of electronic information—I'm guessing that it had to do with a GPS system. But you know them. They won't admit they know anything."

"Did they have assault ships?"

"No," said Grease. "I'm wondering if they might just try sailing into the port."

"Do the Vietnamese still hold Hai Phong?"

"They do. Were you there?"

"No, we didn't get that far west."

Grease asked her a few more questions about the status of things in Vietnam. He commented that the country seemed surprisingly calm for one under siege. Mara wasn't so sure about that; in her experience, sanity and insanity mixed all the time.

"You going upstairs?" asked Grease, glancing at his watch.

"Yeah."

"Well, come on. I'll escort you. We want to get up in time to see your boyfriend testify before the Senate."

"My *boyfriend*?"

"Looks like I hit a nerve," said Grease, opening the door. "I don't think I've ever seen that shade of red on you cheeks before."

"Grease—"

"It does suit you."

3

The Gulf of Tonkin

Commander Dirk Silas edged his finger along the manual focus ring of his glasses, trying to will something out of the dark night before his ship. The moist air pulled a fog from the ocean, reducing the gear's effectiveness.

The Chinese were still there, six miles off the port bow. The frigate was the closer of the two; the cruiser's captain used the smaller boat as a shield and a prod, sending it close, only to have it tuck away. Right now it was doing the latter, sailing into what its captain probably supposed was safe murk beyond Silas's immediate vision.

Ha!

The communicator on the destroyer captain's belt buzzed and vibrated with an incoming message. The wireless system allowed Silas to communicate with all departments on his ship without having to be tethered to a physical control panel. He could switch from voice or text messaging by pressing a small button, changing channels and issuing simple commands such as "save" via voice.

In this case, the message referred him to a longer transmission from his fleet commander via video; he retreated to his cabin to view it.

Admiral Roy Meeve's stone countenance filled the screen. The message had been recorded; it wasn't live. The admiral's face seemed almost gray. That wasn't a function of the video mechanism—if anything it cast it a little more fleshlike.

> "Dirk—we've confirmed now the Chinese have canceled their plan to ship the landing force from Hainan. Continue your patrol in the area. Maintain a course in international waters. Do not provoke or engage. Do not withdraw."

Don't engage, but don't withdraw? Should I just let the bastards run over me?

Silas flipped the video off with disgust and went to find a cup of coffee.

4

Washington, D.C.

Josh sat in the small room in the Senate office building, running his thumbnails together. The *next*-to-last thing in the world he wanted to do was walk from this room into the large conference room next door. He was going to do it, though, because the last thing he wanted to do was let these bastards call him a liar.

The door opened. Josh started to rise, then saw that it was only Jablonski.

"There you are. Ready?" asked the political troubleshooter.

"No."

"Come on now. You have to have a positive attitude." Jablonski somehow managed to look disheveled in a bespoke black suit. Maybe it was his purple tie, which despite a perfect knot at the top was a fraction of an inch too long at the bottom. Or perhaps it was the creases in his white shirt, which suggested the pattern of a psychotic snowflake. "You'll do fine. Senator Grasso loves you. He owes you his life."

"He owes Mara his life. She's being smeared, too."

"We're not going to mention Mara at the hearing. Okay?"

"Mmmm."

"How's the suit? Still fit?"

"It fits."

Jablonski had had the suit made for him in New York. Josh had worn it for the UN speech; it was still a bit dirty from the attempt on his life before the speech but there'd been no time to have it dry-cleaned.

"Tailor's father fought with Chiang Kai-shek," said Jablonski. "Interesting life story. Long struggle."

The door opened again. One of Grasso's aides, a young man about Josh's age, came in. "Ready, Mr. MacArthur."

"It's Dr. MacArthur," said Jablonski.

"Oh, right, I'm sorry."

"It's Josh." He got up and followed the aide into the conference room. It was jammed with aides and seemingly every foreign-interest lobbyist in town. They all wanted to see Josh in person.

Half were undoubtedly spies, Josh thought.

The press was gathered along the far wall of the room. Bulbs flashed and TV lights came on as Josh walked in. He walked stoically to the table opposite the dais and sat down.

Senator Grasso, who chaired the Senate subcommittee on affairs with China—double entendre be damned—sat at the center of the long, courtroomlike platform at the front of the room. He had a grim face—much grimmer than Josh remembered from when they had met in New York. He gave Josh a serious, portentous nod, then leaned back to whisper to one of his aides.

Josh grimaced as a photographer came and took a picture of him. Several more followed. He didn't even try to smile.

Grasso gaveled the session to order. Or at least attempted to— another senator began speaking immediately, saying something about how he wanted to make sure proper procedure was followed.

"The committee will come to order," said Grasso, rapping sharply. "These hearings are being conducted to review the President's request for immediate military aid to be given to Vietnam in light of the gross violation of—"

The senator on Grasso's left pulled his microphone forward to interrupt. "Mr. Chairman, I have a request—"

"Requests will be handled at the proper time," said Grasso. "The chair will make the opening statement."

As seen in television reports, congressional hearings seemed at least somewhat organized, with direction and occasional sparks of order. From Josh's vantage, this one was three-ring chaos, with the senators talking to aides and correspondents at the back of the room doing brief broadcasts. Josh heard the loud clatter of laptop keys; the session was being live-blogged on at least half a dozen sites.

He was completely ignored for a few minutes as Grasso made a statement about searching for the truth, then corralled the rest of his subcommittee into agreement that they would shut up while he swore Josh in.

"Will the witness rise?" asked Grasso finally.

Josh put his hand on a Bible and swore that he was going to tell the truth.

"Absolutely," he added.

Jablonski had coached him to read a prepared statement that was essentially an edited version of the one he had given the UN the day before. As he sat down, he took it from his jacket pocket and folded it out on the table in front of him. The cameramen rose, poised to take his picture as he read.

"Dr. MacArthur," said Senator Grasso. "Do you have a statement you'd like to make?"

"Yes, Senator, I do," said Josh.

His tongue suddenly stuck in his mouth. He looked down at the pages, filled with words Jablonski had written. They weren't his. He couldn't read them.

Everyone waited. The cameras clicked away.

"I . . . A few days ago, I returned from Vietnam after witnessing a massacre." Josh pushed the paper to the side. "Innocent people were killed. I testified about it at the UN yesterday morning. I brought back a video. In the hours since, I've been called a liar. I'm not a liar. I'm a scientist. I know what I saw. The Chinese are murderers. They killed innocent people. It was despicable. It is despicable."

There was collective gasp at the word *murderers*. Jablonski had specifically coached him *not* to say that. You're a scientist, he'd said. Be scientific.

But how the hell could you be scientific when you'd seen what he'd seen? And when people called you a liar?

The photographers began taking pictures furiously. Josh looked at Grasso. He had a worried frown on his face.

"Order," said Grasso, pounding the gavel.

"Mr. Chairman, I must demand that our witness apologize for his intemperate remarks," said Senator Galveston, who despite his name represented Minnesota. "The Chinese are our allies and our business partners."

"I don't see how you can call them our allies," said the senator on Grasso's right.

Something between a discussion and pandemonium followed, as the senators argued back and forth about decorum and adjectives. Josh was shocked—not only did one of the senators want him to issue an apology, that seemed to be the majority view on the panel.

Josh knew that standing up to China was unpopular—the President himself had told him that—but he had thought that his speech and the images he'd presented at the UN had shown Americans, if not the world, what was going on.

Maybe it wasn't fair to call the Chinese murderers. Certainly not every Chinese citizen was in the army, and maybe most wouldn't support the war. Certainly, they wouldn't be in favor of killing innocent civilians. But the Chinese government was another story. And their army had definitely done this.

"Mr. Chairman, I ask for a vote of censure on the witness," said the senator from Minnesota.

"That's preposterous!" said Grasso. He pounded his gavel.

More discussion. Josh glanced toward the door to the small room where he had left Jablonski. But the door was shut. Most likely the political operative was at the back of the room somewhere, but Josh didn't want to give the reporters back there the satisfaction of his turning and looking at them.

Grasso finally gaveled his committee back to order. There would be no demands on the witness, and no further statements from the witness. Instead, he would answer questions posed by the senators.

It was less a Q&A session than an excuse for pontificating. First up was the senator on Grasso's right, who asked Josh if it was true that he had been near the Chinese border when he witnessed the slaughter, and then after getting a "yes," launched into a denunciation of China as the enemy of the free world. The senators were on a time limit, as Grasso noted not once but twice before tapping his gavel lightly to cut off a man who was clearly his ally.

Next up was a member of the opposition party, who sat at the far end of the dais. He asked Josh what his qualifications were.

"I'm a biologist," said Josh. "My specialty is studying the effects—"

"You're a biologist? I thought you were a climate scientist."

"Yes. You see, there's an overlap. In that I study the effects of rapid climate change on biological populations. Now, in Vietnam—"

"So excuse me," interrupted the senator, in a voice that implied no apology whatsoever. "You're not a trained observer? You're not a medical doctor. You know things about the weather."

"Of course I'm not a medical doctor."

"I see," said the senator, his tone triumphant. "And this tape you brought back—"

"Actually, it was a video stored on—"

"The recording," continued the senator, annoyed at being interrupted. "Who gave it to you?"

"No one gave it to me."

"Your CIA handler didn't give it to you?"

"I don't have a handler."

The senator frowned.

"Sixty seconds," said Grasso. His tone made it clear that that was all the senator was getting. He was looking directly at his watch, and his gavel was poised to strike.

"Mr. Chairman, I want to submit that we cannot, and should not, take action based on ephemeral information from a possibly biased source, who may or may not have witnessed an isolated incident in an obscure—"

"Time." Grasso pounded the gavel.

But while the chairman could keep the speakers to their time limits, he had no control over what they said. As the session went on, it became clear that the majority on the committee was unwilling to take any action against China, and would certainly not authorize aid to Vietnam. One said that he would be in favor of aid if the UN passed a resolution condemning China. As China was able, as a member of the security council, to veto any resolution—and already had twice—this was tantamount to saying that he would never support aid, except that he phrased it in a way that made most people think he might.

Josh, thinking of the dead people he'd seen, of the buried hand of the corpse he'd dug up, of the girl, Mạ, whose parents had been killed and whose village had been wiped out, felt sick to his stomach.

At least none of the senators called him a liar. As the meeting went on, Josh tried to lengthen his answers so that they contained actual information. But the senators were on to that ploy, and soon began simply to ignore him, pontificating at will without bothering to ask a question or even glance in his direction. One or two made conciliatory gestures in his general direction—one even said he had been very brave to have escaped the war—but for the most part he was an accessory at best, and a potted plant at worst.

Finally, the ordeal was over. Grasso, clearly worn by the proceedings, thanked Josh for his time and "your unselfish devotion to our country." With a loud clap on the gavel, some of the longest and certainly most frustrating hours of Josh's life came to a close.

5

On the border of China and Vietnam

Zeus saw the Chinese soldier stop, push his head down as if in disbelief, then start to raise his rifle.

From that point, the world became a gray funnel. He couldn't see or hear.

He could feel. And what he felt was his body rushing through the night, legs and arms pumping. He leapt onto the soldier's chest. They fell to the ground.

Zeus let go of the explosive as he rolled to his right. He dropped the plunger. In the same motion he flailed at the soldier's chin and neck, smashing them first with his forearm, then his fists. The gray funnel became a black ball, a hard knot of fury.

He didn't breathe. His heart didn't pump. He just punched.

Something grabbed his back. He spun, ready to strike his second assailant.

It was Christian. He just barely stopped himself from punching him.

"He's down. He's down."

Zeus leapt to his feet, grabbed the explosive pack and the detonator mechanism up. Meanwhile, Christian grabbed the Chinese soldier's legs and pulled him under the nearby APC.

"Take his pistol!" hissed Zeus, grabbing the soldier's assault rifle.

"No other guards," said Christian. "Think they heard?"

"Too late to worry about," said Zeus. He pointed to the right. "We can crawl around that little mound to the truck."

"I don't think I can do it."

"Come on, Win. You got this far."

The men who were loading the fuel tanks were about fifty feet away. Zeus heard them talking as he crawled forward.

He stopped when there were just two trucks between him and the pump apparatus.

If he could make it to the other side of the apparatus without being seen, he could plant the bombs right on the machinery itself. The explosion would very likely take out the tank below.

One of the trucks he had passed began to move. Zeus dropped to the ground.

The men waved it forward. Zeus watched as it was filled. A red light came on near the pump. There was a shout. The light went off. Another truck started up.

He wasn't going to get any closer than this, and if he waited too much longer, he'd be found.

Zeus crawled under the truck he'd been hiding behind. He rolled onto his back. He'd plant the charge against the chassis, and hope that the explosion was large enough and close enough to affect the pumps.

Blood rushed to his head as he flipped around. A wave of blackness shot through his brain and body.

Get through this, he told himself. But his brain remained in the dark static.

Zeus breathed slowly, willing his full consciousness back, but unable really to effect that—unable really to do anything but lie on his back in absolute darkness. The machinery hummed nearby. The ground vibrated. A few voices, nonchalant still, punctuated the deep hums.

Beyond that were the noises of the jungle: *cricks* and *creaks* and *car-rumphs*, the soft whisper of water much farther off behind them all.

Christian, of all people, brought him back.

"Where do we plant these?" he asked, tapping Zeus's side.

"Under the center of the trucks," said Zeus. "Or else near the gas tank—the truck's gas tank. Whatever you can get to."

"One apiece?" asked Christian.

"Yeah. They're awful close," said Zeus.

"They all went over to that truck at the far side," said Christian. "They're grabbing a smoke."

Zeus turned his head. He didn't see anyone nearby, and assumed Christian was right.

"String the wire back toward the berm where we can hide," he told Christian. "You know how to connect them?"

"Yeah. Same way they were, right?"

"Exactly."

Zeus scolded himself. He should have laid this all out before they started. He was flying too much by the seat of his pants—a good recipe for disaster.

"You take the two trucks to the left of us," Zeus told Christian. "I think your wires will reach. Two charges per truck."

"Two?"

"I don't think we better risk doing more than that," said Zeus. "Their break isn't going to last forever. And that missing guard is going to be a problem. I'll get this truck, and maybe two others. Anything happens, get the hell out of here."

"No shit."

Zeus could see again. Gray shades mostly in the dark, but it was something.

He went to work. Setting the charges was easy—Velcro straps were fixed to each, the ultimate in user-friendly destruction. He twisted the wires out, made sure of the connections—the terminals had jumpers so that the bombs were set in parallel rather than series, ensuring the others would blow even if one failed.

He crawled across to the next truck. He had four more packs. He set two, then crawled to the side, gathering his strength before pushing over to the next and last vehicle.

Just as he was about to get up, he heard the rough cough of a truck engine starting above him. He pulled back, centering himself, worried that he would be run over. In the next moment he realized the engine had been started on the next truck over, the one he'd been about to climb under. He watched the wheels move, the vehicle being maneuvered out of its spot.

This is as far as you should go, he told himself.

A second later, another truck pulled alongside the vacated space. He caught a strong whiff of diesel—the truck had just been freshly loaded.

He'd do one more.

The truck stopped and the driver hopped out of the cab. Zeus bellied across the open space to the other truck. His fingers fumbled for the explosives, made the connections, unraveled the wire. There was a knot—he ignored it, stringing back to the other truck, pushing now, careless and frantic, even as a voice inside his brain told him to calm down, to go slow and not leave himself so vulnerable to stupid mistakes and the great weight of chance and disaster that accompanied them.

Christian was waiting for him back at the berm. Zeus took his wires and wordlessly connected them to the plunger, moving quickly.

"When are we going to detonate it?" asked Christian.

Zeus's answer was to press the plunger. In the next moment, the night exploded, a fireball rushing like a volcano across the Chinese fuel trucks.

6

CIA headquarters, Virginia

Mara leaned back in the seat, watching the C-SPAN feed on Peter Lucas's office television. The committee meeting had been a fiasco. Josh looked even more worn than the day she'd rescued him.

"Well, that's the last nail in that coffin," said Lucas, turning the television off with his remote control.

"What'd you expect? Damn China lobby's been working overtime," said Grease. "Half the people on that committee are in Beijing's pocket. Greene is never getting a bill through Congress. He's lucky he won't be impeached for suggesting it."

Lucas fiddled with the Coke can on his desk. It was empty and slightly dented, kept there as a toy. He looked at Mara. "Maybe we can open up the old Sky Acres Express."

"I'm sure it's possible," she said. "If you can get the money."

Sky Acres was the name of an air transport company Mara had used to bring Russian weapons into Malaysia. The company—actually a pair of pilots who would kill their grandmothers if the price were right—had flown a wide variety of gear to the forces fighting the Chinese-backed insurgency. Using Sky Acres had allowed the agency to move much quicker than it might have. More important, it made possible deals with middlemen that might have been embarrassing or even impossible through regular channels.

"You'll never get a go-ahead," said Grease. "Not legal."

"I wouldn't be so sure," said Lucas. "Frost has already floated the idea."

"This is different than Malaysia," said Green. "You have a moratorium you have to deal with."

"The director is working on that," said Lucas.

"I don't want to hear it," said Grease.

"You didn't."

The moratorium—actually a law banning American participation in weapons sales to a long list of countries—was stringent enough to forbid the indirect sales covered by Sky Acres, according to every agency and administration lawyer who had gone over it. That was largely because, while it was never publicized by the congressional aides who drew it up, the law was a response to the shipping of the Russian weapons into Malaysia, which had made use of a loophole in previous export controls.

"They need a lot of help," said Grease. "A lot of it. This isn't Malaysia. The sort of things Vietnam is going to need are big. Hell, they're a third-world country facing a first-world army. They need a lot of weapons. Antitank missiles, SAMs."

"I don't know if we could find that kind of materiel," said Mara. "We tried to get antitank missiles to use against bunkers." She shook her head. "I don't think we could find more than a half-dozen antitank missiles from Syria, or even Iran. Not even if we paid through the nose."

Lucas rolled the can across the desk, catching it with his right hand, then sending it back across to his left.

"You know, bottom line here, Peter," said Grease, "the Vietnamese don't have a chance in hell. They're going to be overrun in a week's time. We'd be better off shoring up Thailand."

"How do you do that once Vietnam, Laos, and Cambodia are gone?" asked Mara. "They won't stand a chance."

"Well, that's your answer right there," said Grease, getting up. "I'll be upstairs if you need me."

"So, what now?" Mara asked after Greene had left. "For me."

"Play it by ear."

"What's that mean?"

"Let's see what shakes out. Officers get outed all the time, Mara. It's not the end of the world. Focus on the job—there's plenty to do. You're still with Josh?"

"What do you mean?" she asked, surprised at the question.

"With protective services. The marshals or whatever."

"I came down to D.C. with them, yes. They got us a hotel in Alexandria."

"You can let them take it from here." Lucas picked up his soda can and put it in the middle of the desk. He started to lean back, in his chair, then almost sprung forward. Mara pictured a thought developing in his head, physically prodding him. "You're not sweet on him, are you Mara?"

"Sweet?"

"You know what I'm talking about."

"My job was to get him here."

"Yeah, but . . . you guys aren't . . . you know?"

"Would that be any business of yours if I was?"

"I, uh . . . I wouldn't think he'd be your type."

"Why?" Mara shot back. "Too smart for me?"

Mara could feel her ears starting to warm with the blood rising to them. She got up to go.

"Hey, listen, seriously," said Lucas. "The marshal service has it from here. You need a place, right? In D.C."

"I'll get a place."

"Don't be like that. Take one of the Tysons Corner apartments. Kevin can work that up for you. Go talk to him."

"Smith?"

"Yeah, he's handling that sort of stuff these days."

What a comedown, she thought. He had once been one of the agency's top people in Europe.

God, was that her fate?

No—her career in the field hadn't been a tenth as long as his.

"Mara?"

"I'll go see him. Thanks."

7

On the border of China and Vietnam

They didn't stay to see the rest of the show.

"We shouldn't run," said Zeus.

But they did run, first to the fence and then on the other side, racing to the shadows of the trees and brush beyond the camp perimeter. They ran as quickly as they could, stumbling along the uneven ground. Floodlights came on, augmenting the red glow of the fire behind them. The lights showed where the sentry posts were—four of them, all along the fence on the Vietnamese side of the border.

Zeus headed west, continuing past the fenceline as it turned. Crashing through the fronds and branches of the low brush, he came to a thicket of trees, five trunks growing from a single hump, a fist of wood jutting from the ground. He slipped as he veered around it to the left. He grabbed one of the trees and spun down, landing on his butt. He collapsed backward, spent but exhilarated—happy and triumphant, as if he'd just accomplished a Herculean task.

And he had.

They had.

Christian collapsed next to him. "God, we're lucky."

"Damn straight," agreed Zeus.

"I thought we'd be blown up, too. Did you see how far the blast threw us?"

"It didn't throw us."

"Hell, yeah, it did. Ten feet at least. Against the fence."

Zeus blinked. He had no memory of that. Had it thrown them? No.

"Look at that goddamn fire," said Christian. He got to his feet as a fireball rose in the air. The ground shook.

Zeus took hold of the tree trunk and pulled himself up.

"Shit," he said.

"Hot damn!" yelled Christian. He started to laugh. "Hot damn!"

"Sssssssh," said Zeus. But he laughed, too.

They *were* lucky. Very, very lucky.

And now they had to get back.

Silently, without another word to each other, they started walking.

————

They walked for what they reckoned was a little more than an hour—both of their watches had stopped, Zeus's because the crystal had been shattered, Christian's for some unknown reason. The clouds parted and the moon moved over them as they walked, showing the way. The Chinese had undoubtedly sent patrols to find the saboteurs; they could hear occasional gunfire in the distance. But the patrols had apparently gone, understandably, in the direction they thought the attackers had traveled, directly across the border.

Zeus and Christian, by contrast, were walking farther into China, though they didn't realize it. They came to a hard-packed dirt road and began following it southward until it ended abruptly in a bulldozed berm. They got their bearings with some difficulty, moving first east and then southward, walking for a few more minutes before Christian spotted a row of cement fence posts on a hill about forty yards ahead. The hill had been stripped of trees; their carcasses lay among the weeds.

"We're still in China," said Christian dejectedly. "I thought we were in Vietnam."

"We can get through here," said Zeus.

"There's barbed wire on top."

"Razor wire."

"That makes a big difference," said Christian sarcastically.

It did—it made it harder, the wire more likely to slice them into pieces. The bottom of the fence was buried in the ground. And there was a second fence farther down the hill, which looked to be configured exactly the same.

"We ain't getting across here," said Christian. He put his hands against the wire. His whole body drooped.

"There'll be an easier place," said Zeus. "Come on."

"I don't think I can walk another mile," said Christian, but he started walking anyway.

As the euphoria of setting off the explosion faded, Zeus thought of starting a conversation to take their minds off their fatigue and hunger.

But even that seemed to take more strength than he had. Subjects occurred to him—they could talk Army football even, which was about as safe and invigorating a topic two West Point grads could ever find. But his mouth stayed closed.

Walking parallel to the fence, they reentered the jungle after about a half mile. Zeus's knee was giving him problems; it didn't hurt but felt as if it had swollen somehow. Yet when he touched it, it felt exactly the size as the other one.

"More woods," grumbled Christian as they treaded into them.

"Gives us cover."

"The only cover I want is on a bed."

"Yeah. A blonde would be nice."

"Blondes aren't cover."

There was a joke in that somewhere, but Zeus couldn't find it.

"I think the most beautiful girl I ever saw," said Christian after a while, "was at a Yankee game."

"You're a Yankee fan?"

"Hell no. But she was . . . I think. She had a Yankee cap on. So I guess she was a Yankee fan. But for her, I'd make an exception."

"Good looking?"

Christian made a whirling sound. "Good looking isn't the start of it. Blond hair. With like this little brownish streak. Not brown, just a little darker blond."

"A highlight."

"And she had a skirt."

"Skirts are always good."

"At a baseball game? They're incredible."

"A tight skirt, or a loose skirt?"

"Like a silky skirt. Very short."

"She had a boyfriend, right?"

"Of course. Otherwise I'd be married right now. To her. Absolutely."

Christian sounded a little drunk, if only on the memory. They talked like that for a while, the way friends would talk if they had no cares in the world, if they were in a distant city on a convention, enjoying an easy evening. It was a surreal moment, full of contradictions.

Zeus tried to think of a story he could tell, but came up empty.

They'd fallen silent again when they came across another dirt road, this one not much wider than a bike trail.

"This way's south." Zeus angled his thumb as if he were a hitchhiker.

Vegetation teased at the sides, at times swallowing the path whole. It took only a few minutes for them to reach the fence.

"Another dead end," said Christian.

"Wait." Zeus stared at the ground to the east of the path, then walked to the other side.

"What?"

"There. Come on." He led Christian past a few bushes to a well-worn spot about thirty feet west of the path. There was a hole cut in the fence at the bottom; some of the metal was pushed back.

"Damn small hole," said Christian, squeezing in behind him.

Christian started past him. Zeus grabbed him.

"Wait," he said. "There's a sign over there."

The sign was posted on a pole about chest high ten or twelve yards away, just visible in the moonlight. He couldn't see its face from where he was standing, but suspected that was immaterial—more than likely it was in Chinese.

Besides, he could guess at what it said.

"Minefield?" said Christian.

"Shit." Zeus dropped to his haunches. He leaned out, and tentatively groped the ground.

"What the hell are you doing?"

"There's a path. You can see how the grass is parted."

"You're out of your mind," said Christian. "This is a minefield."

"People go through here a lot," said Zeus, pushing out a little farther. He knew he was right—it was a smuggler's path.

"No way."

"Any place where there aren't mines, there are going to be guards. It's the only way."

"God, Zeus. What if we get all the way to the other fence and we find there's no hole there? What then?"

"There'll be a hole. I'm telling you. People go through here all the time."

"Crap."

There was a hole, though it was a little tricky to spot. The fence was bent toward the China side, and obscured by a clump of grass and a scattering of rocks. Zeus's shirt caught as he slipped under. It ripped; the fence scraped his back. It hurt like a hot knife.

"I just want to get the hell home," said Christian, falling in behind as Zeus found the trail into the jungle.

———

The trail led to a wide but unpaved road. The road twisted east and then back north, and at first Zeus was afraid he'd gone the wrong way, but then it took a sharp turn south.

The sun had just begun to rise when they came to another road, this one macadam. They walked parallel to it for a few dozen yards, until they heard the sound of a truck approaching.

"Chinese?" asked Christian.

Zeus listened, trying to decide what direction it was coming from. Finally he realized it was behind them.

"It's coming from the north," he said, ducking down. *"Chinese."*

Christian flopped down beside him. Zeus angled himself so he could see the vehicle as it passed. Every ounce of his body began to ache. He could feel his eyelids hanging down, the eyeballs themselves sagging.

The truck rumbled closer. Zeus spotted the olive drab fender moving toward him.

An older truck. He leaned forward, trying to get a glimpse of the insignia. But he couldn't see it.

An open truck. People standing in the back.

They were wearing peasant pajamas.

Vietnamese home guards. He spotted the star on the cab.

Zeus jumped to his feet.

"Wait!" he yelled, crashing through the brush toward the truck. "Wait!"

He reached the road a few yards after the truck had passed. He yelled loudly, waving his arms.

"Wait! Wait!"

The people at the back of the truck stared at him. They were dressed in dull green uniforms.

"Wait!" he yelled, starting after them.

He'd taken only three or four steps when he tripped, his legs simply too tired to remain coordinated. He tumbled down, barely able to get his hands out in time to break his fall.

Zeus heard the truck stop. By the time he managed to get himself upright, two of the people in the back of the vehicle had run to him.

They were women. They had AK-47s. Pointed at him.

"I need to get to General Minh Trung," said Zeus. "You must take me to General Trung. To General Trung. Right away."

8

The Gulf of Tonkin

The Gulf of Tonkin was a veritable bathtub filled with Chinese rubber duckies, the biggest of which were two Chinese aircraft carriers. The carriers were not, strictly speaking, in the same class as American supercarriers.

Silas told his number two, Lieutenant Commander Dorothy Li, they weren't even the match of the Italian ship *Garibaldi*, which the *McLane* had maneuvered with in the Philippines not six months before.

The assessment was grossly unfair. The *Garibaldi* was a capable ship, but she was much smaller than the Chinese vessels. While packing quite a wallop for her size, the Italian vessel was primarily an antisubmarine helicopter ship with an attachment of Harriers to extend its mission to air strike and defense.

A better comparison was the French carrier *De Gaulle*, a ship Silas had never seen. Displacing around 40,000 tons, the Chinese carriers carried the new Chinese J-15 Flying Shark, among the most capable naval combat aircraft in the world; and considerably more capable than the Harriers. While the Chinese vessels were conventionally powered, they boasted forty aircraft apiece (including helicopters). Together they had nearly the same punch as a larger U.S. supercarrier, though with a shorter reach and somewhat less efficiency. Their sensors and defenses were not up to American standards, but they were operating so much closer to their homeland that any disadvantage was marginal.

Their aircraft would give the *McLane* a difficult time. It was conceivable, in fact, that if properly handled, the Chinese fighters could sink the American destroyer, though Silas was loath to admit it.

And, of course, they would do so only over his dead body.

The carriers were a good distance away, nearly ninety-five miles by the last plot. Closer and of more immediate concern was the cruiser and her frigate.

Named the *Wen Jiabao* after a recently deceased premier, the cruiser was the refitted *Moskva*, a Russian ship sold to China ostensibly as scrap two years before. At one hundred and eighty six meters long and nearly twenty-one meters at beam, it was a good bit larger than the *McLane*. The *Wen* carried at least thirty-two long-range YJ-83 antiship missiles, each with a range of roughly two hundred kilometers.

Nasty things, those.

"Cap, have you had a look at the weather report?"

Silas looked over at his chief aerographer's mate, Petty Officer Jondy Moor, who'd just come out on deck. Moor, who had a background as an aviation warfare specialist, had completed training for the meteorology specialty just before joining the *McLane*.

"What do we have?" asked Silas.

"Nasty storm brewin', Cap. It's gonna be a bitch."

Moor had a satellite image with him; it showed a classic tight pinwheel with a dot at the center.

"Category 5 typhoon. Or it will be," said Moor. "That is the real deal." A Category 5 typhoon—the Pacific version of a hurricane—could have winds in the area of 136 knots, generating storm surges over eighteen feet. The storm was a monster.

"It's coming our way?" asked Silas.

"In this general vicinity. Absolutely, Cap." The petty officer began regaling him with possible storm tracks and percentages, talking about probabilities and the difficulty of really knowing which way the wind was blowing. "We'll have a better idea in twenty-four hours," said Moor. "Any way you look at it, Cap, the seas'll be ultra heavy. Even if it veers off, we get a lot of rain. Gale winds. Gonna be a bitch no matter where it goes."

"Good job," Silas told him. "Keep me informed."

"Aye aye, Cap." Moor glanced over Silas's shoulder. "Chinese still out there?"

"Just over the horizon," Silas told him.

"We oughta kick 'em in the balls before they get a chance to kick ours," said Moor.

"Not up to us," said Silas. "Though I have to say, you have the right idea."

9

Alexandria

Josh's appearances at the UN and before the Senate committee made him a popular "get" for the network and cable talk shows. The only problem was that he didn't want to be a "get."

His experiences since returning to the U.S. had so completely depressed him that he didn't want to do anything, not even eat. Much of it was simply fatigue—he was still hungover, physically and mentally, from his ordeal in Vietnam. Nothing in America could quite match the adrenaline rush of what he'd been through, the triumph as well as the fear. But most of what he felt was utter contempt for his fellow human beings, who were simply too selfish to understand what was really going on. They closed their eyes to the outrage, trying to wish it away in hopes that it wouldn't affect them.

But eventually it would.

Jablonski had set himself up as Josh's media broker, and he gave Josh a long list of possible interviews. Josh turned them all down.

"It's completely up to you," said Jablonski. "But it would be in your best interests to take a few. Just a few."

"*My* best interests?"

The political op stared at him.

"I'm going home," Josh said.

"I'll give you a ride to the hotel."

The hotel wasn't what Josh meant. He wanted to go home home.

The problem was that he didn't have one: the Vietnam field work was supposed to have lasted six months, with research following in Australia.

So Josh had given up his apartment. He didn't even have a storage locker: postgrad, his entire accumulation of worldly goods amounted to three boxes of clothes and six boxes of books, all of which were donated to a Goodwill outfit in Kansas where he'd been staying with his cousin's family before leaving for Asia.

He could go back to the farm. His cousin had invited him in their brief phone call right after the UN talk.

Where else would he go?

————

Josh was still brooding when he returned to the hotel. He started to turn on the television, then realized it would only depress him further. Instead, he started to pack, pulling together all of his borrowed clothes.

He had to talk to Mara, say good-bye.

She was the one thing keeping him here, or keeping him around. He didn't want to leave her.

But that was silly. They weren't boyfriend-girlfriend. She'd been doing her job. It was time to go.

He pulled everything together in less than five minutes, checked the bathroom twice, and left the room.

"Hey, champ, where we going?" asked the marshal. By now Josh was calling him Tex, which he didn't seem to mind.

"Home, Tex."

"Home?"

"You can ride with me if you want. But I'm going."

"Where's that?"

"Tex, you don't have that in your little earphone there?"

"Come on now, Doc. I'm on your side, right?"

"I'm going home." Josh walked to Mara's door and knocked, even though he knew she wouldn't be there. He knocked twice, called her name, then decided it was time to leave.

He wanted to see her. He wanted more than that. But it was time to move on.

Tex trailed him down the hall to the elevator.

"I'm not sure about this," said the marshal.

"I'm not under arrest, right?"

"Well, no, of course not."

"Then I'm going home."

10

Aboard the *McLane*

"*Five merchant ships.* They sailed out of Zhanjiang a few hours ago," the communications officer told Silas. "Fleet wants them checked to make sure they're not running guns to the Vietnamese."

"Well, that's bullshit. They're not going to sail from China to Vietnam to deliver weapons."

The communications officer gave Silas an embarrassed look. Obviously, he had no idea what fleet was up to.

"All right. I'll talk to them from my quarters. Where is Lieutenant Commander Li?"

"She was in the Command Center when I left, sir."

"Very good."

Silas went into his cabin, secured the door, and then flipped on his secure link to fleet. The satellite system provided an encrypted, real-time link to practically every Navy command in the world, all the ships at sea, and the Pentagon. It was a double-edged sword, as it gave those sailing the desks back home considerably more opportunity to interfere with the captains on the front line.

In Silas's opinion, of course.

"There are you are, Silas," said Captain Mortez. He was Admiral Meeve's chief of staff.

"What's the story on these merchant ships. Why am I supposed to intercept them?"

"We think they're carrying Chinese troops."

"What? According to this, the ships are registered in the Philippines."

"Don't believe everything you read. Can you get to them?"

"Depends where they're headed. In the meantime I've got a hurricane blowing up my fantail."

"I've seen the weather reports. Can you stop those ships?"

"I can sink them."

"Dirk, why do you give me a hard time?"

"Because you know and I know they should be sunk if they're Chinese."

"Even if I agreed with you—which I'm not saying I do—that isn't the admiral's order. You board them under UN sanction 2014-3-2 and search them. All right?"

"What if they don't want to be boarded?"

"We'll deal with that when we get to it. The admiral will want you to be in communication at that point anyway."

"Doesn't trust me?"

"You're busting my chops."

"You've been ashore too long, Tommy."

"I'm not disagreeing with you. Contact us every hour to let us know what's going on."

No way, thought Silas. But he didn't say it.

"Are our carriers moving in my direction?"

"Not at the present time," said Mortez. "Everything else is staying near Taiwan. You're on your own. You don't think you can handle it?"

"I can handle it," said Silas. He reached for the kill button. "*McLane* out."

11

Hanoi

Zeus woke to a buzz of voices.

Nurses, doctors, and attendants flitted around his bed. He had trouble opening his eyes. When finally they opened, the light was so intense he had to close them again. He gasped for air, struggled, then breathed as if for the first time.

When he finally managed to keep his eyes open and focused, he found General Harland Perry standing next to his bed. To the general's right was Melanie Behrens, the American ambassador to Vietnam.

"Major, are you with us?" asked Perry.

"Sir, I'm good."

"Glad to hear it." Perry gave him a broad smile. "Doctors claimed you'd sleep for a month."

"Nah, I'm awake."

"Maybe you should rest," said Ambassador Behrens. "They said you were dehydrated."

Zeus pulled himself upright. He felt a little woozy.

"How's Major Christian?" he asked.

"Already checked out," said Perry.

No way Zeus was staying in bed now. He looked around the ward. It was a large room with space for about a dozen beds. Those across from him were packed closely together, the space between them barely enough for a nurse or doctor to edge into. His own bed had three times as much space around it—a gesture toward VIP status, he guessed.

Little else about his immediate surroundings could be considered exclusive, however; there were no monitors, and the saline drip was hung from the ceiling by a thin metal chain, which ended in a blunt, oversized fishhook. There were carts of equipment parked near the foot of the bed next to him, and more extensive equipment a little farther down to his left.

"General, the Chinese have tanks on the border," Zeus told Perry. "They're ready to come across. They must already be across. There was a bunker . . ."

"We know all about the bunker," said Perry. "And the fuel accident."

"It wasn't an accident," said Zeus.

"Major, I believe you are mistaken," said Behrens. "You may have a fever. You are in no position to know what is happening on the Chinese side of the border."

Behrens was a small, petite woman; barely five foot. But she had the voice of a tigress, sharp and commanding. It brooked no discussion, let alone argument.

Perry smiled down at him.

"See you when you're rested up," said the general, starting away with Beherns.

"I'll be in soon," said Zeus.

When they were gone, he took stock of his situation. He pulled up the tight pajama shirt they'd dressed him in. The left side looked fine, but there were several large welts on the other. Oddly, he felt pain only on the right side.

A mystery of medical science.

His right knee felt a little funny. It was slightly swollen, but not really painful. There were numerous scratches and tiny cuts along his lower legs, and his arms looked like they were crisscrossed with graffiti.

All things considered, he was in good shape. The only possible complication was the bag of saline hanging from the ceiling. Zeus looked at the needle taped into his arm, then followed the rubber tubing back up to the bag. The drip wasn't surging through his body—obviously they'd given it to him because they thought he was dehydrated, a problem that could have been solved by just giving him a few gallons of water, for cryin' out loud.

The easiest way to deal with these things was quickly: he pulled off the taped bandage holding the tube in place, then, with a good tug, removed the needle.

Saline poured all over his hand, running down to his arm. He swung his legs off the bed and got up, a little unsteadily. His head cleared as he tied the tube in a knot.

He couldn't get it quite tight enough to stop running. He reached the tube up over the bag, hooking it into the chain. Gravity 101, but he was quite proud of himself for realizing it.

Now where were his clothes?

One of the nurses rushed over as he looked for them at the end of the bed. He didn't understand what she was saying, but knowing the exact words was unnecessary; she was speaking universal nurse-patient language, saying something roughly along the lines of: *What are you doing out of bed?*

"Hey, I'm okay. Thanks," Zeus told her.

She looked at him with the outraged stare nurses are trained to use on noncompliant patients. Zeus had seen that stare plenty of times from his mother, herself a nurse, so he simply smiled.

"You have any idea where my clothes are?" he asked.

The nurse threw up her hands, adding gestures to her verbal admonitions. She pointed at his arm where the IV had been.

It was bleeding slightly.

"You could give me a bandage," said Zeus. He pushed down the pajama sleeve to staunch the bleeding.

"What are you doing from bed?"

Zeus looked up and the met the green eyes of the most beautiful woman he had seen in years, if not his entire life. Her dark-skinned face was framed by black hair that was pulled back behind her head into a long ponytail. Her bleached white smock hung loosely off a narrow frame over baggy blue pants. A stethoscope was strung around the back of her neck.

"I'm okay, nurse," Zeus told her. "I'll just be going now."

She smiled broadly. "Oh, are you now?"

"Yeah, all I have are a couple of bruises and stuff," said Zeus.

"Bruises."

"I used to play football," said Zeus. "I had a lot worse than this after a typical practice."

"Your head?"

"Nothing."

"Concussion?" asked the woman.

"Nah."

God, she was beautiful.

"Your knee?" she asked.

"Banged it up, but look." He put his weight on it, walking out from around the bed. "Not a problem."

"No pain?"

"Just feels a little weird. You know what's wrong with it?"

"Hyperextended it," she said. Even her slight mispronunciation and unsteady grammar were endearing.

"You think so?" Zeus asked.

He looked into her eyes. They were definitely the highlight of her face, and her face was extremely attractive without them. The irises were almost incandescent—he'd seen hazel before, but these were more green.

Jewel-like.

So that wasn't a metaphor. It was how some women's eyes really were.

"I am a little hungry," Zeus told her. "What about you?"

"Me?"

"We could get something to eat," said Zeus. "I don't know any places around here. I'd need a guide."

She smirked.

"No no, not like that," said Zeus. "Just to, you know, show me around."

He touched her elbow. The slightest frown came to her face.

"Your English is very good," he told her. "Is your accent British?"

"I went to school in Australia."

Zeus looked around. The nurse who had scolded him had gone off to see another patient. Two attendants were watching from the far end of the room. The patients in the beds across from him were too sick or injured to pay much attention.

A real shame, Zeus thought. Every eye in the place should be on this nurse.

"Where are my clothes?" asked Zeus.

"You must be released by the doctor to leave. Then you can get clothes."

"Good, let's find him."

"You feel okay?"

"Sure. Absolutely. I could do a dance or something."

She smiled, this time amused.

Finally.

"Come this way," she told him.

"I'm Zeus, by the way. Zeus Murphy. Zeus is an unusual name in America. My father was Irish. My mom Greek. Zeus is an ancient god of Greece."

He babbled on, knowing he wasn't making much sense, but not really caring. Maybe they had doped him up.

A pair of metal desks sat at the end of the ward, pushed together to form an L. Folders and papers were stacked high at the one close the door; the other was covered with small wooden baskets that were filled with rubber gloves and common medical supplies like bandages and shrink-wrapped syringes. A stern-faced man in a pin-striped black business suit sat behind the desk, looking over the material in one of the folders—a patient's chart, Zeus assumed. He was about fifty, and even seated looked tall.

The expression on his face could have soured milk.

"Hey, Doc," said Zeus. "I'm good to go."

The man looked up at him. He wasn't wearing a tie, but his Western-style button-down shirt was cinched so tightly at the collar that Zeus wondered how any blood got to his head.

"I'm ready," said Zeus. He made a motion with his thumb, then pretended to scribble. "Can we sign out?"

The man frowned at him and started speaking in Vietnamese. The woman responded.

"Tell him I'm good to go," said Zeus. "Right?"

Neither paid any attention to him. Zeus thought of slipping away, but the idea of leaving the woman's side voluntarily seemed . . . foolish.

Finally the man behind the desk reached to the pile of folders, took the top one, and slid it across the desk. Sighing, he handed the woman a pen. She jotted something in the top corner, and handed it back.

"You're coming with me, right?" Zeus asked her. "For dinner?"

She shook her head. "Much work."

"But you have to have dinner with me. To eat. For my strength."

She frowned, but not in a mean way.

"And my clothes," added Zeus. "You're going help me with my clothes."

"Clothes are at the desk, the hall end," she said, pointing. "To the right."

Zeus leaned out the wide doorway. There was a cage at the end, with a person working behind it.

"I can do that," he said. "When are we having dinner?"

She tilted her head slightly, looking him over though her gaze never moved from his eyes.

"Please," said Zeus. "Tell me when you get off."

"Midnight."

"That's when I'll be back," he told her. "Where should we meet?"

"I . . ." She smiled. "I will meet you upstairs."

Zeus hadn't realized until then they were in a bunker. They went down the hall, where an older woman sat behind floor-length bars that blocked off part of the hall and a side room. She had white hair, sunken cheeks, and a deep frown. Her arms were covered with large liver spots. Before Zeus could say anything, she got up from her chair, said a few words in Vietnamese, and went into the room.

"She'll get your clothes," said the woman.

"Your name," said Zeus. "So I know who to ask for."

"Doctor Anway."

Of course she was a doctor, not a nurse. Duh.

"Doctor," said Zeus, bowing his head.

She smiled, shaking her head—not quite a laugh, but certainly amused.

———

The matron found army fatigues about an inch too tight in the crotch and two inches too short everywhere else. But they were the best she had. The clogs she gave Zeus were a little undersized as well, but better than walking in bare feet. Making his way up the large flight of stairs at the opposite end of the hall, Zeus felt as if he were a character in a play—an elementary school play, the unlucky child who had to play a forest tree in a costume a size and a half too small.

He went up four flights, stiff-legged, clogs clunking the whole way. A guard stood at the top of the last flight. He wore a helmet and a flak vest, and stared at the wall opposite him, unsmiling, his hand near the trigger guard of his AK-47. He said nothing as Zeus passed.

The doors at the end of the landing opened into a large, dimly lit space that smelled like damp concrete. Zeus shuffled toward a red light at the far end, where another stairway led upward. The top of that landing was guarded by two soldiers, who snapped to attention as soon his feet clapped on the first tread.

Zeus walked past them into the ground floor of a building that at first glance seemed entirely abandoned. The wide hall before him extended some twenty feet, where it opened into a wide room of desks and low partitions. The overhead lights were off, but sunlight flooded through from the left side of the building. The air smelled like dust and ozone, as if there had been an electrical fire. When Zeus reached the open area, he saw rubble to the right; two more steps and he realized that the far side of the building had collapsed.

A woman in a light-brown khaki uniform stood at the far end of the room. She was talking on what looked to Zeus like a cordless phone. Looking up, she gestured to him, signaling for him to approach as she continued her conversation.

The floor tiles had been freshly mopped. Aside from the crumbled stone that had been part of the building wall, there was no other sign of wreckage or destruction—no scattered papers, no debris or refuse. The desks Zeus passed were immaculately clean.

"You are the American," she said, still holding the phone. It was a satellite phone, an older model.

"Yes," said Zeus.

"Go through the door that way," she said, pointing to Zeus's left. There was a large red door that opened outward. "That is the exit."

"Is this building okay?" he asked.

"Go through the door to the left," she repeated.

She looked at him, obviously expecting an answer.

"All right," he said. "Okay."

She resumed her conversation on the phone as if he weren't there.

The crash bar on the door gave way reluctantly. Zeus had to muscle the door open, the edges chafing against the sides.

The door opened into a concrete courtyard. The sunlight was intense, washing out his view. Piles of stone and construction rubble lined both sides of the space. A gray-brick building rose some fifty feet away. There were no windows, just a blank wall of bricks.

As his eyes adjusted to the light, Zeus saw that the opposite wall had the outline of another structure—the building, or part of one, that until very recently had stood where the courtyard was. It had been reduced entirely to rubble by the raid.

Zeus found a path to the street. Two troop trucks idled next to the sidewalk, but there were no soldiers nearby.

He had no idea where he was. He was about to go back and ask the woman to get him a ride when a boy of twelve or thirteen called to him from across the street.

"Joe, you need ride?"

"Uh, yeah, I guess I need a ride," Zeus answered.

The boy turned and darted to his left. The buildings across the street were three stories high, storefronts topped by apartments. All were intact, though the closest one to the right had large boards covering what had been plate glass windows. As he stared, Zeus noticed that some of the apartment windows had been blown out; curtains poked through the empty spaces, fluttering with the light wind.

A bicycle rode up to his left. It was the boy who'd called to him.

"Where you go, Joe?" asked the kid.

"Hanoi's Finest Hotel," said Zeus. It wasn't a description—that was the name of his hotel.

"Very good. Five minutes."

"How?"

The boy started describing the directions, speaking in a mixture of Vietnamese and English.

"No," said Zeus. "I mean, where do I get the taxi?"

"No taxi. No more. I ride you."

"On this bike?"

"Very strong." The kid rattled the bike, as if its sturdiness were the actual issue. "It hold you good."

"There's only one seat. Where are am I going to ride?"

The boy stood over the frame; Zeus would sit on the seat while he pedaled.

"I'll pedal," said Zeus.

The kid made a face.

"What's your name?" Zeus asked.

"Lincoln."

Clearly, that wasn't the case. But it made Zeus smile. He took the bike, positioned himself over the seat and the pedals, then told the kid he could sit on the handlebar.

"You pay first," said the kid. "Five dollars."

"Five dollars?"

"Three good."

"I don't have any money with me," said Zeus. "I'll pay when we get to the hotel."

"No pay, no ride," said the boy, grabbing the bike with both hands. His look was so ferocious Zeus laughed.

"I'll give you ten when we reach the hotel," said Zeus. "Okay?"

"Deal, Joe. You pedal." He climbed up on the front of the bike.

"Where'd you learn English?" Zeus asked.

"School."

"Just school?"

"Internet. Very good teacher."

"I guess. Tell me when to turn."

Zeus struggled to get his balance and to get going—the tight pants and clogs made it difficult. He finally kicked off the clogs and managed a steady pace.

The boy began talking, showing off how much he knew about America. His name was Linkin, not Lincoln; he had adopted it not from a study of American presidents but from Linkin Park, the rock bank, which apparently he knew from YouTube. He described a video of the latest *Transformers* movie, punctuating his enthusiastic review with directions to turn.

It took nearly fifteen minutes to reach the hotel, which was guarded by a platoon of Vietnamese soldiers. Zeus had to argue with the platoon commander to get him to allow the kid to come into the hotel so he could be paid. The boy's English was better than the lieutenant's.

When Zeus had been here last, the hotel lobby and bar had been filled with foreigners. Now they were empty except for a desk clerk and four security officers. The security men, all in their mid-fifties, refused to allow the boy upstairs. Zeus told him to wait by the elevator and he would get his money.

"No no," said the kid fearfully. "You leave, Linkin out."

"You think they'll kick you out?"

"You leave, Linkin gone."

Zeus glanced at the guards. The kid was undoubtedly right. He walked over to the desk clerk.

"Major Murphy," said the man brightly. "We are glad you have come back to us."

"I need to pay my friend here," Zeus said. "He gave me a ride."

The clerk glanced at the boy, then made a face.

"You have ten bucks?" Zeus asked.

The clerk began scolding the boy in Vietnamese. The boy answered back, defending himself.

"It's all right," Zeus told the clerk. "I have it upstairs. I'll pay you right back."

"I do not have any money to lend," said the clerk.

Zeus knew the hotel did keep small sums of money, both American and Vietnamese, at the desk; Perry had borrowed some a few days before to pay a local driver.

"Can't you just lend it to me for a minute?"

"These children are thieves," said the clerk, getting to the heart of the problem. "You pay, it encourages them."

"Zeus, what are you doing out of jail?"

Zeus turned around and saw Christian striding out of the elevator.

"Hey, you got ten bucks?" Zeus asked.

"Ten bucks?"

"Kid gave me a ride. I gotta pay him."

"Get outta here."

"Come on, Christian. I'm good for it."

Christian pulled out his wallet. "All I got's a twenty."

"That'll do."

Zeus took it and gave it to Linkin. The worried look immediately vanished.

So did the twenty.

"You need help, you ask for Linkin," he said. "Linkin best guide to Hanoi."

The boy turned and ran from the lobby, undoubtedly escaping before the hotel people could intervene.

"You owe me twenty," said Christian.

"And you owe me your life," said Zeus. "How come you're not in the hospital?"

Christian shrugged. "I'm tougher than you."

Zeus laughed. "Your problem, Win, is that you believe it."

12

Alexandria

Mara knew something was up when she didn't see the marshal in the hotel hallway. She knocked on Josh's door anyway, then called his room from hers. There was no answer.

After changing, she went down to the lobby and sat on one of the plaid-fabric couches next to the plastic ficus tree to wait for him. There was a television in the corner of the room, tuned to CNN. Mara went over and changed the station to a sports network showing a tennis match.

An hour later, when he still hadn't come in, she knew he had left.

Without saying good-bye?

Impossible.

She waited another hour. She had no way of contacting him—she didn't even have the marshal's cell phone number.

She could get it from the marshal's service.

Mara held off, thinking it would seem too . . . what, exactly? Like she was worried about him? Or infatuated with him.

More the latter. Which she wasn't. Except she was.

Finally, after she'd been sitting for nearly three hours, Mara's cell phone rang. She nearly jumped from the couch.

"Hello?"

"Where is he?" demanded Jablonksi.

"What?"

"Mara, where the hell is Josh?"

"I was going to ask you the same question."

"The marshal service says they're taking him home. What the hell is going on?"

"I have no idea what's going on. You're supposed to be helping him. Why did you let him go before that committee? They made him look foolish."

"They're the ones who look foolish. I told him not to say anything about the Chinese," Jablonski added, flustered. "I specifically told him not to call them murderers. I told him not to use that word."

She clicked off the phone and got up. Time to get something to eat, she decided. And think.

13

Aboard the *McLane*

"They're too far away."

Silas looked at the image on the computer screen. The *McLane*'s present course was plotted against the expected course of the merchant vessels he'd been assigned to intercept. The line ended at Hai Phong— about ten miles shy of the vessels.

"That's at flank speed," added Lt. Commander Li. "And it assumes the merchant ships will continue moving slowly. They're only doing about six knots."

"We need to go faster," said Silas.

He turned and looked around the destroyer's combat information center, or CIC. Stuffed with data screens and high-tech gear, the space was the *McLane*'s nerve center, literally the brain and spine of the vessel's warfighting ability.

Long before Silas's time, a destroyer's chartroom served as a primitive information center, in some ways as much a library as think tank. But the advent of sensors such as radar and sonar greatly increased the size and function of the combat information center, and by World War II, the CIC was the most important compartment on the ship, with due respect to the bridge. Its function since then had not so much changed as it's been refined and expanded with advances in technology. The destroyer's sensors—and the information beamed from elsewhere, generally via satellite—put unparalleled intelligence at the commander's beck and call.

The downside of all of this information was that it had to be processed, which meant not only machines but people who could help make sense of what the instruments told them, and not bombard the captain or weapons officer with isolated bits of intel. The modern CIC—also known by the more modern names of Combat Display Center and Combat Direction Center—was as high-tech as the bridge on a fictitious starship, and in her own realm just as dangerous.

"Commander, with due respect, we're moving as fast as we can," said Li.

"Good," said Silas. "Find me a few knots more. Let's get to those merchant ships before the storm hits."

14

Hanoi

In the first hours of the war, the Chinese planes and theater-launched conventional missiles had been aimed primarily at radar, SAM, and antiaircraft sites, following the time-honored strategy of reducing the enemy's ability to contest control of the skies. But with most of those sites neutralized, and the Vietnamese air force a marginal factor, the Chinese had intensified their attacks on the Vietnamese command and control centers. This meant a step up in their attacks on government buildings, including the one in Hanoi whose basement housed the hospital ward where Zeus had been treated.

Vast swaths of the capital had been struck over the past two days as part of this campaign. The accuracy of the bombs and missiles was impressive—for the most part, they had avoided the area of west Hanoi where foreigners had their embassies and hotels like the one where Zeus stayed were located. And where they hit, the damage was generally contained to the actual target, as Zeus had seen leaving his building.

The effect of this was to make the war seem almost bizarre. One could go several blocks with everything looking normal, then suddenly come upon a street where half the buildings were reduced to rubble. After the first raids, the authorities immediately mobilized and organized relief parties to clear the debris and restore some sense of order. But now the workers, who were mostly volunteers, were tired. Their work dragged, and the continued onslaught was wearing the city down.

A few bombs, apparently strays, had struck the Old City in the center of Hanoi during the day. Fires continued to burn there, smoke wafting over the city. The smell in the air changed from that of an electrical fire to something sweeter, an incenselike aroma of charred, ancient wood.

The city's businesses had largely shut down, with their workers recruited for the country's home guard, or organized into volunteer brigades for various chores. The regular army soldiers who had been manning checkpoints just a few days before had been moved on to more important tasks. Many of their posts were now abandoned, though sandbags and barrels they left behind still slowed traffic. Others were manned by men who had served in the army earlier, primarily during the early stages of the war with America. They were gray, frail figures, more ghostlike than soldierly, dressed in ragtag combinations of military and civilian clothing. Still, motorists obeyed them, stopping and explaining their business, often asking for directions around the streets that had been barricaded due to the strikes, and exchanging information and rumors about the war.

Rumors were a great currency. Information about a pending attack, no matter how far-fetched, could get a citizen very far, opening the doors of shuttered shops and even obtaining extreme discounts in price for necessities.

Hoan Kiem Lake, the romantic soul of Hanoi just east of the now devastated Citadel, was a rallying point for the brigades that were organizing citizen volunteers for the defense. This was at least partly for symbolic reasons—the lake commemorated a successful uprising of the Vietnamese against the Chinese in the fifteenth century, when General Le Loi received a divine sword from a golden turtle there and used it to rout the Ming Dynasty rulers from the country. The park around the lake was overwhelmed by the outpouring of citizenry. Crowds overflowed into the nearby streets, completely choking off traffic.

The necessary detours sent Zeus and Christian wending their way through much of the rest of Hanoi as they headed toward the Vietnamese command bunkers south of the city. Most of the streets were deserted, the residents either enrolled as volunteers or hunkering down in basements and other places thought to be safe. In a few cases, they were still working—a barbershop overflowed with customers, two men shared a single cup of tea at a table in front of a café.

At the start of the conflict, the Vietnamese military command had moved its operations to a set of bunkers south of Hanoi. The bunkers had escaped the opening rounds of the Chinese attack, but now were a primary target. They were very deep underground; Zeus believed they could only be taken out with American-style bunker busters, which the Chinese were not believed to have.

The Chinese had nonetheless made a considerable effort to destroy them. The radio towers that marked the northern fringe of the compound area had been destroyed in one of the first attacks. The small airstrip at the western end of the reserve area had been bombed until it looked like the far side of the moon.

The Vietnamese had moved some antiaircraft guns and missiles into the area before Zeus and Christian left on their mission to Hainan. All were now twisted wrecks, mangled metal arms and flattened torsos dotting the distance. The security fences tilted and swooned in different directions, and the road leading into the complex was so cratered that a new path had been marked with cones. Only the deepest potholes had been filled in; the jeep bounced back and forth as the driver did his best to navigate through the shallowest ones.

The bunker entrances were contained in low-rising buildings hugging the field. The nearest one to the road had been hit by a succession of bombs. It had not been totally destroyed, but the Vietnamese had opted not to use it until their engineers could examine the overhead concrete that covered the stairs to the doorways. Following a set of gray cones, the driver took Zeus and Christian around to the next one. It had survived a near miss that had gouged about ten feet of earth away from its northern end.

There were no guards aboveground. Zeus, who'd been in the bunkers several times now, went down the stairs to the ramp that led to the first security area. He nodded at the soldiers who came to meet him, holding out his arms so they could perform the mandatory weapons checks. He and Christian were wearing civilian clothes, as they had for most of their stay here; the presence of American soldiers in Hanoi, even as advisers, was still top secret.

"You notice there are fewer sentries," said Christian as they were cleared to enter a second hallway.

"Need them to fight the war," answered Zeus.

"Or they got killed in one of the attacks."

"Or that."

The floor they were on had been used for a meeting when the Americans had first arrived. But the actual Vietnamese command offices were lower, and the Chinese attacks had convinced the Vietnamese to close off these conference rooms. There were no elevators down to the lower level—in fact, there were no elevators in the complex at all. Zeus and Christian walked down the long hallway to a wide green door. Though the soldier here had seen the man at the other end check them, he nonetheless looked at the IDs they had been issued before stepping aside.

The door led to a stairway lit by battery-powered red lights. After descending two flights, the stairwell stopped at a steel door. They went through that door and descended another set of steps, repeating the process two more times. The offset shafts were designed to make it difficult for an enemy to send a missile down to the command area.

The door to the last stairwell opened on to a ramp similar to the one they had started on. The walls and ceiling were made of concrete, polished smooth. The floor was covered with a thin industrial carpet. The lighting fixtures embedded in the ceiling were low-powered LEDs, and shaded the corridor with a dim yellow light.

The Chinese attacks had damaged one of the venting units, and the Vietnamese had shuttered it to make repairs. This made the air even staler than it had been, to the point that Zeus felt his lungs were being pressed in his chest.

A young woman in civilian clothes met them a short distance down the hall.

"Major Christian?" she said.

Christian nodded.

"I'm Major Murphy," said Zeus.

The young woman flushed, and bent her head.

"We are most grateful for your brave gallantry," she said softly. Her English pronunciation was impeccable. "You will please come with me."

They followed her past a few closed doors to a small conference room. General Perry was hunkered over some reports at the far end of the table that dominated the room. He was all alone. They had to squeeze past the chair backs to get close to him.

"The Chinese have moved a fair-sized force into the border area where you were last night," said Perry. "I have the morning satellite images. I'd welcome your opinions."

Zeus struggled to fit into the seat.

The images showed the situation in western Vietnam about where they had left it; the Chinese forces were arrayed along the flooded Song Da lake area. But Zeus immediately noticed a key change: the water had retreated by nearly 50 percent. It surely wouldn't hold the Chinese back much longer.

He paged through the images. They were raw, without notations or accompanying explanations. The Chinese had moved their tanks and many of their troops to the northwest area of their assault, taking them out of range of the Vietnamese artillery. There were concentrations near Moc Chau, Doan Ket, and farther north at Bac Yen.

If this were the war game simulation, Red Dragon, Zeus would launch a counterattack from the area of Yen Bar, or even farther north through one of the passes in the Hoang Lien Son Mountain Range. It would break the strength of their drive.

Of course, he'd also have American troops to do that with. *Very* big difference.

The Vietnamese had launched their own strikes on the flank, but the effect of these was negligible. They didn't have the firepower to push across the Da River, let alone blunt the offensive.

"This is where you were," said Perry, handing over another series of images. "The division commander is a fellow by the name of Ho. You should make some sort of gesture of thanks. He contacted his headquarters right away, and they got an ambulance up to evac you. You don't remember any of it?"

"No," said Zeus. "I guess I slept the whole way down."

"I don't blame you," said Perry.

The marshalling area was clearly delineated in the photos. A huge black crater sat where the tank farm had been. There were a dozen vehicles, including APCs, that had been hit by the explosion; even at the scale of the photo the damage was visible. Several other vehicles nearby had probably been damaged as well.

There was a large concentration of tanks, close to fifty, about thirty miles farther north into China. A short distance away was a collection of APCs and trucks, about twice the size.

"You stopped them for a day, maybe more," said Perry. "We've been preparing the defenses."

"That's a huge force," said Christian. "Assuming a three-to-one ratio of infantry to armor."

"I think it's safe to say there'll be more than that," said Perry. "The highways are being booby-trapped and mined. The road net through the mountains is sparse. The Vietnamese have a chance."

"They're going to isolate Hai Phong," said Zeus. This major port on the Pacific was some fifty-five miles east of Hanoi, and another hundred or so south of the border.

"Why bother if they've got it blockaded?" asked Christian.

"Because they want to use the port," said Zeus. "They can land troops there. And more important, ship material out. Which is really the reason they're attacking like this. They want to get it intact. That's why they're coming along the coast."

"Could be," said Perry. "It hasn't been bombed or mined. Which would tend to prove your theory."

Zeus looked at the images from the Gulf of Tonkin and the rest of the waters off Vietnam. The Chinese invasion force was still gathered at the southern tip of Hainan Island. The Chinese aircraft carriers remained close to the western side of the island—roughly where Zeus had seen one of the ships from the window of the airliner.

There was another force, three destroyers and a Corvette-sized craft, steaming south.

"They're thinking of taking the oil platforms," Zeus told Perry, pointing to the destroyers.

"Possibly," said Perry, reaching for the images.

"This is an American ship," said Christian, pointing to the destroyer tagged as *McLane*. "What's it doing up here all by itself?"

"Testing the blockade," said Perry.

"It's not going to take on the carriers, is it?" asked Zeus. "If they come west?"

Perry made a face. "He's under orders to avoid conflict."

Zeus knew from the simulations that the Chinese ships were not as potent as their American counterparts—a Chinese aircraft carrier couldn't hope to project the sort of power an American carrier did, and one Chinese destroyer or light cruiser was no match for the USS *McLane*. But even an American destroyer would be overmatched by the carrier's planes; a coordinated attack would send it to the bottom.

Especially if the destroyer wasn't allowed to fight.

"He's got two Chinese warships tracking him," added Christian, looking at the map. "One of them's a cruiser."

A good match, Zeus thought. The American *should* win, but . . .

"We'll let the Navy worry about their assets for now," said Perry. "The first problem is how to stop those tanks."

"The Chinese are making a mistake using the heavy tanks that close to the coast," said Christian. "There are only a few highways. Route 18's their main route—take that out and they're stuck. We dynamite a couple of bridges, and they grind to a halt."

"They don't think the Vietnamese can stop them," said Zeus. "And they're right."

"There's a possibility we'll get American assets to fight them," Perry told them, his voice hushed. "We're working on it."

"A-10s?"

Perry nodded. Zeus realized that meant he had approved the force plan they'd been working on before the mission to Hainan. He wondered, though—the politics back home did not favor intervention.

"Proceed as if they're not coming," Perry added. "Figure out a way for the Vietnamese to stop the tanks, if possible."

"Prayers?" quipped Christian.

"Hopefully, a little more than that," said Perry as he rose from his chair. "I'm meeting with the Vietnamese commanders in an hour. I need ideas by then."

———

"They're aiming at Tien Yen," said Christian. He pointed to a small city a few miles from the coast in northern Vietnam. "It's a crossroads. From there they have a couple of ways to get to Hai Phong."

Zeus nodded. It would be a good first-day goal, reachable within hours; they could even bypass any strong points without losing access to the roads. Once that was taken, they could stay on 18, which became a coastal highway farther south, or they could move inland and take Hai Phong that way. The Yen Tu Mountain Range would push them eastward, but also cut the Vietnamese options for attacking their flank.

"The first line of defense is to blow up the bridges on both parts of National Road 18," continued Christian, referring to the branches of the highway that ran along the Tien Yen River and the other farther east. Again, this was a no-brainer, very basic strategy that would slow the Chinese advance, not stop it—none of the bridges were very steep or long. Still, it could delay them by more than a day.

Whether that would be enough was an open question.

The Vietnamese army had ten armored brigades. On paper at least, this was a considerable force—there were over 1,300 main battle tanks alone, with an assortment of light tanks and fighting vehicles to complement them.

But the bulk of the Vietnamese tanks were T-54s and T-55s, excellent tanks in their day . . . which had ended somewhere during the late 1960s or early '70s. They were no match for the Chinese 99s, or even the lighter tanks in the Chinese army. The heavier T-62s the Vietnamese had were every bit as vulnerable, though they had better guns.

There were three armored brigades in the north. One was dedicated to Hanoi and would not be taken from the city for any reason. Both of the others were in Lang Son, the province to the west of the area where the Chinese tanks had been spotted. It was far too late to get either brigade into place to meet the advance at the border.

The obvious thing to do would be to slow the Chinese advance with the forces in place. As the Chinese advanced, a counterattack might be organized to cut behind the spearhead, striking at its flank. There was a certain amount of wishful thinking involved in such a strategy, even though it wasn't exactly radical—it presupposed that the Chinese flank would be weak enough to hit.

Slowing the advance was itself problematic. The infantry forces in place consisted of one Vietnamese regular division, just called to regular strength, and two regional divisions—militia units that had been promoted to regular status under the Vietnamese mobilization system. None were equipped to deal with the sort of armored assault the Chinese were about to launch.

The regular division had a smattering of Russian antitank weapons, including a few vehicle-mounted AT-2s and man-portable AT-3s. Neither missile could be counted on to penetrate the Chinese tanks, though lighter vehicles such as APCs would be vulnerable to well-placed fire. The AT-2s were older, line-of-sight missiles; the AT-3 was wire-guided. Both could be fired from a little over a mile away, though in practice much closer ranges were greatly preferred.

Unless you were the operator under fire, of course.

The steeps hills and slim road net suggested that land mines would be particularly useful, but Zeus knew from their earlier briefings that most of the mines the Vietnamese had were ancient, a good number left from the American war, and were mostly of the antipersonnel variety, useless against heavy armor. Squad-level antitank weapons were virtually nonexistent—primarily RPGs that would bounce off the hulls of the Chinese main battle tanks and even some of the infantry fighting vehicles Zeus had seen.

Experience had shown over and over that a determined enemy could improvise tactics to defeat tanks if they had enough time and the right weapons. Typically, armor became more vulnerable as it slowed down and lost its advantage of mobility and speed.

But where would they get the weapons?

Zeus stared at the map. He'd concentrate on the time element first.

Maybe if you blew all of those bridges, it would take longer than a day. There hadn't been bridging equipment in the depot they'd attacked, and none had been spotted in the last set of reconnaissance photos.

The tanks could ford some of those crossings. Maybe all of them.

The Chinese were cautious, though. He'd seen that in the west.

Blow the bridges. That meant two days' delay, more if you could set up additional traps near them.

Highway 4A cut straight down from Lang Son. If the Vietnamese sent one of their tank brigades in that direction, then swung the second down and around so that it blocked off the approach to Hai Phong, they *might* have a chance at a flank attack.

Not really, thought Zeus. Their weapons would be hopelessly outmatched.

They could get more artillery into the area. Once the tanks stopped, the artillery fire could take at least a few out.

He sketched the ideas out for Christian. They weren't much; even Christian could see through them.

"Look, if we blow up every bridge, that's still only a few days at most," he told Zeus. "A few days. I can't imagine it taking a whole week to get to Tien Yen, even without the bridges. You get there on Day Three, you have the whole rest of the coast open to you. South of Dam Tron, everything really opens up—you don't have to be Patton."

Zeus stared at the map. If he were using that route, he would count on the bridges being blown, and use much lighter vehicles.

"If I were the Chinese, I'd welcome a counterattack," added Christian. "It'd make them easier to kill."

Zeus knew he was right. Still, there must be something here, something else they could use.

He straightened, and walked across the room. *Put the attack in perspective*, he told himself. *What is the goal?*

Hai Phong. Had to be.

Nothing else?

Hai Phong was more than enough.

How did it fit with the rest of the strategy? The main attack was in the west. It was an armored strike, a lightning move designed to get deep into the country. They would be moving south and east soon, cutting the country in half.

You took Hai Phong and the northern coast, and the capital would be completely cut off.

And yet, something about it didn't completely ring true. There were better roads farther west, and a decently wide valley if you were pushed off it.

"There's going to be another attack somewhere," said Zeus. "This has to be setting something else up."

"Besides the amphibious landing?" asked Christian. "That must have been part of the plan."

Zeus nodded. That was the context to see this in—it should have been launched with the attack they'd forestalled.

Too much fatigue, too much pressure. Zeus sat back in the seat, moving forces around in his head. There was always a danger of over-thinking things. A lot of times you gave your enemy too much credit. Hell, he'd done that against Christian during Red Dragon.

Zeus watched Christian prepare some notes. He had to admit that Christian was holding up far better than he thought he would—that, in fact, Christian had changed over the past few days and had become much stronger, while he had become weaker, or at least felt weaker.

Zeus's eyes started to close. The air was fetid down here. He could use a nap, or a walk to the surface.

A knock on the door stopped the downward drift of his eyelids. Two Vietnamese officers entered the room. They were the staff translators. One was a major, the other a captain.

"We are ready?" asked the major.

"Good to go," said Christian.

The captain looked blankly at Zeus.

"Yes, we are ready," said Zeus. "Can we get some coffee?"

"There will be tea. Apologies; it is all we have."

———

Zeus and Christian rose as the Vietnamese generals and their staff officers came into the room. They reshuffled the chairs, moving around so that the Americans were on the right side of the room. Zeus wasn't sure if this was a feng shui thing or related to some sort of ritualistic honor he wasn't aware of.

Or maybe they just wanted to keep them far from the door.

General Perry came in, his face grave. He'd gone back to the embassy to talk with Washington; obviously he didn't like what he'd heard.

The last person to enter the room was General Minh Trung. Except for the army uniform—which was the plainest available, baggy at the knees and sides, with no ribbons and no insignia—Trung could have looked like one of the Buddhist priests conducting ceremonies in the orientation film Zeus had seen on the way over. He was several inches taller than Zeus, a veritable giant in Vietnam, but thin. His neck and forearms were sinewy; he stood extremely straight, his posture textbook perfect.

He nodded to Zeus, a smile appearing at the corner of his lips, then took his seat at the head of the table.

A colonel began the meeting by lowering a screen from the ceiling opposite Trung. One of the other officers opened a laptop on the table and took out a small digital projector. Flashing a situation map on the screen, the colonel gave a brief summary of the situation. He spoke in Vietnamese, stopping every so often to let the translators explain what he was saying. He ended with the sighting of the tanks and the action by the Americans.

"A most valuable contribution," said the colonel, looking over at Zeus and Christian. "We are very grateful for all your help."

"Several times now," added Trung. They were the first words he had spoken.

The Vietnamese colonel turned back to the map. He predicted that the Chinese would launch their assault down the east coast by dawn. He swept his pointer downward, showing the projected path.

The Vietnamese had arrived at roughly the same conclusion Zeus and Christian had: The attack would come down the coastal road, aimed first at securing Tien Yen, then sweeping southward toward Hai Phong. The tank brigades would be rushed to that area.

"How do you plan to stop them?" Perry asked.

The colonel seemed a bit put off by the question, and began answering in Vietnamese even before the translator translated.

"We will fight with conviction for our homeland," he said, using English.

"I know," said Perry. "But the rounds in the T-55s aren't going to penetrate the Chinese armor."

"We have strategies."

"What are they?" asked Christian.

The Vietnamese were not completely unrealistic, Zeus thought; there must be some reason for their confidence. He took a guess at it.

"How many *Boltoks* do you have?" he asked. Turning to Perry, he explained. "Missles. For the tanks."

The Boltoks were missiles that could be fired from the T-55's gun;

they would also fit in the 100mm smoothbores of the ancient SU-100s the Vietnamese had as well. They were relatively expensive missiles, manufactured by Russia. As far as Zeus or anyone else in the States had known until now, Vietnam did not possess any.

The Vietnamese colonel turned pale as Zeus's comments were translated. He turned to Trung.

"The major is, as always, knowledgeable and prescient," said Trung from the end of the table. "You will understand, Major, that the existence of this weapon is, of course, a state secret."

"I do understand," said Zeus. "But I also have to tell you, they're not necessarily going to stop the Type 99s. The latest versions can penetrate armor to 850 millimeters. The tanks you're coming up against are thicker than that."

"We will adapt to the realities of the battlefield," said Trung. "The difficulty is to slow the tanks down. Our forces need time to prepare."

"General, if I might interject," said Perry. "We can be of most use if we know exactly what the situation is. Not informing us of your weapons is your prerogative, but it does hamper our ability to help you."

"An oversight," said Trung.

The meeting resumed. The Vietnamese colonel outlined a plan of harassment and delay, hoping to stall the Chinese drive long enough to launch a counterattack. Christian offered a few technical points. Zeus listened silently, taking stock of the Vietnamese. Not telling them about the antitank weapons was counterproductive and petty. More important, though, it indicated that some of the Vietnamese on Trung's staff didn't trust them.

Ridiculous at this point, but there it was.

The Boltocks alone wouldn't overcome the Chinese offensive. There were just too many Z99s. After the first blow, the Chinese would adapt their tactics. They'd concentrate on the T-55s if they hadn't already. In a war of attrition, the Vietnamese would inevitably lose.

They moved on to the other fronts: the preparation for the amphibious attack, which the Vietnamese now believed would come near Hue if it came at all, and the dagger that was stuck deep in its western side. In both cases the Vietnamese seemed to be optimistic, placing a great deal of faith in the ability of the reserve troops—the older men and women who formed what would be colloquially termed a home guard. The colonel spoke of guerilla attacks against Chinese pickets as if they were major victories. Blowing up a troop truck here and a depot there were certainly good for local morale, but they were pinpricks against the Chinese juggernaut.

Zeus suggested a spoiling attack against the Chinese before they moved across the swollen water in the west. If placed properly, it might provoke the Chinese into shifting their forces once more away from the offensive. But the Vietnamese didn't have the troops to pull this off, and the colonel told him that they were quite content with their "defensive posture."

The meeting lasted two hours, a relatively short time given the gravity of the situation and the amount that was discussed. Zeus began to look forward to his dinner with Dr. Anway.

He pictured her again, this time trying to replace the medical clothes with something more attractive.

"You have done us great service," said Trung as the session closed. "We are deeply in your debt."

Christian grinned like a stuffed pig.

"Thank you," said Zeus.

Trung nodded at Perry, then left. The rest of the Vietnamese officers filed out.

"What's up, General?" asked Zeus when they were alone.

"Trung wants to have a word," he said. "He wants you and Christian to talk to his troops. It's voluntary."

"Sure."

"He also wants to thank you personally. It's the least he can do," added Perry, with just the slightest hint of sarcasm. "Good work figuring out what they were thinking."

"They don't trust us, do they?"

"Not completely. How potent are the missiles?"

"Depends on how many they have. In the end . . ."

Perry nodded.

"I don't know that we're getting outside help," he told him. "We may be it."

Zeus had feared as much.

"They'll get their asses kicked," said Christian.

"Yes, Win, that does seem likely."

"If the goal is to slow them down, they might let them get south a bit before attacking," said Zeus. "The Chinese stop when they're surprised—it's a pattern. They get overconfident, then once they run into something they didn't expect, they stop and look around. They're really cautious."

"What are you thinking?" asked Perry.

"Let them get down to Tien Yen. The armor moves quick—they'll stretch out, the tanks ahead of the infantry units. Just like they did in the west. We make the attack behind the forward units. Hit them really hard."

Zeus laid out his plan. They would concede territory initially, and at the end of day, the Chinese would be in control of Tien Yen and possibly farther south. But if things went well, that force would be cut off.

"But you give up Tien Yen," said Perry.

"True."

"Why would they stop there?" asked Christian. "If you're going to hit them, why not get them at the border?"

"Because they expect resistance at the border, and all the way down to the city. It's the unexpected that throws them. They don't adapt quickly. That's really the key. Their generals are too cautious."

"Tell Trung," said Perry. "And what he's asking is purely voluntary. You've been through enough already. I'd send you home if I could spare you."

———

Trung spoke without an interpreter.

"We are very grateful for your heroic efforts," he told Zeus and Christian. "You have done much for the Vietnamese people."

Zeus bowed his head slightly, in the Vietnamese way.

"Many of the commanders have heard of your achievements," continued Trung. "If you were to speak to their troops before the battle, it would be a very good for them. Their bravery would be reinforced."

"It would be an honor," said Christian.

"Thank you, Major," said Trung. He turned to Zeus. "Your wounds?"

"I'm fine," said Zeus. "Sure, we'll talk to your men. If it'll help."

"Major Chaū will be your guide," said Trung, nodding to the senior translator. "He will see to your needs."

Trung started to leave.

"I did have an idea, General," said Zeus. "A way that you might be able to slow the Chinese down for a while."

Trung turned back to him. Their eyes met, as if the older man was studying the younger.

"Tell me," said Trung.

Zeus sketched the strategy. As he spoke, he realized that it implicitly assumed that the Vietnamese were overmatched and desperate—a realistic assumption, though certainly not one that the commander of their forces would want to hear. Trung said nothing. He seemed barely to hear what Zeus said at all.

But he did, in fact. When Zeus was finished, Trung turned to the translators and spoke in Vietnamese. Chaū nodded.

"Please, Major Murphy, go with Captain Nuhn to General Tri and explain your idea to him," said Trung. "Tri is in charge of the corps defending the area. Major Christian, if you would proceed with Major Chaū, it would be greatly appreciated."

15

The White House

"I'm ready for my daily dose of bad news, Peter," said President Greene, spotting CIA director Peter Frost as he walked down the hallway. Frost was standing near the wall where visitors typically queued to go into the Oval Office; it was a little too early in the morning for a line, or Frost would have been at its head.

Greene was on his way to NSC chairman Jackson's office. He had just come from an early video recording in the Rose Garden for the morning-news programs, with a quick stop in the kitchen for a doughnut and coffee. He'd finished his doughnut; the coffee was about half done.

"Come with me," he told Frost.

"They say you have a lot of appointments this morning," said Frost apologetically.

"I do," said Greene cheerfully. He took a sip of coffee. It was cold, but some days that was the best he could manage. Today was going to be one of those days.

Walter Jackson's secretary had not yet arrived for work. Jackson was inside, on the phone.

"I think he was born with a phone attached to his ear, don't you?" asked Greene, winking at Frost as he took a seat.

Jackson's office was small to begin with, but it was made even tighter by the presence of large bookcases that lined three of its four sides. The shelves overflowed with books, papers, and journals. There was also an old, well-oiled catcher's mitt, alleged to have belonged to Yogi Berra—an interesting artifact, given that Jackson claimed to be neither a baseball nor a Yankee fan.

"Arghhh," said Jackson, hanging up the phone. "Mr. President."

"Problem, Mr. Director?"

Jackson frowned. "Have you read the morning briefing?"

"Of course."

"The Chinese are preparing a second offensive down the east coast of Vietnam," said Jackson.

"I read that," said Greene. "I also read an assessment that said this was a particularly poor area for them to try to attack through. Very limited road net."

"General Perry's assessment is considerably more pessimistic than the Army's," said Jackson.

"What do you think?" Greene asked Frost.

"I'd stick with Perry," said Frost. "The five merchant ships that are mentioned in this morning's briefing. We're pretty sure now that they're heading for Hai Phong. It could be to hook up with the attack down the coast."

"The Navy is supposed to check them out," said Greene.

"The destroyer is too far away to reach them in time," said Frost.

"Why the hell wasn't I told about that?" said Greene. The coffee shook in his hand—he reached over and put it on the edge of Jackson's desk.

"Operational detail," said Jackson drolly.

"Your only option may be to blow them out of the water," said Frost.

"We can't do that," said Greene. "What if we're wrong?"

Frost nodded. "I'm just saying, it may be too late to get in there."

"Even if the *McLane* did get close," said Jackson, "they're being shadowed by a cruiser and frigate. They might interfere."

"I need that damn vote," said Greene.

He glanced over at Jackson. The national security director was silent, his expression neutral, but Greene had no trouble reading his mind: *You're not going to get it.*

16

Northern Vietnam

General Tri was the army commander responsible for the defense of the three northeastern provinces, including Quàng Ninh, where the Chinese were expected to make their attack. He had moved his headquarters from Bac Giang city to be closer to the expected fight.

The new command post was in Tien Yen.

Zeus and his guide flew there in a Mi-24 Hind, a Russian-made helicopter that was half-transport, half-gunship. This particular aircraft was somewhere in the area of thirty or forty years old, and it bore a number of scars, including a set of patches in the side and floor that Zeus imagined covered bullet holes older than he was.

The exterior of the helicopter was freshly painted in a jungle camouflage scheme. The interior, however, showed its age. Many of the metal surfaces were worn bare and shiny. A pair of simple metal benches had been welded into the center of the hold. These, too, were worn, with silvery spots showing where passengers typically sat. The aircraft smelled of oil and exhaust.

Captain Nuhn sat next to Zeus for the flight. Outside of headquarters, Nuhn had proved to be a jovial guide, friendly and talkative. His English was as good as his jokes were bad. But the Hind was far too loud for a conversation. Zeus spent most of the flight on the bench staring at the floor.

The helicopter landed in a bulldozed field about three miles south of Tien Yen. Zeus ducked as he stepped out, instinctively flinching as the blades spun overhead. Nuhn came out after him, trotting away from the helicopter with a childish gait, pumping his arms energetically. The Hind's rotors revved and the helicopter pitched forward, scattering large clods of mud as a farewell.

"This way, Major!" shouted Nuhn, leading him toward a path at the edge of the bulldozed field.

General Tri had established his command post in a copse of trees on a hill above the field. The post was remarkably simple.

Two trucks, both canvas backed and both built before 1960, were parked wedged between the trees at the top of a winding trail. An open-sided tent dominated the small clearing behind them. This was the general's office, with his staff performing their various functions around a pair of small tables beneath the canopy. A thick set of wires ran across the clearing and up the hill; Zeus guessed there was an antenna or a satellite dish, or more likely both, on the opposite slope. A pair of Honda electric generators were clunking away a few feet from the tent; jerry cans containing their fuel lined the northern edge of the clearing, guarded by a lone soldier. Two other soldiers, both armed with AK-47s, were pulling security duty nearby. A handful of privates, all very young, were standing at the opposite edge of the clearing, near a pile of bicycles.

General Tri was speaking on a field phone as they approached. While Zeus couldn't understand what he was saying, Tri's manner made it clear he was giving orders. His right hand tapped the table as he spoke, unconsciously emphasizing what he was saying. He spoke in sharp, hard tones.

Nuhn waited at the edge of the table without speaking. The others continued to work over their maps and papers, taking no notice of them. Zeus wasn't surprised; they undoubtedly had a great deal to do.

Tri finished his call with an emphatic slap against the table. He slid the phone onto the cradle of its field pack, and said something to Nuhn.

Whatever he said made Nuhn feel uncomfortable. The captain started to answer, but Tri cut him off. The two men began arguing. It was one-sided; Nuhn strained to be polite while making his point. Finally, General Tri ended the conversation by picking up his phone.

"What's up?" Zeus asked his guide.

Nuhn shook his head. General Tri, meanwhile, began a conversation with one of his officers, once more giving orders and making his points with the help of his fingers.

When he was done, Nuhn began speaking to him again. Or trying to—General Tri rose from his seat, pointed his finger at Zeus, and began speaking very sharply.

Zeus imagined he was being called several names at once, none of them flattering.

"General Trung told me to come here," Zeus said. "It wasn't my idea. If you don't want my advice, that's fine."

Tri turned to Nuhn and began berating him even more harshly than before.

"Hey, don't pick on him," said Zeus. "We're going. Come on, Captain."

Nuhn seemed a little shell-shocked.

"Major," said Nuhn. "General Trung has ordered you to give your advice."

"General Tri doesn't want advice. Why waste his time?"

"Major, we must." Nuhn caught Zeus's arm as he started to leave. He turned back to Tri and started to talk to him again, this time his voice very soft.

"*Không!*" said Tri adamantly. Even Zeus understood this meant *no*.

The general turned and called to one of the men at the bicycles. Ignoring Nuhn and Zeus, he took a piece of paper and wrote something on it. Folding it, he handed it to the man with a brief set of directions. The man immediately set off on his bike.

The rest of his staff, meanwhile, kept their eyes fixed on their work, steadfastly refusing to look in their direction, let alone get involved.

"Come on, Captain," said Zeus. "I'm tired."

He went back down to the field, admiring the bright-green fields and hills in the distance. It was a peaceful, near idyllic scene—one that would shattered soon.

Nuhn followed a few minutes later.

"I apologize deeply for the insult," said the captain.

"It's not a problem. He probably wouldn't have liked what I was going to suggest anyway."

"He should have listened. It is an insult to you and General Trung."

That was the real problem, Zeus knew. Nuhn now had to go back and tell the supreme commander that the general he was counting on to hold this sector was insubordinate.

An isolated incident? Or a sign that Trung was losing his grip on his army?

"We will find a ride in Tien Yen," Nuhn told him. "But we have to walk there."

"To the city?"

"I guarantee we will find a ride," said Nuhn. "I am sorry—the helicopter was needed elsewhere."

———

Evening was settling over the hills, but the weather was mild. Though Zeus's legs were tired, he had no trouble keeping up with Nuhn, whose pace slowed as they went.

In the States, Nuhn would be considered a little overweight, though not portly. By Vietnamese standards he was Falstaffian. Though it was doubtful he had any idea who Shakespeare's hero-clown was, his swinging arms and cheerful manner amused Zeus, easing some of his fatigue. Nuhn's smile returned little by little.

"We have a lovely day for a walk," said Nuhn. "A lovely day."

Zeus asked the translator where he had learned English. It turned out that Nuhn had two brothers who were born in America, though both had returned to Vietnam just before he was born.

"I am the baby of the family," he said, detailing a Nuhn family tree that had eight members in the present generation. Originally from the Central Highlands, several members of the clan had left for the U.S. just before the collapse of South Vietnam. These included Nuhn's father and mother, along with a hodgepodge of uncles and aunts. The family owned two restaurants in Los Angeles, but Nuhn's mother had been homesick and the family had made its way back to Vietnam clandestinely about a year before Nuhn was born.

"English was always my best subject in school, even better than math," said Nuhn. "No one knew why." He laughed.

"I'm sorry the general gave you such a hard time," said Zeus.

"He's a fool," said Nuhn. "But we are stuck with him."

The road they were walking on had been made from hard-packed gravel coated with oil. It was about three car-widths wide. The sides fell off sharply into fields that seemed fairly wet. If the soil held the Chinese battle tanks at all, it wouldn't let them move very quickly.

About a mile after they started walking, the road intersected with a highway. This was made of thick asphalt, and was wide enough that two columns of tanks could easily travel down it, with space for other vehicles to pass. A hill rose sharply on the left, but on the right the fields were green and level. Water was channeled across by a pair of deep ditches; tanks would have no trouble getting through here.

You could ambush the Chinese from the hill, come at them from the trees at the far side as well. They'd never expect an ambush from the Vietnamese on the open plain like this, not so close to the city after just having taken it.

If you hit them hard quickly, they might fall back to the city. But ideally you would want them to move even farther south, hopefully along this road where they could be bottled up.

Zeus tried to turn off his brain. There was no sense thinking of this. The commander didn't want help. He had better things to do.

Give speeches. See the doctor.

Not in that order.

"You know a good restaurant in Hanoi that's still open?" Zeus asked as they walked.

"A restaurant?"

"I want to thank the doctor who worked on me," said Zeus. "I thought I would take her someplace nice."

"Ah, a lady doctor. I understand," said Nuhn. "You want to impress the lady."

"Something like that."

"Then she will fall into your arms," joked Nuhn.

"That'd be nice."

"Before the war, there were many places," said the captain. "Now, you would be best in the hotel area. You will do best finding a place for tourists."

"My hotel looked deserted."

"That is not bad for you, is it?"

Zeus nodded. It might not be bad at all.

"We will find you some flowers," added Nuhn enthusiastically.

"Great idea."

"I have often impressed women with flowers," said Nuhn confidentially. "They are like magic."

He sunk into full Falstaff mode, regaling Zeus with a story of how he had wooed a woman in Saigon some years before. He had found a perfect flower—he couldn't translate the Vietnamese word, *hoa cruc*, but the description made it sound like a mum to Zeus. He brought it to her at work just before she was due to take lunch. This scandalized her, as she had been avoiding him for weeks. But her boss insisted on her going to lunch with him, and they ended up having a love affair that lasted for months.

"Lucky for you the boss was on your side," said Zeus.

Nuhn winked. "Ten dollars American makes many friends."

———

The war had upended Tien Yen, even though the fighting hadn't reached there yet. A good portion of the population had been moved by the government or fled on their own. Most of the people who remained were working on various defenses, filling sandbags and posting them on street corners, erecting barricades, preparing gun positions. Twisted pieces of metal intended as tank obstacles were piled on one side street, waiting to be deployed. There weren't many troops in the city; most were north, waiting warily for the Chinese attack.

A company of home guards were being drilled on one of the side streets as Zeus and Nuhn passed. Nuhn told Zeus to wait at the intersection and trotted over to speak to the captain who was supervising the drill. A few minutes later he appeared with a member of the guard in tow. The man was well into his fifties, and nearly as chubby as Nuhn.

"This is Uncle Vai," said Nuhn, introducing the soldier. "He will drive us to Hanoi."

Uncle Vai was a farmer who lived at the edge of the city. He led them back the way they had come, turning northward near the center of town and then wending through a series of narrow alleys behind a warren of tiny houses. Zeus was beginning to feel a little dizzy when finally Uncle Vai reached over a gate and undid the wire holding it in place. He led them into a narrow yard between two brick garages. Both buildings pitched toward the yard; it wouldn't take much to knock them down.

A small truck was parked behind one of the buildings. The hood and windshield were covered with a tarp. Zeus and Nuhn helped Uncle Vai remove the tarp, following his directions to fold it carefully so it could be tied beneath a pair of large ropes on the flat back of the vehicle. Then they stepped out to the small alley and waited as Uncle Vai maneuvered the vehicle from its parking spot.

At some point in its life, the vehicle had been a panel van, the sort used to deliver goods to small shops during the 1960s and '70s in Europe. The rear compartment had been removed, replaced by planks to make a flatbed. If the condition of the planks was any indication, this had happened many years ago.

The front of the van had been altered as well. The original seat had been replaced by one slightly larger; the edges of the seat stuck out into space where the door closed, so that when Zeus got in on the passenger side he had to slam the door several times before he could get it to latch. About half of the dashboard was missing, leaving Zeus with an open space in front of him—a blessing, really, since it left him more room for his feet. The vehicle had a manual transmission, mounted on the floor. Nuhn had to pull his legs back and hold his breath every time Uncle Vai shifted.

How could a country whose cars and trucks were falling apart hope to hold off the Chinese?

More to the point, why would anyone want *to take them over?*

The answer to the second question was in the fields they passed as they drove back to Hanoi. The generously watered crops would feed a good portion of the Chinese population in the south, particularly hard hit by the climate shifts over the past few years.

There was no good answer to the first question.

———

Nuhn had Uncle Vai stop by the Nhat Tan flower market when they arrived in Hanoi. It was well after nine o'clock. All the shops in the district had been closed for hours. But that didn't deter Nuhn. As Zeus waited with the truck, he ran around the corner, promising to return with "something special." A few minutes later he reappeared, carrying a long branch of blossoms.

"Your doctor will be very impressed," he told Zeus.

Zeus stared at the blossoms. He'd never seen flowers this beautiful before. He barely thought of flowers as pretty—they were gifts, accessories. He felt as if he were seeing flowers for the first time.

His mind drifted from the flowers to the doctor.

"Major, this is you!" said Nuhn cheerfully.

Zeus looked up. They had reached the checkpoint to his hotel.

"Right." Zeus squeezed his hand into the door latch. The door sprang open, a bird released from its cage. "Thanks."

Nuhn slammed the door behind him, then opened the window and leaned out.

"Good luck!" shouted the captain cheerfully.

The men at the barricade pretended not to be watching Zeus as he walked past them. They didn't bother checking his identification; the fact that he was a westerner was ID enough.

There were more people inside than there had been that morning. Even so, the lobby was hardly full. Zeus walked to the elevators, curious about who might be still in the city, but not wanting to talk to anyone. He pushed the button and stepped to the side, waiting.

He had a few hours before she got off. The first thing he was going to do was take a shower. After that . . .

After that he had to make sure he didn't fall asleep. His body was starting to droop.

A man in his twenties came up next to him, tapping the elevator button even though it was already lit. He gave Zeus a sideways glance, then an embarrassed smile.

"Never trust them," he said in English. His accent seemed British.

The elevator doors opened a second later. Zeus let the other man go in first, then got in himself. They were headed for the same floor.

"Nice flowers," said the man as the doors closed.

Zeus glanced down at them. "Yeah."

"Do you think the hotel is safe?"

"Probably as much as any place."

"Bret Cannon." The man stuck his hand out. "AP."

"Uh, Zeus Murphy." Zeus shook hands awkwardly.

"Been here long?"

"Few days. What's AP?"

"Associated Press." Cannon smiled again, this time looking like a man who had just confessed that he had inherited a great deal of wealth. "I'm covering the war."

"I see."

"You?"

"I work for the embassy." He didn't say U.S.; it would be obvious.

"Ohh," said Cannon knowingly.

"I'm not actually a spy," added Zeus, "but it does sound more ro-mantic if I leave it open-ended."

"What do you do then?"

"I'm not really supposed to say, but basically I keep machines work-ing."

"A copy machine repairman, eh?"

"Pretty much."

Cannon gave him a smirk. He thought they were playing a game—that by saying he wasn't a spy, Zeus had in fact admitted that he was. Zeus didn't mind that; spies were expected. What he didn't want to do was let on that he was here as a military adviser.

"How long do you think the Viets can last?" Cannon asked.

"Got me. A long time, I hope."

"I give them a week. At most."

The doors opened. "See ya around," said Cannon, stepping out. "I'll buy you a drink sometime."

"Sure."

Zeus thought of stepping back into the elevator and going down-stairs; he didn't want Cannon to know which room was his. But it would be a waste of time; anyone with ten bucks could probably bribe a hotel worker for the information.

Inside his room, Zeus peeled out of his clothes, then tried to take a shower. The water trickled from the spout, and it was cold. He washed anyway.

How long can the Viets last?

Not long. A week wasn't a bad estimate.

There was a knock on the door as Zeus toweled off. He thought of ignoring it, sure it must be Cannon. But where was the sense in that?

"Yeah?" he yelled.

"It's me," said Christian.

"Hang on." Zeus wrapped a towel around his waist, then went to the door, undoing the lock.

"What's up?" he asked as Christian came in.

"Jeez, you got water?"

"A trickle."

"Across the hall there's nothin'." Christian plopped down in one of the chairs. The bottom of his jeans was crusted with mud. "God, put some clothes on, would you?"

"I wasn't expecting company." Zeus pulled some underwear and a fresh pair of pants from the dresser. He was getting low; pretty soon he'd have to resort to his BDUs.

"So they go for it?" Christian asked.

"The general wouldn't even see me."

"Figures. I don't know what it is with these guys. Inscrutable Asians. And we saved their butts. You and I." Christian got up and went to the minifridge. "All they got here is Chinese beer."

"That stuff costs a fortune."

"I wouldn't sweat it. They won't be around to collect. Bar is crawling with reporters," added Christian. He held out a bottle for Zeus.

"I better not. I don't want to fall asleep."

"Why, you got a date?"

Zeus started to grin.

"You *do* have a date. What the hell, Murph? With who?"

Zeus shrugged.

"I'll find out if you don't tell me. I'll have you trailed."

"The doctor who worked on me. A woman."

"Yeah, no shit?" Christian took a slug of the beer. "I think I know who you're talking about. Good choice. That's what the flowers are for, huh?"

Zeus looked at the branch of blossoms on the dresser. He should probably put it into water.

"We went to eight different units. Eight," said Christian, leaning back in the chair. "They're going to get their asses kicked. I don't think I saw one weapon less than twenty years old. You really think they have Boltoks? Or was that a pipe dream?"

"Probably a few."

"A few won't do it." Christian took another slug. "Hell, those aren't going to go through a 99 anyway. Unless you get a really good hit. The damn tank was designed to deal with that crap."

Being outgunned didn't necessarily mean that you would lose an engagement, let alone a battle. During World War II, the main American battle tank was well overmatched both in firepower and armor by the German Panzers. But the Americans were able to develop tactics to overcome that disadvantage.

Not easily. And generally those tactics relied on numerical supremacy, something they didn't have here.

"But what the hell are we supposed to do, right?" continued Christian. "Tell them to give up? I wouldn't give up."

"You wouldn't?" It was halfway between a question and a statement.

"No way."

That was one thing about Christian—even when his ass was being kicked in the simulations, he kept fighting to the bitter end.

Stupidly, since it meant they'd usually missed the start of happy hour. Probably not a concern for Christian, as Rosen and Zeus had never invited him.

"I met a reporter in the elevator," said Zeus.

"No shit."

"He asked why I was here. I told him I was a repairman for the embassy."

"No more trade specialist?" That had been the suggested answer.

"I don't think he'd believe that shit."

"And he believed you're a repairman?"

"No. He thinks I'm a spy."

Christian drained the rest of his beer, then went back to the minifridge. "Sure you don't want one?"

"I'm sure."

"The women always liked you. I can understand that." Christian twisted off the top, took a swig, then sat back down. "It was Rosen I can't understand. How the hell did he get women?"

Zeus shrugged.

"I mean, could there be a more obnoxious wise ass in the army? And he was nothing to look at. At least, not that I could tell. Not that I would know. But . . . the women. Cripes! What did he do, make some sort of deal with you to take the rejects?"

"They did go for him, didn't they?" said Zeus. "Hard to explain."

"You know, I have a different opinion of you over here," confessed Christian.

"Huh?"

"You used to be an asshole. War brings out something better in you."

"Gee, thanks," said Zeus.

"No, I mean it. You're a lot more humble. No more big head, no more 'I got the solution to the world's problems.' You're very focused. It's good."

Look who's talking about having a big head, thought Zeus.

"What time's your date?" asked Christian.

"She gets off at midnight."

"Midnight? Hell, you better get over there. It's quarter of."

———

There was a curfew, but it could be broken for official business.

Which translated into a bribe, both for the driver and anyone who happened to stop them.

Zeus was surprised that there was a line of cars waiting near the street, a product of the hotel's sudden popularity with foreign correspondents. The driver used a variety of backstreets, wending his way around checkpoints and blocked streets. The Chinese had not bombed Hanoi so far that night. Zeus wondered if they were saving their ammunition for the assault in the north.

Despite all the detours, they managed to get to the square near the building a minute or two before midnight. Zeus practically leapt from the car.

"Wait!" yelled the driver, chasing after him. "You will call me." He handed Zeus a card with a cell number. "I cannot stay for you."

"All right. I'll call when I need you."

"You call," said the man.

Zeus crossed the street, walking briskly toward the battered building where the hospital was located. But when he found the door he'd come out of, he discovered it locked. He pounded on it, but no one came to answer.

He took a few steps back, surveying the area, looking for another entrance. There *had* to be another entrance.

On the block behind the building, he realized. He must be at the back.

Zeus started running. It occurred to him that he probably shouldn't run—a soldier seeing someone running might easily draw the wrong conclusion. But it was hard not to. He dropped to a trot, then walked, then trotted a bit.

When he reached the front of the building he managed to slow to a deliberate walk. There were people ahead, a half dozen about a third of the way down the street on the right. He picked up his pace, then slowed down, nonchalant, trying to relax. He scanned the faces, but didn't see her. She must be inside.

Two soldiers stood near the door. One raised his hand as Zeus approached.

"I'm here to see Dr. Anway," he told them.

Neither man said anything. Zeus took a half step toward the door. The soldier who had raised his hand moved in front of him.

"Dr. Anway," Zeus said. "I'm here to meet her. The doctor."

Zeus held up the branch of blossoms.

"I have to see Dr. Anway."

The soldier on the right said something in Vietnamese. His voice was soft; the words came slowly and distinctly, but of course Zeus didn't understand what he said.

"I'm an American," he said, though this would be rather obvious. He reached into his pocket and took out his passport.

The soldier who had barred his way took it, leafing through slowly.

"Dr. Anway?" said Zeus hopefully.

The other soldier said something in Vietnamese.

"I'm sorry but I don't understand. I was told to meet her here." Zeus glanced back at the people on the street. None of them seemed to be paying any attention to him.

"Does anyone speak English?" he asked.

No one responded. Zeus turned back to the soldier who had the passport.

"Dr. Anway," said Zeus, pointing to the flowers.

The other soldier reached over for the branch. It wasn't a violent gesture; Zeus thought he was offering to take them to her.

"I want to give them to her myself," said Zeus, holding them.

The other soldier handed his passport back.

Zeus started for the door, but the soldiers immediately raised their rifles to bar him.

"Does anyone speak English?" asked Zeus loudly. He turned and repeated the question.

One of the men on the street looked back at him.

"Do you understand?" Zeus asked.

"No to go inside," said the man. "Only worker."

"I'm supposed to meet someone," Zeus explained.

Just then the door opened. Two older Vietnamese men came out. Both were dressed in button-down Western-style shirts, and wore well-tailored trousers and dress shoes. Zeus guessed they were doctors.

"Excuse me," he said. "Do either of you know Dr. Anway?"

"Anna?" said one.

"Yes," said Zeus, guessing that was her first name.

"She left hours ago. Her shift ended early. We sent her home. She needed rest."

Zeus felt as if his lungs had collapsed.

"Oh," he managed.

"You should check in the morning," said the man. "She will be here by eight."

"Thank you."

The man glanced at the flowers in Zeus's hand and smiled. He and his colleague stepped over to the knot of other people. A van was just driving up the street.

"The van will take you to your hotel," said the man who'd been speaking with him.

"No, that's all right. I have another ride."

"You should be careful," warned the man.

Zeus walked to the corner, dejected. He fished the card out from his pocket, and took out his satellite phone. Then he put both back—he'd rather walk. It would do him some good.

He dropped the flowers on the ground. He should have known.

A bell rang behind him. It was an odd sound in a war, a light ring.

When he was younger, he thought of war and peace as two very separate things, different parts of the universe. Now he knew they were entangled, shards of each poking through the fabric of the other.

The bell sounded again, louder. Zeus turned to see a bicycle bearing down on him. He hopped back as the bicyclist pulled up.

It was Anna.

Anna.

"I am sorry to be late," she said, sliding down off the seat.

"Anna."

"Yes?"

"I . . . they didn't let me in. Someone told me you had left."

"Yes. I was able to get out. Come."

She turned the bicycle around.

"I can call a cab," Zeus said. "A taxi."

"It is only a short way."

"Oh . . . great," said Zeus, starting to follow.

They came to the flowers. Zeus scooped the branch up and handed it to her.

"I . . . I got this, but I dropped it." He winced, suddenly realizing he was underlining his loss of faith.

"It's very beautiful," she told him.

"Like you."

"Hmmmm."

Was she blushing? He couldn't tell in the dark.

"You speak English so well," he told her.

"I left Vietnam as a child. My parents sent me to Australia. Where I went to school."

"Why did you come back?"

"I was always to come back," she said, as if the question were odd. "Vietnam is my home."

They walked past the street where the hospital was. Zeus felt his energy coming back.

"Do you like being a doctor?" he asked.

Another dumb question. *Where is my brain?*

"I like helping people." She glanced up at him. "Do you like being a soldier?"

"Sometimes."

"We are very grateful for your help. I have heard of your sacrifices. You destroyed enemy tanks."

"Actually, the trucks that would supply them. We blew up their fuel."

"Ah."

"Where's the restaurant?" asked Zeus.

"I have made dinner," she told him. "At my apartment."

"Oh," he said. "We can do that, too."

———

Anna's apartment building had so far escaped damage. Eight stories high, it was a plain, boxy building, the sort of nondescript structure that would have been anonymous in the West and even in most of Asia. Here, however, the newness and size of the apartments made it a place of luxury. Little cues signaled its status: a black wrought-iron fence around the small courtyard, a well-tended if small garden at the front, a fancy plaque that held the address.

Anna used a key to open the building's front door. Zeus held it for her as she wheeled her bike into the darkened foyer.

"The electricity has been turned off," she explained. "The city has to conserve."

"Sure."

"I'm at the top."

"I'll take your bike," he told her, picking it up. "Show me the way."

The bicycle was heavier than he expected, and by the first landing Zeus felt the strain in his arms. But pride kept him going. A skylight at the top of the stairwell supplied a faint grayish light, making it easier to see the steps as he worked his way up behind her.

"Here," she said, putting her bike next to the door of the apartment at the end of the hall. "Wait."

Anna put her key in the lock. A yellow glow spilled into the hallway as she opened the door.

"Candles," she told him.

The door opened into the kitchen. A pair of candles sat on the stove. A table was pushed against the opposite wall, with two places set. The appliances were all new. Zeus recognized an LG logo on the refrigerator.

"Sit, sit," Anna told Zeus.

Zeus watched her bend down in front of the oven and gingerly touch a covered casserole dish inside, testing with her fingers to see if the handles were still hot.

They were. She straightened, retrieved a pair of pot holders from the nearby counter.

Zeus admired the curve of her body as she squatted back down in front of the stove. She removed the pot with the grace of a dancer, pulling it out and setting it in on the table, deftly maneuvering the pot holders so that they formed a place mat for the dish. She went to the refrigerator and took out a small plate of sliced garnishes: bean sprouts, radishes, and bits of lime.

"This is *pho*," she told him, lifting the cover of the dish. "Noodle soup."

She'd forgotten that the top was hot. It dropped from her hand. Zeus jumped up, grabbing not the pot but her.

"Are you okay?" he said, holding her protectively.

"I'm—" She turned toward him.

Time melted away. Their eyes met, and they were kissing.

If there was anything beyond that kiss—a room, a war—Zeus didn't know it. If there was pain or fatigue or fear—if there was courage or foolish bravery, thought or planned—it evaporated in the warm press of her lips.

Their lips. It was an infinite moment, a sensation of grace or bliss, of nothingness beyond the moment.

He held her for a long time, his arms pressed against her as gently as he had ever held anyone, or anything.

"I—" He tried to speak, but couldn't.

"We should eat," she said finally, easing away.

———

How that moment occurred, or why it occurred, was inexplicable to Zeus. It was not lust, or at least not solely lust. If he were to analyze it, the only words he could have used would have come from the language of religion. It was a feeling he had never had before, through countless encounters and relationships, with past loves and flings. If it was not perfection, then he had no possibility of ever understanding the term.

———

They ate mostly in silence. Zeus used chopsticks, fumbling a bit though he was used to them. The *pho* was excellent, spicy and exotic. Anna had only water for them to drink, but it was just as well; alcohol would have gone to his head. He luxuriated in every sensation.

"So you studied in Australia," he said when he'd finished eating.

"I went to school there. Yes. And my residency. First year."

"It must have been difficult, leaving your home."

She smiled faintly. "I went to study. It was good to have few distractions."

Anna reached her right hand to the side of her face, where a few hairs had fallen. She swept them back into place. Zeus had never seen such a graceful gesture.

"I always knew I wanted to be a doctor," she said. "To help other people."

"And you are."

"Yes. Though I was trained to work with children."

"You don't do that now? Because of the war?"

It had nothing to do with the war. Anna explained that the state, which had paid for her education, had initially assigned her to work with older people. Grandmothers, she said.

Two months before, she had been called to Hanoi to help open a clinic for older people. She dealt largely with women, since the men tended to be shy of a lady doctor. The first night of the war, the clinic had been destroyed, apparently by an errant bomb.

"No injuries. We were lucky. But there has been much work since then."

"So you were assigned to the hospital where I was."

"Yes. It is more a special clinic than a hospital. As you can imagine, we are stretched thin."

Anna's voice trailed off. She got up and began clearing the table.

"And you . . . Why did you come to Vietnam?" she asked, taking her plate to the sink.

Zeus rose to help. "I was assigned. It's not really much of a story. I, uh . . ." He stumbled, not sure exactly how much he should say. "I'm like an adviser. I know a little bit about Chinese tactics."

"They are very evil."

"They're not nice," said Zeus. He didn't see them as particularly evil; they were simply trying to win the war.

"They don't care who they kill."

Part of Zeus wanted to tell the truth: killing was what war was, ugly and ruthless. The Chinese were not purposely targeting civilians, but no matter their intentions, innocent people would die.

The greater part of him didn't want to talk about it at all.

"What part of Vietnam does your family come from?" he asked.

"Yen Bai Province. Many of my relatives are still there. We lived in Hanoi when I was small. My father is with the government."

Yen Bai was in the west, part of the area the Chinese had already overrun. It wouldn't be pleasant for anyone there.

"Now my father is in the south," Anna continued. "Ho Chi Minh City. Saigon to Americans. To everyone. It is an ancient name."

She began running the water to clean the dishes. Then suddenly she stopped.

"We should conserve water," she said, turning off the tap. "I forgot."

Zeus reached to touch her.

She started to object.

"I don't think—"

"It's okay," said Zeus.

He put his hand on her arm, gently running it down past her elbow to her forearm, to her finger. She closed her eyes.

His satellite phone began to buzz. Zeus ignored it for another moment, his fingers lingering on hers.

"Your phone," she said.

"Yes," he said finally, pulling his hand away reluctantly.

————

"*Where are you?*" demanded Christian as soon as the line connected.

"Why?" said Zeus.

"Trung needs us right away. The Chinese have launched their attack."

"I don't know—"

"Jesus, Zeus."

Zeus glanced at Anna. Her eyes were wide, searching him.

"Zeus! I have a driver. We'll pick you up."

"Do you know the hospital where they took me?" Zeus said finally. "Meet me there in an hour."

"An hour! No—right now."

"Ten minutes, then," said Zeus. "I need ten minutes to get there."

17

The Gulf of Tonkin

Commander Silas put the night glasses to his eyes. The ocean was already heavy, even with the storm front some hours away. The waves had white crusts; the bow of the *McLane* crashed hard against them.

The Chinese cruiser *Wen Jiabao* loomed on his starboard side, pushing through the waves in a blatant attempt to cut the *McLane* off. She had her lights blazing, spotlights playing across the American destroyer.

Silas was strongly tempted to shoot them out.

"Steady as she goes," Silas told the helm. "We've played this game before."

"Aye, Captain."

Bearing long, classic lines, the *Wen* extended some six hundred and ten feet, a good hundred longer than the *McLane*. When she'd sailed in the Russian navy, her decks were littered with unsightly ash-can tubes for missiles. The Chinese had replaced those with modern four-pack YJ-83s. The deck was still crowded, but the newer, more potent missiles added an ominous beauty.

She was a pretty ship, Silas thought. The *Wen* displaced in excess of 11,500 tons—again, a good deal more than the *McLane* or her sister Arleigh Burkes. The additional bulk did not slow her down; on the contrary, she was capable of mustering a knot or two more than the American destroyer, at least on paper.

At the moment, she had an angle on the *McLane*. One of the ships was going to have to turn off soon, or there would be a collision.

These weren't a pair of canoes. Even a glancing blow would do considerable damage to both vessels.

"So, tell me, Captain," Silas muttered to himself, as if speaking to the master of the Chinese vessel. "What will happen to you if your beautiful ship comes back to port with a big gash in her bow? Do they still hang captains in the Chinese navy?"

The only answer was a howl in the wind. Silas could see across to the ship's lighted bridge, though he couldn't quite make out the captain.

He couldn't afford a collision, either. Not only was the *McLane* likely to sustain more damage, but any damage would undoubtedly mean that he wouldn't reach the merchant ships before they got into Hai Phong, if that's where they were going.

The *Wen* closed in.

"Hard right rudder," said Silas suddenly.

"Starboard, Captain?"

"Aye, into the bastard," he told helm. "Don't worry. We're cutting inside him."

The destroyer began to pivot. As she turned in the choppy water, Silas gave another order to cut their power. The heavy waves quickly tugged at their momentum. The big Chinese ship continued past. The

McLane's bow came within a few yards of clipping the cruiser's stern. If the Chinese had been towing an array, it would be Silas's now.

Advantage mine, Captain, Silas thought. *Your move.*

The *McLane* turned smartly, straightening her course back to its original mark. The *Wen*, meanwhile, slowed. Silas watched for another few minutes—she drew to a parallel course aft, unnerved perhaps by the close call.

"Helm, if you need relief, holler," said Silas.

"I can do this all day and all night," said the man at the wheel.

"You may have to."

18

Hanoi

Zeus walked from Anna's apartment in a hollow, silent fugue, everything outside him numb and his own mind blank. He was not so much smitten as consumed, absorbed in what he felt for her.

Under ordinary circumstances, such a sensation would have shocked, if not repelled him. Zeus had always compartmentalized his life, carefully separating his feelings into easily handled boxes, partitioning love affairs far from his everyday life.

And certainly from work.

But this was not an ordinary time.

He found the street. He was about halfway to the hospital when a yellow light swept up across the pavement behind him. He turned and saw a large, black Hyundai sedan approaching, using only its running lights to illuminate the roadway. Christian opened the rear window.

"Hey, lover boy—sorry to interrupt your date."

Anger snapped Zeus out of his fog. He jerked open the door and grabbed Christian by the neck of his open-collar shirt. He pulled him from the car, holding him close to his face.

"I'll break every fucking bone in your body," growled Zeus.

"Major!"

It was Perry: he was in the back, on the other side.

Zeus released Christian, who tumbled down out of the car and onto the sidewalk. Zeus ignored him. He pulled open the front door and got in. He could feel the heat rising to his head. He knew his face would be beet-red.

They drove in silence to the bunker.

———

The Chinese advance had begun an hour and a half after midnight, along exactly the lines the Americans had predicted.

Which was not surprising. The night attack was a page directly out of the American Army playbook, doctrine the Chinese had thoroughly dissected and learned following the famous Shock and Awe campaign during the Second Gulf War. The advances during that war, using a force much smaller than the enemy's but highly leveraged by technology, had shocked the Chinese. Until that point, Chinese military doctrine had been based on the idea of numbers: vast numbers of soldiers, using relatively simple but dependable weapons, could defeat any enemy. It was an idea not all that much different from Soviet doctrine during World War II, or Chinese doctrine during the Korean War. In both contests, the superior technology (and, at least arguably, superior soldiers and leadership) of the enemy had been overcome by the sheer size of the victorious army. While there were contradictions—the American counteroffensive in Korea, for example—by and large the philosophy behind the doctrine had seemed stable throughout the postwar period.

But the ease of the American advance during the Second Gulf War showed that the time had passed for that strategy. An overwhelming attack leveraging technology could produce such destruction in the opening phase of a campaign that numbers became meaningless.

So the Chinese went to school. The most obvious lesson they had learned was that their technology had to be improved. They didn't necessarily have to exceed the U.S., but they had to close the gap to an acceptable level, at least close enough so that numbers could once more make the difference.

There were many other lessons. One was that certain "environments" enhanced the power of technology. That was what fighting at night was all about. Nighttime gave a technologically superior army a clear advantage over a poorer one, since it had sensors (and extensive

training) that turned the night into day. The Chinese had installed infrared sensors in their tanks, and had trained to attack in darkness.

In that context, waiting an extra twenty-four hours to launch the
tank attack made sense. Though they had lost strategic surprise, the
Chinese still hoped to press their technological advantage. Choosing
the exact timing of the attack preserved, to some slight degree, a narrow tactical advantage. And since the attack on the fuel depot would
have taken several hours to compensate for under the best of circumstances, waiting a full twenty-four hours to attack would make sense.

And yet, the slavishness of the original plan—or what Zeus inter-
preted as the original plan—spoke volumes as well. If you had such little regard for the Vietnamese, why not simply launch the attack as soon
you were ready? What was it that the darkness gave you, really?

"The beauty of waiting twenty-four hours is, you don't change anything, just the calendar," said Zeus when Perry remarked that the timing
seemed to coincide with what had been planned the night before. "D + 1
is now D. All the times, etc., are the same."

The mood inside the command complex was glum. Perry left them,
presumably to talk personally to Trung. Zeus sat next to Christian, but
made sure to keep his eyes fixed in the other direction.

Perry and Trung weren't there for the start of the staff briefing. A
Vietnamese colonel gave a situation report with only a large map for a
reference. In Zeus's experience, intelligence briefings of outsiders fell
into one of two categories:

1. The superoptimistic kind, like the one telling Custer there were a
   few Indians ahead, and
2. The seriously pessimistic kind, where Sitting Bull's ancestors'
   failure to make the proper prayer to a minor god several eons ago
   would hang heavy over the battlefield.

This briefing was a fine example of category one. The forces under
General Tri, said the briefer, were resisting fiercely. No inch was being given freely. The Chinese were stalling all along the roads they had
taken.

That was the strategy? Fight for every inch? They were just making
it easier to be annihilated.

Zeus walked over to the side of the room as the officer continued.

There was a large steel pot of tea there. He would have greatly preferred coffee, but at this point any caffeine would do.

"Do you agree with this interpretation?" asked the interpreter.

Zeus looked over and realized that everyone was looking at him. "I'm sorry?"

"The assessment," said the interpreter.

"The Chinese are attacking as we predicted," said Zeus. "They'll be at Tien Yen by morning."

"We will stop them beforehand," answered the briefing officer, using English and not bothering to wait for the interpreter. "The attack will wither and die."

There was no sense arguing with the man. He seemed genuinely to believe what he was saying.

Christian asked a few questions, trying to get some information about the Chinese infantry units that were accompanying the armor. The Vietnamese couldn't give detailed answers, another bad sign.

Zeus blew on his tea to cool it. He thought of Anna, then pushed the image away.

Briefing over, the Vietnamese officers left.

"You still mad?" said Christian when the room was empty.

Zeus just stared at him.

"Look, I was out of line," said Christian. "I apologize."

God, he really *has* changed, thought Zeus.

"It's all right," he told him.

Christian got up and went to get himself some tea.

"Thanks for getting us out of China," he said.

"Yeah."

Christian grimaced. "That . . . I screwed up. I lost my head. I was tired; I felt like I was possessed or something. I'm sorry . . . I just about got us killed."

"Yeah."

"I'm glad we got through it. Thanks."

Zeus nodded.

"This tea sucks," said Christian. "We should find some coffee."

"I'm for that."

They sat silently until General Perry came in a few minutes later.

"Lost in thought, gentlemen?" said the general.

"Trying to figure out where we can get some coffee," said Christian.

"Well at least you're not fighting," said Perry with a sour face. "We're making progress."

"Sir, that was my fault," said Christian. "I was an idiot."

"It wasn't anything," said Zeus softly. "I was a jerk, too."

"Vietnam may be lost, but there's hope for the U.S. Army," said Perry. His tone remained stern, sour even. "Zeus, General Trung would like to speak to you. I think he wants to apologize for yesterday."

"He doesn't have to apologize."

"He knows that. Be gracious."

"Yes, sir."

"What's our next move, General?" asked Christian.

"Watch and wait," said Perry. "If they want our advice, they'll ask."

"How about the A-10As?" asked Zeus.

"Even if they were coming, which they're not, it may be too late," said Perry.

———

General Trung met Zeus in a small office on the lowest level of the complex. It was bare, even by Vietnamese standards. There was nothing on the cement walls, and the only furniture was a solitary wooden chair. Trung stood behind it as Zeus entered. His eyes had deep rings below them, circular welts that seemed to penetrate far into his face.

"General Tri was in error," Trung told Zeus. "I deeply apologize." He bent forward.

"General, there's no need to apologize," said Zeus. "I wasn't offended. I understand the stress very well."

Trung straightened.

"We're guests here," continued Zeus. "Some people may not want our help. It's not a problem."

"Thank you, Major, for your understanding."

"General, I have a question," said Zeus. "Do you believe the Chinese are aiming at Hai Phong?"

"It would seem a logical conclusion."

"Why did you put your forces in Son Duong then?"

"Do you have a better suggestion?" asked the general.

"I certainly don't know the tactical situation of your forces and bases as you do," said Zeus. "I was just curious. You have a large force there, and it's going to waste."

A faint smile appeared on Trung's lips, but it slipped away quickly.

"Curiosity in a commander is always a good thing," said Trung. "I wonder, Major, would you like to tour the battlefield? By plane, I mean."

"I'd like to, yes."

"I would be grateful for additional insights. Captain Thieu will be your pilot."

Thieu had taken Zeus west to scout the Chinese advance in a jet trainer a few days before. He was an excellent pilot. His plane, though, was a little shaky.

"I'd be happy to fly with him," said Zeus.

"It will be arranged for first light," said Trung.

19

Hanoi

Harland Perry was too young to have fought in Vietnam; his introduction to combat came as a very green lieutenant in the Kuwait War conducted by the first President Bush. But the Army that he joined had been molded by men who had been through Vietnam and the dreadful years immediately afterward. Many of their lessons stayed with him, including one about how easy it was to get sucked into a conflict you had no intention of fighting.

Like this one.

Perry's original mission of fact-finding made enormous sense; by offering advice to the Vietnamese, he had in turn been granted an inside look at the country's military situation. What he had seen firsthand pretty much jibed with the intelligence reports he'd read and viewed before coming: Vietnam had an earnest and courageous force that was thoroughly outnumbered and ill-prepared to fight in the twenty-first century.

If there was a surprise, it had come from the Chinese. Their equipment was better in many respects than had been predicted, but their leadership was much worse. The generals running the war had been more timid than Perry expected, shutting down drives when dealt the slightest setback.

On the one hand, this was a valuable psychological insight: it told Perry that the Chinese army had quite a distance to go before it would truly achieve its potential. On the other hand, it was the sort of flaw that might be reversed quickly, if the right general were found to lead the charge and then clean house. But whether a Chinese Ulysses S. Grant emerged or not, the advantages the Chinese held over the Vietnamese were so extensive that even a McClellan would win this war in a matter of weeks.

Which brought Perry to the question of what the U.S. should do.

The United States could defeat China in a head-to-head battle. No war was easy; Perry knew from his experiences in Iraq and Afghanistan that even a lopsided battle brought heartache and pain to the victor. But defeating China in Southeast Asia was possible. The key was acting quickly and decisively, with massive amounts of force.

A-10As and Apaches were only the tip of the spear as Perry saw it. He needed a lot more force. And he'd asked for it.

The idea wasn't simply to stop the Chinese and get them out of Vietnam. They had to be soundly defeated—a strong punch in the nose that sent them to the mat. Such a strike would convince their army that the Americans weren't to be messed with. Better, it would undermine China's premier. And that was the key to a peaceful future: ousting Cho Lai from power.

The Chinese had seen decades of wise leaders. While they certainly hadn't always acted in America's best interests, they had recognized the importance of peace to their, and the world's, prosperity. Cho Lai was a different character entirely, a throwback to times when brutality ruled. That approach would eventually be disastrous for everyone; the sooner he was removed, the better.

So, massive involvement by the U.S. now made a lot of sense . . . but what if that wasn't possible? What if the best the U.S. could do were wing-and-a-prayer operations along the lines that Major Murphy had undertaken against Hainan?

By conventional measures, the operation there had been a success— the Chinese had completely overreacted, apparently scrapping all plans for a seaborne assault, at least in the near term. But that had had minimal impact on the longer term. The war continued and would continue, as the new assault proved.

While certainly valuable from the Vietnamese perspective, such small tactical victories would not change the overall outcome of the war if the U.S. stayed out of it.

They were poisoned victories from the American perspective. For one thing, the longer the war went on, the more likely a Chinese Grant would emerge. The longer the Chinese army fought, the more experience their "middle managers"—the NCOs and junior officers—would gain for the future.

If the U.S. was eventually going to have to fight China, and couldn't (or wouldn't) do it now, then it was definitely in America's best interest to have the PLA as inexperienced and even overconfident as possible. In that sense, small setbacks aided them immensely.

Perry also feared that any revelation that the U.S. was involved would provoke a severe reaction among the American public. Everyone he spoke to at the Pentagon made it clear that public sentiment was against intervention. Throw in a congressional investigation and a bunch of headlines about dead Americans in Vietnam, and they might turn against the Army itself.

The longer the war in Vietnam continued, the more tempting it would be for the president—*any* president—to continue adding troops and support on a piecemeal basis. Perry could frame the argument himself: Look at what Zeus Murphy had accomplished with a handful of men, most supplied by Vietnam. What might an entire SEAL team and an attachment of Rangers, a few Delta boys, and some clandestinely inserted CIA paramilitaries accomplish?

And once they were there, the logic for more would be inescapable.

Incrementalism killed you: put a full force in at the very beginning, and you could win. Play into battle piecemeal and watch yourself get ground down. That was a basic lesson of just above every battle in history.

Harland Perry stood at a crossroads. The President—who happened to be a personal friend—had sent him here for advice.

He had made a suggestion for extreme force, and been rejected. Not yet in so many words, but the delays showed Greene lacked enough public support to commit troops.

So now Harland Perry had to make another recommendation. His advice would be to withdraw completely and quickly—to simply stand aside.

It was almost certainly not what the President wanted to hear. And while it was extremely logical, it went against Perry's own wishes and emotions—his instinct was to fight, and much better sooner rather than later.

But emotions didn't win battles; logic did. And it was his duty and responsibility as an officer to present the President, most especially this President, with the best recommendation he could make.

20

Hanoi

It had been about a week since Zeus had seen Captain Thieu and his Aereo L-39C, a small jet trainer used by the Vietnamese for a variety of tasks. In the interim, Thieu had flown several sorties a day, and the plane bore the scars. The little warbird had been hit by nearly a hundred rounds of ground fire, including a few from Vietnamese guns. Fortunately, the bullets had been both small and unlucky, missing the Aereo's vitals. The majority of holes had been patched, though there seemed to be a few perforations in its rear belly from the most recent mission—a quick hop north to check on the Chinese formations a few hours earlier.

If the rings under his eyes were any indication, Thieu had had less sleep in the past twenty-four hours than Zeus. Yet he seemed energetic as he walked Zeus around the aircraft prior to their takeoff. A quartet of small bombs had been fastened to the wings; they supplemented the 23 mm twin-cannon mounted beneath the fuselage. Aircraft were so precious that even his recce mission would be combined with an attack sortie.

"Think those holes will be a problem?" Zeus asked, pointing to a few fresh notches in the belly.

Thieu laughed. "Ha-ha, Major Zeus, always making jokes."

"Those are holes," said Zeus.

"No worry. Board now."

The Albatros was a two-seater, and Zeus sat in the rear. He had a flight stick and throttle, and Thieu insisted on giving him a quick orientation on how to use the controls if something happened.

"This way, if I am shot, you will land," said Thieu over the plane's interphone circuit. "Plane is very valuable."

"What makes you think they'd get you and not me?" said Zeus.

"Ha! You are very lucky man, Major Zeus. The captain is very lucky to be flying with you today."

"Oh yeah. I'm just oozing luck."

The oxygen pumped into his mask gave Zeus a jolt of energy. Having flown with Thieu before, he had skipped breakfast—a decision vindicated by the roller-coaster takeoff that buried his stomach somewhere behind the tailplane.

"See—we miss all potholes!" said Thieu triumphantly as they climbed out.

The sun wouldn't rise for another half hour. The dim sky and darker ground made it hard for Zeus to orient himself. The course Thieu laid out was due east to the sea, then north along Route 18 in the direction of Tien Yen.

Zeus strained to see out the sides of the cockpit, looking for lights or other signs of life. But there was nothing, just shades of gray.

"Do you prepare for bombing?" Thieu asked.

"I'm sorry?"

"We will drop our bombs first, then make our observations," said the pilot.

"Are we that close to the lines already?" Zeus glanced at the compass for the heading. They were still going east.

"We turn and be prepared," answered Thieu. "Ready?"

"Anytime."

The plane took a slow bank. They were traveling just under seven hundred kilometers an hour by the plane's gauges—in the area of 375 knots, or nautical miles an hour. That put them a little more than five minutes from the front line, by Zeus's calculation.

Something red sparked in the distance. Zeus stared at it, unsure what it could be. It looked like a splash of paint on a photograph, something that didn't belong.

More red appeared, a line of splashes.

Tracers!

They were a lot closer to the front than he'd thought. The Chinese were at Tien Yen already.

"Gunfire ahead," said Thieu.

"Ours or theirs?"

"No matter."

Zeus heard Thieu speaking to someone over the radio. The aircraft took a sharp bank to the left, then swung its nose back northward. The altimeter indicated they were at five thousand feet above ground level—well within the reach of whatever was firing ahead.

Probably Vietnamese antiair, thought Zeus. But what were they shooting at? Not them.

Zeus saw the answer in a string of black dots behind the flashes.

Chinese helicopters. Two of the dots were flying to the right, the others were slightly behind in echelon.

The dots at the right glowed red. They were firing rockets or something at the ground.

The antiaircraft fire intensified. Yellow-red streams leapt from the ground, bullets hosing the air. One stream turned black; another died. The ground flashed. A fire erupted.

"Hold on, Major," said Thieu. "Our fun begins."

The jet suddenly twisted on its wing, pushing down to Zeus's left. The nose angled down, gently at first, but then in a flick of the pilot's wrist almost ninety degrees. The plane became a dagger aimed at the earth. Zeus felt his stomach push toward his spine.

The left wing lifted; the nose swung hard to Zeus's right. He strained to see, raising his head over the side of the cockpit, but gravity pushed him back down into his seat. The plane shot upward—straight up it seemed, though by this time Zeus was so dizzy he had no real idea of the direction they were going. His head slammed back against the rest. The engines surged behind him.

"I think we got him!" yelled Thieu. He could have been at a baseball game, cheering a grand slam.

"What?"

"The tank," said Thieu. "You see it?"

Zeus struggled to look out the canopy. The ground was dark. If there was smoke or fire from the explosion it was lost in a blur of shadows as they zoomed away.

"I don't know," said Zeus.

"Look on next run. Will be to your left."

"You didn't drop all the bombs?" Zeus asked, but his words were swallowed by the engines as the pilot coaxed more power for another plunge toward the battlefield.

Everything outside the canopy blurred. The Albatros was not a particularly fast aircraft as jet fighters went, yet it seemed to be flying at the speed of thought.

Fingers of red fire appeared at the side, uncurling from black fists. Angry hands grabbed at the plane. The jet bucked ferociously as the pilot neared his target.

Crap, thought Zeus. *Let's get this over with.*

He glanced at the handle he was supposed to pull if they needed to bail out. They were so low here . . . Would he even survive to be captured?

Hoo-rah.

They pulled up sharply, the aircraft gaining several hundred feet as the bombs were dropped. Zeus strained to keep his head where he could see outside the cockpit. There were black boxes on the ground— armored personnel carriers, he guessed, not tanks.

Or maybe they were tanks, or armored cars, or infantry fighting vehicles, or just trucks—it was too dark and they flitted by so quickly, who could tell?

Something hit the right wing. Zeus heard a screeching sound, something like metal being torn in two. The plane bucked for a moment, then righted itself. He pushed himself up against the restraints, craning his neck to see the wing, but he couldn't quite see anything.

"Close one, Major," said the pilot.

"Were we hit?" asked Zeus.

"Two bullets, maybe. Nothing. It would take many to harm us."

Zeus doubted that. Just one bullet in the right place would surely be enough.

"Now we ready look on your mission," said Thieu. His English got shakier as he became more excited, and he was clearly in the middle of an adrenaline rush at the moment. "We go to north."

"More to the northwest, right?"

"Oh ho, Major, you are remember your compass."

Thieu sounded absolutely high, as if he were stoned on cocaine. It was just adrenaline—and the excitement of survival. Some men pressed down under the continuing strain. For others, the stress became a drug, something you almost lived for.

Had Zeus been craving that high when he decided to take on the tanks at the border?

"Are you still with me, Major?" asked Thieu.

"I'm here."

"Do you see the river on the right? That is Ky Cung."

Zeus looked out the side of the cockpit. The sun was just below the horizon, and the ground still blurred into different shades of gray. But as his eyes adjusted and his mind focused, the dark blotches turned into colors, the shapes into objects that he had some hope of recognizing. He saw hills first, then a road they were passing, and finally the river, a surprisingly straight slit of black almost parallel to the aircraft's path.

The Chinese border lay a few miles beyond the river. Zeus stared from the aircraft, straining to see activity.

"I am going to fly up Highway three-one," said the pilot. "We will see what we can see."

Zeus held his breath as the plane turned almost ninety degrees in a matter of seconds. Thieu dropped lower, edging the plane down toward the mountain that the highway ran through. This wasn't so Zeus could get a better look—the lower the plane was, the harder it would be for any Chinese patrols or radars to spot.

The road tucked left and right, disappearing under the canopy. Zeus examined the terrain, trying to get a feel for how it would be to run a division through it. This was the real reason he'd come—it was one thing to stare at satellite photos and Global Hawk images, and quite another to see the land in person, even from three or four thousand feet.

What puzzled him was the fact that the Chinese had not come through here. But now it was clear. If you attacked on this route, you would be limited to the main road. The road net was limited and the sharp terrain made it exceedingly difficult to find an alternate route. Unlike the area farther east, there were no interconnected farm fields that could be used as temporary passages.

"Border is near," said Thieu. "We may have shots."

The pilot laughed. The aircraft had been steadily slowing; they were now doing only a bit more than a hundred knots, closing in on the plane's stall speed—the speed at which it stopped staying in the air. But the low altitude made it appear as if they were going much faster.

There were houses ahead, on both sides of the road. The war seemed not to have reached here; smoke curled in thin lines, breakfast fires only.

Jungle.

Thieu raised his nose slightly. Zeus saw a line ahead—a fence, he thought, but it turned out to be a power line, or maybe telephone wires.

More houses, buildings. There was a barrier in the road.

"Guns on the right," said Thieu.

Zeus raised his head, staring. He spotted what looked like tanks on a hilltop. They were ZSU-57-2s, ancient Russian-made antiaircraft guns. They didn't fire. The Albatros continued northward, deeper into China. Its straight-line path took it away from the road, which curved left.

The ground was thick jungle, a deep green that undulated with the hills. Just as they started to bank westward, the color changed from green to a dark brown. The trees were dead, killed by a three-year drought—the rainfall pattern changed dramatically on the other side of the hills.

A good place to stage armor for an attack, Zeus thought. But he couldn't see any.

"Uh-oh," said Thieu.

"Problem?"

One of the warning systems began to bleat.

"They are finding us on their radar. No worry," said Thieu.

Zeus's stomach jumped very close to his mouth as the pilot put the plane into a sharp dive and turn. The sensor stopped beeping.

"We have to turn south," said Thieu, reluctance creeping into his voice. "Pingxiang is ahead."

Pingxiang was the largest Chinese city in the area, and it was ringed by sophisticated air defenses.

"Have you seen what you want?" added Thieu.

"I guess." Zeus hadn't seen much.

Thieu kept the Albatros pitched about thirty degrees after they came out of the turn. The Vietnamese city Lang Son was ahead, on their right as they approached the border. The entire area around the city was well developed—until the war, the area had been popular with Chinese men looking for a very quick vacation from their wives. It was like a Vietnamese version of Las Vegas: what happened there, stayed there. A good portion of the businesses there were owned by Chinese businessmen—obviously the reason it hadn't been attacked.

"Fly over 1A, will you?" asked Zeus, naming the major road south.

They angled eastward. There were patrols and emplacements all along the highway. They flew over the road at about six hundred feet, following the highway for about ten minutes until black puffs appeared in front of them. Thieu laid on the fuel, deepening the angle right as he took a very sharp turn and began to climb.

"They think we're Chinese," he said.

"Can we go back east?" said Zeus. Now that it was light, he wanted to see where the armored brigade General Tri commanded was.

"I will have to go north," said Thieu. "It will take a few minutes."

"North? Why?"

Thieu didn't answer.

"Thieu?"

"Restricted. We cannot fly the area."

Zeus reached to the pocket on the leg of his flight suit and took out the map, folding it open on his lap. What were they avoiding?

They'd flown south of the Yen Tu Mountains on the way out, and were now flying north of them. Was that the Luc Nam River below?

Zeus studied the map, trying to triangulate their position by what they had passed.

Why would the mountains be restricted? It wasn't part of the defense zone around Hanoi.

"We are ten minutes from Tien Yen," said Thieu.

"I wanted to be farther north, along Route 4B," said Zeus, turning his attention back to the armored brigade.

"Ah."

Thieu immediately began a turn. Within a minute or two, Zeus spotted a highway clogged with traffic—it was the armor brigade and part of the infantry division, rushing toward the battle at Tien Yen.

They turned and followed the highway back in the direction of Lang Son. There were two columns of vehicles along the road, then nothing.

Now would be the time to attack Lang Son. Blow through the crust of the defenses, then sweep down the roads parallel to 1B.

Except the Chinese saw no reason to destroy a city they in effect already owned.

Of course, that also meant that they were not on their guard here. They thought so little of the Vietnamese.

Not without reason, Zeus reminded himself.

"Our fuel becomes low," warned Thieu.

"I've seen enough," said Zeus. "We can go back whenever you want."

"Very good, Major."

Thieu bent the nose of the plane upward. Zeus felt his blood rushing from his head. How did pilots learn to live with this?

As they leveled off, an alarm began to blare. The plane jerked hard left, then pointed toward the ground.

"Major, we are being tracked by Chinese fighter," snapped Thieu. "Watch out!"

Before Zeus could reply, the warning tone went two octaves higher.

"Launch warning!" intoned an English voice.

The Chinese fighter had fired a pair of missiles at them.

21

Beijing

"We can crush the American destroyer," offered Lo Gong, the defense minister. "If that is what you wish."

Cho Lai put his hands together on the desk. Yet another move by the American President to thwart him.

This one he should have anticipated. But it was ingenious—the American ship would claim it was inspecting cargo. It was a matter of enforcing neutrality—a position China itself had encouraged. The fact that the ships were registered in the Philippines—what could the Chinese possibly object to?

Simple, yet ingenious. And of course, as soon as the Americans went aboard the ships, they would see they were filled with Chinese soldiers.

And so what? Besides a public relations coup, what would the Americans win, exactly?

Public support to interfere. That was Greene's real aim.

If they stopped the ships, that would be disastrous. That would ruin the plan to take Hai Phong.

Sink the destroyer and be done with it. That was Cho Lai's true wish. But it would invite open conflict with America. A shooting war. And if his generals and admirals were timid now, what would they do against the Americans?

It would be a fiasco.

Time. He needed time. Eventually, the Vietnamese would collapse. And eventually, his generals would gain the confidence they needed.

"The destroyer seems very far from the ships," said Cho Lai.

"On the present course and speed, the ships will beat the destroyer to Hai Phong," said the defense minister. "But that assumes the drive in the east will proceed on schedule."

"You told me it is ahead of schedule," said Cho Lai.

"It is."

"Well, then, there is no problem," said the premier, somewhat more relaxed. "The ships will beat the destroyer to the port, and that will be the end of it."

"And if something delays them or the operation?"

Cho Lai ground his back teeth together. Now he was the one being forced to act as a coward. But he must take the long view. He *must* take the long view.

"Make sure that it doesn't," he said darkly. "Take Hai Phong. And make sure those ships return with rice."

Lo Gong bowed his head.

22

In the air over northern Vietnam

Zeus lurched against his restraints as Thieu threw the Albatros toward the earth, trying desperately to lose the missiles on their tail. Buzzers and bleeps and voices warned of their impending doom. Zeus felt as if his stomach and lungs were being torn into several pieces inside his body. Gravity crunched against his chest, and his face mask felt as if it were edged with a steel knife, cutting deeply into his face.

The Albatros jerked right, heading straight for a huge rock outcropping. Then it spurt back left. Something popped behind Zeus. He thought they'd been hit. But as the plane hurtled ahead, he realized Thieu had launched decoys—"tinsel," or chaff, the pilots called it, pieces of metal shards that confused radar.

The Albatros shot straight up, then turned upside down. Zeus caught a red flash in the corner of his eye—one of the missiles that had been chasing them, blowing up harmlessly a mile or more away, suckered by the decoy.

The other missile mysteriously vanished, just gave up as its radar lost contact. The cockpit went silent.

But not for long.

"Bandit, ten o'clock!" said Thieu. "Hang on, Major!"

If air combat had ever held any fascination for Zeus, it was lost in the sharp plunge the Albatros took as it knifed away from its attacker. Zeus saw a yellowish triangle moving through the valley at his left. It was the Chinese aircraft—a Jian-10B multirole aircraft, a plane Zeus knew only from the dry specs in the Red Dragon war game simulator he had used back in the States. The aircraft bore a striking resemblance to the Israeli Lavi, not exactly a coincidence or accident, as the Israelis had helped the Chinese develop the plane.

Having already fired its radar-guided missiles, the Chinese plane had to maneuver into position to use its heat-seeking missiles. In practical terms, this meant it had to get behind the Albatros, something that Thieu aimed to prevent, jinking back and forth sharply and staying low to the ground.

"Look for his wing mate!" said Thieu over the plane's interphone. "He should have a wing mate. He is not on my radar."

Zeus searched the sky for a second airplane. He couldn't see any aircraft, not even the one that had attacked them.

The Albatros pushed hard to the right, seemingly bending itself in half. Zeus saw fire on his left as they bounced back around

Decoy flares, launched by Thieu.

There was a low rumble. The plane bucked up and down. The engine seemed to stutter behind him, as if choking. They slid down on their left wing. Then Zeus felt a shake from the center line of the aircraft—the cannon strapped to the forward underside began firing.

More flares filled the air, this time directly from the Chinese plane, its pilot apparently fearing the Albatros had a missile similar to its own.

And then it was gone.

The whine of the Albatros's engine dropped a dozen decibels. The plane slowed and banked eastward. Zeus thought for a moment that they had been hit again, or had run out of fuel. But Thieu was only recognizing that the fight was over. The Chinese pilot had laid on his afterburner and was rocketing away. The Albatros lacked the speed to catch up, and was low on fuel besides.

"We gave him a good fight!" yelled Thieu.

"Oh yeah."

"What do you think of that, Major? We have chased off a bigger plane. Do you think we damaged him?"

"I'm sure of it," said Zeus.

23

Suburban Virginia

As an institution, the CIA had almost unlimited resources for finding someone.

As an individual, a CIA officer was surprisingly limited. He—or in this case, she—couldn't simply type in a name into a computer bank and receive reams of information on the person, even if the information was stored in the agency's computers. There were protocols and safeguards and procedures that had to be followed.

Assuming they were followed.

Within a few minutes of deciding that she really, *really* did want to find out, Mara knew exactly where Josh was headed. The problem was deciding what to do about it.

What she wanted to do was hop on a plane and fly out to the cousin's farm. She could get there before he did; he was driving, which meant it would take probably another half day if not a full day.

But doing that would be messy. Doing that meant she had to tell him that she was in love with him.

And if she told him, then what happened? Obviously he wasn't in love with her, because he wouldn't have left the way he did.

He had kissed her. But it was just a kiss, a good-to-be-alive kiss, nothing more.

A nothing kiss, in the end.

She'd go there, and be rejected; he'd look down at the ground and stammer. What the hell was the sense of that?

How the hell could she have let herself fall in love with him? She was such a goddamn *girl*.

Be a woman, Mara.

Oh, but the woman in her wanted him as well. The woman in her— the woman who knew that she was no great beauty, but that she was, and could be, a good companion, a good lover, someone who would hold a man and make him whole—the woman pined for him as well.

In the end, she decided to call the marshal.

"Terrence, this is Mara Duncan," she said when he answered the phone. "Where the hell are you guys?"

"Ms. Duncan." The marshal's Texas accent blossomed. "We're in a car. He wanted to go back to his family place. I'm watchin' him. You don't have to worry."

"I understand that. Let me talk to Josh."

"He's kinda sleeping right now. In the backseat."

"Terrence, are you lying to me?"

"No," he said. There was enough surprise in his voice for her to believe him.

"I'm supposed to be watching him," she said. It was lame, but it was all she could manage.

"I have it covered. He hated that hearing," added the marshal. "That guy Jablonski keeps calling. Josh doesn't want to talk to him."

"Tell him he didn't do as badly as he thinks." Mara wanted to keep talking; maybe Josh would wake up and take the phone. "He gets . . . Josh gets too down on himself. You have to tell him that things are going okay. Not great, but okay. He just loses perspective. We've been through a lot."

"Hey, you want me to wake him up or something?"

She did. She definitely did.

"No," said Mara. "It's all right. You take care of him. Have him call me. I'm . . . I have some things I have to do. But you have him call me. You have my number, right?"

"It's right here on the phone."

"Okay. Have him call me."

"Got it."

She hung up, wishing she hadn't repeated her plea to have him call.

24

Hanoi

After they landed on the patched tarmac of Hanoi Airport, Zeus and Thieu examined the fighter. A good portion of the tail had been eaten away by ground fire and the exploding head of one of the missiles that had just missed them.

Thieu gestured at the damaged aircraft with a laugh, and shouted something at Zeus. A jet landing nearby made it impossible to hear, but Zeus guessed that it was some sort of boast along the lines of, *Is that the best they can do?*

"Do you think we shot the other plane down?" he added, his voice a little stronger as the other plane's roar subsided.

Zeus had seen it fly off and knew they hadn't come close to hitting it, let alone shooting it down. Yet somehow it didn't feel right to let him down.

"It's a very good chance," Zeus told him.

Thieu patted him on the back.

————

An hour later, Zeus waited outside an office at the U.S. embassy to talk to General Perry. He was beyond exhausted. The injuries he'd received in his foray behind the lines, though minor, screamed at him. Even the spots on his chest where the restraints had pressed against him during the flight hurt.

He thought of Anna. She'd be on shift now. He wanted to take her in his arms and fall into her bed, sink past the war, sink past everything for a week, a month, forever.

God, she was beautiful. He could feel her lips on his. . . .

"You sleeping, Major?"

Zeus jumped to his feet. A woman in her early thirties was standing a few feet from his chair in the hallway, suppressing a smile.

Barely.

"I'm s-sorry," stuttered Zeus. "I haven't gotten much rest lately."

"Join the club."

If she was tired, it didn't show in her face. She wore a long white sweater over black pants, very basic, yet flattering. Anna was prettier, but the woman in front of him was no slouch.

"I'm Juliet Greig," she said, holding out her hand. "Acting Consul General. We haven't met."

"No. I'm sorry."

"You're here to see General Perry?" she asked.

"Yes, ma'am."

She smiled indulgently at the word *ma'am*.

"He's in with the ambassador and would like you to address them both. They're downstairs. If you'll follow me."

She led Zeus to the secure area of the embassy, where a suite of rooms were protected from electronic eavesdropping. Greig stopped in front of a thick door. She drew a magnetic card from her pocket and ran it through a reader, then pressed her thumb against a flat plate of glass beneath the card slot.

The lock snapped open. Greig and Zeus entered a small, narrow vestibule covered in what looked like cork. There was a second door, this one operated by a numerical keypad.

"Please don't peek," said Greig over her shoulder.

Zeus stepped back.

"It was a joke," she said as the door unlocked. "Peeking wouldn't help you—the combination changes every hour."

She pushed open the door, then stood to the side as Zeus entered. He brushed against her arm ever so gently, catching a whiff of her perfume.

It made him think of Anna.

General Perry and Ambassador Behrens were on phones at the far end of the table that dominated the room. Behind them were a pair of boxes that looked as if they were part of a very upscale home entertainment system. Blue lights flickered on both. A single laptop sat on the table.

Perry gestured to Zeus, indicating he should sit down on one of the chairs scattered nearby. They were folding chairs, the sort you would see in a church basement.

"Yes, sir, Mr. President," continued Perry. "I understand."

He frowned, and glanced at the ambassador.

"We will," she said, and hung up.

"How was your flight, Major?" said Perry, placing the phone on the receiver.

"It was . . . interesting," said Zeus. "We, uh . . . we got fired on a couple of times."

"No damage?"

"Plane got banged up, but we got home. The Chinese are moving past Tien Yen," he added. "The Vietnamese were overrun farther north. Part of the armored brigade hasn't even reached the city yet."

"Are they going to launch a counterattack there?" asked Perry.

"It didn't look like they were organized at all. Frankly, hitting the city now would be a waste of time. They'd have to get farther north if they wanted to cut off the Chinese supply lines."

"Or go farther south if they want to confront the spearhead," said Perry.

"Could you show me where we're talking about on the map?" asked Behrens. She touched a few keys on the laptop and pushed it over toward Zeus.

Zeus showed her.

"There's vacuum north of Lang Son," he told Perry. "You could attack north and get pretty far."

"The Vietnamese can't even defend their own soil," said Perry, with some disgust.

The general pulled the laptop closer to him. Zeus noticed his arm brush against Behrens's; he wondered if they were lovers.

Certainly not. They pulled their arms away almost instantly.

He was seeing sex in everything because of Anna.

"There's something else," Zeus said. "The Yen Tu Mountains are a no-fly zone. Why do you think that is?"

"What do you mean?" asked Perry.

"We couldn't fly over the area," said Zeus. "We detoured around it around it the whole flight. I definitely got the impression that I wasn't supposed to see something there."

"Show me," said Perry.

Zeus pointed out the area over the mountains. It was a large swatch east of Hanoi.

"Could that be where the government is going to evacuate to?" the general asked Behrens.

"I doubt it. Their bunkers are all in Hanoi and to the south, where the military headquarters are."

"Well, something's there," said Zeus. "Can I get a look at the satellite data?"

"Absolutely," said Perry, rising. "They're in the other room. Come with me."

————

Zeus didn't know exactly what he hoped to find in the satellite imagery of the Yen Tu Mountains in Quàng Ninh Province. But whatever it was, he didn't find it. The mountains looked like crusty patches of tan and green, crisscrossed by strings of blue. These were intersected by a spider web of gray lines—small local roads.

The sheer number surprised Zeus. Some were related to the Yen Tu Buddhist relic, a holy place marked by a massive bronze statue and surrounding pagodas. The ancient Vietnamese king Trân Nhân Tông was said to have sat in meditation at the spot in the mountains. Located about midway through the range, the relic was popular with pilgrims and hikers.

Away from the relic, the mountains were heavily mined, with coal and bauxite among the more plentiful minerals. Titanium, chromium, copper, and tin were also found there, as were rare earth metals.

Temples and mines were hardly a reason for a no-fly zone. Zeus studied the images, looking for signs of a bunker that might serve as an emergency retreat for the Hanoi government. But if it was there, it wasn't obvious. The mines were almost exclusively open pits: big holes in the ground where mountain peaks had once stood. Nor were there defenses ringed around them.

"It doesn't make all that much sense," Zeus told Perry. "A no-fly zone over a bunch of mines?"

"Maybe they're not hiding anything at all," Perry suggested, rubbing his eyes. "Maybe they're worried about damaging the pagoda."

"There are shrines all over the place. Dau Pagoda's just outside Hanoi. That's not a no-fly zone."

"This one's more important."

Zeus wasn't convinced, but he had no other explanation. And there were other problems to worry about.

"If you were the Vietnamese," said Perry, "what would you do?"

"Assuming they're heading toward Hai Phong? I'd swing down here and try and trip them up. Separate the armor from the infantry. It's almost hopeless, though."

"What if it weren't? Where can you stop them?"

Zeus tapped the area near Dam Trong, west of Cai Bdu Island. It was an area made for ambushes, with small bridges and a myriad of irrigation ditches feeding the inland rice fields that had been built in the past two or three years.

"Slow them down here," added Zeus. "Maybe you can get the infantry units that retreated to hit their rear."

"Will it work?" asked Perry.

"If those A-10As were here."

"Forget them."

"More weapons. I don't know."

Perry shook his head. "See if you can figure out a place for an ambush, even if it's hopeless."

"All right."

Zeus pulled over the magnifying glass and started going over the images and maps. A buzzer sounded; Perry went to the door near the intercom.

"Yes?" asked Perry.

"It's Juliet Greig. I brought you some coffee, General."

Perry unlocked the door from the inside. Greig was standing with a tray holding a carafe of coffee, milk, sugar, and two large white cups.

"Ms. Greig, thank you very much. You know Major Murphy?"

"I showed him in earlier." She smiled at Zeus. "Coffee, Major?"

"Sure."

Greig put the cups down at the far end of the table, then poured the coffee.

"General, the ambassador asked me to remind you that the meeting with the premier and General Trung is a half hour from now. She wanted to make sure you had time to get ready."

"Yes, of course." Perry rubbed his chin, whose stubble hadn't been trimmed in nearly two days.

"You want me to come, General?" asked Zeus.

"No, I think I can handle this on my own, Zeus. Listen, it's possible . . . we may . . ."

His voice trailed off. Zeus guessed what he was going to say from his eyes—it was possible they were going to bug out. They didn't want to get caught in Hanoi, which could happen if the tanks came far enough south and the offensive in the west started up again.

"I'll be ready," Zeus told him.

Perry nodded. "Why don't you get some sleep?"

"I'm okay."

The general turned to Greig. "Ms. Greig, would you do me a favor?"

"General?"

"See that Major Murphy gets a ride back to his hotel, would you?"

"Absolutely. I'll tuck him in if you want."

She smiled, then left. Zeus packed everything up. He was surprised to find her out in the hall when he came out.

"All done?" she asked.

"I didn't realize you were waiting," he said.

"That's my life. Don't worry about it. Where's the coffeepot?"

"Oh, I forgot it. I'm sorry."

"Don't worry. They'll get it later. You want me to take those?"

She pointed at the folders with the photos and map.

"I have to check them back in," he said.

"I'll do it for you if you want."

"No, that's all right."

She gave him another of her indulgent smiles, as if she were sharing a private joke with someone.

"I'll see you, Major. Unless you do want me to tuck you in."

"That's all right."

"The offer stands," she said before going upstairs.

————

Zeus had the driver take him to the hospital. The Vietnamese soldiers on the day shift seemed to recognize him; as he reached for his American

ID, they nodded and waved him inside. No one seemed to notice him as he walked through the battered interior of the building.

Anna was looking over a patient's chart about midway down the room where he had woken up. Zeus stepped up to the wall, watching her for a moment as she worked. She was as pretty as he remembered. Even the most mundane acts—jotting a note, closing a folder—were things of beauty.

The nurses watched her intently, as did the nearby patients. It seemed to Zeus that every eye in the place was watching her. And why shouldn't they?

Anna glanced in his direction as she finished. A smile broke across her lips.

Zeus started to push away from the wall to go toward her. She made the slightest motion with her head, telling him not to. Then she pointed at a patient next to the bed she had just checked—one more, she was telling him, then they could be together.

He understood perfectly. It was as if their minds were already joined.

There was a commotion out in the hall, people arguing. Zeus stepped around and looked out the door to see what was going on.

Two men in hospital scrubs were wheeling a gurney quickly down the hall. A third chased after them, his white lab coat flying open. He was angry, his face red. A patient lay on the stretcher, a bag of plasma on his chest. He was moaning, covered with blood.

The men rushed past. A nurse came out of the room behind him. Then Anna, her perfume sweet and pungent in the air. She passed as if she didn't notice him, walking briskly after the others.

They all went into a room a few doors away across the hall. Zeus followed in time to see the nurse who'd come from the ward bending over the patient. The angry man in the lab coat yelled something; the nurse stepped back. Everyone except Anna froze. Anna, glancing at the man who had yelled, stepped over and lifted the sheet from his midsection. He was covered in blood.

The angry man took hold of Anna's arm. Pain seized her face.

Zeus sprang forward, grabbing the man's shoulder so hard he let go of Anna and started to fall. Zeus spun him around and held him upright.

The angry man looked up at Zeus.

"Leave her alone," said Zeus sharply. "Don't touch her."

The man began stuttering something. Zeus let go, pushing him back as he did. The man stumbled but caught his balance. He backed out of the room.

"Please, you must leave," Anna told Zeus.

By the time he turned to look at her, she had gone back to work on the patient. She spoke quickly in Vietnamese to the nurse, who went to a side cabinet and began pulling out packages of gauze and other items.

Another nurse rushed in, wheeling a tray of instruments. Another came in, pushing a machine. The room suddenly smelled of rubbing alcohol and antiseptic.

Anna continued to work, hands moving swiftly and surely. The others moved around her frenetically, but she stayed calm, completely in control.

Zeus backed against the wall, mesmerized. A heart monitor was hooked up. The machine beeped erratically. Zeus noticed the man had his boots on—he was a soldier, in a dark green uniform.

Not Vietnamese. He must be a Chinese prisoner.

An airman, maybe. His uniform was baggy—a flight suit.

Footsteps clicked down the hall, then into the room. The angry man had returned. He had an officer with him.

The angry man in the lab coat began haranguing Anna. Zeus started to go forward, determined to pull him off again.

The officer stepped up next to the man in the lab coat and raised his arm. He had a pistol.

Two shots echoed in the small room. The noise was the loudest Zeus had ever heard, louder than any explosion, louder than any shout or scream. Before he could react, before anyone could react, the officer turned on his heel and left the room.

The man on the gurney was dead, the top of his head blown away.

25

Washington, D.C.

Walter Jackson hated going to diplomatic receptions for a host of reasons. Now President Greene had given him a fresh one—he had to speak pleasantly to the Russian ambassador, a man he loathed. It didn't help that the end result of the conversation might or might not be legal, in his opinion. The fact that it would help a country he'd never been particularly fond of was icing on the cake.

But such were the riddles and twists of national security in the twenty-first century. Greene needed someone at a very high level to push through the deal, someone he could trust if things went wrong.

Jackson had studied the Nixon presidency for his doctorate. He had been deeply ambivalent about Henry Kissinger, whose Realpolitik had opened China to the West and balanced it against the USSR, contributing greatly to the eventual end of the cold war.

Kissinger had also overseen a policy toward North Vietnam that was an utter failure.

And here it all was again: same players dancing in different roles.

The crisis helped Russia in several ways. The price of oil had skyrocketed. Meanwhile, they were selling a good amount of weapons to China, and to other countries—notably India—anxious about China. At the same time, the conflict was absorbing China, a neighbor they increasingly worried about.

The longer China's war in Vietnam went on, the better for Russia. So it was in their interest to help Vietnam, as long as it could be done covertly.

Things could be worse, Jackson told himself as he stepped from the back of the town car that had taken him to the embassy. The reception could have been black tie.

Jackson ran the gauntlet of the reception area, bowing to the hosts and a few celebrity guests, a smile pasted firmly on his lips. Inside the nearby ballroom, a band that didn't look particularly Polish played light jazz. Guests mingled in front of easels of abstract landscapes said to be inspired by the Polish countryside. To Jackson's jaundiced eye, they looked more like nightmares of color, with purple being a particular favorite.

He moved with purpose toward the bar at one side of the large ballroom. A broad-shouldered man with a Fu Manchu mustache greeted him.

"Would you be able to make a Manhattan?" Jackson asked.

"Of course," said the bartender.

"Good. Then hold the whiskey, and just give me a sweet vermouth."

Fu Manchu smirked and reached back for the vermouth. "Rocks?"

"Yes."

"With a cherry?"

"Hold that."

Jackson took the drink and stepped aside. As he lifted the glass to his lips he was shocked to see a former student standing in front of him. He recognized him a second before he could put a name to the face, then suddenly it came back: James Ferico.

"James?" said Jackson.

"Professor?"

They exchanged the mandatory how-are-you's and why-are-you-here's. Ferico knew Jackson's answers, but Jackson was surprised and somewhat cheered by his former student's: he had just published a biography that the Polish ambassador, for some unknown reason, had read and liked; the ambassador was so taken with it that he had invited him to the reception.

"Trying to pad the crowd, probably," said Ferico self-deprecatingly. "Maybe the first set of guests saw the paintings beforehand."

Jackson smiled. "I didn't know you published a book."

"I'll send you a copy."

"No, I insist on buying one," said Jackson. "Then you'll have to autograph it for me. Tell me, what else are you doing?"

Ferico was working as a "creative" with a Madison Avenue advertising company. "A little art, little video, sometimes writing."

"No foreign policy?" said Jackson.

Ferico laughed. "Not if I can help it."

They refilled their drinks. Jackson was having such a good time talking to him that he almost forgot why he came. But then he saw the Polish ambassador, holding court on the other side of the room. He excused himself after extracting a promise from Ferico to have lunch.

"I am surprised to see you here, Dr. Jackson," said Gregor Goldena-chov after Jackson sidled over. "Usually you do not join the social swirl."

"I make exceptions."

"An art lover," the ambassador told the two women hovering next to him. Jackson calculated that, if their ages were added together, they would still be about a third short of Goldenachov's.

"It is a lovely night," said Jackson.

"Indeed."

"A good night for a stroll."

Goldenachov raised his eyebrow. "Perhaps you would care to share a cigar," he suggested. He reached into his pocket. "Cubans."

America still had a ban against certain Cuban exports—including cigars. Technically, Jackson was violating the law by smoking one.

The things one was forced to do in the name of national security.

"I suppose I might," said Jackson, taking the long Figurado.

Goldenachov turned to the women. "If you would excuse me for a moment, we are going to pollute the air."

———

President Greene was sitting up in bed, one eye on the television, the other on a briefing paper relating to suggested changes in the upcoming health care legislation. It was almost 11:30. He'd switched off the Lakers game—they were being pummeled—and was waiting for Jon Stewart to come on. Even though Stewart rode him unmercifully, his show was a secret pleasure.

A top-secret pleasure. But damn, the guy was just *funny*. And Greene's wife was away, which meant she wouldn't needle him for watching it.

The phone rang. The White House operator told him Jackson was calling.

"Put him through."

His National Security adviser's voice boomed in his ear a second later. He sounded out of breath.

"Good evening, Mr. President. I'm just on my way back from the reception."

"Walter, how did we do?"

"It's set. We'll use the arrangements we used in Malaysia. The sales will appear to come from Georgia through Syria. The agency can go ahead."

"Were there complications?"

"The only serious ones were to my lungs," said Jackson.

"To your lungs?"

"I'll explain tomorrow." Jackson started to say something, then stopped.

"What is it?" asked Greene.

"I don't know that this is a good idea."

"Stopping China?"

"Working with the Russians."

"It's a terrible idea, Walter. But at the moment, it's the best one we have," said Greene. "Excellent. I'll call Frost at the CIA in the morning and have him make the arrangements. Good work, Walter. Have a good sleep."

"I'll try," said Jackson. "First, I'm taking the world's longest and hottest shower. I may even douse myself with disinfectant."

26

Hanoi

It was Anna who moved first. Everyone else in the small hospital room was frozen in place. She took a step back from the man she'd just been working to save, turned, and walked from the room.

Zeus had trouble getting his legs to work. He'd seen plenty of deaths before, had killed more than his share of men. It was a necessity, a duty, a job in war.

This was different.

He pushed his feet to move, shuffling at first, then striding, moving purposely. He went out of the room and turned into the hall, looking for Anna.

She'd disappeared. He walked quickly to the large ward room and looked inside. She wasn't there. His eyes met the gaze of a nurse, who was looking at him for an explanation: *What had the shot been about?*

He broke her gaze quickly and hurried down the hall, looking in each ward. He went to the end of the hall, where the woman who had given him clothes the day before looked at him with a blank, shocked expression.

"Where did Anna go?" he demanded. "Dr. Anway?"

But of course the woman didn't speak English. She could only stare, uncomprehending, speechless. Zeus turned and went up the stairs, trotting, then running.

He caught up to her on the sidewalk outside, near the end of the block. She was still wearing the gloves she'd had on in the hospital room. Blood had splattered on her.

Spots stained her face.

Zeus reached to wipe them off, and she collapsed in his arms.

———

He found her apartment without difficulty. She didn't have her keys, but the lock was easily forced with the help of Zeus's identity card.

He carried her into her room and put her on the bed. Then he went to her kitchen and looked for the kettle to make some tea.

There was no running water. Zeus opened the refrigerator, and found there was no light—the electricity was off as well.

A jug of water sat on the counter. He poured some into the teapot, then went to the stove. There was still gas, and there matches at the side. The burner lit with a loud *pul-ufff.*

The sound was odd—Zeus's ears were still shocked from the sound of the gun.

God, why had they had killed the man? Because he was Chinese?

I should have stopped him. But how? It was over before I realized what was happening. I never expected it.

The kettle began to shake. Zeus started looking for tea.

He found a canister on the counter filled with loose tea leaves. He looked through the drawer for something to hold them in, but all he could find was a strainer in the sink washboard. Examining it, he vaguely remembered what Anna had done the other night—the loose tea went directly into the kettle, and was strained when the liquid was poured into the cups.

How much should he use?

Zeus poured water into two cups, then dumped what was left into the sink. Belatedly, he realized he should have poured it into another pot, saving the water—who knew if it would come back on? But it was too late for that now.

He poured the hot water back into the kettle, measured out two spoonfuls of tea, and dumped it in. He stirred it around, and watched it steep.

The result looked too weak. He added a third spoonful.

Zeus maneuvered the pot and strainer carefully, filling the cups.

Anna met him at the door to the bedroom. She wasn't wearing any clothes.

"I—" The words died on his tongue. She took his arm and tugged him toward the bed, wordlessly asking him to join her there.

Zeus put the cups down on the floor, and did as she asked.

27

American embassy, Hanoi

The phone seemed to weigh twenty pounds. General Perry pressed it harder against his ear as he spoke.

"Mr. President, if we're not all the way in, we should be all the way out. As I've said."

"You're saying, give up," responded Greene.

"I'm saying, we have to play our cards wisely. It's a long game."

"You sound like a defeatist, Harland."

Perry was surprised by Greene's tone. He'd disagreed with him countless times before; almost always he had been logical, willing to at least listen to the argument. Now it was clear his mind had already been made up.

"Doing something is better than doing nothing," continued Greene. "You have to agree."

"Not necessarily. And not in this case, if we take the long view."

"That's where you're wrong, Harland. I think we can give them enough of a bloody nose here that they'll be deterred. It's in our best interests to drag it out. I'll bring Congress around eventually. You needed more weapons; here they are. You don't think Russian equipment is good enough?"

"George, history suggests—"

"History is on my side, Harland. Look at the Russians in Afghanistan. What happened there? Carter and Reagan helped the rebels. They drew it out. It helped collapse the Soviet Union."

"I don't know that that conflict is a good example," said Perry.

Greene didn't respond for a moment. Perry saw him shaking his head, squeezing his lips together. His mind was definitely made up; he was dealing with a recalcitrant subordinate.

"I always follow orders, Mr. President," said Perry. "My orders here, your orders, were to give you my opinion without prejudice. And that's what I've done."

"Yes." Greene was silent again for a few seconds—a very long few seconds. "I'll consider your advice," he told Perry. "In the meantime, tell the Vietnamese their weapons are on the way. Someone will forward the details."

28

The White House

Greene held the phone for several long moments after General Perry had hung up. He couldn't remember a time when he had disagreed with Harland on anything more substantial than the probable outcome of a baseball game.

Perry was telling him to stop helping Vietnam—now, rather than later.

Was that really the wise thing to do? If they didn't get some weapons, they had no chance of surviving. There were downsides, certainly. And *real* intervention—real *assistance*—was the right approach. But when you were President, you had to compromise. A lot.

He put the handset back, then immediately picked it up.

"Get me Peter Frost, please."

Frost came on the line moments later. He was still at home.

"Peter, I didn't wake you, did I?"

"No, sir, Mr. President. Just about to head in."

"The project we spoke of regarding the Russian arms—let's move ahead."

"Uh, yes, sir. Of course."

"Problem?" asked Greene, noting the slight hesitation.

"I did take the precaution of having the legal review so we could expedite things."

"And?"

"Divided opinion."

"That's fine."

Legal reviews had been de rigueur at the CIA for some time. There were more lawyers involved in some operations than officers.

"I should tell you, even Bindi's opinion was borderline," added Frost. "And that was our lone positive."

Bindi was a CIA attorney known for taking very pro-administrative stances. Frost was telling Greene that the weapons procurement and transfer would be on extremely shaky ground legally.

"The nonaggression law of 2011 specifically outlawed third-party sales to allies," Frost explained. "The three negatives pointed that out."

"Vietnam is not an ally," said Greene, switching into his own lawyer mode. "Congress's refusal to authorize the bill to enter into a treaty with Vietnam proves they're not an ally. So the law doesn't apply to them."

"That was Bindi's position."

"Slam dunk. I like that man." Greene chuckled. "It's fine, Peter. Don't worry about it. I take full responsibility."

"Mr. President . . ."

Greene waited for Frost to complete his thought. Instead, Frost took a deep breath.

"We'll make it happen, Mr. President."

"Very good, Peter. I'm counting on you."

29

Hanoi

Zeus woke with a start.

He was in Anna's apartment, in her room, in her bed. It was nighttime. She wasn't there.

He got up slowly, body stiff from his ankles to his neck. He turned his head against a knot in his neck, teasing against the pain.

His first step was a stumble, feet moving awkwardly. Zeus pushed his arms back, gathering himself. He was in a fog, his mind in cotton, distant from his body.

Where was Anna?

Zeus stooped down and picked up his clothes from the floor. He dressed awkwardly, off-balance. With each piece of clothing, he regained more of his equilibrium, became more of himself. By the time he buttoned his shirt, all of his senses had returned. He was a soldier again, at least most of him was . . . Some part remained with her, with Anna, resting in a dream.

Zeus walked into the kitchen. A single candle on the stove provided light. She wasn't there.

"Damn," he said to himself. He rubbed his eyes, then the top of his head.

What should he do? He had to get back—

Just then, there was a sound at the door: a key placed into the lock. The door opened; Anna came in with a bag of food. She pushed the door closed behind her, slipping in quietly without looking, so that when she finally turned back and found him staring at her across the kitchen she was startled.

"I got some things," she said, her voice a soft whisper.

"Good," said Zeus.

He took a half step to hug her, but she was in motion, moving around the kitchen. Zeus retreated to a nearby chair, pulling it out to sit on and watching as she lit the burner.

Anna put the tea kettle on the burner, then lit another candle, putting it on the table. Zeus caught her hand as she placed it down. She turned and gave him a look of such sadness that he felt as if his heart had been stabbed.

"Are you all right?" he asked.

She managed a smile, then slipped her hand away. She got out two cups, and retrieved a small bottle from her bag.

"I found you coffee," she told him, holding up a jar of instant. "Good?"

"Thanks."

She put the groceries away.

"What time is it?" Zeus asked, though he had a watch.

"Eight."

"God, I slept all that time."

"You are very tired."

Anna poured the water, then sat. She blew gently on her tea.

"Are you hungry?" she asked.

"No," said Zeus. "Are you?"

She shook her head.

"My legs feel restless," Zeus told her. The aroma of the coffee reminded him of soggy cardboard. He hated instant, but he treated the liquid as if it were the most precious in the world, nursing the cup in both hands, the steam rising against his face. "Do you think we could go for a walk?"

She answered with a question. "When do you have to be back?"

"Eventually." He took a tentative sip. The liquid was still very hot. "What happened in there?" he asked. "At the hospital. Who was the man who was shot?"

She looked straight down at her tea. Her features seemed to harden, the soft frown she'd worn turning into a grimace.

"Can you tell me?" Zeus asked gently.

"He was a Chinese pilot. A bandit. The director's family had been killed by a bomb two days before."

"Who was the officer who shot him?"

She shook her head.

"I'm sorry," said Zeus. "Bad things happen in wars."

"My grandfather was killed by bombs in the American war. And two of his brothers."

She stared at him for a moment, then sipped her tea in silence.

"Let's try that walk," he told her finally. "Come on."

———

There had been no attacks on Hanoi that day, no bombings. But the quiet only increased the tension. Smoke curled in the far distance, the remnants of fires that the emergency crews had not yet succeeded in putting out. Zeus felt torn—his place was at the battlefield, but he wanted to be with Anna as well.

"I saw the bombs fall the first night," she told him. "I was standing at my window. There was a floodlight in the sky. Sticks fell through it. I thought there was something wrong with my eyes."

Distance grew between them as they walked shoulder to shoulder, her arm occasionally jostling against his. The closeness that he'd felt in bed, making love, sleeping next to her, dissipated. His mind pulled toward duty. It was like gravity.

She stiffened when he took her hand.

"I want to see you again," he said.

"In Vietnam, it is not usual to hold hands in public," she said in a voice so faint that he barely heard.

"It's dark. The streets are deserted." He squeezed her fingers, looking down into her face. "Okay? You'll see me again?"

"Yes."

He leaned down and kissed her softly, gently, on the lips. She hesitated but then surrendered, her lips meeting his. It was a tantalizing shadow of what he had felt earlier, being pulled into bed.

But just a shadow.

———

When they turned the block on the way back to Anna's house, Zeus saw a Honda Accord sitting in front of her building. He kept walking, hoping it wasn't waiting for him.

But of course it was.

"Where the hell have you been?" demanded Christian, opening the door and getting out as he approached.

"Taking a walk," said Zeus.

"All night?"

"Major Christian, this is Anna Anway," said Zeus. Anna stiffened. She held her arms close to her body, as if she were trying to present as tiny a front to the world as possible.

"Hi." Christian nodded, then frowned as he turned back to Zeus. "We gotta go. Perry's going to have a cow."

"He told me to get some rest."

"Yeah, well, he thought you disappeared. You weren't answering your phone."

Zeus had left it upstairs. Christian had used the GPS tracking function to find him.

"I knocked on every door," Christian told him. "Nobody answered."

Upstairs, after he retrieved his phone, Zeus told Anna gently, "I'll see you as soon as I can." She gazed into his face, then took both of his hands and squeezed.

Their bodies were about a foot apart, an immense distance.

"Will you be at work tomorrow?" he asked.

"Of course."

"I'll get there. Somehow."

She nodded, then closed her eyes as he kissed her.

———

"*She's a dish*," said Christian as they drove away. He was sitting in the front seat, next to a driver hired by the embassy. Zeus sat in the back. "What a babe."

Ordinarily, Zeus would have been angered by the comments, but he felt immune to them now. Immune to Christian.

"You know Perry was trying to get A-10 Warthogs here?" asked Christian.

"Huh?"

"There was a wing in Korea, already on the way. Some sort of political deal crushed it. Now we're on our own." Christian's voice had a note of disgust in it as he continued. "I talked to these commanders yesterday. Pep talks? What a waste of time."

"What's the military situation?" asked Zeus.

"Chinese consolidated around Tien Yen during the day. Some of the Vietnamese armor's engaging them outside the city. Thinking is they move farther south tonight. Probably already started by now."

"Any action near Lang Son?"

"Lang Son?" asked Christian.

"The place on the border I showed you."

"Nothing going on there that I heard," said Christian.

The driver took them to Trung's bunker. The general was in a conference with his commanders, but he smiled when Zeus came in. Perry was sitting in the corner, grave-faced.

"Our American friends have arrived," said Trung. "Just in time to hear of the bad weather."

The others smiled, as if this was some sort of inside joke. And perhaps it was; Zeus still felt a little off balance.

"A typhoon is approaching," explained Major Chaū, the senior translator who had led Christian around on his tour of the Vietnamese troops. "The estimate is that it will strike the coast in less than twelve hours. The path is unpredictable, but it is highly likely to make landfall."

Zeus looked over at Perry. "I didn't think this was typhoon season."

Perry nodded as the translator explained that while typhoons were rare in February, they were not entirely unknown, averaging one every other third year prior to 2005. Over the past few years, the frequency had increased, possibly, though not definitively, as a result of global climate change.

This was a reasonably strong storm, with winds up to 125 knots projected. Rain was falling at over two inches per hour near the center. Total rainfall in the path of the storm would depend on its route, but could be anywhere from a "scant" ten inches to fifty and beyond.

Zeus realized the implications immediately.

"We can use it to stop the Chinese advance in the east," he said. "As long as we can keep them near the coast. Once they get west, they'll be free."

Trung nodded. The situation was somewhat more complicated than that, not least of all because the typhoon would affect the Vietnamese as well as the Chinese. Still, it was an extremely fortunate development, one that could be capitalized on. The generals had been examining topographical maps in the area of the Chinese advance. The area in the vicinity of Dam Tron would be flooded early during the storm.

The only problem was that the lead elements of the Chinese advance were only a few miles north of it.

"It's better if it floods behind them," said Zeus. "We let the lead elements get beyond it, then cut them off."

The battle materialized in his mind as he looked at the map. He pictured the area he had seen the other day from the plane—long fields of rice, which would be easily washed over.

"We keep them close to the coast," said Zeus. "We mine the roads to the west, and ambush the forces that reinforce the spearhead. At some point with the rains, they start to bog down. We attack them during the storm."

"The major has never experienced a typhoon," said one of Trung's generals dryly, using English.

————

Besides the ferocity of the weather, the strategy to slow the Chinese advance along the coast faced numerous obstacles, not least of which was the disorganization of the Vietnamese forces. The armored brigade that had approached from Route 4B was now engaged outside Tien Yen. Entered into combat piecemeal as Zeus had feared, the T-55 and T-54 tanks had been outgunned by a handful of Chinese main battle tanks and infantry manning the outer defenses. To the east, the battered remnants of General Tri's infantry division had failed to reorganize themselves. Some were fighting on the city's outskirts. A few had gone south along Highway 18. Still others were in Ha Duong and the other small port villages nearby.

General Tri had offered his resignation, but Trung had refused it. There was no sense in changing commanders in midbattle, especially given that he had no suitable replacement.

The Vietnamese asked if Zeus could help formulate the defense plan. Perry, who said little during the session, agreed.

When the meeting ended, Trung asked if Zeus could come with him to his office for a moment.

"I apologize again for the other day," Trung told Zeus. "You will not be treated as you were. Your advice will be followed."

"Okay."

"You look more rested," added Trung, his tone lighter. It was almost fatherly.

"I got a little sleep."

"Sleep is an important ally."

"I'll help with the plans, General," said Zeus. "But I have to say that the situation is not a very positive one. Your forces are very much outnumbered."

"We have always done much with little," said Trung. "It is our way."

30

Washington, D.C.

The hot water came full force out of the showerhead, a fire hose compared to what Mara had been used to in Asia. She turned her back to the flow, letting it pound into her skin, soaking her muscles in warmth. She bent slightly, letting the water massage her lower back and then her thighs and calves. It splashed against her side and then her breasts; she arched backward and let it hit her stomach, the front of her legs.

God, it felt good. But she had to get to work. She was already late.

The only shampoo in the apartment was a supermarket special, a rip-off of a boutique brand that Mara had never heard of. It glopped into her hand like granulated maple syrup. Glancing at it dubiously, she ran it through her hair cautiously, not entirely trusting that it wouldn't leave her bald.

Her hair felt short—short and thin. Long hair was a pain in the field, but if she was going to be in the States for a while, then she was going to let it grow past the shoulder length she had it at now.

In the States for a while. *Send that idea away*, she told herself. She was getting the hell out of here as soon as possible.

Dressed, she checked her phone.

Still no call from Josh.

Downstairs, she hunted through the kitchen cabinets for coffee. She found two choices: Maxwell House and New England. Neither particularly appealed to her, but she needed caffeine.

She had to use a paper towel for a filter. Mara flipped the TV on while she waited for the coffee to brew. The cable news anchors were talking about the latest charges from China that the American CIA had helped Vietnam stage the photos and incident. Josh MacArthur, said a reporter on a remote in front of the capitol, had gone into hiding.

Draw your own conclusions.

Mara flipped the television off.

———

Grease was waiting for Mara when she came in. He took her downstairs and explained that the Vietnamese needed Russian weapons, that the conduit was to be the same as she had used in Malaysia, and things had to move as quickly as possible.

"And it's been authorized on the highest level," Grease added.

"Peter signed off?" said Mara, meaning Peter Lucas.

"Much higher than that," said Grease. "Make it as long an arm's length as you can."

———

The key to the arrangement was a man named Sergei, whom Mara knew and loathed from her days in Malaysia. Sergei traveled extensively, and Mara never really knew where he might be. She had only met him twice, both times in Paris. The last had been in an after-hours sex club, an experience imprinted on neurons she'd never use again.

She left Langley and bought a cell phone specifically for the purpose of contacting him, using an agency-supplied ID and credit card. She found a coffee shop and placed the call. Not surprisingly, she remembered the number by heart.

An answering machine picked up on the second ring.

"Leave a message," said a mechanical voice.

"This is Turpentine." Mara winced at the ridiculous code name he'd picked for her when they'd started. "There are some new arrangements. I need to work quickly. Call this number."

She hung up. Sergei's system would have this number, so there was no need to leave it.

He called back ten minutes later, before she'd even finished her coffee.

"This is Mara."

"You have a Washington number. Is that to be trusted?"

"I doubt it's to be trusted," Mara said. "But if you mean, am I in D.C., the answer is yes."

"Then for lunch, Union Station. There is a bar there. I like the fries."

Sergei hung up before she could ask what time to be there. With nothing better to do, she headed into the city.

———

Mara killed time in the bookstore and some of the other tiny shops before going over to the restaurant, which opened at eleven. She nursed a light beer for forty-five minutes before ordering a second. She was halfway through that one when Sergei showed up.

"The beautiful but volatile Miss Turpentine," said Sergei, far too loudly as he pulled a chair away from the table to sit down.

Intentionally or not, Sergei projected the image of a Russian fat cat, complete with the macho assumption that every woman he met was cast instantly under his spell. This might actually have been true when he was younger—there was a certain twinkle in his eyes, and his face was not unpleasant to look at. But he was past fifty now, and not aging particularly well, with a full paunch and a rather odd balding pattern on the top of his head. The leather jacket he wore looked almost comical. But at least he didn't smell of cologne.

"So, it is a pleasure to be working with you again, Turpentine," he said brightly as the waiter approached. "Such a pleasure."

The restaurant was located in the center of the station, which didn't bother Mara as much as Sergei's booming voice. She'd taken a table off to the side, with no one else around. Still, a modicum of discretion was in order.

But discretion wasn't Sergei's style.

"I will have a vodka gimlet," he told the waiter. "You will use Standard."

The waiter nodded.

Sergei looked at Mara. "You are wondering why Standard? It is the best."

"I was wondering if your voice had a lower volume," said Mara.

"But if I am too quiet, your microphones can't hear me."

"I'm not miked."

Sergei smiled and gave a little knowing laugh. Mara caught a glimpse of a nondescript, middle-aged man taking a seat not too far away.

One of his bodyguards, she guessed.

"So. You have wishes, yes?" asked Sergei.

"Yes."

Mara saw the waiter heading toward their table. They ordered—she asked for a Caesar salad with grilled tuna, Sergei a burger with cheese and bacon, along with a double order of fries.

"And, I will take beer," said Sergei. "You have this Boston Ale."

"Pint or glass?" asked the waiter.

"The pint."

"It's not 'this,'" said Mara when the waiter left.

"This?"

"You said, 'this Boston Ale.' You don't know the adjective . . . just say, 'Boston Ale.'"

Sergei smiled. "Ah, Turpentine. It is always an education to be working with you. Now you will correct my grammar. When will you allow me to teach you Russian?"

"We need antitank weapons," she said softly. "Big enough to take out main battle tanks."

"Hmmmm. Very expensive."

"I understand. We need Kornets."

"I could get, perhaps, the Konkurs," he said, referring to a Russian wire-guided missile that could penetrate about 800 mm of armor—not enough to deal with the Chinese tanks the Vietnamese would be facing.

"Kornet or nothing."

"Miss Turpentine, so crass today. Vietnam was not agreed with you."

The waiter appeared with their orders. Mara asked for another beer.

"You know, it is not always easy to find what you wish," said Sergei offhandedly. "Have you considered the Sheksna? Very nice."

Mara made a face.

"You would refer to it as AT-12. This good weapon."

"Sergei. Really. Just get what we need. Okay?"

"So we work on your request. What else?"

Mara worked down the list. Sergei was relatively agreeable, even when it came to spare parts for the Vietnamese MiGs.

The price, of course, was ridiculous. But Mara agreed, as long as delivery could be arranged within hours.

Sergei, much to her surprise, agreed.

"Some things already on way to Manila," he told her. "From there, your problem."

This *had* been approved at the highest levels, Mara realized. The Russians clearly wanted the Vietnamese to give the Chinese a bloody nose.

Good for business? She wondered what else was involved in the deal.

"We'll confirm through the usual channels," she said, getting up.

"What? You don't stay for lunch?"

"I have to put things in motion," she said. "Leave a good tip."

31

The Gulf of Tonkin

They played cat and mouse with the Chinese cruiser for several more hours, the night growing darker and the weather growing stormier as they went. The merchant ships were almost in Vietnamese waters now—which was fine with Silas; he could board them more easily there.

What wasn't fine was that they were still a good two hours away—that would put them in Hai Phong before he could get there.

Though given the intensity of the storm, maybe not.

The cruiser was faster than the *McLane*, but it was clear that her captain was not willing to actually risk a collision. The first encounter had been the closest; since then, the captain had taken a few feints, but hadn't presented an outright threat.

He might have been more willing to risk his frigate escort, but the smaller ship couldn't keep up her speed. She fell farther and farther behind in the heavy seas.

"She's turning off!" yelled one of the extra lookouts Silas had posted. "Turning to port."

The synthetic radar plot confirmed it. The Chinese captain was giving up, battening down to cope with the storm. Now was their chance.

A strong wind echoed through the ship. The gust pushed the *McLane* down against the water. A white cloud of ocean rose, enveloping her from bow to amidships.

The typhoon was faster than them all.

"Captain, should we come about and face into the wind?" asked helm.

"Belay that," said Silas, as if it had been an order rather than a question. "Steady on course."

The ship rose from the fantail and crashed forward. The wind howled over the deck, the hush of a ghost clawing at the bridge's glass.

"Steady!" repeated Silas. "We've got to intercept them."

A hard roll sent him to the deck.

"Steady!" he repeated, climbing back to his feet. "Keep me steady!"

32

CIA headquarters, Virginia

Peter Lucas was surprised that Mara had made the arrangements so quickly, even though he tried not to show it. He pressed his lips together and nodded solemnly as she filled him in on the details.

"How do I get to Manila?" she asked.

"Manila?"

"The first shipment should be there in a few hours. I should be there already."

"You're not going."

"What?"

"We'll find someone else to take care of this."

"Why?"

"For one thing, you're now world famous. Your videos on YouTube are up to a million hits apiece. Give it a rest, Mara," he added with a bit of an edge. "You're going to have to accept that you're in a new phase of your career."

Mara had half-convinced herself that Peter would let her go. In fact, more than half-convinced: she felt honestly disappointed, and angry.

"I don't see, after everything that's happened, why I can't get a break," she told him. "I think I'm owed a break."

"You're not thinking rationally. Come on." He picked up his empty soda can, twirling it between his fingers. "I want you to look over the material that's coming in from Vietnam. I want to figure out who the mole is."

"What's Grease doing?"

"Grease has different priorities," Lucas answered. "I want you to look at everything. I need a second set of eyes to go through it. You're the best we've got. Really."

Mara didn't want to concede.

"Who's going to handle this?" she asked.

"Don't worry about it."

"Well, I can give them a heads-up. If it's somebody from Thailand—"

"It won't be from in-house," he told her. "I have somebody in mind."

"Do you want me to talk to him?"

"No. That's all right."

"You don't trust me?"

"Jesus, come on. You're taking this whole thing way too hard. Way, way too hard." He put down the can and frowned at it, as if it had somehow crossed him. "We'll figure something out together, all right? When this . . . passes, we'll sit down and think about where you can go next. It's not going to hurt you, believe me."

"Passes—like a kidney stone."

A faint smile came to Lucas's lips.

"It'll pass," he told her. "Go upstairs and get up to date. I'll arrange things for you in the vault. All right? Somebody took your money in Hanoi, right? That should be your focus."

"You think I can figure that out from here?" she asked sourly.

"I think you can do anything."

33

Quàng Ninh Province, south of Dam Tron

The helicopter that took Zeus and Christian east to General Tri's head-quarters was even older than the Hind they had flown in the other day. It was an Mi-8 Hip that had belonged to Poland and was sold secondhand. Though it had been transferred at least a decade before, the outlines of the Polish insignia still peeked through the hull paint.

The Russian-made aircraft wheezed and whined as it made its way eastward, flying over Route 18—avoiding the mountains as the Alba-tros had, though in the case of the helicopter it could be argued that the altitude would have presented a hazard.

A more immediate problem was the fact that the pilot had only the most primitive navigation instruments at his command. He lacked night-vision gear, and "GPS" was just a set of letters in an unfamiliar language. He put his forward light on and flew low to the highway, following the roads to General Tri's command post.

The headquarters was now in a field outside Vu Oai, an agricultural settlement along Route 18. General Tri was some ten miles west of the intersection of Route 18 and 329, a critical intersection the Chinese would undoubtedly attempt to seize.

The search beam caught a large farm building as they turned to-ward the CP. The helicopter pilot pulled up suddenly, barely missing a power line, then settled into a field about twenty-five yards from the road. A pair of old American tanks, M48s Zeus thought, were set up on a slight rise, guns pointed east. The rest of the headquarters sat behind them.

General Tri was working in the barn. The space dwarfed his table, which had seemed so large when Zeus saw it outside earlier. The gen-eral and three staff officers were poring over a set of maps when Zeus and Christian entered.

Tri rose and stood stiffly at attention as Major Chaū announced them. The general turned his gaze silently from Major Chaū to Zeus, fixing him with the rigid stare Zeus might have expected from a newly minted private.

The gaze made Zeus uncomfortable. The only thing he could think to do was salute, but this was a mistake—Tri held his hand at his forehead, waiting for Zeus to lower his—another sign of submission.

"General." Zeus leaned toward Tri, lowering his voice to almost a whisper. "I'm not here to give orders. I'm just an adviser. I want to help you, not command you."

Tri stared at him, stone-faced. The three Vietnamese staff officers—two colonels and a major—remained frozen at attention next to him.

"Maybe we should discuss the situation," said Zeus. Major Chaū, rather than translating, pulled out a chair. Tri only sat down when Zeus did.

The general's G-2 began pointing out the disposition of the forces, speaking in haltering English though occasionally glancing at Chaū when he hit a hard word. He knew English reasonably well, and Zeus had no trouble with his accent.

The situation was a little worse than Zeus thought. The spearhead of the Chinese force was about twelve miles north of the highway intersection. Harassed by stragglers from the overrun division, the PLA forces were dropping off infantry units to control their flanks. This was a positive, if only a small one—the more stretched out the Chinese became, the better the odds of slicing a gap through their line.

Christian had brought the latest Global Hawk imagery with him. The staff officers grabbed at them like kids reaching for goody bags at a birthday party. They laid them on the table, speaking rapidly in Vietnamese.

"General, could you and I speak privately for a second?" said Zeus.

Tri rose and walked with him toward the back of the barn. Chaū stayed with the others.

"I didn't mean to embarrass you," said Zeus. "I know this is a difficult situation for you."

Tri didn't answer.

"I'd suggest that we let the Chinese get past the intersection. Entice them . . . make it look as if we have a major force that they can engage. The faster they go, the better off we are."

Tri took a long, slow breath.

"My commander is trying to find more antitank weapons," said

Zeus. Tri did speak English—he had at their first meeting—but did he understand it well enough to know what Zeus was saying? "Once the bulk of the storm hits, the Chinese tanks will have to stop. The farther they are from the rest of their force, the better. Once they're on the defensive, we can pick them off."

"You are a young man," said Tri finally.

"Yes, sir, I am."

"Your father fought in our war?"

"No, sir."

"You have studied Vietnam?"

"Mostly the Chinese."

"You know it is a diff-i-cult—" Tri stumbled over the word, finding it hard to pronounce. "A diff-i-cult position. They outnumber us greatly."

"Yes."

"You will desert us when the battle goes poorly."

Was it a statement or a question? Zeus wasn't sure.

"I'm not going to leave you," said Zeus. "I've already fought against their invasion force. And the tanks. I'm not a coward."

Tri nodded.

They went back to the table and mapped out a plan. Zeus wanted the armor brigade to disengage in the north and come south, where it might be more useful. But the only good route was on the roads already held by the Chinese.

"Use bad roads," said Christian when Chaū told him the problem. "They're useless up there. They're getting cut to pieces. At least save them so we can use them against their infantry, for Christ's sake."

They found a succession of mining roads that might be used, but the travel would take considerable time—the tanks wouldn't be available until after the storm hit. But this was better than having them waste themselves against the Chinese at Tien Yen.

One of the Vietnamese officers objected. He worried that the people in the city, seeing the fighting stop, would think that they had been abandoned.

"We can't worry about what people think," said Christian. "We need to win the fight."

"Don't let them think it's over," said Zeus. "Leave a small force to engage the Chinese. That's better in any event. The Chinese will stay there."

Zeus's ideas were not particularly foreign to the Vietnamese, who realized the Chinese became more vulnerable the faster their tanks moved. The roads and surrounding areas were already mined. The home guard was dug in. The situation was far too dire to be optimistic—that would have been foolhardy. But as a long shot, it was at least doable.

The storm would arrive, and the Chinese advance would slow by necessity. After that, who knew?

At the end of the session, Zeus volunteered to go with one of colonels visiting a battalion directly in the Chinese path, a little north of the intersection.

"I'll go, too," said Christian.

"One of us probably ought to stay here," Zeus told him.

"Hell no, I'm not missing the fun," said Christian.

Chaū reluctantly agreed to go with them.

They hopped into the bed of a Toyota pickup that had been requisitioned from a civilian several days before. Zeus had to insist that he didn't want to sit in the front seat, claiming to the translator that he had a problem with his legs and needed to be able to stretch out.

Glad to have ducked the privilege of squeezing four across in the front of the truck, Zeus checked in with Perry.

"Major?"

"General, I'm sorry to bother you. I didn't know if you were still sleeping or—"

"No, no, just having something to eat." Light music was playing in the background; Perry had gone to one of the Hanoi hotels. "Give me a minute to get somewhere secure. I'll call you back."

Zeus turned the phone off, holding it in his lap. Christian was curled against the side of the pickup, trying to catch a quick nap despite being constantly jostled. Chaū stared at the road behind them, lost in his thoughts.

Zeus's sat phone buzzed a few minutes later.

"What's the situation?" said Perry as soon as the connection went through.

"Not the best, but not lost, either." Zeus told him about the plans. "How about the Stabbers?" he asked Perry after his brief. "They have some T-55s and T-54s. We could possibly get a volley or two, take out the first Chinese tanks."

"We're arranging weapons," said Perry. "I wouldn't count on much within the next twenty-four hours."

"Yes, sir."

Perry told him that artillery was being brought in from the south. But even that seemed tenuous.

"Latest figures are thirty-eight tanks in the lead group coming down the highway," said Perry. "Another eighteen about five miles behind. The Chinese are running them without infantry."

"Interesting," said Zeus.

"They may know about the storm and are trying to get to Hai Phong ahead of it. Or else their infantry is just slow. Take your pick."

Tanks without troops around them were vulnerable. Though it was not necessarily easy to convince a soldier facing them of that.

"Zeus, before you sign off . . ."

"Yes, General?"

"Things get sticky up there, you and Christian are to bail out. You understand me?"

"Yes, sir."

"No 'yes, sir' bullshit, Murphy. You understand what I'm telling you? You've taken far too many risks—far, far too many. Do you understand? I want you back here in one piece."

Zeus suddenly felt his throat tighten. He remembered his promise to Tri.

"Yes, sir," he told the general.

"You bug out *before* the Chinese tanks get there. That, Mr. Murphy, is an order. And I'll court-martial your ass if it's not followed. Assuming I can find an ounce of it left to court-martial."

"Understood."

Zeus clicked off the phone.

———

The Vietnamese battalion was scattered along a bend in the highway where the road dipped through a run of reclaimed marshes. It was an excellent spot for an ambush.

The problem was, their biggest caliber weapons were rocket-propelled grenades and man-portable mortars—nothing big enough to take out a main battle tank.

Zeus and Christian walked along the highway with the commander of the company charged with facing the Chinese at the road itself. This was the hardest task, and the best troops had been assigned to it.

A drizzle started as they set out. A light, on-and-off spritz, it seemed almost pleasant. The wind, not yet that strong, felt warm and tropical.

The company's entire store of antitank mines—a dozen—had been placed about a half mile from a small bridge crossing. Vietnamese sappers were installing demolitions on the bridge when they arrived.

"Better to put the mines in the ravine," suggested Zeus. "Blow the bridge when the lead tank gets to it. Then the tanks are likely to hit the mines once they try to cross."

The commander agreed. Christian went to inspect the engineers' work, then came back with an idea.

"They've got some explosive left over," he said. "We can make an IED."

They drove the truck across to the other side of the bridge and arranged it to look as if it had been abandoned. Christian loaded the explosives in the cab. Meanwhile, Zeus and the company commander moved the infantry back, trying to get them hidden so they could fire at the tanks from behind once they were stopped. If there had been support vehicles with the tanks, the ambush would have made more sense, providing them with easier targets. Zeus thought the grenades would simply bounce off the tank's thick skin.

There was a second bridge about a half mile farther west. When Zeus went to inspect it, he found a trio of young soldiers crouched at the edge of the ravine. Each had two grenades in his hand. When the tanks stopped, they would run behind them, climb up, and drop the grenades in the open hatches.

The plan bordered on suicidal. Two more teams were similarly armed and prepared on the other side of the road.

"This doesn't have a snowball's chance in hell of working," whispered Christian as they walked back to the small rise where the platoon commander had stationed himself. "Maybe they knock out six tanks."

"Better than nothing," said Zeus, though in fact he wasn't sure it was.

There's wasn't time to come up with a better plan—the sound of approaching tank engines rose above the growing howl of the wind.

34

The Gulf of Tonkin

The sea crashed heavily over the bow, spraying clear to the bridge. This was nothing, just the spray ahead of the storm. The typhoon itself was still several miles behind the *McLane*.

It was coming. The darkness seemed to focus its intensity. The deck hurled upward and down, again and again, the hard hand of Poseidon slamming against the waves.

"Captain, we're still five miles from the nearest merchant ship," said Lt. Commander Li. "But the storm—we can't keep moving this way much longer."

"We have to get between them and the port," said Silas.

"Captain, even the Chinese warships have moved off. We have to head into the storm."

"We can take hundred-knot winds," said Silas. He meant they could take a wind that strong at the side without rolling over.

"These winds are one-twenty, one-thirty!" The howling outside the bridge was so loud Li had to shout to make herself heard.

"We're going to do it," said Silas calmly. As if to mock him, a heavy gust bit at the ship, pushing her over a good ten degrees. "Helm! More power."

"She's to the limit now, Captain."

"Pour it on!" insisted Silas. He looked at Li. He knew what she was thinking. "I know the ship, Dorothy. We're not capsizing. We're going to accomplish our mission."

She grit her teeth, then nodded.

"Steady!" yelled Silas as the vessel lurched again. "Steady!"

35

Quảng Ninh Province

Zeus pushed himself into the wet grass, waiting for the first tank to come around the bend. The rain had picked up to the point where it interfered with his night glasses.

Good. The tanks' infrared sights would be useless as well.

He thought of Anna, remembered her body pressing against his.

The first Chinese tank came around the turn, gun pointed toward the hill where Zeus was lying. In the dark, it looked exactly like an M1A1, the low silhouette grinding through the night.

"Come on, baby," muttered Zeus.

A second tank came around the bend, about ten yards behind the first. A third followed almost on its bumper, with a fourth right behind that.

Zeus turned toward the bridge. Would the engineers be patient enough to let the first tank pass? If they were, they could get three in one shot.

Perry's warning and orders came back to him. But there wasn't time to bug out. The Chinese had come down too quickly. It wasn't his fault.

The first tank rumbled onto the bridge. It paused for a moment, then burst across toward the pickup truck on the far side. The second tank moved onto the bridge, then the third and fourth.

Blow it now, thought Zeus. But nothing happened.

36

The Gulf of Tonkin

The wind and water worked together, sliding a long hand beneath the stern of the *McLane* and then dashing her into the ocean like a fly caught in a stabber. The vessel rolled forty-five degrees, staying there for a long moment.

Silas realized he had erred, gravely. He had thought he could best not simply the Chinese but nature. It was a foolish, fatal bit of egotism, the hubris of an idiot—and too late to be retrieved.

The vessel smacked back upright. He had two men on the helm now, and another to help if either needed relief, but they were nothing against the storm. The *McLane*, for all her dash and technology, was not the equal of God. Nor was she intended to be.

A new wave sent him to the deck. The pit of his stomach opened. He felt nauseous—something he hadn't felt even as a freshly minted ensign. He began to get sick; in an instant, vomit spewed from his mouth, over his shirt.

It was the ultimate humiliation for a captain. He cowered on the deck, humbled.

Now, he told himself, now that you are stripped of all your dignity, now that you stand before your crew exposed as a fool—now you must decide what you will do.

Will you stay at the deck like the broken dog you are? Or will you rise and scream against the wind, take one last stand, even if futile?

Every muscle, every bone in his body screamed for the deck, for oblivion. Only the voice in his head remained defiant.

"Into the wind, mister!" he said, voice so faint the wind kept even himself from hearing. "The wind!"

The lights blinked, went out, came back. Silas grabbed onto a piece of the forward panel and pulled himself up. There was no one at the wheel—his men had tumbled to the deck, one unconscious, the other moaning with a hand clapped to his bloody scalp.

Silas leapt up and took the wheel.

"We're into the teeth of it!" he yelled, talking not to his crew, not even to himself, but to his ship. "Steady against the waves! Steady!"

The wind whipped hard against the *McLane*'s side, and she rolled hard with a strong swell.

"Into the storm. The teeth of the storm!" said Silas, checking his bearings as best he could as the ship lifted and turned at the same time.

He had her. He had her.

"I feel the wind at my face," he said, reciting an old sailor's poem as the rain pelted the bridge windscreen. "Come around, come around, there's fight in us yet!"

37

Quàng Ninh Province

Zeus held his breath. The first tank was now beyond the pickup truck that had been fashioned into an IED. The second tank was just reaching the end of the bridge. The third and fourth were about midspan, bumper to bumper.

The night cracked. Zeus thought it was thunder from the storm. Then there was a flash from the road—the truck being detonated.

Then a louder, deeper explosion, and a rumble that felt as if the ground were being pulled away. The bridge went down, taking two tanks with it.

Shrapnel and dirt flew in the air. Zeus pushed his head down. He smelled wet grass and metal.

Two more tanks came around the bend. There was a whistle in the air—mortar fire.

The shells popped around the two tanks, black hammers pounding through the dark curtain of rain. One hit against the hull, but did no damage. One of the tank commanders began firing his 12.7 mm gun, though he couldn't possibly have a target.

More mortar shells. More tanks. The ground rumbled with explosions.

Zeus raised his head. The platoon commander had been a short distance away on his right. As soon as the bridge exploded, he had jumped up with one of his men and run down to a position near the road, covering the ravine where the tanks had fallen in.

"Zeus, we gotta get across to the other side!" yelled Christian behind him.

Another tank came around the bend. The tank commander in the turret was firing his 12.7 mm machine gun, spraying the road near the blown-out bridge. He was firing blindly, but the spray of bullets was deadly nonetheless.

A line of mortar shells walked up toward the tank. There was a flash and a puff of smoke; an acrid smell filled the air.

The tank stopped dead. One of the mortar shells had struck the top of the open turret, scoring a direct hit inside.

"The Vietnamese are damn good with those mortars!" yelled Christian. He tugged at Zeus's arm. "Come on! Back!"

Zeus turned and ran back up the hill. Three tanks seemed to burst around the corner. The mortar shells rained down; the tanks continued forward. Two entered the ravine. There was another explosion—one had hit a mine.

Zeus slipped and fell. A tank round whipped through the air. It didn't land anywhere close—the large shell cleared the hill and traveled several miles—but the sound was frightening, as if the air was splitting wide open. He was wet, drenched; the rain pounded him.

Zeus struggled to his feet. He started moving again, toward what he thought was the ravine, only to realize he was moving toward the road. He slid down on his butt, freezing in place as he tried to make sense of the scene before him.

He was supposed to cross the ravine and the creek at its bottom about seventy-five yards from the bridge, well away from the antitank mines. He began moving backward, then turned and finally found the edge of the drop. He ran alongside it for a few strides, then slipped and fell, tumbling down toward the water. Along the way he hit his head on a rock, smacking it hard enough to hurt, though not enough to do any real damage.

Thunder cracked overhead, and the sky flashed with lightning. In the flash he saw that he was still close to the bridge—not more than twenty yards away.

He stood, then saw the leading edge of a tank coming straight for him.

Zeus threw himself down as the ZTZ99 loomed overhead. The driver attempted to steer through the ridge at a right angle, but either the wet grass or his own lack of skill made that impossible.

There was a roar. Exhaust and mud packed into Zeus's face and body.

He thought he would be run over, but in fact the tank missed him by six or seven yards. He lay there for a moment, stunned, unsure exactly what had happened. Then something took hold of him, something deep in his soul. He got to his feet and began running after the tank as it climbed the other side of the ravine. It was in its lowest gear, sure-footed against the mud and rocks. Zeus grabbed onto the light at the right rear, pulling himself onto the back of the tank.

There was a rail at the back of the turret. He took hold and hung on as the tank stood nearly straight up, rising up the side of the ravine. The angle was so severe he thought the tank would fall off backward, and he would be crushed beneath it, this time for real. But it pitched down sharply as it neared the top of the ridge, gravity helping it over the summit.

Zeus pulled himself forward to the hatchway. It was closed, the tank buttoned down.

"Open up, you bastard," he screamed, pounding on the hatchway.

He'd lost his mind. It was worse than when he'd been at the border, when they'd attacked the depot. He was completely insane, rain pounding through him.

And yet he was confident he was going to take this tank. He was going to wait until the hatch opened, and pull out the man who popped up, kill him, and then take the tank. He pushed over to the side, grabbing the machine gun, steadying himself as the tank rumbled across a patch of rocks and uneven ground.

Something moved behind him.

Zeus turned, saw two men leaping upward. Thinking they were Chinese soldiers, he started to swing the gun around, then realized they were part of the antitank team—the volunteers with the grenades.

One of them gave him a raised fist, recognizing him.

"The hatch is locked!" yelled Zeus.

Neither man made any sign that they had heard him. Instead, one placed a charge on the hatchway. His companion pulled Zeus off to the side.

The charge exploded as they hit the ground. As Zeus rolled down, the Vietnamese soldiers sprang to their feet. Already the third man in the team, who'd been running alongside the tank as they set the charge, had scrambled to the top. He had a long pry bar, and in one smooth motion, pushed the damaged hatchway far enough aside to squeeze in a grenade.

He jumped, then all three men on the team ducked down, signaling at Zeus to do the same.

There was a barely audible pop. The tank stopped moving.

Zeus followed the Vietnamese soldiers as they ran back toward the second bridge. The mortars had stopped firing. The tanks were launching their own shells, though all seemed to be aimed too far away.

Christian met him a few yards from the bridge.

"What the hell happened to you?" he shouted into Zeus's ear.

"I went crazy."

"You look like it. Come on."

The Vietnamese engineers were still configuring the explosives under the structure. Though six or seven tanks had been destroyed, the Chinese had found a route across the ravine. They mustered the tanks on the road near the burned out shell of the pickup and the Z99 it had damaged.

"They won't go over the bridge," predicted Christian. "They'll be too careful now."

"That's fine with us," said Zeus. "We want them to stop."

The company commander was in a small building about a hundred yards from the bridge. Zeus and Christian ran across the open field toward it. With every step, Zeus was sure the tanks would spot them and begin firing.

When they made it to the building, they saw the CO standing in the front room behind the blown out window, gazing intently at the bridge with his binoculars.

"You can't stay here!" yelled Zeus. "The Chinese will blow up any building they can see."

The commander gave Zeus a puzzled look.

"You gotta get out," said Zeus. He motioned with his hands and arms.

The commander stayed put.

"Where the hell is Chaū?" asked Zeus.

"Damned if I know," said Christian. "I thought he was with you."

"Out," said Zeus. "We gotta get out."

Two of the Chinese tanks had been sent down the road as scouts. They drove at about five miles an hour. Both commanders had their tops open and were scanning the ground ahead, firing their machine gun indiscriminately. They couldn't have many targets—the rain was heavy and the Vietnamese ambushers were well hidden.

There were several more tanks behind them. A few had lights, but the others had either been damaged or turned off by the crews, who realized they were helping the Vietnamese attack.

The two lead tanks stopped.

"Out of here now!" shouted Zeus.

He grabbed the Vietnamese commander and dragged him shouting from the building. One of his men jumped on Zeus as he pulled him out of the door, and they collapsed in a tumble. Christian threw himself against the scrum, trying to push the men away from the building.

The first round from the tanks missed very high, whipping well overhead. But that was enough to convince the Vietnamese that Zeus's idea was the right one. They stopped fighting and scrambled away from the building.

The next round from the tank shot clear through the front of the wooden structure. The shell, designed to pierce a tank, exploded halfway into the field.

The third obliterated its target. By that time, Zeus and the others had joined the two-man demolition team behind some rocks thirty yards from the far end of the bridge.

"Ten bucks says they stop right there," said Christian, watching the Chinese tee off on the few splinters that were left of the building.

Zeus raised his head as high as he dared, looking at the area. The surrounding marsh was relatively deep and muddy; even without more rain the tanks might not be able to make it through.

Assuming the bridge was blown.

There was a loud clap overhead.

"Is that them or thunder?" asked Christian.

"I think it's thunder," said Zeus.

"Man, we are soaked."

"We need all the rain we can get."

"They're moving!" said Christian.

The Vietnamese commander had apparently seen it as well. He huddled next to the engineers.

The tanks moved forward slowly. They must be blind, or nearly blind; in this downpour, their infrared sensors would be useless, and it was a good bet that their optical sights were fogged and cloudy as well.

But obviously they'd been given orders to advance. Did they realize that was a bridge they were coming close to? In the rain, the guardrails didn't look like much.

First one, then the other went onto the bridge. When the first one was about halfway across, the commander raised his hand and gave the order to blow the bridge. The engineer pushed the detonator.

Nothing happened.

They tried again. Twice. Nothing. The first tank reached their side.

"Shit!" yelled Christian, rising.

"Where the hell are you going?" said Zeus.

"You're not the only nut!"

Christian started running for the bridge. One of the engineers joined him.

Zeus stared for a moment, then got up and followed.

Hate

厭恨

1

Quàng Ninh Province

Zeus ran across the field toward the marsh and the bridge. His feet sloshed through the wet field, the water sucking at the soles of his boots. The rain felt like a hose, washing him down as he ran.

The storm intensified with every step. It was a blessing—it meant the Chinese would be trapped—but it was a curse as well, limiting the Vietnamese counterattack. And if they didn't blow the final bridge right now, everything would be lost—the Chinese tanks would ford the first ravine and stay on the road past this low area, moving to Hai Phong despite the rain. The tanks would simply speed past any effort to stop them, and once in the harbor, the armored spearhead could wait for reinforcement, which would surely arrive as soon as the winds died down.

So they had to blow the bridge.

He heard a splash in front of him, then saw something moving on the ground. The first thing he thought was that it was an alligator. Then he saw an arm—Christian's. He'd fallen.

Zeus grabbed his arm and pulled him upright.

"Goddamn rain," complained Christian as he pulled away. "Come on."

Zeus followed. The two tanks that had headed the column were now across the bridge, moving down the road. Zeus heard the rattle of a machine gun over the roar of the rising wind, but it was impossible to know if the gunfire was coming from the tanks or the Vietnamese.

Zeus cupped his hands over his eyes, trying to see through the rain. Someone was moving on the right side of the bridge. Assuming it was the Vietnamese soldier, he started in his direction. After only a step he slipped and fell facedown into the flooded marsh. The water pushed hard against his side. The rain was falling so hard that the marsh was becoming a stream, and an angry one at that.

It'd be a river before this was done.

A man was climbing along the steel understructure. Zeus made his way toward him. The water was already above his knees.

It was the Vietnamese engineer, checking the wire lines. He yelled something to Zeus. The wind carried his shout, but it was in Vietnamese, and Zeus had no idea what he was saying.

The steel beam that supported the bridge was just wide enough so he could put his knees on either side of the rise that split it. He began crawling upward, grasping the metal to steady himself against the wind. He found a wire running up the support and followed it to the charges.

"Got it! Got it!" Christian's voice came on the wind, but Zeus couldn't see him. And he had no idea what he meant.

The first charge was taped around the beam about a third of the way up. Zeus followed the wire to the posts. He tightened the screws though they were already hard against their stops, and moved on.

Zeus ducked down as the arch approached the underside of the bridge. A charge had been planted at the very peak, in the little triangular curve at the top of the arch. To reach it, Zeus had to lay down across the steel, the metal rib in his face and chest. He hugged the beam as the wind picked up, his fingers crawling across the charge as he attempted to find the connection posts. He found them. The wire seemed secure. He tightened the bolts, his fingers so slippery he couldn't even tell if he was turning them or not.

The beam began to vibrate. Zeus let go of the charge and hugged the bridge, wrapping his legs as well as his arms around the metal. He thought it was the wind, gusting, then realized from the heavy, throaty sound that another tank was approaching . . . was, in fact, already on the bridge, driving above him.

And maybe another and another.

It was too late. *Too late.*

They could still blow the bridge. It would still slow them down. Four or five tanks weren't going to make a difference.

Go.

Go!

Zeus started to crawl back down. He couldn't see where he was going because of the rain. He raised his hand to wipe his eyes clear, but as he did, he slipped and started to fall.

He threw himself back against the beam, clinging for dear life.

It was no good. He was too wet to get a grip. He let his feet down, then fell into the flooded marsh below.

Zeus smacked into a deep puddle of water. His feet collapsed beneath him and he slipped backward, falling so his head plunged below the surface of the water. Though it was just barely over his face, he still managed to get water up his nose. Coughing, he rolled over and staggered to his feet, pushing away from the bridge.

A light moved across it—one of the tanks.

A gust of wind slammed so hard against his back that Zeus felt himself turning around involuntarily. He hunched down and began making toward the field, trudging through the water and mud. What had been just a wet field just a few minutes before was now a torrent of water.

The way the water was rising, it might go over the bridge. Maybe the Chinese would be stopped after all.

Zeus heard a series of rumbles. Unsure whether they were thunder or cracks from the ZTZ99's 120mm guns, he turned back toward the bridge to see what was going on. A flash of lightning revealed the silhouettes of two tanks on the bridge, just starting to cross. Several more approached behind them.

There were already five across. The first two were about fifty yards from the bridge, each on one side of the road. Three more clustered in a row, moving slowly toward them.

Something ran by on his left.

Three figures—one of the attack teams.

Zeus started to follow, trailing by about ten yards. Part of him knew it was foolish. The madman that had taken him over just a short while before had vanished. But the soldier left in control had no better plan.

"Christian!" he yelled. "Christian!"

Something moved on the tank ahead.

Tracers flew.

Zeus threw himself down.

A red light flashed to his right, too large, too jagged, to be gunfire. Zeus turned his head, and saw a black jumble falling in his direction, moving in slow motion against the howling wind. There was a scream above the roar, a cry for help, and a terrible reverberation that shook deep into the earth.

The Vietnamese had managed to blow the charges on the bridge.

2

Manila, the Philippines

Ric Kerfer pushed the glass toward the bartender, contemplating the critical question of the moment: another bourbon, or switch to beer?

There were good arguments either way. Lately, bourbon messed with his stomach, not a particularly pleasant situation. It wasn't automatic, though. There was some sort of equation involved: X amount over whatever it was yielded problems. But what X was, and whether those problems increased geometrically or not beyond it, had yet to be determined.

On the other hand, the beer in this allegedly first-class Manila establishment was decidedly second-rate. The Japanese offerings were basically Japanese. Kerfer liked much that was Japanese, but nothing involving alcohol. Tsingtao—Chinese—was out of the question. Which left Stella, an Italian lager. And what the fuck did the wops know about beer?

Espresso, sure. Grappa, definitely. Wine, eh. But beer?

"Sir?"

"Yeah, I'll take another bourbon," said Kerfer. It was research.

He leaned back on the barstool, surveying the *lounge*, as the Manila First-Class Oasis called itself. The bar was about the last place anyone in the world would look for a hard-ass SEAL leader like Kerfer, which was exactly why he was here.

Unfortunately for Kerfer, he wasn't quite so impossible to find as he had hoped.

"Either you hit the lottery or you're getting some money under the table from somewhere."

Kerfer glanced up into the mirror behind the bar. One of his old sea daddies, Jacob Braney, was standing with his arms folded about twenty paces away.

Kerfer scowled into the mirror.

"Fuck you, chief," he said as Braney came next to him.

"And yourself back, asshole."

"Drink?"

"At these prices? You're buying."

"Scotch," Kerfer told the bartender. "Worst crap you got."

Chief Braney had served under Kerfer during his first SEAL command. While officers didn't admit it, old sea dogs like Braney had a hell of a lot to teach them, especially when they were still wet behind the ears as Kerfer had been.

One of the things that made Kerfer different was the fact that he admitted it. He considered Braney one of his best teachers in the service, and one of the few men he was truly close to now.

Not that an outsider would ever know it from their conversation.

"God, how the hell do you live with yourself, drinking in a place like this?" asked Braney after his drink arrived. "Look at this—all these guys are wearing suits."

"I think of it like I'm goin' to the zoo."

Braney laughed. He'd left the Navy a few years before; after six months catching up on all the sleep he'd missed, he'd gone back to work, first as a contract CIA worker, then with the National Security adviser's office. He'd never been forthcoming with the details of his employment in either case, though Kerfer knew the general lay of the land, and had even worked with him a few times.

"So, to what do I owe the pleasure?" asked Kerfer.

"Can't a guy just wander in to see an old friend and bum a drink?"

"Sure. And Cinderella's sittin' upstairs with her legs spread, waiting for me."

Braney smiled and drained the Scotch. "Another," he said, pushing it toward the bartender.

"We need something done really fast, in a place you've been very recently," said Braney.

"Uh-huh."

"Boss asked for you specifically."

"I'll bet."

"Well, I think they thought you were in the States," said Braney. "I was sent to track you down."

"You really should get a better job," said Kerfer.

———

A half hour later, driving to the airport, Braney handed Kerfer a sat phone and gave him the outlines of his mission.

"There are some goodies from our Russian friends that need to be delivered to Vietnam. They'll tell you where once you're in the air."

"Why not tell me now?"

"I don't think they're sure themselves. It's all quiet, you know."

"That country is one big fuckup." Kerfer stopped talking as Braney passed a pair of slow-moving trucks. Driving was not the chief's forte. He'd once nearly driven straight off a bridge in Venezuela on a clear, dry day when he hadn't had a drink for a week.

Which, come to think of it, might have been half the problem.

"I don't get much input on foreign affairs," Braney told him as he pulled back into the lane, barely missing an oncoming Suzuki compact. "I'm just the messenger."

"Well, send them back the message that it's one big fuckup."

"I'm sure they'll listen with all ears. Don't use the phone to call out unless it's an A-1 emergency. And if things fuck up bad, they aren't gonna want to know you."

"Feeling's mutual, I'm sure."

3

Quàng Ninh Province

Zeus watched as the bridge fell into the marsh, the tanks falling like toys. He was twenty yards away from the edge of the bridge, if that, but the howl of the wind was so strong that he couldn't hear the crash.

He felt it, though, the earth moving beneath his chest in a long, violent ripple. He watched from his knees, shielding his eyes with his hand. A bank of steam filled the air where the bridge had been. He rose, leaning forward to see through it, then immediately threw himself down, ducking below the tracers from one of the tanks that had already crossed.

A yellow light moved into the space where the bridge had been, crawling forward at a snail's pace. Had the driver not seen the bridge go down? Suddenly the light dropped, the dark shadow behind it disappearing.

Zeus crawled to his right, toward the edge of the ravine. The water was rising rapidly, filled not only by the rain but the runoff from higher ground.

There were figures in the water, and big black boxes—overturned tanks.

Another ZTZ99 started firing from the right side of the ravine, before the bridge. Men moved. Zeus heard shouts on the wind.

Where the hell was Christian?

Zeus heard a motor whine nearby. He looked to his left and saw one of the tanks that had already crossed. It was backing up in his direction. He got up and began to run to his right, trying simply to get out of the way.

A flash of lightning revealed a soldier on the top of the tank. He whirled the machine gun around and began firing into the ravine, raking it with gunfire.

One of the other tanks began returning fire. The tank reversed course, starting back onto the road.

The soldier dropped from the tank.

Zeus found him curled up in the field a short distance ahead. A fresh volley of rain fell in a ferocious swoop, pelting him from all sides as the wind shifted back and forth, unable to decide on which path offered the maximum chance for destruction.

The body didn't move. Zeus reached the legs and pulled himself forward, turning the man over as he crawled next to him.

It wasn't a Vietnamese soldier. It was Christian.

———

"Hey!" yelled Zeus. "Hey!"

Christian remained motionless.

Zeus pulled himself up to a kneeling position, then tucked his shoulder down into Christian's chest. He gathered the major's legs and rose, staggering in the slippery, wet grass. There was gunfire somewhere—the high-pitched metallic sound of the machine gun cut through the whine of the wind—but he ignored it. Zeus took two steps. Realizing he was heading the wrong way, he changed course and began moving to his left in the direction of the road.

The tank that Christian had fallen from had stopped about twenty yards ahead. Zeus decided it would be safer to pass behind the tank, cross the road, and move toward the spot where the Vietnamese company was supposed to fall back to.

He'd just started behind the tank when the turret began to move. The gun barrel swung in his direction, so close at first that Zeus thought it was going to hit him. He jerked right, nearly losing his balance, then staggered forward, clear of the gun.

A shadow came at him, moving.

Zeus started to move to his right, to get out of the way. The shadow came right at him, materializing into a man. They collided, falling down.

"Leave the tank," Zeus shouted, figuring that the man was one of the Vietnamese soldiers attacking the tank. "Help me get my friend out of here! He's hurt!"

The other man didn't move. Zeus pulled Christian up over his shoulder. He heard a groan—the first sign of life.

He turned back to the soldier he'd run into. The man was two or three feet away, saying something. In the wind and the rain it was impossible to hear what it was, or even make out the language.

Lightning flashed. Zeus saw an insignia on the man's lapel. He was an officer.

Chinese. With a gun in his hand.

Zeus dove at him, using his body and Christian's to bowl him over. The gun went off near his head, and Zeus felt something burn the side of his face.

There was a rumble. A whistle—the mortars were firing again.

He couldn't see where the Chinese officer was, even though he had to be very close. Still holding Christian over his shoulder, Zeus pushed up to his knees, then to his feet. And began to run with every ounce of his strength. His feet sunk deeply into the soft, mucky earth.

I have to get away from the mortars.

The shells exploded everywhere, fists pounding the earth. Zeus spotted a low mound on his left and headed for it.

It was the house that had been blown up earlier. He detoured right, barely avoiding a crater that had been left by one of the tank shells.

His lungs ached. The rest of him was numb.

His pace, slow to begin with, slacked until he was barely making progress.

A figure rose about thirty yards from him. Another.

"I'm a friend!" he yelled. "American!"

He kept moving forward. They yelled again. Their guns were pointed in his direction.

God, it's the Chinese, he thought.

Exhausted, he slipped to his knees. As he crumbled, he felt a hand catch him and looked up into the face of Major Chaū, the translator.

4

The Gulf of Tonkin

And with a sudden crash, the worst of the storm was over.

The wind, still strong, shifted. The waves, still high, continued to pound. But the *McLane*, struggling for hours in the darkness, stood upright in the waves.

There was no longer a question of survival. The worst of the typhoon had passed.

Silas, still manning the wheel, turned to his crew. A relief team had come up; the seamen who'd been injured had been helped to sick bay.

When? Hours ago? Minutes? He couldn't remember or calculate.

His hands trembled when he took them off the wheel, turning it over to petty officer Gordon.

"Lieutenant Cradle, I'm going below to check on the ship," he told the officer of the deck.

"Sir."

It was a good, bracing response. Silas nodded.

Lt. Commander Li met him in the CIC. Her face looked bleached white, except for the purplish welts beneath her eyes.

"Commander, you were right," he told Li. "I owe you and the ship's crew an apology."

Her lower lip trembled. She half nodded, then struggled to respond. "Commander, the merchant ships . . ."

Silas frowned, waiting for the news.

"The ships are three miles from us," she told him. "East."

"East?"

"Yes, sir. We're between them and the port," she told him. "You did it."

"*We* did it," said Silas. "Get the boarding teams ready. I'll be on the bridge."

5

Quàng Ninh Province

Christian was dead.

There was no way of knowing which of the several bullets that had hit him had killed him. Most had left large gouges in his body, thick angry welts.

The hole near the middle of his forehead was small, cut by a 9 mm bullet. Probably the same one that had grazed Zeus on the cheek, though no one would ever know for sure.

For much of the time he had known him, Zeus had despised Christian. He'd been an uptight prig at West Point, an insufferable know-it-all as Perry's aide.

A crazy idiot when they'd escaped through China.

But now Zeus remembered him as a valuable soldier. He'd proven himself on the Hainan mission.

And in China, and again blowing the last bridge. Maybe he'd been the one who fixed the charge—no one would ever know, because the sapper had died as well.

You're not the only nut.

———

The storm and the destruction of the two bridges broke the Chinese tank brigade into three different knots. The rising water and flooded fields made it impossible for the tanks to advance. Using coordinates from the company near the second bridge, the Vietnamese began sending 120 mm artillery rounds against the five tanks that had come farthest south.

Their marksmanship left something to be desired. Out of two dozen shells, only one had struck a tank. The commander, who had precious few armor-piercing rounds to begin with, called a halt to the shelling, deciding that his men would do better once the storm subsided. But the shelling convinced the Chinese that it would be foolhardy to remain where they were, and the lead element attempted to pull back. All but one of their tanks floundered in the flooded ravine.

The bullet that had grazed Zeus had done only superficial damage, but it was a wound nonetheless, and Major Chaū insisted that Zeus go to a hospital to get it cared for. Chaū was already spooked by Christian's death, worried that General Trung would hold him personally responsible.

"I'll tell him what happened," Zeus assured the translator. "It's not your fault."

Chaū's eyes brimmed with tears.

"The company commander says there is a car we can use in the village about two miles back. I'll bring it back."

"I'll go with you," said Zeus.

They left Christian's body in the rain. There was nothing to cover him with.

Zeus and Major Chaū trudged down the road nearly shoulder to shoulder, silently. When they reached the village, Chaū asked Zeus if he wanted something to eat. Zeus shook his head. His stomach was wrenched tight; he'd never get anything into it.

What he wanted was to see Anna. He wanted to see her and hug her and hold her in bed, to stay there for days and weeks.

The car wasn't where it was supposed to be. They went to the nearest house and pounded on the door. Zeus thought the house was empty and the village abandoned, but that wasn't the case: the door opened and a middle-aged woman, bundled in a raincoat, appeared.

She knew nothing about a car, but gave them directions to the police station. They weren't of much help. It took nearly an hour before Major Chaū managed to find a vehicle. The owner gave them the keys, deciding it was safer to remain at home.

They drove back to the company, put Christian's body in the trunk, then reversed course.

A few minutes later, there was a fresh crack in the storm, a loud thud. By the time the second one came, Zeus realized it wasn't thunder—the Chinese tanks were firing their guns at the village where they'd found the car, deciding to take revenge on whatever they could. Surely they were firing blind. Even if there hadn't been a storm, the topography and distance made it impossible to see the village from where they were. The only guidance they had were their maps.

Major Chaū stepped on the gas.

"They'll kill everyone in those houses," said Zeus.

Chaū didn't answer. It was too late to get the people out—the shells were falling rapidly now, and it would be just a matter of luck where they exploded.

Zeus dropped his head on his chest, rubbing the rain from his hair.

———

Calling Perry to tell him about Christian's death was the most difficult thing Zeus had ever done. He punched the numbers on the sat phone tentatively, then put it to his ear. He hoped the general wouldn't answer.

Perry picked up on the first ring.

"General, it's Zeus."

"Major?"

"We stopped the tanks. They're definitely stopped."

"Good."

"The advance is definitely slowed. For now at least. It'll take them some time to regroup. They may be able to find a place to get across the fields once the storm stops and the water goes down. But they won't get to Hai Phong tonight. Or probably not tomorrow."

"Excellent. Good work, Major. How's Christian holding up?"

Zeus couldn't speak for a moment. When he did, his voice trembled.

"Major Christian, sir, didn't make it."

Perry said nothing. The silence grew until Zeus couldn't stand it anymore.

"He . . . the Vietnamese put demolitions on one of the bridges and something went wrong. He went back and fixed them," said Zeus. "We went back. And then, uh, he went into the field. There was fighting there, and then, he was trying to make his way back."

"Where's his body?" said Perry.

"I have it."

The silence lasted for only a few seconds, but they were painful to Zeus. Finally, he had to speak.

"Should I bring him to the embassy?"

"Take him to the hospital where you were treated. Someone will meet you there. What shape are you in?"

"I'm fine."

"Report to me at Trung's headquarters."

"Yes, sir."

———

Chaū suggested that they put Christian in the backseat and make it look as if he were injured rather than dead. Once inside the hospital, they could take the body directly to the morgue.

"I would guess that the general does not want people to know it is an American officer," said Chaū. "That is why he would be taken to the hospital."

Zeus closed his eyes as they opened the trunk. A wild thought sprang into his head: it had all been a dream, it hadn't happened, at least not the way he remembered it.

But Christian's body, drained of blood, sopping wet, was curled in the small space before him. In the darkness, Zeus couldn't see his face. He was thankful for that.

———

By now, the hospital seemed familiar, as if it were a place Zeus where belonged. A gurney and two nurses met them in the long hall. Zeus stepped back, pushing against the wall as the medical people took over. Water dripped from him to the floor, puddling around his feet.

He watched the stretcher disappear. He kept thinking Christian would rise and hop off.

A hand folded gently around his arm.

Anna!

It was only a nurse. She tugged him lightly.

"Your cheek," said Major Chaū. "She wants to see to clean it."

"I want to be seen by Dr. Anway," said Zeus, going with her. "Dr. Anway. Tell her."

Chaū told the nurse. She shook her head as they spoke in Vietnamese.

"You have to go with her," said Chaū. "She'll treat you."

"I want Dr. Anway."

"She says she's not here," said Chaū.

"She works the night shift. Did she leave?"

Chaū spoke to the nurse again. This time she said very little, instead prodding Zeus toward the wards.

"She doesn't know. You better go with her and get treated," said Chaū.

"Where are you going?" Zeus asked as Chaū started to turn away.

"I will look after the arrangements. Then I must go to General Trung. I will have a car for you, to wait. I will meet you back at the bunker."

Zeus let himself be led downstairs. The nurse sat him in a small, nearly empty room right off the stairwell. A polished steel stool sat in the middle of the room. There was no other furniture, no med cart, no instruments or monitors.

She told him something in Vietnamese, then left.

The wet, muddy clothes weighed Zeus down. As he stared at the floor, a haze seemed to fall over him. He sat and stared, unable to think.

A short time later, the door opened. Two nurses, neither of whom he'd ever seen before, entered. One had a tray with a basin and cloth; the other carried what looked like a tackle box.

"Is Dr. Anway here?" he asked them. "Dr. Anway?"

The nurses glanced at each other.

"Do you speak English?" he asked. "I know I'm probably messing up the pronunciation. I'm sorry."

The nurse with the tackle box told him something in Vietnamese and put her hand gently on his arm.

"I'm not nervous or anything," said Zeus. He pointed at his face. "This probably looks like hell, but I'm okay. It doesn't even hurt, really."

It stung when they cleaned it, spraying it with a liquid that the nurse had in the box. Zeus tried not to flinch.

The women discussed something in Vietnamese, then motioned that he should take off his clothes. They wanted to see if there were more wounds.

"I'm all right, really," said Zeus.

They insisted. The one who had brought in the basin to wash him put her hands on his shirt to unbutton it.

Zeus jerked to stop her, grabbing her hand. She shrank back. He let go.

"I'm sorry," he said. "I'm sorry. I'll do it."

Zeus peeled off his sodden shirt. They were on their guard now, afraid of him.

There was nowhere to put the shirt. He let it drop to the floor. It made a loud *ker-plunk*, almost a splash. He peeled off his undershirt.

His arms and his chest were crisscrossed with bruises and scrapes and cuts. They were a map of his war.

Their war. He was just a bystander, an adviser. Or at least was supposed to be.

As was Christian.

You're not the only nut.

The nurses cleaned him up gingerly. None of his cuts was fresh enough to sting as they sprayed and daubed. After his chest, they wanted to work on his legs.

Zeus, reluctant, got off the stool and pulled down his pants, leaving his sodden underwear in place. They were nurses, but he felt embarrassed before them.

"Dr. Anway?" Zeus asked as they inspected the bruises on his shins. "Is she working tonight? I'm pretty sure she is."

Neither responded. Zeus resigned himself to finding Anna on his own.

A male attendant entered as the room with a small tape measure, and used it to take the roughest of measurements of Zeus's body—across the shoulders, legs, torso.

"I could use some underwear, too," said Zeus as the boy started to leave.

He nodded, then went out the door. A few minutes later, he returned with a pair of surgical scrubs, handing them directly to Zeus. They were stiff and scratchy, but dry. There was no underwear. The boy said something in Vietnamese that Zeus took to be an apology.

"That's okay," Zeus told him. "Thank you. Thanks."

He stood up. The nurses, who were trying to bandage his right knee, backed away quickly.

"I'm going to get dressed now," he told them. He repeated the words slowly and motioned with his hand. "I want to get dressed."

One of the nurses said something sternly. Zeus pulled on the shirt, hoping they would get the hint and leave. When they didn't, he turned away and faced the wall.

Taking off his underpants felt as if he were pulling off a bandage. But the cool air on his skin was a relief. He balanced on one foot, then the other, pulling on the scrubs.

They were too short by about an inch. Barefoot, he turned around.

The nurses were gathering their things, facing the other way.

"Do you have any shoes?" Zeus asked. "Something for my feet? Shoes?"

As he pointed, the door opened. The boy had returned with a pair of sandals.

"It's like magic," said Zeus. He smiled and sat on the stool. To his surprise, the sandals fit perfectly.

He took his sat phone and put it in the pocket of his shirt; it hung out precariously. He bent down to the pile of sodden clothes on the floor and folded them into a bundle as best he could.

The nurse who had wheeled in the cart began talking to him, pointing to his arms and legs, giving him directions on how he should care for his injuries. Zeus nodded solemnly; in truth, he probably paid as much attention to these incomprehensible instructions as to any medical instructions he had ever received.

"Dr. Anway?" he asked when she finished. "I want to see her."

The nurse held out her hands, indicating she didn't know what he was saying.

Zeus trailed the women out of the room, his legs stiff and a little wobbly from sitting. The hospital was quieter than he remembered, almost serene.

He went to the ward where he had first seen Anna, then stopped. What if she had changed her mind about him?

She wouldn't.

He stepped into the room, sidestepping along the wall so he wouldn't be in the way.

The ward looked bigger than it had the other day. Zeus saw a woman's back at the far end of the room. His heart jumped.

He was about halfway there when she turned and he realized it wasn't Anna. She gave him a quizzical glance.

"Dr. Anway?" he asked. "Is she here?"

"Who?"

"You speak English?" Zeus asked. "I'm looking for Dr. Anway. I'm, uh, Zeus Murphy. Major Murphy? She worked on me . . . I was her patient. I *am* her patient." He looked down at his scrubs. "I was just patched up. I wanted to make sure . . . I thought, you know, she was a doctor so I wanted her to check me out."

The nurse shook her head, her mastery of English overwhelmed by the sheer amount of words that had flooded from Zeus's mouth. She pointed to the floor: a small puddle had dripped there from his wet clothes.

"I'm sorry," he told her.

"You are a patient?"

"Yes. Dr. Anway's."

She came over and put her hand on his arm. He let her guide him out of the ward. When she turned in the direction of the stairs, he stopped.

"I wanted to see Dr. Anway before I left."

She frowned at him, then turned and walked in the other direction. Zeus decided his best bet would be to follow.

The room where the shooting had occurred was on his right. He glanced in as he passed, only to make sure Anna wasn't there. It was empty.

A middle-aged man in a lab coat came out into the hallway. "You are Major Murphy," he said.

"Yes."

"I am Dr. Quan."

Zeus moved his clothes to his left arm and held his right hand out to shake. The doctor hesitated a moment, then clamped his hand around Zeus's.

"You need something for your things," said the doctor. "Come into my office."

"Thanks."

Zeus followed him into the room, which was more like a small alcove off a narrow corridor that ran perpendicular to the main hall. The nurse Zeus had followed was standing at the edge of the alcove, watching apprehensively.

"Thank you," Zeus said as she started to leave. "Thanks."

"Here," said the doctor, taking a mesh bag from behind a filing cabinet near the wall. He held it open. Zeus squeezed his clothes in. More water dripped on the floor.

"I'm very sorry," Zeus told him.

"Someone will clean it up. Don't worry."

The office space was small, with a metal desk pushed up against the side, and the filing cabinet taking most of the space opposite it. The doctor seemed not to have a chair, not even behind the desk.

"I wanted to see Dr. Anway," Zeus said. "She had helped me before. We're friends now."

"Dr. Anway."

"Anna." Zeus couldn't believe that anyone who worked here, let along another doctor, wouldn't know her. "Where is she? Is she working today?"

"Dr. Anway is not here." Dr. Quan pushed his lips together, his cheeks pinching inward.

"Where is she?" Zeus asked.

"I don't know."

"What happened to Anna?" said Zeus, leaning closer.

"She was arrested as a traitor," said the doctor, looking down. "I know nothing else."

6

South of Hanoi

Perry needed to make the call to Washington from outside the bunker, not just because the signal for his scrambled sat phone wouldn't reach from beneath all the cement and metal grids, but because he could not trust the Vietnamese not to listen in. He certainly would under the circumstances.

Unfortunately, that meant standing in the rain and the wind to make the call. He pulled the collar of his raincoat up and took his cap out and put it onto his head, pulling the beak down over his eyes until he could barely see.

The phone rang once on the other side before Walter Jackson, the President's National Security adviser, answered.

Personally. One measure of the importance of his mission.

"Walter, this is Perry."

"General."

"I need to talk to the President. As soon as possible."

"That's not a problem, General. He happens to be right here in my office."

There was a slight delay as the President picked up another phone.

"Harland. Bringing good news, I hope."

"No, Mr. President. I'm not."

"Okay." Greene's voice dropped about a half octave, and the cheeriness was gone. "Tell it to me straight."

"One of my men died in action."

Perry explained the circumstances briefly. Neither Greene nor Jackson interrupted.

"I think that, unfortunately, under the circumstances, it was a necessary sacrifice," said the President.

His voice was so emotionless a shudder ran through Perry's body. The general immediately upbraided himself. The President's attitude was hardly surprising; it was exactly the way a commander ought to think. The stakes were much higher, much more important, than the life of any one individual.

It was the way Perry should think. It was the way he had thought in the past.

"Our read on the situation is a little more positive today," said Jackson, filling the silence. "Between the action in the east and the storm, the Chinese advance is stalled. If you can capitalize on that, delay it even further, that would be a good thing."

"The Russian missiles should be there soon," said the President. "I'm still working with Congress. Eventually, you'll have real support. I may send SOCCOM; we're discussing that right now."

SOCCOM was shorthand for Special Operations Command— Special Forces, Rangers, SEALs. Covert units the President could essentially sneak into the country without telling Congress.

"Continue helping the Vietnamese," added Greene. "Spare no effort. We have to slow down the Chinese."

Perry's throat suddenly thickened. "Mr. President, I think under the circumstances we're going too far. Given the status on Congress, if we have more casualties—"

"Not to be crass, Harland," said Jackson, "but what casualties are we talking about? We haven't committed troops."

"One of my majors just died."

"I'm sorry about your man, Harland. Those are my orders," said Greene.

"George—"

"If you're unable to carry out your mission—"

"That's not necessary," said Perry, almost under his breath.

"Good," said Greene.

Perry struggled to articulate his objections to escalation by pieces. Bringing in special ops troops now for more missions wasn't going to change the war. The only effect would be dead Americans—more people like Christian.

But the President had already hung up. He punched off the phone and went back inside the bunker.

7

Hanoi

The door to Anna's apartment was open. There was no one inside, and the place seemed neat and completely in order, as if she had just gone down to a neighbor's. But she hadn't.

No one in the building answered his or her door when he knocked. Not that he would have been able to talk to them anyway.

Zeus had no idea what to do. Finally he went back to the hotel, changed into his BDUs—the only clean clothes he had left—and had the driver Chaū had left him take him to the bunker.

—————

"What the hell did you do?"

General Perry's words slapped Zeus as harshly as the rain had. He curled his fingers into fists and looked at the ground.

"Excuse me, sir?"

"What did I tell you? I told you to stay away from the action. Why the hell aren't you in civilian clothes?"

"This is all I had that was dry."

"What the hell did you think you were doing?" Perry shook his head. "You're out of control, Major. I gave you orders—you know what our mission here is. We are *not* here. We are *not* involved. I thought you understood that."

There were any number of things Zeus could say, but Perry was in no mood to be interrupted. His stars were screaming, and the only option was to shut up.

"What the hell got into you, Zeus? You were the responsible one."

"General, I can't say—"

"You're damn straight, you can't say. Why did you let Christian jump on that tank?"

Perry had obviously gotten a report from the Vietnamese.

"I didn't let him do anything, sir," said Zeus. "He ran before I could stop him."

"Christian did that? Christian ran into the line of fire?"

"It wasn't like that. There were explosives set to a bridge, and they didn't go off. Christian thought he could fix them. He went with the demo guy and I went after him."

"What the hell does he know about demolitions? Jesus, Zeus! You should have stopped him."

"I *did* run after him. In the storm, it was hard to tell what was going on."

"Damn it, Murphy! I told you to stay away."

Zeus felt his cheeks burning. Part of him realized that Perry was just unleashing his frustration, fairly or unfairly, on the object that happened to be closest at hand.

Unfairly. Perry's attitude was one hundred and eighty degrees from where it had been only a few days before. He'd approved the mission to Hainan, which was even more suicidal than what he and Christian had just done.

"Go back to your quarters," said Perry finally. "Don't come until you're called for."

Zeus turned on his heel and left without a word.

———

Perry folded his arms in front of his chest, angry with himself for losing control. He'd been unfair to Zeus.

But then everything about the situation was unfair. They shouldn't be here in the first place if the country wasn't going to support them.

Now he had to deal with Christian's death.

There was a knock on the door. One of Trung's colonels leaned his head inside.

"General, if you have time," said the colonel, "General Trung would request to talk to you."

Perry walked with him to Trung's office, his mind still fixed on the problem of Christian. It was the lying to the family that bothered him. He couldn't tell them what had happened because of where it had happened, so he'd have to make up a story. That was lying.

It dishonored everyone.

Trung was talking to General Tri, the commander in the northeast whom they'd been helping. Perry stopped just outside the doorway.

"General Perry," said Trung in English. "We would be honored if you could join us."

"General." Perry nodded at Tri.

"We are very grateful, once more, for your help," said Tri. "And for the sacrifices of your men."

"Yes."

"Were you successful in obtaining the weapons?" asked Trung.

"I've been told two planeloads of Russian AT-14s are en route," said Perry. "There will be more."

"We have only the missiles for the infantrymen?" said Tri. "Nothing for the tanks?"

"That's all so far."

"As we are constituted," said Trung, "the best strategy would be to use these weapons in the north immediately. In the west we still have time."

"Agreed," said Perry.

"If Major Murphy is agreeable, we would appreciate his tactical advice," said Trung.

Perry stiffened.

"Major Murphy needs to rest," said Perry.

Trung stared at him. Perry stared back.

"The Vietnamese people are grateful for your sacrifices," said Trung finally. "As is General Tri."

"Thank you."

"We have no experience deploying that weapon," continued Trung. "We would be grateful for assistance."

Perry had been ordered to provide assistance—which meant that he should allow Murphy to help.

It was his duty.

"Once the major has rested, he can assist in developing a proper strategy," said Perry. "I'm sure he'd be happy to do so."

"Thank you, General. We are most grateful."

"Yes," said Perry. "I'm sure."

8

Hanoi

Zeus needed someone to help him deal with the Vietnamese so he could find Anna, but it was pretty clear to him that General Perry wasn't going to help. The only person he could think of who might was Ambassador Behrens. So instead of returning to the hotel, he went back to the embassy.

The rain had slackened to a light mist. That was bad, he thought; the more water, the better for the Vietnamese.

The Marine in the center hall told him the ambassador was out. He suggested he see Juliet Greig instead, and pointed Zeus toward her office.

Zeus sneezed as he went up the stairs. "That's all I need now, a cold," he muttered.

Greig's office was a suite, with two outer offices and a larger inner one. When he didn't see her in any of the rooms, Zeus decided to stand near the hallway door and wait for her. He'd been standing a few moments when he realized he smelled coffee being brewed somewhere in the vicinity. He walked toward the end of the hallway, and found a room that served as a kind of kitchenette, with a counter and a small refrigerator and a microwave.

Greig was standing in front of a Mr. Coffee, watching as fresh coffee poured into the carafe.

"Real coffee," said Zeus.

"Major Murphy." Greig, surprised, gave him an exaggerated sideways glance, then took the pot from the holder and poured a cup. "Would you like some?"

"That'd be great."

She reached up and opened the cabinet, taking down a cup. Stretched, her arm muscles showed strong definition.

"And how would you like it?" she asked.

"I'll just drink it black."

"Good choice." She handed him the cup she had already poured. "We don't have any milk. And the sugar supply is getting low."

Zeus took the coffee and held it under his nose. The steam felt good on his sinuses.

"Smell good?" she asked, her tone slightly mocking.

"My nose is a little stuffed up. I think I'm getting a cold."

"That's too bad. How's the storm?"

"It's, uh . . . wet."

"I see." She glanced down at the floor. He'd trailed rain onto the rug.

"It was worse before," said Zeus.

She poured herself a cup, then took a sip.

"Are you here for a meeting?" she asked.

"I kinda have . . . there's a problem with one of the Vietnamese doctors who helped me. She's in trouble. I was wondering if the ambassador could help."

"Let's discuss this in my office," she told him.

————

For the ambassador to intercede in a case of treason would be highly unusual, Greig told Zeus after he explained why he had come. There were all sorts of political nuances involved, and Behrens would almost certainly refuse to be involved on an official level.

Unofficially, Greig might be able to do something herself. She was the acting consul general, and as such, used to helping Americans deal with the Vietnamese authorities.

Still, she didn't hold out a lot of hope. Her body language—arms furled in front of her breasts, legs crossed in a tight wedge—emphasized the point. She sat at the edge of her desk, a few feet from him in the large inner office.

"The Vietnamese government is very hierarchical," Greig told him. "They don't take very kindly to outside interference. They're very touchy."

"I'm not trying to interfere. I just want to get her out. She's not a traitor."

"They may see things very differently. The Chinese are massacring their people."

"That doesn't give them the right to kill injured prisoners of war," said Zeus. He started to get up from the overstuffed chair. "I'm sorry to waste your time."

"Wait, wait. Relax, Major." Greig put her hands on the desk behind her, as if bracing herself. "I didn't say I wouldn't try to help. I'm just putting things into their perspective, that's all. If you're going to help her, you're going to have to understand the system she lives in."

"You don't sound very optimistic."

"I'm trying to be realistic. I'll talk to some people in the government whom I know. That's where I'll start. But with the war, obviously, I don't know how much help they'll be."

"I risked my life for them. One of my friends got killed."

"Which friend?"

Zeus was surprised that Greig didn't know about Christian.

"Some of the Vietnamese I met," he told her, deciding to backtrack. "They didn't make it."

"Mmmm." She didn't seem to believe him, but she didn't press. "Let me ask you a personal question, Zeus. What's the nature of your relationship with Dr. Anway?"

"There is no relationship."

"None?"

"She helped me, that's all. And I . . . I saw what happened."

"I'll do what I can, Major. But don't expect miracles."

9

Forthright, Ohio

Josh kicked the clod of dirt, watching it burst into a dozen small pieces as his toe launched it into the air.

His cousin had recently turned over the ground of what they called the house garden behind the barn, ready to plant some of the early vegetables. The small garden was separate from the actual farming operation. It was a full acre, elaborately laid out and carefully tended by hand. In a few months' time, it would be filled with tomatoes and cucumbers and melons, several different kinds of lettuce, and huge, long green beans that Josh remembered from his childhood as veritable swords.

The farm had been in the family for generations, through good and bad times. Mostly, they'd grown wheat and soybeans, though a good portion of the land supported dairy cows for a while, and forty acres had been devoted to corn, supposedly since the days of the Indians.

It was on the farm that Josh had first become interested in how things worked together, how different plants thrived under different conditions, and it was in the house garden that his interest was piqued. Some of the varieties they grew had been passed down for several generations. Among the prize vegetables was a particularly squat but juicy striped tomato that bore no resemblance to anything Josh had seen anywhere else.

Josh was not a farmer, for many reasons. But he did love to stand in the middle of a farm, close enough to the barn to feel its smell, or near to the machines, or out in the middle of fields that seemed to go on forever.

This was the American core, at least as he knew it. Ironically, while the rest of the world was sinking fast into depression, agriculture in America was booming. The climate pressures were helping.

Temporarily, and in select places; much of the southeast was facing a severe drought, which Josh knew would only get worse. It was a slow-motion disaster, which meant there was still some time to deal with it.

Ironically, that made people less likely to face the problem. As he'd seen in China.

Josh shook his head. The rest of the world was not his concern. War was not his problem. He was a scientist, and his job was science. The war would end. Science would not.

He kicked another clump of dirt.

Josh left the garden and walked up the little hill where they had gone sleigh-riding as a kid. He wondered if his cousins still did that.

His parents had died not far from here, in a massacre that the newspapers had compared to the much more famous *In Cold Blood* crimes. He could almost see where the house had been from the hill.

He could see it, actually, if he looked hard enough. But he didn't.

He could see it even more clearly if he closed his eyes and thought about that day. But that he never did.

Josh headed back for the house. It would be good to go back to work soon, but where exactly would he go? He was still on a stipend from the UN Climate Catch program. He had to talk to them, see what they wanted him to do.

He smelled the strong scent of coffee a good twenty paces from the back door. He went into the kitchen, where his cousin's wife, Debra, was just cleaning up.

"There you are, Josh. Fresh coffee's up."

"Thanks." He went to the cupboard and took out a large mug. When he was little, the farm had belonged to his grandfather. With the exception of the appliances and TV sets, very little had changed. The kitchen stove, a massive eight-burner, two-oven behemoth, was so old it had to be lit by hand.

"How long's your friend staying?" Debra asked.

"I, uh . . . I don't know. He's supposed to be protecting me."

"There are a lot of crazies out there," said Debra.

Josh wondered if she was worried about her kids. She didn't seem to be.

"I can talk to him and find out."

"It's no bother," she said cheerfully. "Jim might put him to work."

"Might not be a bad idea."

"I have some errands in town this morning. Want to come?"

"Nah, I'm just going to take it easy if that's okay."

"That's good." She smiled at him and disappeared to get her things.

The morning paper sat on the kitchen table. Josh folded it over and pushed it aside.

"Good morning," said Tex, coming into the kitchen.

"Morning. There's coffee."

"Thanks." The marshal went over to it. "Sleep well?"

"Passably."

The marshal filled his cup. He took three sugars.

"You leaving today?" Josh asked.

"Uh . . . I'm supposed to hang around for a few more days. We have a couple of more agents coming out."

"More?"

"We usually work in shifts. Can't be too careful."

"You really think it's necessary? I'm old news."

Tex grimaced slightly, then sat down with his coffee.

"Deb's on her way out," Josh told him. "If you're hungry, there's plenty of food."

"Some eggs, maybe."

Tex looked at him—he seemed to be expecting that Josh would make them.

"I'm not much of a cook," said Josh finally. "There's a pan under that cabinet there."

"Yeah, yeah, no—I'm, uh . . . do they mind?"

"They won't mind."

Tex went to the refrigerator and looked inside. He took out two eggs and some butter.

"Damn, I forgot to tell you last night: Mara called. She wanted you to call her back."

"Oh, okay."

Josh felt bad about just leaving her like that, but really it was the best way. A clean break. He felt too . . . if he hadn't just left, he'd probably never leave her, like a puppy pining for a master it couldn't have.

"I got the number on my phone," said Tex. "You want it?"

"When you get a chance," said Josh, getting up to refill his coffee. "Later's fine."

"Okay." The marshal looked at him for a moment, then turned back to the stove. "How do you get these burners on, you think?"

10

Hanoi

Major Chaū was waiting in the hotel lobby when Zeus got there.

"General Trung was hoping you could give us guidance on the anti-tanks weapons," said Chaū. "After you have rested."

"Let's go now," said Zeus.

———

The Chinese had devoted a Group Army to the attack in the northeast. Roughly the equivalent of a western army corps, this amounted to four divisions on paper, potentially a little more than 46,000 troops. But so far only about a quarter of the force, if that, had made it into Vietnam.

The intelligence data showed that only one armored regiment—eighty tanks—had crossed the border. About a third of the tanks had been kept near Tien Yen to deal with the counterattack there. The rest were stalled along Route 18 between Tien Yen and the bridges Tri's men had destroyed. Elements of two infantry divisions had gone south with the armor, but most of the soldiers were either in Tien Yen or farther north. Though mechanized, these soldiers would be severely hampered by the storm for at least the next twenty-four hours.

A shipment of Russian AT-14s was expected soon. General Tri wanted to take the weapons and use them against the tanks. But Zeus had a different idea: hit the infantry coming to support them instead.

"The tanks will be ready for an attack," he explained. "And they're not going anywhere. You can keep pounding them with artillery."

There was a shortage of armored-piercing shells, Tri's logistics officer explained. They were trying to get more to the front, but there was no guarantee that they would be successful.

"You have to find them," said Zeus finally. "And anyway, you're not getting AT-14s to take out all of those tanks. You're going to have to leverage what you got."

Zeus's idea of leverage was to strike the mechanized infantry as it came south in its APCs, striking from the east rather than the west. He wanted the Vietnamese to organize themselves into three-man teams that would set up multiple ambushes. The Chinese commander was conservative, and would be even more so after having had his nose bloodied with the tanks. He'd be bound to slow down his offensive.

That would give Tri time to stiffen his defenses. He could bring the rest of his tanks down from Tien Yen. If more Russian munitions arrived, they could take on the tanks.

The idea was to slow the Chinese assault in the east for a week. It would take them that long to maneuver the rest of their Group Army— and perhaps bring a second one to reinforce the attack.

"Delaying them is useful," said Trung, speaking for the first time. "But it is not a substitute for victory."

"No," said Zeus. "The idea is to stop their offensive completely. To do that, you have to do something very bold."

"And what is that?" asked Trung.

"Attack China."

————

China had obviously prepared for an offensive war. They had made their calculations and moves, and while there were still some big mysteries— Zeus still wondered why they hadn't attacked in the Lang Son area, for example—the overall shape of their strategy was clear: basically they were going to roll over Vietnam.

Since Vietnam couldn't really prevent that, the only way to upend that strategy was to get China to reevaluate it. And the only way that was going to happen was if China saw a threat to their own homeland.

"Hit Nanning with your mobilized division, and the war will grind down to a stalemate," said Zeus. "The Chinese will panic and pull back. Look at the satellite photos—there's nothing in their way. You get through the border defenses, and you have a clear drive. It's a hundred and twenty miles; you'll be there inside a day. Maybe two."

Trung appeared stunned. He looked at each of his commanders in turn, then at Zeus.

"The major has a provocative idea. It will be discussed. In the meantime, we will arrange for the strikes against the mechanized infantry, as you suggested. If time can be bought, it will be useful. Major, I am told the missiles are to arrive at Hanoi Airport within the hour. Can you retrieve them and instruct the men in their use?"

"My pleasure," said Zeus.

———

The plane was a C-130 that belonged to the Philippines army, an old "slick" as the Air Force might have called it. It landed fast on the Hanoi runway, bouncing hard on the fresh patches covering the results of earlier Chinese bombing raids.

Zeus waited near the terminal building as the plane came across the long cement apron. The storm had passed to the north, leaving humid, heavy air and a light wind in its wake.

The aircraft pirouetted around and the rear ramp slowly lowered. The pilots clearly weren't being paid by the hour.

Zeus turned to Major Chaū. "Have two of the crates carried into the hangar so I can check the weapons," he told him. "Pick them from the middle. In the meantime, load everything into the Ilyushin as fast as you can. These guys are going to want to get out of here real quick."

Zeus gestured toward the propeller-driven cargo plane sitting in the drizzle a few yards from the hangar. The Ilyushin IL-14 was a Thai commercial cargo carrier that had had the misfortune of landing in Hanoi just a few hours before the war began. Grounded during the first air raid, it had been commandeered by the Vietnamese military; it was about to be used on its first mission, delivering the antitank missiles to General Tri's men.

Watching from the hangar, Zeus saw a tall, athletic figure dressed entirely in black amble down the ramp. It was too dark to get a good view of who it was, yet the figure was familiar.

"Ah for Christ's sake, it is a small *goddamn* world," said the man, his voice loud enough to carry over the whine of the engines and the howl of the wind. "Let's see—you are Major Murphy. No relation to the infamous maker of the universal law governing how often shit rolls down in my face."

Zeus held out his hand to Ric Kerfer, the SEAL officer he'd met helping Josh MacArthur escape from Vietnam some days earlier.

"You got the money?" Kerfer sneered, looking at the hand.

"Money? I thought it was all paid for."

"It is, Major. I'm janking your chain. What the hell are you still do-ing in this shithole of a country, huh?"

"My duty."

Kerfer laughed. "You're outta your fuckin' mind."

"Is everything here?" Zeus asked.

"How the hell do I know? You think they tell me?" Kerfer walked into the hangar. The large expanse was lit by dim red lights. "Yeah, yeah—it's all here. Ninety-six AT-14Es. All with HEAT warheads. Bang-bang. What are you thinking of doing with these?"

"Blowing up some APCs," said Zeus.

"You know you gotta get pretty close." Kerfer's voice was suddenly all business. That was the way he was, Zeus knew—a cynical, screw-the-world type until things got serious. Then he was the one man you wanted watching your back. "Even with a personnel carrier. You're not going after tanks?"

"Not if we can help it."

"That's good. Because these things ain't as powerful as they claim. They'll go through some tanks. Chinese X99s?" Kerfer shrugged. "Fifty-fifty."

"I know they work," Zeus told him.

"You've used them before?"

"Once."

Kerfer scoffed.

"And you've shot them a lot?" retorted Zeus.

"More than you. Shit. Once."

Kerfer looked at the Vietnamese soldiers carrying in the two boxes for Zeus to examine. They were men in their fifties and sixties, and they strained mightily to get them inside.

"These aren't the guys using them, I hope," said Kerfer.

"No. We're taking them east."

He gestured toward the plane. Kerfer looked over.

"Fuckin' plane is older than you. Older than me," said Kerfer. "What the hell is it? A DC-3?"

"No. It's Russian."

"Fuckin' Russians. They're makin' a mint on this war." He looked at Zeus. "Tell you what, Major. Why don't you tell me what the plan is, and I'll shoot holes in it for you. Before the Chinese do."

———

Actually, Kerfer was surprised at the plan, because while not necessarily the most innovative in the world, it wasn't half bad for a blanket hugger. Leaving the tanks alone made some sense, and not just because he personally doubted the effectiveness of the Russian weapons. The Chinese would be expecting the attack there, and would undoubtedly be better prepared than the infantry supposedly running to its rescue.

But there were two big problems with Zeus's strategy. First of all, getting the teams into place to use the weapons wasn't exactly a gimme— the forces were currently southwest of the Chinese troops; Zeus wanted them northeast.

More important, the Vietnamese soldiers hadn't been trained to use the weapons.

"The ragheads used these weapons against M1s in Iraq," Kerfer explained. "They worked at night, mostly, and they had night goggles, the whole deal. Supposedly, they trained for years. What I heard is that most of the weapons were fired by Russian mercenaries who knew what they were doing. Which we ain't got."

"I don't think these weapons are hard to handle at all," said Zeus. He hadn't heard that mercenaries were involved, and doubted it. "They're point and shoot."

"They're point, shoot, and shit," said Kerfer. "You have to sit there and keep your sight on the target. The missile follows a laser. So you have to keep beaming the bad guy. Even when they shoot at you. You need a clear sight, straight line to the target. You need balls to use it right."

"They got them. I've seen them work basically suicide attacks without flinching."

"Hmmmph."

"Listen, it's their best shot," said Zeus. "I agree with you against the tanks. But I think they can take on the APCs. The armor's a lot lighter."

He walked over to the pile of crates. They were made of wood, and had Russian lettering on them.

"Says 'kitchen utensils,'" said Kerfer. For once he wasn't joking.

"You check them out?"

"You think the 'S' in SEALs stands for stupid? Of course I looked at them. They're all there."

Zeus wanted to see anyway. He went over to the side of the hangar to look for a crowbar. By the time he came back, Kerfer had already pried open the crate using a combat knife. The missiles were packed into large cases that looked like oversized suitcases made of aluminum and plastic. Kerfer laid one on the floor.

"Go to it." He gestured.

Zeus snapped open the case. He'd never actually assembled one of the weapons—the only time he had used one was during a weapons familiarity training course, and they had already been put together and mounted. Fortunately, they were made to be assembled quickly and easily in the field. The mechanism consisted of a tripod mount, a large box that had the sights and laser beam mechanisms, and the missile tube itself. The device was aimed by peering through a large optical sight tube attached to the lower tripod area.

"Careful," said Kerfer. "That launch tube comes with a missile in it."

"It's safed."

"Oh, yeah, I'd trust that shit. This is a Russian weapon, remember? Always remember, *Amerikanski*," he added, using a hackneyed Russian accent. "We win cold war."

"I think the Vietnamese can handle them," said Zeus.

"Maybe."

"If you got a better idea, I'm all ears."

"Yeah." Kerfer frowned. "My idea is to bug the hell out of here."

The Vietnamese soldiers brought over the last crate. There were a total of ninety-six missiles, with an even dozen launchers. It was far less than Zeus had hoped for.

"What you need is a training session with your guys, then set them out on their own," said Kerfer. "But you got less than a hundred missiles. So you really can't afford to lose any."

"Yeah."

"You're not thinking of shooting them yourself?"

"I might."

Kerfer frowned.

"You want to help me?" asked Zeus.

"I would," said Kerfer. "But suicide is against my religion. Besides, I gotta go pick up more weapons."

"Where?"

"Jesus, blanket hugger. I tell you that, I'm going to have to kill you."

"You bringing back artillery shells? That's what they need."

"Not my call." Kerfer shrugged. "If you're going to get out there before daylight you better get moving. And tell those guys they're not hauling rocks. I'd be a hell of a lot more gentle than that."

Kerfer watched Zeus and the Vietnamese interpreter wrangle their Vietnamese helpers. His plan wasn't a bad plan at all—*if* it were being done by SEALs.

But with untrained troops? They might be dedicated, they might even be suicidal, but ninety-odd missiles against a division's worth of APCs? To say nothing of the odd tank or two that might show up.

Kerfer couldn't help but admire the major a little. He'd changed somewhat in the days since Kerfer had seen him. Or maybe just more revealed: harder, determined.

Too determined, maybe. He was sliding down a hill Kerfer himself had gone down many times.

Not this time.

Kerfer started to turn back for the C-130, which was waiting for him to take off. He stopped and called to Zeus.

"Hey, Major—"

"Yeah?"

"You mind if I give you a little friendly advice?"

"Shoot."

"This isn't your war."

Whatever Major Murphy had been expecting to hear, it wasn't that. He gave Kerfer a puzzled look.

"It's not your war," repeated Kerfer. He turned and began walking to the plane, knowing his words would be ignored.

11

CIA headquarters, Virginia

Before she could figure out who the traitor was in Hanoi—and even if there definitely was a traitor, as opposed to a more run-of-the-mill thief—Mara Duncan needed to familiarize herself with what was going on in the country. To do that, she spent her time sitting at a computer in a secure room reading and reviewing data from a wide range of sources.

The room looked very much like an ordinary office suite, with partitions and desks clustered in different areas. Two sections were partitioned off by thick glass from the rest, which made it easier for the people inside to have conversations, though generally they didn't.

Three analysts and Grease were using the room as well. Grease was the only one who took notice of Mara when she came in, and he barely nodded before going back to his screen.

After clearing her security code and putting her thumb on an ID pad, Mara punched in a temporary password. Within seconds, she was scrolling through a list of recent situation reports and analyses. She started by looking at the news reports that had been filed online over the past twelve hours. It was always best to start with fantasy before proceeding to real life.

The disconnect between reality and what was reported wasn't surprising, of course, though she hadn't quite realized how strong the sentiment against Vietnam was in the U.S., let alone realized how it colored the news reporting.

Josh's revelations hadn't had much impact. Just within the hour, a statement had been released by several retired generals urging the U.S. to remain neutral.

The statement was a dead giveaway that the highest ranks of the Army were adamantly opposed to any involvement. They couldn't say that publicly, of course, but it was very unlikely that these retired generals would have gone public without at least some backing at the Pentagon.

Mara moved from the press reports to diplomatic cables, and then on to Army and Pentagon intelligence assessments and estimates. From there it was on to the other agencies, starting with the NSA. Somewhere in the middle of looking at the eavesdroppers' updates and estimates, she realized the Vietnamese were limiting the movements of their armies in an unusual way.

Several decrypted communications between different Vietnamese commands indicated that a no-travel zone in the north was to be strictly enforced at all costs. At first Mara thought this related to the area south of Hanoi proper, where the command bunkers were, but it turned out to be a large swatch of the Yen Tu Mountains.

An armored brigade being rushed to meet the Chinese advance in the east had been warned away from the area. Which didn't make a lot of sense.

She pointed it out to Grease.

"Yen Tu Pagoda is very sacred, not just to Buddhists but to all Vietnamese," he told her. "That was where a famous uprising against the Chinese was centered historically. You can see the symbolic significance."

"The pagoda is nowhere near the roads they were warned away from," said Mara.

"Tanks would never make it up those mountain roads," he said. "They were probably just being practical."

But a no-fly zone as well?

"Huh," said Mara out loud. She went back to the computer and started reading more.

12

Outside Hai Phong

The Ilyushin couldn't handle the weight of all the missiles, and so a second plane was pressed into service. The jet, an old 727 airliner, nearly ran off the end of the short Hai Phong runway as the pilot tried to brake on the wet pavement in the dark. Its tail swung hard to the left, threatening to spin the aircraft onto the grass infield. When it finally came to a stop, one set of wheels was off the runway.

By the time Zeus got there with Major Chaū, the platoon of soldiers detailed by General Tri to unload the weapons had managed to push the plane back onto the runway apron. The missile crates had been stacked in the aisle between the seats, wedged sideways so they couldn't move. Thanks to this, all were intact. Major Chaū gave the order to have them unpacked as quickly as possible.

Drawn from volunteers in his regular division, General Tri's strike force had been assembled at the airport. There were exactly twenty-four soldiers, ranging in age from eighteen to forty-three—a fact that somehow seemed significant to the youngish-looking captain named Kim who led them. He told Zeus proudly that every man had heard of the Americans' glorious victory against the tanks, and was hoping to live up to his inspiration. General Tri had told them personally that Zeus was one American who would never desert the Vietnamese, and he had proven that with his blood.

Zeus glanced at Major Chaū as he finished translating.

"He's sincere," said Chaū. "They all feel that way. We all do."

"All right. The first thing we do is divide everyone up into three-man teams," said Zeus.

"Already done," said Chaū. Captain Kim had even managed to divide the teams up so that at least one man on each team had had some training with antitank missiles.

Zeus showed the men how to set up the launcher. Ideally, he would have had each squad assemble the missiles on their own and take a practice shot before setting out. But there wasn't enough time for the former, and not enough missiles for the latter. They'd have to learn in the field.

Tien Yen was located beyond an estuary off the South China Sea. There was another large peninsula to the south. Rice fields, probably completely flooded, lay on the south side of the peninsula, which was heavily treed and marshy. Zeus thought they could sail up the far side of the southern peninsula, land near one of the roads to the south, then march inland about a mile and a half to the area of Ha Dong. A regiment of Chinese infantry had stopped here before the rain; their vehicles were the primary target.

"There is another depot here, farther down," said Zeus, tracing the route on the map. This was held by a platoon's worth of infantry and their vehicles. "Ideally, we can hit them at the same time. If we move out now, we can get them and withdraw before dawn."

By the time Major Chaū finished translating, Captain Kim had a worried look on his face. Zeus knew there was a problem.

"You better have him tell me what the problem is," said Zeus.

With some reluctance, Kim explained that the Vietnamese had been able to muster only two patrol boats for the operation. They weren't nearly big enough to carry all of the missiles and the men in one trip.

"How many can they carry?" Zeus asked.

Kim wasn't sure. The weapon crates were bigger than they had thought.

"All right," said Zeus. "We'll figure it out when we see the boats. Let's load up the trucks."

———

The two boats the Vietnamese had mustered couldn't have been more different. The first was a Stolkraft with a trimaran hull, an extremely fast, wide-bodied craft designed as a customs patrol boat. In smooth waters, it was capable of hitting close to 90 knots. With the remnant of the typhoon still beating the waves, the vessel would move considerably slower, but the design made it reasonably stable despite the heavy seas.

The other boat was an ancient U.S. Navy PBR, a Vietnam War–era riverine patrol boat that had somehow made its way up from the delta. It was a tiny vessel, originally designed to handle only four crewmen, and never meant for rough water.

The Stolkraft could have taken all of the men, but not the missiles. Even with some of the men sitting in the life raft on the aft deck, they could only bring five three-man teams with all of their gear. The PBR could take one squad, with all of their missiles loaded aboard the Stolkraft.

"It'll have to do," said Zeus. "We'll take one group up first. They'll hit the northern depot. The Stolkraft will go back and load up. I'll meet the second group farther south. We'll strike the second point."

"You're going with them?" asked Major Chaū.

"Yes. I have to show them how to shoot."

"The procedure seemed easy."

"I'm going with them. Ask Captain Kim if I can get a rifle. All I have is my Beretta."

"Captain—"

"I'm probably a better shot than most of these guys," Zeus told Major Chaū. "It makes sense that I have a gun."

"I don't believe General Trung envisioned your joining the troops," said Chaū.

Zeus just shrugged.

———

They set out just as the rain started whipping up again, a last arm of the storm punching them. Zeus stood on the bridge with Major Chaū and the boat's captain, gripping a handhold for dear life.

It was anything but smooth, but it beat what was happening on the other boat, which bounded up and down like a ball bouncing across the floor.

As long as he remained focused on the mission, Zeus was all right—not only did concentrating on what they were going to do help stave off seasickness, but it kept him from thinking about Anna.

"Another two kilometers to the inlet," said Major Chaū. "Almost there."

"Good."

"You should go back with the boat," suggested Chaū. "Your own general would surely prefer it."

Undoubtedly. Perry would surely have a fit when he found out, but Zeus had decided he was going anyway. He couldn't have said exactly why. Some of it may have been the speech the captain had made, some of it his promise to General Tri. Some of it was duty; despite General Perry's comments, he felt his orders to help the Vietnamese meant that he had to actually help them, not leave them in the lurch.

And some portion, too, had to do with Anna. If he helped the Vietnamese now, maybe they would release her to him.

A war prize.

The waves calmed considerably as soon as they turned into the narrow strait of water that would take them to their landing area. The captain cut the engines, waiting for the PBR to join them.

Zeus took a long, slow breath and stared out at the blackness in front of the boat. The Chinese army was only a mile and a half away on their right.

It was a foolish plan. He should never have proposed it.

Too late now.

The boat began easing forward. Zeus left the bridge, climbing down the short ladder and walking to the forward deck. A sailor manned the machine gun there; four of the soldiers were crouched nearby, hunched over their knees as they waited to land.

"Looks good," said Zeus, trying to sound optimistic.

The sailor on the gun raised his hand, catching the spirit if not the precise meaning of what Zeus had said.

The night smelled of metal and wetness, the air thick with the typhoon's passing remnants. The boat's captain had predicted a fog would rise from the land as the storm passed. That would help them, Zeus thought, at least until it came time to fire the missiles. The laser needed a clear line of sight to the target, and too much moisture would interfere with the beam.

So they'd wait for dawn then. No turning back now.

The Stolkraft jerked against something. There was a muffled shout from the cabin, a command from the bridge. They moved backward, the craft stuttering in the water. Though shallow-drafted, the vessel had run aground.

They maneuvered a little back and forth. Two sailors stripped to their underwear, and jumped into the water ahead of the bow. One disappeared completely. The other stood in water to his waist.

The sailors guided them farther up the strait toward the land, until finally the boat's captain decided they were as close as they were going to get. They brought the other boat alongside, then began to unload.

Zeus was the third man off. He slipped into the water as quietly as possible. It was a foot and a half deep.

Before the storm, this had been a rice field. The berms that separated the fields were covered, leaving only those with trees visible.

It took nearly five minutes before the scout at the head of the group found a hump of dry land and a path to two small hovels beyond the field. The men quieted as they neared the buildings, unsure whether they were occupied or not.

Taking no chances, Captain Kim detailed two of his teams to check the first building. It was empty, as was the second. He left a trio of men there to guide the others still coming up from the boats, then continued with the rest to a narrow gravel road a short distance from the houses.

Zeus didn't have a GPS unit, and had to get his bearings with a Vietnamese map and some Global Hawk images he had brought with him from the planning session. He turned his map sideways, retracing the path they had taken on the water, then moving his finger up through the land toward the hamlet the Chinese had seized as a command post before the storm. He double-checked it against the photos, making sure he was right.

If they went due north, then cut west, they should see Chinese troops. There were two companies waiting out the storm inside the trucks along the road. Another was back in the hamlet.

"We have to get through that lane over there," Zeus told Captain Kim when he'd collected all his men. "There are some buildings where it meets the local highway. That should give us a vantage point to see up the road. The Chinese stopped about three miles farther north before the rain hit. We should be able to take the road."

He waited for Major Chaū to translate. The captain nodded vigorously.

Ten minutes later, Zeus and the two Vietnamese privates who were acting as point men drew close to the back of the buildings at the southeastern quadrant of the intersection. There were three structures, all squat and dark. The tallest was a service station.

Zeus used two garbage cans as a makeshift ladder, scrambling up the garage roof. It was made of metal, and between the pitch and slippery rain, Zeus had to climb on all fours.

Just as he reached the apex, his AK-47 slipped off his shoulder and clanked against the metal roof. He cursed himself, pulling the gun strap back in place.

When he put his head up, he saw dozens of Chinese armored vehicles scattered along the road around the intersection. A pair of Z99 tanks sat in the middle of the crossroads.

The Chinese had moved south during the storm.

13

Forthright, Ohio

"Pretty damn warm day," said Tex, putting down the ax to take off his jacket. "Must be all this global warming you're studying, right?"

"Believe it or not, no," said Josh. "I mean, it could be, but a warm day like this in February? That sort of thing has been happening forever. Climate change is more subtle."

"Droughts are subtle?"

"I mean, the effects of climate change are very complex." Josh picked up his sledgehammer and positioned the splitting wedge over a log. It had been Tex's idea to cut the family some firewood. Josh had readily agreed, not so much because it was an easy way to thank them for putting him up, but because the exercise would make him forget about Mara.

If he could forget.

He swung the hammer down, getting the wedge in place for the real blow.

"So droughts—they're the result of climate change?" said Tex, picking up the ax again.

"Yeah. Well, in aggregate."

"Jesus, Doc. I hate to say this, but you sound like a politician. Mincing your words. You never say what you mean."

Josh sighed. Actually, he could be extremely precise, talking about numbers and percentages and statistics.

"It's the trend that's important," he told Tex. "Climate change means more droughts. More warm winters like this. Which, for some places is good."

"I like it," said Tex. "Don't need a coat."

Josh swung the sledge. The log split cleanly in half.

God, he missed Mara. He'd tried calling twice, but his calls went straight to voice mail.

He hadn't bothered to leave a message. Too much to say.

He bent and took another piece of wood from the pile.

14

South of Halong Bay

Zeus pushed his eye against the aiming sight, whispering just loudly enough for Major Chaū to hear. The tank was zeroed in.

The two team leaders peering over his shoulder mumbled something as Chaū translated the aiming procedure. Zeus leaned back, letting them take a look.

The clouds were moving away. Though it was still a good hour before the sun would rise, the sky was already light gray with a false dawn. The dark smudges they'd seen when they landed were now reasonable facsimiles of trees and buildings.

Zeus had set up two teams on a small rise on the west side of the road, with a clear line to both tanks. Two other crews were gathered around a launcher a short distance away, their weapon aimed at the second tank. Little more than a kilometer separated the launchers from their targets. Easy shots.

"They are ready," said Chaū.

"All right. Wait until I say fire."

Zeus trotted over to the other teams. He'd already sighted their weapons.

Just as Zeus reached them, there was a loud pop behind him. Zeus turned to see smoke billowing from the rear of the launcher he had just left.

Shit!

"Fire!" he yelled. "Fire! Fire!"

The missile leapt from the launcher next to him. There was a hiss and a low *thur-rump-the*. The Russian antitank projectile flew across the field and road, streaking along the line set by the laser beam. Racing against the reddish light, it didn't stop when it came to the steel hull of the Chinese tank. The missile didn't realize it had found its target, much less know what its mission was. It kept flying, penetrating into the steel shield and body, exploding in madness and frustration as the red laser light disappeared.

The men inside the tank never knew that they had been fired on. From their perspective, there was a brief, terrible premonition of death, then nothing.

"Load the next one, the next one," Zeus told the men. "Aim at the APCs. As we planned. As we planned."

"Yes, Major," said the team leader. He spoke a little English. The others were already loading a second missile.

Zeus ran to Chaū. "Why the hell did you fire?" he yelled.

"The top of the tank opened. We were afraid we had been seen."

The other missiles were launching, whizzing across the field. Zeus ran to the squat flat-roof building next to the service station, where he had set up two more teams. As he started to climb, he heard one of the missiles being launched. He got to the top and saw steam furling from the nearest APC.

More missiles fired. Figures began stumbling from the houses up the street. The Vietnamese began firing their AK-47s, gunning them down.

It was working.

"Major! Major!"

Zeus went to the back of the building, where Chaū was calling up to him.

"We have to get back to the boat," said Chaū. "We have to get back for the second attack."

"You're right," said Zeus. He leapt off the back of the building, rolling to his feet after he hit the ground.

"*Everything is running late,*" said Chaū, glancing at his watch as the PBR skittered southward, away from the peninsula where they'd landed and launched the attack.

"Yeah," said Zeus, steadying himself against a spar at the side of the boat.

Chaū's point was that the second attack would be made during the day, greatly increasing the danger. But there was no sense waiting now. The other units would be on alert because of this attack.

As soon as they fired all of their missiles, Captain Kim and the teams would work their way south toward the second attack point; with luck they would meet up by nightfall to be evacuated.

The Stolkraft met the PBR about two miles north of Hai Phong, the rest of the teams crowded so tightly on the deck of the boat they looked like refugees escaping the war. The PBR took on three men, a full team, then turned and followed the Stolkraft north to the second landing point, a marshy area inland from Dong Dui.

The two boats treaded through a run of islands and jutting fingers of land, heading for a narrow estuary stream that extended nearly sixteen miles from the ocean. They were near Halong Bay, an upended jaw of earth, where some two thousand limestone and dolomite teeth poked through the water, flashing at the dragons said to haunt the area.

A bridge ran over a creek about three miles inland. About a mile north of the bridge was a hamlet where two companies of Chinese APCs had parked before the storm. The units were the farthest south of the Chinese infantry.

Fog drifted in from the ocean, the mist curling around islets of pillar-shaped rocks and tree-covered spits of land. The sun played through the mist, cutting it like a sword, flashing against the white rock sides to reveal intricate clefs and scars. The storm had pulled many trees down, and the two boats had to trim their engines to tread through the debris. The ends of tree trunks poked up like the elbows of dead sailors, and the dark hulks of the submerged branches loomed just below the surface, shifting like mythical beasts waiting to spring from the water and swallow the small PBR whole.

Zeus rubbed his arms, suddenly cold. The rounded crags towering over him made him feel puny and small, showing him just how insignificant he was, how tiny, how unimportant.

Kerfer's words came back to him:

It's not your war.

Standing on the forward deck, he realized nothing was his, not these looming green and white shadows around him, or the still-angry water. And especially not the hulking green earth behind them.

By that logic, too, not one thing he possessed was his—not the gun loaned to him, not his boots, not his own arms or legs. The earth was the possessor of all things, not him; he was just another speck flicking across the sun, throwing a momentary shadow across the water.

And as he contemplated that puniness he thought of Anna, thought of the soft way she had fallen into him, thought of her kiss and the touch of her lips. It was an antidote to his depression—the sunlight that pushed away the fog.

This wasn't his war, but it had brought her to him, and for that reason alone—for that reason beyond fate or chance, beyond even his duty—he would fight this war. He would find her and free her. Because they couldn't deny him anything. He was their hero.

The debris thickened as they began inland. Two soldiers were detailed to push some of the logs away. They began cheerfully enough, one of the men even laughing at some joke. But within moments one had slipped and fallen into the water, and by the time he was pulled out he was covered with bruises, and his arm seemed to have been badly sprained. There was no more laughter after that.

Finally, they reached the mouth of the stream that would take them up toward the bridge. They passed into what looked like a clear lake: the typhoon had swelled the stream far beyond its banks, and rather than the farm fields Zeus expected they passed telephone lines and the tops of trees. The shoreline had completely disappeared. Even the boat captain was amazed at how high the water level had risen.

"The water is much higher than normal," Chaū explained, translating what the boat captain told him. "Higher even than during some rainy seasons. He expects that the area you wished to land will be flooded. It may be flooded all the way to the bridge, if the water is this high here."

Ordinarily, that might not have been a problem, but their experience farther north made Zeus worry that the Chinese might have moved down to the bridge. He took out his map and conferred with the boat captain, trying to decide on an alternate spot.

"The captain says there is a stream that runs beneath the highway a little farther north," said Chaū. He pointed on the map. "There is high land on the west side. If we landed there, we would be only about two miles south of the hamlet."

"All right, let's try it," said Zeus.

They pulled across to the Stolkraft, and after a few words the PBR captain slid his vessel ahead, steering it through a patch of muddy water. They passed a set of wooden staves on the left, fence posts that separated small fish pens from the rice paddies behind them. The boundary had been erased.

A fork loomed ahead. The boat captain started spinning the wheel, pushing the PBR to port side. As he did, something shot through the air a few inches from Zeus.

Zeus's first thought was that it was a swarm of insects; they'd passed several already. Then another part of his brain pushed him to his knees.

They were being fired on.

The soldier manning the forward machine gun started blasting the trees to the right. Soldiers on both boats started yelling and returning fire with a vengeance.

"Cease fire! Cease fire!" yelled Zeus, seeing that the Chinese had already stopped shooting. There had been one or two men at most. "You're wasting ammo!"

He turned around and shouted at the captain. "Get us out of here! Get us upstream! Go! Go!"

The captain had already gunned the throttle. The PBR lurched forward, pushing toward a group of houses on the left. Meanwhile, the soldiers on both boats continued shooting. Zeus scanned the opposite shore, but saw nothing—no flashes, not even an area of cover where someone could be firing from.

"Chaū! Chaū! Get them to stop firing!" yelled Zeus. "Just get the boats up to a place to where we can get off. We're wasting ammo."

He looked behind him but couldn't see Chaū. One of the sailors had grabbed a rifle and was standing next to the captain on Zeus's left, firing wildly. From the wild look on his face Zeus knew he was simply firing from fear, without any target. He kept shooting until he'd run through the magazine.

Zeus saw Chaū crawling across the deck toward him. He ducked down and yelled in his ear.

Chaū yelled something from his crouch, but his voice was hoarse and even Zeus, right next to him, couldn't hear.

"Tell me the words for 'cease fire,'" yelled Zeus. "We need to get us ashore."

Chaū's voice was gone, and even leaning against Zeus's ear, couldn't make himself heard over the din. The boat lurched hard to port, then back, swerving wildly. Something clunked hard against the side, and Zeus thought they'd been hit by a shell or a grenade. But it had only been the top of a fence post, brushing against the hull.

Zeus rose, pulling Chaū with him.

"There's a road ashore," Zeus yelled at the captain. He pointed ahead, where he saw the crown of a dirt road rising above the water. "Get us there! Go!"

The sailor on the deck gun had run through his second belt. As he paused to reload, some of the soldiers on both boats heard the lull and stopped firing themselves. Finally, the firing died.

"We go ashore near the road! We get out here!" yelled Zeus. "Chaū—tell him. There! We land!"

Chaū squeezed over to the captain, cupping his hands to his mouth to try to amplify his weak voice. The captain altered his course, aiming just to the south of the road.

Zeus slipped to the stern of the PBR. The Stolkraft was behind them, separated by almost twenty yards and listing serious to starboard.

"Land the men ahead!" Zeus yelled. He spun around and tried to mime what he wanted them to do.

The Stolkraft tucked toward its port side, angling to come up next to the PBR. Zeus decided it would have to do.

He turned back to find Chaū. Just then, a black brick flicked overhead. Zeus started to react even before the brick materialized into a shell, exploding about a hundred yards beyond the two boats in a burst of water and mud.

"Get us to the shore!" he yelled.

A few seconds later, there was a whistling scream as a full volley of shells, seven or eight at least, flew overhead and crashed into the swollen stream behind them. Hoisted from at least two miles away, they were well off the mark, hitting the water three hundred yards behind the boats.

The next volley came close enough to splatter water over the PBR. The wake of the explosion shoved the boat sideways against a fallen tree. The vessel lurched, then stopped short. The motor revved but Zeus knew they were never going to reach the spot he'd picked out.

"We land, now!" he yelled. "Off the boat! Everyone onto land! Get away from the shells!"

He started for the side, thinking he would jump off onto the tree, then realized Chaū wasn't with him. Turning back, he heard the whistle again, a brief—all-too-brief—high-pitch whine of the air unable to resist the inevitable rush of the Chinese shell. And then the next thing Zeus knew, he was face-first in a pile of wet green slime.

He pushed upright, only to fall into the water as the branches he'd lodged against gave way. Zeus rolled to his right, dug his foot down, and found ground just solid enough to support his weight.

Straightening, he heard something wallop the air behind him. It was a strange sound, one that didn't correspond to anything he knew or had experienced before. Before he could decide what it was, the water rose up and hurled him forward, throwing him up over the tip of the tree into a patch of mud.

Zeus punched down with his arm and managed to get to his knees. Something grabbed his side—one of the soldiers. Zeus leaned down, hooking his arm beneath the man, and together they dragged themselves toward a clump of weeds. To Zeus's surprise, the man had a missile box in his right hand.

Zeus turned, expecting there would be a whole group of soldiers with their gear struggling after him. But there was nothing, just a clear patch of flooded field. He couldn't even see the boats. The felled tree he had landed on poked out of the water about forty feet away. Beyond that, the flooded stream rippled with white froth, extending sixty or seventy yards to a green bank.

Zeus's AK-47 was still strapped over his shoulder. But the extra ammo he'd had in a small field bag was back somewhere on the boat; all he had now were two banana magazines, one loaded and the other taped to the first magazine.

"The road is up this way somewhere," Zeus told the soldier who'd come out with him. "There are some buildings—let's get up there and get our bearings."

The weeds were actually a berm separating two fields. Though flooded, the next one was only ankle-deep with water. There was a pair of buildings at the far side, maybe thirty yards away. Zeus, the AK now in his right fist, began trotting in their direction.

The shelling had stopped.

The buildings were small farmhouses, similar to the hovels he'd seen before. Zeus pounded on the door of the nearest one.

The words he'd heard earlier came to him: "*Xin chào!*"

Hello! A strange thing to say in the middle of a war.

No one answered. He looked at the soldier, gesturing that he should say something as well. The man yelled something of his own, a different phrase, but again there was no answer.

They ran to the next building. This one had a window at the front, next to the door; Zeus knocked on the glass and yelled. When no one answered, he pounded on the door, then found it unlocked.

They went in. The front room was some sort of family room, with chairs and cupboards. There was a wet spot in the corner opposite the door, apparently where water had come up from below. They searched the house quickly—there were only three other rooms: a kitchen, a bedroom with a small bed and a crib, and a bath. All were deserted.

"Stay here," Zeus told the soldier, gesturing. "I'll be back with the others."

He went outside, calmer now, heart no longer throbbing. The road they'd been headed toward was across another field directly in front of the house; he could see the crown running in a backward Z to the north.

There were more buildings on his left. From here they looked deserted.

Starting back toward the flooded paddy, Zeus tried to triangulate where the other boat would have been when he was thrown overboard. Somewhere to his right, he decided, and he angled that way, climbing over a row of half-submerged vegetation dividing the fields. Another cluster of houses, four or five them, sat along a flooded lane just beyond a sparse cropping of trees. These were much bigger houses than the one he had left the soldier at, a much more logical place to gather the missile teams. Zeus decided to head for them and check them out.

The closest building was a bamboo-roofed two-story house whose lower level was perched on stilts, apparently protection against flooding. A porch ran around this level, plantation style.

When he was ten yards away, he saw a man emerge from the lower level of the house, walking out of a basement room. Zeus raised his arm to wave at the man. The man froze, then threw himself down.

"Friend! Friend!" yelled Zeus, running toward him. He couldn't remember the Vietnamese word.

"Friend!" he repeated, leaping over a small hedge. As he landed, he saw the man cower. Zeus raised his eyes, looking toward the corner of the building. There was another man there, and a second, and a third.

"Hey!" he yelled.

One of the men spun toward him. He had a uniform, and a gun. The rifle barked.

Zeus hit the dirt. The rifle was a QBZ-95 bullpup, easily identified as Chinese.

As was the uniform of the man aiming at him.

15

The Gulf of Tonkin

The lead ship, the *Filipino Star*, was less than a half mile off the port bow when Silas had her hailed via radio.

"We are an American warship, and we intend to inspect your cargo according to UN sanction 2014-3-2 forbidding the passage of military aid to the belligerents in Southeast Asia," declared Silas. "Prepare to be boarded."

The seas were still heavy, and sending a rigid hulled craft across would be risky. But with the sun up now and the last squall of the storm drifting northward, Silas would do so anyway. The *McLane* had no helicopter at the moment; it had been used to transport the SEALs and had not yet returned.

"No answer, Captain," said the communications mate.

"Try it again, broadcasting on all channels," said Silas. "We've been patient all night."

Indeed, the merchant ships had sat off his bow now for quite a while. Since they weren't moving forward and with the Chinese cruiser and her frigate nearly thirty miles to the east, Silas had bided his time.

Those were, after all, his orders. The merchant ships were just to the east of Vietnam's coastal waters, in open seas. Technically, he could stop them whenever he wanted to inspect the manifest, but the admiral had directed that he wait until the ships were clearly embarked toward Hai Phong—which to Silas meant inside the twelve-mile limit.

But the cruiser had just changed course for him. It was time to bring things to a head.

After the message was repeated, Silas had the helmsman adjust his course to get a little closer. He wanted to make things as easy as possible for the boarding craft.

He had a sudden inspiration and ordered weapons to have the forward gun track across, making it very clear to the cargo vessel that he was prepared for business.

"Boarding party, stand by," ordered Silas over the ship's intercom system.

"Captain, the merchant vessel is turning off," said the helmsman. "Moving northeastward, sir. All ships."

A few seconds later, Lt. Commander Li reported that all of the Chinese merchant ships had changed direction. They were heading back toward China.

"Do you plan to pursue?" Li asked.

Silas wanted to. But his orders were to get the ships to leave peaceably if possible.

He could go ahead. But if they really were packed with men, his boarding party would be in a dangerous situation. In the end, he'd probably ending up sinking every damn ship around him, which was what he wanted to do. But he'd also lose some good men in the process.

"I intend to hold my position off Hai Phong," he told Li. "If the Chinese want to just turn and run, that's okay with me."

Belatedly, Silas remembered that the admiral had directed that he contact him before issuing the Chinese an ultimatum.

Ooops.

He smiled to himself. Even when he didn't do it on purpose, he seemed to drift toward insubordination.

"Arrange a secure video link to fleet," he told his communications mate. "I'll take it in my quarters, after I've changed."

16

Inland from Halong Bay

Neither Zeus nor the soldier who'd spotted him moved, both too surprised by the other to react.

A burst of gunfire cut through the weeds. The soldier ducked back around the corner. Zeus dropped to the ground.

The gunfire came from beyond the house. It was from AK-47s.

Zeus guessed what was happening, though he couldn't see—the Vietnamese soldiers had come ashore and stumbled on the men here.

He had their retreat cut off. Zeus edged to his right, trying to work himself into a position where he could get an angle on the Chinese soldiers if they stayed where they were. Dampness seeped up his pants legs, and from his chest around toward his back. The ground oozed with water.

The Chinese soldiers were at the front of the building, behind a barricade or a wall under the porch between the stilts. They didn't seem to be returning fire.

Were they simply conserving ammo? Or were they out of bullets.

They ought to conserve their ammo, Zeus thought. Sure as hell they're going to need it.

A low berm ran across the field a few yards away, disappearing into the water on the right. He got up, intending to throw himself against it, but just as he reached it he fell into a drainage ditch that ran along the other side. As he struggled to pull himself against the raised dirt, gunfire stoked up, from both sides this time. Zeus pushed along the ditch until he was parallel with the front of the house. He saw a green uniform moving beneath the porch and fired a quick burst; the man jerked almost upright, then slumped down.

There were two or three men behind him, maybe a fourth. Zeus fired a burst, but couldn't see into the shadows to even know if he'd hit them.

They didn't fire back. The Vietnamese stopped firing as well.

The truth was, the Chinese were in a good spot. They could probably hold their position for some time unless the Vietnamese rushed them. And in that case the Vietnamese were sure to take at least some losses.

They hesitated, probably calculating the odds. Zeus looked to his left, toward the back of the house. He might be able to backtrack, and come up from the other side. As long as the Chinese remained pinned down, he could probably sneak close enough to surprise them.

Should have thought of that earlier. Now it would be harder.

There was a shout from the area of the house. Zeus looked back. One of the Chinese soldiers had tied a piece of cloth to the end of his gun, and was waving it in front of his position.

The cloth was green, but it got the message across. They wanted to surrender.

What a break, thought Zeus.

He moved to his right, trying to get into a better position to cover the Chinese soldiers as they came out.

Someone shouted something from the Vietnamese side. There was an answer from the Chinese.

The man who had raised his gun to signal the surrender started moving along the front of the house, toward Zeus, holding the flag. The Vietnamese barked something. The man stopped, threw down the gun, and held his hands high.

Zeus was close enough to see the private insignia on his uniform.

The Vietnamese soldier said something else. The Chinese private began moving out. Two more men popped up and joined him. Their hands were high in the air.

"All right! All right!" yelled Zeus, wanting the Vietnamese to know he was there. "I'm here! It's Zeus! The American!"

He rose slowly, his AK-47 pointed in the direction of the house. He was ready to drop; he glanced to his right, trying to see if the Vietnamese saw him.

There were two Vietnamese soldiers moving forward in the field in front of the house, sloshing through the water. Four more men were behind them. All had their guns trained on the three Chinese soldiers.

One of the men had been wounded; his arm hung down.

The Chinese soldiers waited. One of them glanced at the body of the man Zeus had shot. He lay facedown in the mud, clearly dead.

They were kids, eighteen maybe at most. They were shivering, probably with fright.

One of the Vietnamese soldiers told them to drop on the ground, and they complied.

Zeus moved to his left, peering toward the bottom of the house to make sure there was no one left inside. He glanced at the Vietnamese soldiers, waved to make sure they saw him, then cautiously moved under the house, his finger resting ever so lightly against the trigger.

It was empty.

He started to relax, backing out.

Something flashed on his right.

He turned in time to see the Vietnamese soldiers who'd come forward to accept the Chinese surrender lace the prisoners with several dozen rounds.

———

There was nothing, no sound except the bullets leaving the gun. Zeus heard nothing—not the cries of the boys killed, not the tears of their betrayal, not the unrequited hatred of their murderers.

———

Zeus fell to his knee, unsure what exactly was happening, ready if there were more Chinese, if it was a trap. He told himself not to fire until he saw a target.

He reminded himself that bullets were more critical than fear.

The Vietnamese were shouting. Zeus remained on his knee. Finally, he heard someone yelling in Vietnamese-accented English.

"Clear!"

Zeus rose slowly. Two Vietnamese soldiers ran up, nodded at him, then went into the underside of the building. One fired into the body Zeus had already killed.

"Don't waste bullets," Zeus told him.

He walked toward the front of the building. Eight soldiers were standing near the bodies of the dead Chinese.

"What the hell happened?" demanded Zeus. "Why did you fire?"

"Major Murph!" said one of the team leaders, a sergeant. "Major Murph, you found us."

"Why did you shoot them?"

"Chinese."

"Yeah, but they were surrendering. Did one of them fire?"

The sergeant looked at him as if he didn't understand. Maybe he didn't.

"You killed them when they were surrendering," said Zeus.

The man shook his head lightly, not comprehending. It was possible someone had gotten nervous and pressed his trigger. Maybe there were other extenuating circumstances. It was too late to undo now.

Zeus felt his stomach grip him from the inside.

"How many of us?" he said, struggling to stay calm. He raised his hand and made a circular gesture. "How many?"

The sergeant said something in Vietnamese.

"Is this all?" Zeus asked. He circled again with his hand.

"All. Yes."

"We have a man in that house, over there." Zeus pointed beyond the field. "*Our* man." He tapped his chest. "Do you understand?"

"Our man. One."

"Right. Hook up with him, and meet me near the road," said Zeus. He tried miming it with his hand. "Okay? I'm going down to the water and see if I can find anyone else. Where is Major Chaū?"

"Chaū?" The sergeant shook his head grimly.

"By the road. Meet me. Don't kill our guy."

"Yes," said the sergeant.

———

The field was separated from the stream by a row of trees and submerged rocks. Zeus slipped through the trees, trying to see where he was.

A boot floated in the water nearby. It turned on the current, revealing the hacked edge of a lower leg.

Zeus steeled himself, balancing amid the trees. He could see the semisubmerged hulk of the PBR ten yards away, on his left. Two bodies floated in the water near it.

Both sailors.

Slinging his rifle over his shoulder, Zeus shimmied up one of the trees, trying to get a better view. He could see at least one other body beyond the PBR. It was a soldier's.

Chaū?

Zeus hugged the tree and turned in the other direction, looking for the Stolkraft. He found it grounded on some debris about thirty yards downstream. A shell blast had broken the hull in two, and the sides bowed up, as if the boat were a deck of cards waiting to be shuffled.

Zeus counted three bodies on the deck. Several missile containers, and ammunition boxes were there as well. A few were stuck in the mud nearby. They could all be salvaged.

Zeus pushed himself higher on the tree, looking toward the opposite shore. He saw no sign of the Chinese there. There was a rise a little more than a mile beyond. He guessed that there was a roadway through or near the swamp, and that the Chinese had gathered their tanks there. A scout near the water would have seen the boats, and sent back information about them. Or maybe he'd just fired to provoke the Vietnamese and alert the tanks.

The theory gave him a working target. They'd move up in that direction and look for the tanks—or whatever it was that had hit them.

Zeus shimmied down the tree trunk, his legs and palms scraping though the trunk was smooth.

As he started back up through the field, he heard the whine of vehicles moving in the distance. He put his head down and started to run. He crossed to the right side of the house, running past the bodies of the Chinese soldiers, who'd been left where they fell.

A mistake, thought Zeus. If the Chinese saw them, they'd know exactly what had happened.

But there was no time to do anything about it. The ground was shaking with the approach of the armored vehicles, moving on the dirt road in the field beyond the houses. Zeus ran up along the woods to the opening where he had crossed earlier. He was about five or six steps away when he heard the swoosh of a Kornet missile streaking across the open yard.

A loud crack followed, as if lightning had hit a massive redwood and felled it with one burst. A second missile zipped into the air, but this time there was no explosion. Instead, a Chinese ZTZ99's 120mm began to fire, tossing shells in the direction of the house where Zeus had left the soldier.

Another missile—an explosion, small-arms gunfire, a shout and a scream.

The air reverberated, the ground shaking as the Vietnamese engaged the force of tanks that had moved down the road. Zeus, realizing that he would not be able to run across to the buildings without being caught in the crossfire, changed course and headed toward his left, hoping to come up around the Chinese force.

He remembered the crates of missiles lying back at the shore, and considered going to grab them, but it would take considerable time to fish out even one, and he might be more useful in the meantime. At a minimum, he had to know what he was up against.

Zeus sprinted across the field, crossed a muddy lane, then circled around a small shed that bordered the road before finally reaching a point where he could look in the direction of the firefight. Four Chinese tanks, very closely packed together in a column, sat in front of the house. Smoke billowed from the lead tank. Black smoke and gray steam furled behind it, from at least one other Z99 that Zeus couldn't see.

The others were firing their machine guns in a steady hail, the sound a kind of steel-tap chorus.

The house was engulfed in flames and smoke.

Zeus laid down flat and began easing across the field on his belly, trying to get a better angle. After about ten yards of crawling through the mud he came to a water-filled ditch. Slipping into it, he found himself in water almost to his neck. Holding his rifle just above the surface of the water, he followed the ditch as it slanted behind the tanks' position, moving away as it drew parallel to them. The depth of the ditch decreased as he went, until finally when he was even with the tanks he had to kneel to avoid being seen.

One of the four tanks was still firing. The empty building was on fire as well. If the Vietnamese were still alive, he couldn't see them, or hear their guns.

More vehicles were moving in the distance, on his left, coming to join the fight.

The smartest thing to do at this point—aside from running away—was to backtrack, get some of the missiles, and get into position to either take this tank out or, more likely, ambush whatever was coming up as reinforcements. Zeus turned and looked back down the trench, calculating whether it might not be easier to back out here and make a wide circle back.

It would certainly be drier. Zeus looked back to make sure the Z99's turret was buttoned up. When he didn't see anyone on the machine gun, he climbed out of the ditch and crawled straight back, aiming for a row of foliage separating the field from another. He reached the bushes and turned around, got his bearings again, and started to run along the brush to angle back toward the water. He kept his eyes on the tank and the road some fifty or sixty yards away.

He'd gone no more than a few steps when the top of the tank popped open. Zeus dropped down immediately. By the time he looked up, the tank commander had grabbed the machine gun on the turret and begun firing toward the two burning houses.

If he was thinking logically, Zeus might have seen this as an opportunity to get away—the man was focused on a target one hundred and eighty degrees in the other direction.

But Zeus wasn't thinking logically. Instead, he saw a threat to the men he'd been with, and he reacted instinctively, jumping up through the brush and starting across the field. With a different, more familiar weapon, he might have fired from the brush itself—fifty yards was not a particularly difficult shot with an M-16 or even an AK-47 for that matter, so long as the shooter was used to the weight and pull of the gun, and the weapon itself was in good repair. But Zeus had little experience with an AK, and he'd already seen that the weapon could be unreliable except at very close range.

He stopped ten yards from the tank.

The Chinese tank commander hunkered over his machine gun. The man ceased firing and straightened, looking over the field to see where his enemy was hiding.

Now, thought Zeus. He dropped to his knee, almost too close to have an angle.

But he did have an angle, and he did have a shot, dead-on in the middle of the iron sights.

Zeus pressed the trigger.

Nothing happened.

He tried again. The gun had been fouled in the water.

He cleared, tried again. Nothing.

In the next second, the sound of a steam engine about to blow rose in his ears; the noise merged into a loud screech and boom. One of the Vietnamese had fired an AT-14 at the tank.

———

By the time Zeus heard the noise of the missile strike on the tank, he'd already pitched to the ground. The AT-14 hit the bottom of the turret on the left side of the tank, away from Zeus. The missile half-penetrated the armor as it exploded, rocking the top upward as if it were bottle opener popping a soda can that had been in the sun all day.

Steam exploded from the fissure. The lower half of the tank thumped down hard against the ground, shaking it in a rumble that reverberated through Zeus's chest. The top of the tank peeled back, metal spitting off.

The tank commander was blasted into pieces. His right hand and forearm flew in a somersault across the air, landing a few inches from Zeus's face. Zeus saw the fingers in front of him, extending from the palm as if beseeching God for mercy.

He jerked his head away, closing his eyes involuntarily.

Someone shouted behind him. He was caught off guard, still stunned from the vision of the hand.

They shouted again. He didn't know what they were saying.

Was it Vietnamese, or Chinese?

Only when Zeus closed his hand did he realize he didn't have his gun; he'd lost it when he threw himself down. It would have been useless anyway.

He started to spread his arms. Someone shouted, then kicked him down, face-first into the ground.

He rolled to his back, raising his arms to ward off another blow. A rifle was in his face.

A Chinese rifle. The soldier, uniform battered, helmet missing, yelled something in Chinese. Zeus shook his head, trying to show that he didn't understand.

The man thrust the rifle barrel at Zeus. If he'd had a bayonet, he would have pierced him in the heart.

Zeus started to push himself backward, not sure what the man wanted him to do. The Chinese soldier screamed at him again. Blood trickled from the man's temple. His face was bright red, as if he'd been burned, as if he was still burning. His eyes were wild and open; he could have been a caricature of hell.

"*Séi!*" the soldier yelled in Chinese.

He continued, telling Zeus that he was a dead man, that there was no hope or escape. He screamed the same word over and over, but the one word was an entire paragraph, a long demand.

"*Séi!*"

He wanted to see Zeus's fear. He wanted him to run before he killed him. For it wasn't Zeus he was going to shoot; it was his own terror and dread. The horror of battle had unnerved him.

Zeus had no way out. The Chinese soldier prodded Zeus with the barrel of the gun, smacking it against his chin.

If he tries it again, I can grab it, he thought.

But there was a second thought: *Maybe he wants me to stand so he can take me prisoner.*

He knew from the man's expression that this couldn't be true—the man was possessed, acting according to some logic only his unhinged mind understood. But even so, Zeus wanted the second idea to be true—it offered some hope.

The man yelled his word again. Losing hope that Zeus would do what he said, the soldier drew back his gun and aimed at the American.

"*Séi!*"

There was loud crack, a single shot.

To Zeus's amazement, the Chinese soldier fell down to his right, so close to him that blood splattered across his face.

"Major Murphy," croaked Chaū in his hoarse voice, running up and standing over him. He was huffing. "I am glad you are still alive."

17

Mariveles, the Philippines

Ric Kerfer folded his arms in front of his chest and took a step backward. In all his time in the Navy, he had never seen so many goddamn weapons gathered in one place before. The dock was literally overrun with boxes and crates, and the warehouse behind it was already half-packed. All manner of Russian ordinance was stacked all over the pier. There were bullets and shells and seven different varieties of antitank weapons. There were AT-14 missiles and jellied petroleum for flame-throwers. There were five-hundred-pound bombs, and cases for SA-7s. Most the munitions were older than he was, but the sheer amount of them was damn impressive.

Too impressive. He only had the single C-130 to get all this crap to Vietnam.

What to do?

The Filipinos he'd recruited as stevedores looked at him anxiously.

It would have helped if someone told him what the damn priorities were. Good ol' Braney hadn't given him a clue.

He'd taken antitank weapons on the first trip. But you could never have too many.

Kerfer began walking down the row of crates. He'd elected to study Russian at one of his schools way back when, but the truth was, he didn't remember crap from those days, and the Cyrillic letters might just as well have been inkblots.

Besides, they all claimed to be things they weren't, like kitchen utensils. One of the Russians had given him a sheaf of papers with the key, but it was all confused.

Kerfer stopped at a crate he thought held more AT-14s. When he opened it, he saw Boltoks—missiles that were launched from tanks.

"Take these for the plane," he told his stevedores. "Two boxes, no, four. We'll keep the numbers even."

A little bit of everything. That was the key. Definitely throw in some artillery shells. Army guys always like that.

And as soon as he had everything picked out, he'd call for another plane.

Or maybe twenty.

18

Inland from Halong Bay

Chaū had been separated from the others when the boats were hit, falling into the water and then swimming or floating—he wasn't sure which—north. By the time he got himself together, the other firefight was already underway. He slipped down through the fields, arriving at the houses after they had been destroyed. There he'd found Sergeant Angkor hunkered over the last missile, waiting for the smoke to clear so he'd get a shot. They'd stalked the tank, then found Zeus by accident.

"There are more tanks coming," Zeus told Chaū. "Hear them? Do you have more missiles?"

"That was the last," said Chaū.

"There are more cases by the water," said Zeus. "Let's get them."

He started to run, then looked back when he realized they weren't following.

"What's wrong, Chaū?"

"We have wounded."

"We'll come back for them," said Zeus. "We're not leaving them."

Chaū and Angkor began talking, apparently debating what to do. Zeus didn't wait. He started trotting again, then running, crossing the field and heading back toward the shore where he had seen the floating boxes. He was soaked, his uniform and face covered with mud and blood.

As Zeus approached the shoreline, he noticed a narrow lane running to the water, which he hadn't seen before. It took him a little to the east, out of his way, but the path was high and mostly dry all the way out to the water. There it gave way to boulders and carefully positioned logs.

Three of the missile cases had washed in. Zeus grabbed them, sliding them onto the path. There were four other boxes nearby, all half-submerged in the water. He took a step toward the closest, and immediately felt his leg sinking. He pushed back and fell rump first onto the rocks.

The rocks extended in a kind of submerged ledge to the left. He stepped out on it tentatively, then worked his way sideways a few feet until he was almost parallel with one of the boxes. He reached out and dragged it up through the water, pulling it to land.

He was eyeing another when Chaū burst onto the shoreline through the weeds about thirty yards on his left. Zeus yelled to him, and waved, signaling that he should loop around and come up through the path.

"There's a path," he said. "Come out this way; it's drier."

Zeus went back to work, fetching out two more boxes by the time Chaū reached him.

"Where's the sergeant?" Zeus asked.

"With the men. We must go back."

They had five missiles, but no launchers, and no launcher boxes that he could see. Zeus went back out onto the small ledge, but couldn't reach the other two boxes. He waded into the muck, then stepped forward onto one of the boxes. He pulled the other out and gave it to Chaū. The one beneath his feet was too embedded to retrieve.

"There aren't any more launchers," Zeus told the major. "We're going to have to go back to the houses to get one."

"Yes," said Chaū, his voice still hoarse. "That's where Angkor is."

Zeus opened the boxes and, by stripping away some of the protective interior material, managed to get three in each box. That gave them only one box to carry apiece.

"It would be better to attack the tanks from the far side of the road," said Zeus. "We can move back a lot easier. But we need a launcher."

"Maybe we should not attack them," said Chaū. "We are so outnumbered."

Chaū's point was utterly logical, yet it caught Zeus by surprise. The only options he was even considering involved the location of the attack.

"What happened to your phone?" Chaū asked.

"I lost it in the water. We're not getting any help here anyway." Zeus pointed in the direction of the smoldering ruins. "Where is Angkor and the launcher?"

"We were right in front of the smaller house," said Chaū. "There was a ditch."

"All right. We'll come up from behind the houses."

Zeus led the way back toward the smoldering ruins. The air smelled like burning wood and dead fish.

The tanks had stopped, somewhere up to the right, out of sight around a bend. It was impossible to tell from the sound exactly how far away they were, though Zeus assumed they were very close.

"We have to watch for scouts," Zeus told Chaū. "They have infantry with them. Where's Angkor?"

"He was to meet me here."

"Angkor!" Zeus yelled. "Sergeant Angkor!"

He turned to Chaū.

"Can you call him?"

Chaū tried, but his voice was still far too hoarse.

"Give me the words," said Zeus.

"Just say his name."

Zeus tried again, but he got no answer.

"He must have moved to a safer spot when he heard the engines," said Zeus.

Passing the hovels, Zeus saw two bodies lying a short distance from it. He veered in their direction, dropping to one knee to stop next to them. Both men were covered with blood, their eyes glazed.

He wanted a gun. Neither man had one.

Back on his feet, he started after Chaū. Something moved on the other side of the road, a short distance from one of the blown-out tanks. It looked like a gust of wind, knocking through the tall weeds. Zeus eyed

it as he ran, mind and sight not entirely coordinating. Green materialized beneath the weeds as they popped up: Chinese soldiers, wearing
the equivalent of gillie suits.

One of them started firing. Zeus leapt the rest of the distance into a
ditch near the road, clutching his missile case to his chest like a gigantic
football. He twisted on his shoulder as he went in, spinning and landing sideways.

Chaū and Angkor were already there, about ten yards away. Angkor
fired a single burst, then another. The Chinese responded with a full
fusillade as Zeus scrambled over.

"How many?" he asked.

Chaū shook his head. The ditch was wide but shallow, with a foot
and a half of water at the bottom. It ran a few feet from the road, possibly to help drain it during heavy rains. Two wounded Vietnamese
soldiers sat against the side to the left. One looked as if he had already
died; the other didn't look too far behind.

Besides a single AT-14 launcher, they had Angkor's AK-47 and a box
of ammo—nowhere near enough to hold off the soldiers across from
them, let alone whatever vehicles were around the bend, waiting for
these guys to tell them what was up.

Zeus leaned against the side of the ditch, trying to gauge the distance from where it ended to the nearest tank. The vehicle was perhaps
ten yards from the shallow end.

"I have an idea," he told Chaū. "Start firing when I'm at the far end
of the ditch. Get their attention."

"What?" asked Chaū. But Zeus had already started away, leaving his
missiles. He scrambled until the ditch became too shallow, then crawled
on his side, making sure he didn't rise high enough to be seen. He
glanced back, and gave Chaū a thumbs-up.

Angkor began firing. Zeus waited until he heard the Chinese respond, then threw himself forward, sprinter style, from a four-point
stance. He ran behind the tank and sprawled on the ground, unsure
whether he'd been seen.

The gunfire died. Zeus curled himself as tightly as possible and scurried around to the second tank, reasoning that it would be harder for the
Chinese to see him there. He slunk around the side, then climbed gingerly up to the tank's turret, crouching by the side.

The hatchway was still locked though the front of the tank had been destroyed. He reached across for the machine gun, but couldn't quite reach it from behind the turret without exposing himself to fire.

One of the soldiers popped up in the field and took aim at Angkor and Chaū. Zeus boosted himself upward, grabbed the gun, and swung the barrel in the man's direction. He stabbed his finger at the trigger and fired. The gun jumped as the bullets flew from the barrel, flying high and wide from their intended targets. Zeus pulled himself up behind the machine gun, bracing his knees against the turret. He fired again, this time lacing the field where the soldiers were. Mud and bits of green and brown leaves flew into the air.

He let off the trigger, waiting for the soldiers to show themselves amid the thick grass and weeds.

Something moved about thirty yards ahead. Zeus swung the barrel over and began firing again. The stream of bullets seemed to just start when suddenly the gun snapped and the stream ended—he'd run out the belt.

He couldn't see another. He raised himself higher, looking for an ammo box.

Something flew from the area he'd been firing at.

A grenade.

Zeus dove forward between the two tanks as it sailed overhead. The grenade landed behind the third tank, which had stalled crosswise in the road. It didn't explode at first, and for that long second Zeus considered whether he should have tried to grab it and throw it back. Then there was a sharp boom and a flash, most of the explosion muffled by the tank.

As Zeus hunkered down, he glimpsed a boot a few yards away. One of the Chinese tankers had fallen there; a gun poked its nose out from under his body.

The gun was a small Chinese Type 79. Intended mostly for internal security forces, it was a 7.62 lightweight submachine gun occasionally used by tank crews as an emergency weapon. Its small box was full.

Another grenade sailed through the air. This one, too, overshot. Zeus pulled the submachine gun next to his chest and ran from the tanks into the field behind the Chinese soldiers. The grenade exploded as he ran. He counted to three, then belly flopped to the ground inelegantly but in time to avoid being seen.

He could hear the Chinese talking. They were between ten and fifteen yards away, to his left.

Throw another grenade, boys. Throw one.

They obliged. Zeus saw the soldier rise, then drop down immediately as it left his hand. Like most soldiers, he was inordinately fixed on the device's explosive power, and took no chances once he let it go.

Zeus figured he was ten yards away at most, and directly ahead of him.

As the grenade exploded, Zeus jumped up and began firing. Sweeping three quick bursts into the grass, he ran to the spot where the soldier had ducked down.

Someone moved. Zeus fired another burst, then went down as gunfire erupted on his left. He pulled his legs under him, curled on the ground, and waited.

He wasn't sure how many bullets he had left in the gun, but it couldn't be many.

Someone groaned a few feet away. It must be the grenade thrower, Zeus thought. He scanned through the weeds, not sure where the others were. He tried to quiet his breath, listening, but he could get no clue either from sound or sight.

Slowly, Zeus shifted his weight in the direction of the man he had gunned down. He leaned forward onto his elbows and knees, crawling in the man's direction.

The groans got louder. There was another—there were at least two men wounded here.

Farther back in the field, someone shouted something in Chinese. The moaning got louder, but there was no answer.

Zeus pushed through the weeds until he saw a dark-green blotch in front of him—one of the soldiers. The man was sprawled on the ground, eyes gaping. Zeus's bullets had caught him in the throat. He'd drowned in his own blood.

The soldier had a Type 95 assault rifle still in his hands. Zeus pried it from his fingers, then pulled two spare magazines from his belt. Stuffing the boxes into his pants, Zeus crawled away. He held the rifle in his left hand, the submachine gun in his right.

The groans were getting louder. But now there was a new sound: tanks again, engines revving.

Huddling against the wet weeds, Zeus crawled in the direction of the nearest moan. It was the grenade thrower, who'd been hit in the side of the face and arm. He lay on his back, blood seeping around him in a pool. He blinked his eyes when he saw Zeus.

Zeus crawled next to him. He couldn't see the man's rifle, but he had a sidearm in a holster. Zeus, covering him with the rifle, let go of the submachine gun and reached to the holster. He undid the catch and pulled out a small semiautomatic pistol.

The man tried to speak, but the only sound he could manage was a choking cough. There was a green canvas bag a few feet away. It looked almost like a shopping bag, bulging slightly with fruit.

There were three grenades inside.

There were several Chinese soldiers still alive nearby, scattered in the field, but Zeus wasn't exactly sure where, and without getting up and drawing their fire—a dubious proposition if they were close—he had no way of finding out. He decided to simply throw the grenades in a spread left to right.

Someone whispered in Chinese on his right. Zeus tried to guess at the words. Was the man calling to a comrade? Or was he talking to someone next to him?

The man whispered again, a little louder.

Zeus groaned in response. The whisperer said something else, a little more urgently.

Zeus didn't answer. The brush nearby rustled—the soldier was crawling toward him, assuming he was a fallen comrade. He was very close—only a few feet away.

The man's face poked through a clump of tall strands of grass. He wore small round glasses barely large enough to cover the whites of his eyes.

He had a pistol in his hand.

He tilted his head, puzzled when he saw Zeus.

Zeus pressed on the trigger of the submachine gun. It flew upward, his one hand not sufficient leverage against the blowback. Several bullets passed into his enemy's forehead.

Caught between surprise and understanding, the man seemed to hover in the air a moment before collapsing, dead.

Zeus dropped the submachine gun and the rifle, and grabbed a grenade. He pulled the pin—it was smoother than he thought—and threw it to his left, arcing it upward as if throwing a long pass downfield. He grabbed a second and did the same.

The pin on the third stuck. He pulled but it wouldn't budge. He tried again, then ducked as the first grenade exploded. Letting go of the grenade, he took hold of the rifle as the second exploded. He rose to his knee and doused the field with the entire contents of the magazine. His fingers fumbled over the unfamiliar weapon as he changed the box. Slamming it home after what seemed hours, he poured on the gunfire, once more running through the magazine.

There was no return fire.

Zeus rose tentatively, looking over the field. He stood, then turned slowly.

"Chaū!" he called.

"Down!" came a voice. It was Angkor's.

Zeus started to turn toward it, then realized what the warning meant: an armored vehicle was rounding the corner ahead on the left. It was a Type 77-2, a tracked armored personnel carrier.

A missile shot from the ditch where Angkor and Chaū were hiding. The front of the troop carrier vanished in a cloud of smoke and dust. Zeus stared at it, forgetting for a moment where he was, let alone understanding that the shrapnel from the hit could kill if it reached him. The vehicle slumped behind the cloud, smoke furling to either side. Finally Zeus remembered the danger, and pulled up the assault rifle, ready to shoot at the soldiers escaping. But there were none—the missile had penetrated the interior and detonated inside, obliterating the passengers.

A second vehicle appeared behind the first, to its right, moving up the shoulder of the road. Zeus retreated to his left, back into the field. He threw himself down as he heard the whiz of the missile leaving the trench. The AT-14 hit home before he reached the ground, crushing through the front of the carrier with an unworldly sound.

There were more vehicles behind them. Two troop trucks—Zeus could hear the engines revving as the vehicles went off the road, trying to avoid the broken APCs.

He'd thrown himself down near the body of one of the soldiers he'd killed earlier. An ammo box sat a few feet away.

It held bullets for a machine gun. Zeus couldn't see the weapon until he noticed a thick clump of grass about five feet away. The grass was camouflage, wrapped around the barrel and the main works.

He turned the weapon on its tripod, bringing it to bear on the troop trucks clearing the APCs. Situating a belt of bullets into the feed, he sighted and began firing. He was too low at first, then overcorrected, spewing bullets wildly around the field. Letting off the trigger, he pulled his body closer to the weapon and tried again. This time he was accurate enough to get a stream of slugs into the engine compartment of the lead truck. It continued a short ways, coasting on momentum until suddenly it stopped and began rolling backward down the slight incline it had climbed. By that time, Zeus had laced the rear of the truck with bullets and put a few into the cab of the second vehicle.

The belt ran through. Zeus fumbled with the cocking mechanism, trying to pull up the cover assembly to accept a new belt. The troops who'd been in the trucks were peppering the field with gunfire. A burst hit only a few inches away. Zeus left the gun and pushed himself face-first into the ground as bullets hit all around him.

Still under fire, he crawled next to the machine gun, reaching up and trying to reload it blind. Finally, he gingerly fit a round against the stop and got the cover down. But a fresh volley of bullets made him lurch backward.

An AT-14 spit from the ditch across the way. It slammed home into a vehicle Zeus couldn't see, though he heard the explosion.

The launch gave the Chinese soldiers a new target. As soon as Zeus realized he wasn't being fired at anymore, he pulled himself back to the machine gun. He laced the field, covering it with bullets.

Either one of the Chinese soldiers set off a smoke grenade for protection or one of the tracer rounds in the machine gun set fire to the grass. Smoke began rising from the Chinese position, a thick curtain of it.

Something moved at the far edge of the smoke on Zeus's right, near the bend in the road. Zeus aimed and began firing; within a few shots the machine gun choked, jammed. Reaching to clear it, he felt something slice against his neck, hot and sharp. The next thing he knew, he was on his back, bullets whizzing overhead.

He didn't realize he'd been shot until he felt something wet drip across his neck bone. He reached and touched it, then brought his hand close to his face. His fingers were black with dirt and the oil and grime from the gun. The blood was black as well, a strange shade of grim.

He put his fingers near his neck gingerly, then pulled them away as soon as he felt the sting.

I'm not really hurt, he told himself. *It's like sunburn.*

19

Beijing

Cho Lai could barely contain his anger as the report continued. The plan to sneak troops into Hai Phong harbor had been thwarted by a single American destroyer, which had outmaneuvered one of the best ships in the Chinese fleet and managed to call the Chinese bluff. Meanwhile, the assault down the eastern coast of Vietnam, designed to reach the harbor at the same time the ships did, had stalled because of the storm. They might not reach the city for days.

The premier rose from the briefing table. The general at the podium stopped talking in mid-sentence. Cho Lai glared at each man in turn.

"We have stalled because of incompetence and cowardice!" he thundered. "I will have a new commander!"

He turned to his defense minister.

"Get my nephew from the front."

"Colonel Sun is only a colonel," said Lo Gong softly. "If he were put in charge—"

"I have work to do," said Cho Lai. He waved his hand. "You are all dismissed. Leave!"

20

Inland from Halong Bay

A train rushed over Zeus, the undercarriage and all its connected pipes and wires whipping a few inches from his face. A jet followed, wheels an inch from his brow. The world stormed by, flashing its color and speed.

He smelled the earth, the water, the thick brown soil around him. He smelled the soldiers he'd shot, lying dead or dying nearby.

It's just sunburn, he told himself, reaching again for his wound.

Just sunburn. Get up.

Get up!

He turned slowly onto his elbow, pushing up and looking for his machine gun. Something grabbed him and threw him down, twisting him over.

It was Chaū.

"Major Murphy—stay down!" gasped Chaū, his voice even hoarser than before.

"Okay," Zeus muttered.

Angkor was nearby, rifling through the bodies of the Chinese for ammo. He yelled something to Chaū, who rose, then lobbed a grenade.

It didn't explode. There was a hissing sound instead.

Smoke.

"Come on!" barked Chaū in his hoarse voice. He grabbed at Zeus and started pulling him. "Stay low."

Fresh automatic rifle fire filled the air. But it was off the mark, closer to the road and the ditch. They were moving to the west, toward a line of trees.

"When we make the jungle, we can rest," said Chaū.

"Okay," said Zeus, pumping his legs as his strength returned.

———

"Major, are you with us?" asked Chaū.

Zeus, resting against a tree, looked up. "Yeah."

"Your neck is bleeding."

Chaū bent over and pulled the collar of Zeus's uniform away. The wound had already scabbed, the blood coagulating with the cloth, and it stung.

"Ah—it's okay, stop," said Zeus.

"Sorry."

"Is the bullet in there?" asked Zeus.

Chaū leaned close. "I don't think so. It's all red."

Another close call. Sooner or later, his luck was going to run out.

Angkor had a small first-aid kit in one of his pants pockets. They took a large gauze bandage that came packed with ointment and taped it to Zeus's neck. The collar pulled some skin with it as they got the bandage in place. Blood trickled from the wound.

"I'll be all right," said Zeus.

"What should we do now?" asked Chaū.

"Where are the Chinese?"

"Back in the field. They are firing at the house. They think we are still there. Over a hundred men," added Chaū. "We destroyed three APCs, killed many."

"All right. We should get out of here."

Zeus rubbed his face, then reached into his pocket for his map. It was sodden. He unfolded it, examining the roads, trying to remember where exactly they were.

"There should be a village in that direction about two miles," said Zeus, pointing due west. "If we can get there, this road looks like it will take us to the road General Tri's tanks were using to get south. You see?"

He showed Chaū the map.

"We have three more missiles," said Chaū. "Should we make another attack?"

"They'll trap us in these woods if we make the attack from here," said Zeus, pulling himself to his feet. "They'll get south of us on the road and come around. We'll be trapped."

Chaū looked disappointed.

"The best thing to do, is wait a little while," said Zeus. "But not here. I think we can swing a little more to the north, cross the stream, and keep going until we're north of the hamlet we were going to hit. We'll attack them there. If we can take them by surprise, hit a few vehicles, and then run west, they'll never catch us. We may even be able to hook up with the others."

"Yes," said Chaū. "It is a good plan."

———

They walked for over an hour, Zeus in the lead with the map. He had the Chinese assault rifle and several magazines that Angkor had pilfered from the dead. Chaū was next in line, carrying a Chinese gun he, too, had found, along with the box of missiles. Angkor had the rear, hauling the launcher as well as a pair of rifles and a bag of extra ammo.

The day turned more humid with the sun. While the jungle kept them in shade, between the humidity and the insects Zeus felt as if he were being pelted and pulled with every step he took. The thick vegetation snapped at him, petty lashes to add to the persecution.

A hollow hunger bit at his stomach. At times his eyes drooped toward the bottom of their sockets, his fatigue welling up.

To keep himself going, he thought of Anna. And yet thinking of Anna made things even more difficult. She was a prisoner.

"The water ahead must be deep," said Chaū as they walked toward the creek. "I can hear it."

"Yeah," muttered Zeus.

The stream had overflowed its banks. It rushed through the jungle, flooding a good eight or ten feet up into the trees on either side. Zeus paused when he reached the edge. The water's path was wide but not particularly deep.

"Should we cross?" asked Chaū. His voice had recovered to the point that he could speak normally without too much strain.

"I wonder if we could float down the stream," said Zeus. "We could hit them at the bridge instead of the hamlet."

"What?" asked Chaū.

"If we lashed a few logs together, and just kind of floated down, you think it would work?"

"What would we use?"

"Just logs, and we could make some rope from the grass. They wouldn't expect us to come down the stream."

Chaū said nothing. It was an outrageously impractical plan—a dream, really. Zeus was losing his mind.

"There are some rocks here," said Zeus, wading into the water. "We'll get to the other side and move down."

The water was only a foot deep, except in the middle, where it quickly dropped another two feet. But they were able to scramble across without their weapons getting wet.

Building a log raft à la Tom Sawyer and Huck Finn—no way. But a canoe was perfect.

"Look at that!" said Zeus, shouting as he spotted the boat pushed against a pair of trees upstream.

It was a wooden boat, slightly battered and small, but perfect.

A dream, even. But it was real.

They loaded the missiles and launcher inside. Both of the long oars were missing, but it was easy to tug it along downstream. Chaū, the lightest, sat inside, while Zeus and Angkor pulled it along. Snakes slithered by, and once Zeus swore he saw the eyes of a crocodile.

Swarms of flies buzzed around them. Every so often Zeus had to let go of the boat to swat at them. The only thing that really worked was to dip under the water to get away, and even that provided only a temporary respite.

"Bitchin' flies," he said to Chaū.

"Maybe they are Chinese."

Angkor said something.

"We are getting close," Chaū told Zeus. "Listen."

They stopped. Zeus held his breath, but heard nothing. Then through the jungle came a familiar hum on the breeze.

Motors. Tanks or APCS.

"We're getting very close," he said.

––––––

Ten minutes later, they were close enough to feel the vibration of the motors in the air. They were about two miles farther north of the spot where they'd fought earlier in the day—much closer than Zeus had reckoned from the map.

A long highway bridge spanned the swamp. Peering from the trees at the bankside, Zeus could make out a quartet of trusses arching above the swollen water below the roadway. There were perhaps a dozen vehicles on the south side of the bridge—and what looked like an endless armada on the north.

"We can have our pick," said Chaū, standing next to him.

"I have a better idea," said Zeus. "Let's take out the bridge."

21

American embassy, Hanoi

Among the great difficulties for an American seeking to help Vietnamese were the ironies involved. Harland Perry was surrounded by them.

Trying to rally the populace against the Chinese, the state media had begun a series of interviews with common citizens who had survived the war with the United States. The interviews were interspersed with old news footage from the war. Among the images that particularly bothered Perry were those showing American prisoners of war being marched through Hanoi and other Vietnamese cities.

History could easily repeat itself now in Beijing.

What would history say of his role? It wouldn't know much about it, especially if the war escalated. Someone else would be in charge.

He had more pressing concerns.

"Sorry to keep you waiting, Harland," said Melanie Behrens, appearing at the door. "I had to talk to our consul in Saigon. Are you ready to go?"

Perry nodded at the ambassador. She glanced across the thick-paneled room where he'd been sitting.

"You're not watching that propaganda, are you?" she asked, nodding at the television.

"Thought it might raise my spirits," he said sardonically, following her out.

22

Inland from Halong Bay

Zeus slipped along in the water, half-swimming, half-walking, pulling the missile box along with him as he scuttled toward the bridge.

When he'd set out, he'd thought the north side would be the safest to use as an approach. But as he got closer to the bridge, he saw that the Chinese had troops on the south side patrolling near the bank. Thankfully the long shadows of the sun covered his side of the water. Still, he had to move carefully, half-holding his breath. He had no gun; it would have been ruined in the water.

Angkor and Chaū were upstream, watching. If he was caught, they were to fire the missile at the center support, hopefully hitting and exploding it.

That was a long shot, and not just because it would take a steady hand to keep the targeting beam on the support. There were several supports around the beam, and blowing that one strut up probably wouldn't take the roadway down.

Zeus had come up with an alternate plan—he'd arrange the two remaining warheads like an IED on the top spar at the center. They'd strike them with the third missile.

That was a long shot as well. But he'd seen the Iraqis do that at least twice on one of his training tapes. So he knew it could be done.

The Chinese were moving their forces very slowly, mustering on both side of the water. It wasn't clear why, whether it was just their normal caution, or if the road farther south was submerged. It might also be that the firefight had given them enough of a bloody nose that they were now going to be extra cautious.

An APC sat in the water about fifty yards from the bridge. It was a Type 77, similar to the ones they had battled before. It was supposed to be amphibious, but it had bogged down in the thick muck.

The vehicles he could see on the shore to his left were more modern—wheeled WZ 523s—M1984s as far as the U.S. Army was concerned. There were a lot of them on the northern side of the bridge, perhaps an entire regiment.

Zeus slipped around the abandoned APC. The side door was open. He was tempted to stick his head inside, look, and see if anyone had forgotten their weapon in the rush to get out. But that was unlikely, and there was no sense besides: he couldn't carry a rifle easily without getting it wet.

Tugging the case behind him, Zeus stopped as he spotted a trio of soldiers standing beneath the northern side of the bridge. His throat tightened—it would be impossible to get to the bridge if they stayed there.

But they weren't standing guard. They were relieving themselves in the water. One after the other they finished, zipping up and walking to the embankment. One stopped, scooped up a rock, and spun it back across the water. It hopped three times across the ten yards or so, then sank near the other side.

The others laughed.

Zeus took a deep breath. Stooping down so the water came to his neck, he began walking toward the middle of the stream, trying to drift gently and not splash. The water was not very deep even in the middle; if he'd stood it would barely come to his chest. He held the case under his arm, fighting against its buoyancy.

A truck started across the span. Zeus pushed faster, finally reaching the shadows next to the stanchion as the vehicle passed directly overhead.

Zeus pulled the missile box up and opened it. He dipped water inside and let it settle down, holding it against the current. Then he took the missiles out, one at a time, placing them on the cement pier the girder rose from. Climbing up onto the curved archway, Zeus examined the strutwork to find his target.

From the distance, the idea had been easy: he would tie the warheads against the steel X where the upright met the arch; the explosion would topple the bridge. But up close it didn't look anywhere near as easy. The steel was thick, and while the shaped projectile would undoubtedly go through it, Zeus wasn't sure that it could both penetrate the steel and explode the warheads at the same time.

He'd have to be a goddamn engineer to figure it out.

So why the hell had the Iraqis succeeded when he couldn't?

Or rather, what exactly had they done?

A swell of despair clamped over him. Paralyzed, Zeus stared hopelessly at the struts, unable to move. Fatigue, hunger, and exhaustion were his real problems, but explaining his paralysis could not erase it, and understanding it was no help in dealing with it at all. Zeus hung under the bridge, his body vibrating with the rumble of one of the heavy APCs passing above. All his courage and strength were negated in that moment; he was a black hole, empty of everything, even fear, just a collection of frayed nerves and taut muscles clinging to the underside of a highway far from home.

Then, in the pit of his mind, a single thought rose up:

Anna.

It was not love that brought him back to himself. It wasn't his concern for her, or even his need to save her. It wasn't even his lust for the softness of her body against his.

Anger broke his paralysis. Rage at the injustice of her persecution.

It was a ferocious anger, a madness—*truly* an insanity, a righteous rising up against the cruel, cruel injustice of a world that would harm a woman who tried to save others. And while logic might have directed that anger more properly toward the Vietnamese, in Zeus the emotion focused on the Chinese, Evil's agent in the war.

The rage that had driven Zeus at different points over the past several days, the blind craziness that even he mistook for courage, merged with the deepest parts of his soul. It became something he could control, something that would allow him to do what had to be done, to act with the logic and directness of a warrior.

Zeus pulled off his belt and slipped the missiles against the beam. He tied the belt as tightly as he could, then started to slip into the water. As he stepped down, a vehicle came onto the roadway and stopped almost directly above him. The bridge vibrated with its motor.

Zeus stopped, concerned that the warheads might slip from his knot. He glanced upward, trying to get a glimpse to make sure they weren't coming loose.

A soldier began to shout. Zeus barely heard his yell over the engine, but the gunshot that followed was loud and clear.

23

Washington, D.C.

The tall bastard with the pockmarked face pushed him down against the floor of the prison cell. Greene gasped for air—he couldn't breathe. Hands grabbed him—dozens of hands, gripping tightly against his arms and legs and side. Someone hit his genitals and he felt a pain rise in the pit of his stomach. Tears were streaming from his eyes, and he was ashamed. . . .

———

President Greene lurched upright in his bed. He knew was just a dream, but for a moment he was confused, lost. Was he home? Why was he alone?

He was in the White House. His wife was gone, visiting relatives.

He was in the White House. *Home.*

The dream was somewhat familiar, a not-quite accurate replay of some of his experiences as a guest of the North Vietnamese government. They *had* beaten the hell out of him, and the tall bastard was a real guard, and a genuine tormenter.

Not that the session had taken place the way he saw it in the dream. And many of the details were off. In the dream, for instance, the cell was spacious and well lit. It had been the opposite in real life.

Am I doing the right thing helping the bastards now?

Yes. Unfortunately. China had to be dealt with.

The bigger question was: *What should he do next?* The Russian weapons would help, but clearly they weren't going to be enough. How far was he willing to go? Already some would say he was breaking the law, or at least its spirit.

Greene glanced over at the clock on his sideboard. It was a little past two.

Too early to get up, even for him.

He slipped back beneath the covers, thinking of how much he missed his wife.

24

Inland from Halong Bay

Zeus turned toward the sound of the bullets. They were striking the water just to the side of the highway.

They couldn't be firing at him. But what?

The vehicle above him started moving again. There were shouts, but the sound of the APC drowned them out. He considered dropping into the water and making a run for it, but decided it was wiser to climb up higher against the bridge and see what happened.

Worst case, Chaū would fire at the beam. He'd be dead either way.

There was more gunfire. The vehicle reached the south side of the roadway. There were shouts—three or four different voices. Zeus saw a pair of legs coming into the water on his left, then another.

The men shouted and pointed. Zeus leaned over, watching as they grabbed the missile case from the water.

The men shouted something in Chinese.

Zeus waited in the shadow of the bridge. He didn't dare move, didn't dare look.

If they come for me, Chaū will kill them all anyway.

An eternity and an instant passed. Finally, Zeus heard the sound of another vehicle starting across. The bridge began to vibrate heavily.

Slowly, he leaned out from behind his perch. The men had moved on.

———

Zeus ran the entire way back, hugging the shadows, trying not to slip or splash in the water as he pushed through the flooded brush. With every step, he thought to himself that now was the moment that Chaū and Angkor would fire.

With his first steps, he felt relief. But as he continued, disappointment crept in, and finally concern: Why hadn't they fired?

Chaū stepped from the brush as Zeus approached.

"Major Murphy?"

"Sight on the middle post," said Zeus, running to them. "The warheads are behind it. Fire! Fire!"

Zeus ran to them, dropping to his knee in a soggy slide. The Chinese were streaming across the bridge in a thick convoy, APCs lined up bumper to bumper.

Angkor moved back to let Zeus look through the eyepiece. He pushed his face against the rubber, saw that the aim was a little low.

"Chaū, explain where I put the warheads," said Zeus. "He has to hit right there."

Chaū said something to Angkor. The sergeant replied in Vietnamese, gesturing with his hands. Zeus immediately understood.

"He says that the missile rides slightly higher than the beam," said Chaū.

"As long as he understands. Tell him to fire." Zeus stepped back. "Tell him to fire. He's got one shot. Get them now!"

Angkor knelt in front of the launcher. Zeus rose, not caring if the enemy saw him. There was a click and a swoosh, air rushing away; the missile faltered, nudging left, then corrected itself, pushing back at the beam.

It flashed through. Zeus saw a bolt of lightning—a white sheet rustled under the bridge. The roadway seemed to rise, as if lifting itself away from the missile. But the weight of the carriers pushed it back down into place.

A black and gray cloud of steam and smoke erupted from the water. The bridge caved into it, the APCs sliding downward like so many toy trucks kicked by a malevolent three-year-old. They rolled and twisted and fell on their tops as the entire bridge collapsed, and the sole road to the south held by the Chinese was destroyed, their path to conquest temporarily blocked.

25

Quàng Ninh Province

Zeus and the others moved silently after the bridge collapsed, abandoning the launcher and trotting upstream. Their boots splashed in the muck. Zeus felt his side strain and his groin starting to pull but kept on. Every so often he felt the heavy, now sodden bandage at his neck. It surprised him—he'd almost forgotten he had been shot there.

Grazed. A talisman of luck rather than a wound.

Gradually, their pace slowed to a jog, then a walk. The Chinese began scrambling behind them, but the initial confusion as well as the thick foliage made pursuit difficult. With no roads to follow, the Chinese soldiers had to move through the jungle, and had to suspect an ambush at every moment. They fell farther and farther behind.

"It will be dark soon," said Chaū, after they'd been walking for more than an hour. It was first time any of them spoke.

"Yes," replied Zeus.

"We should find a place to cross the water."

"We will."

The stream had narrowed, but it had also deepened. They walked for another half hour, moving northward until they found a series of rocks that were easy to scramble across.

Zeus led the way.

"Maybe we should take a rest," said Chaū on the other side.

"If we stop, we may not be able to get up," said Zeus.

But the look on Major Chaū's face showed they had to rest. They found a clearing a few yards away from the water—a small space between the trees, barely big enough for the three of them to sit.

"Here," said Zeus, sliding down against one of the trees.

They looked at each other: Angkor, Chaū, Zeus.

"We did it," Zeus told them.

Angkor said something. Chaū translated: *Have we beaten them?*

"For today," answered Zeus. "Tomorrow we will do something else."

———

Zeus gave them exactly fifteen minutes, then pulled himself to his feet. Every part of his body was stiff, tired, exhausted, but if he didn't move now they would end up staying the night, and even if it didn't seem as if the Chinese were following them, he couldn't take that chance. The more ground they got between them and the force they had just thwarted, the better.

Blowing up the bridge would stymie the Chinese, stalling whatever they had planned. Eventually, though, they would figure out a way around it. Their APCs would be able to ford the marsh eventually, or they might even bring in bridging equipment. At best, the Vietnamese had gained two or three days, largely because the Chinese were extremely cautious. An American commander would surely have found a way to push the APCs and tanks through the mud, and even risked stringing his forces out, realizing the attacks Zeus had engineered were pebbles from a slingshot against a vast armada.

That was the way the Americans had dealt with the Iraqis in the Second Gulf War: as annoying as the antitank attacks were, ultimately they were no match for the juggernaut of the American forces surging toward Baghdad.

Would that be the Vietnamese fate as well?

Zeus wasn't sure. But he had already decided on what their next move should be.

And what he, too, would do.

———

The sun had already set by the time they came across a winding dirt trail that cut southward. By now it was too dark to use the map for reference. Zeus guessed that the trail was too obscure for it to be marked in any event, but the direction was right. It seemed obvious that they should follow it.

The path intersected with a slightly larger trail, this one occasionally used by vehicles, if the muddy ruts were any indication. They walked along it, moving to the southwest and then west, climbing along a ridge that shadowed the larger mountains to the west. The trail ducked in and out of the jungle; for most stretches there was more than enough light to see by, although the shadows were so deep that Zeus had to feel the brush with his hands to guide them.

They walked for another hour and a half before coming to a *Y*. There they went to the right, treading past a confused intersection of ruts and trails. Finally, they found a road heading due south and took it.

A few minutes later, Chaū stopped and held up his hand.

A truck was coming.

"Send Sergeant Angkor down the road," Zeus said. "We'll hide on the side as it passes. If it's Vietnamese, yell to him and he can jump out and stop it."

Chaū explained. Angkor started to run.

There wasn't enough time to get very far. Zeus and Chaū stepped off the road, waiting as the truck came up.

Zeus had no idea what he would do if it was a Chinese scout, looking for an alternative route south. Run into the jungle and hide? Fire at the truck, kill the driver, take it?

The latter, surely, though he felt too exhausted to even stand straight.

Fortunately, a decision wasn't necessary. It was a Vietnamese patrol, crammed into a commandeered pickup, scouting the advance of General Tri's armored brigade as it moved south.

Within a half hour of stopping the truck, Zeus and the others were en route to Hanoi.

26

Beijing

As was his habit, Cho Lai missed the opening curtain at the Huguang Guild Hall in Beijing, settling into his seat a few minutes after the opera had begun. There was a rustling in the audience; the performer on stage turned to the premier's box and bowed. Cho Lai rose, accepting the applause of the audience, then gestured for the show to continue.

The applause seemed genuine, at least. The people still appreciated his leadership.

He settled back to watch. The opera was a new interpretation of the *Qing Ding Pearl*, a classic that dated to the Song Dynasty. This was China at its best—the old traditions preserved, yet updated tastefully. It was proof, Cho Lai thought, that the country was moving forward beyond the chains of foreign interference and into the future.

The villains of the play were corrupt officials. As the reviews had noted, one could interpret them as the men Cho Lai had ousted to gain his position.

The premier was just starting to appreciate the lead actor's strong voice when an aide tapped at his shoulder. Cho Lai sighed, then rose.

He was surprised to see Lo Gong himself in the small antechamber behind the seats.

"The offensive in the east has stalled," said the defense minister. "Hai Phong cannot be reached."

Cho Lai had known this would happen and had prepared himself. He closed his eyes and nodded.

"We are ready to resume the attack in the west," said Lo Gong quickly. "Your nephew will be placed in charge, as you wish. He has been promoted."

"General Sun will do a good job," said Cho Lai calmly.

Lo Gong glanced at the door.

"What is it?" said Cho Lai.

"The intelligence services have been speaking with a source in North Korea," said the defense minister. "We believe the Vietnamese have obtained a serious weapon. More dangerous than we believed."

"How dangerous?" said the premier.

"It should not be discussed here," said Lo Gong.

Cho Lai was about to order him to talk, but Lo Gong's plaintive expression made it clear he shouldn't.

"Meet me in the war room," Cho Lai told him. "I will be there within the hour."

27

CIA headquarters, Virginia

"*Five minutes*," Mara told Lucas. "That's all I need."

"Five minutes," said Lucas. "And no haranguing me about getting back in the field. I'm busy as hell this morning."

"Peter, this is important."

"All right," he said reluctantly. "But five minutes is all I got."

Mara closed the door behind her.

"You have a map of Vietnam?"

"Not detailed."

"Doesn't have to be."

Lucas dug through his papers. He had to be one of the most unorganized station chiefs—make that *area* chiefs—she knew. Without someone like Gina DiMarco—a cryptography clerk who doubled as his administrative assistant and general gal Friday—he was lost.

"Your BlackBerry," she said, finding it under the pile. "Aren't you supposed to leave that downstairs?"

"Mine's cleared," Lucas told her.

Damn! She'd forgotten to check her messages. Josh must have called by now.

Had he?

"Will this do?" Lucas asked, pulling out one of the military sit maps.

"As long as it has the Yen Tu Mountains," said Mara.

"The no-fly zone? Is that what this is about?"

"Partly. You know what's going on there?"

"The pagoda and the mines."

"No."

"No?"

Mara sat down. "North Korea," she said.

"What North Korea?"

"Two years ago, the Vietnamese bought twenty old MiGs from North Korea."

"And?"

"Why would the Vietnamese buy old MiGs?"

"Mara, I really only have a few minutes."

"There's a series of sat photos in my share queue," she said. "Can you access them?"

Peter swung his chair around and faced his computer. It took him a while, but eventually he navigated to a secure folder set up so Mara could share items with selected people. She had already set it to allow Peter to open the photos.

"They're working the mines," he said.

"Go all the way through."

Lucas went through the sequence slowly. They showed an old-fashioned mining area, one where miners took a small train down under the ground, being widened into a strip mine. Then the work stopped for two months. At the end of the sequence, the mine entrance had been closed.

"I'm missing this," said Lucas.

"They closed the mine up at night," said Mara. "In one night. I checked the sequences."

"Help me out here."

"They were working on it all along at night, after the satellite passed. They're hiding something big there. I don't think the Koreans sold them old MiGs. I think they sold them missiles."

"Missiles?"

"And more. Nuclear waste from their reactors."

"Well, we know that—"

"Doc File 2," said Mara impatiently. "Look at that. It's a design for a sub-nuclear bomb. A kind of dirty neutron weapon. I think they have a bunch of them. And I think they're getting ready to use them. Go back to that last image; the mine has been reopened."

28

The White House

President Greene had just picked up the phone to call over to the kitchen for a morning snack when his chief of staff knocked on the door to the Oval Office.

"We need to talk to you," said Dickson Theodore, poking his head in.

"Who we?" said Greene, trying to make a joke of it.

Theodore pushed in. Linda Holmes, his legislative coordinator, came in behind him. Both had serious expressions. Holmes, in fact, looked as if someone in her family had just died.

"We need to look at C-SPAN," said Theodore, walking toward the TV.

"Here," said Greene, picking up the remote control from the edge of his desk.

The television snapped on. C-SPAN was broadcasting from the House floor. Thurman Goodwell, a first-year congressman from New Jersey, was making a speech.

"And I tell you solemnly, and with the utmost sincerity, that I have absolute proof, absolute proof of what I am saying." Goodwell was a short man—no more than five-four. He was young, too—no more than thirty. Greene thought he looked like a child dressed up as a congressman. "I have absolute proof that American troops are fighting and dying in Vietnam."

"Shit," muttered Theodore.

Holmes's face was white.

"I am asking this house, this body, this duly elected body of repre-sentatives, to conduct a hearing, to start an immediate investigation into this and other illegalities," continued Goodwell. "An investigation that will lead, inextricably, to the impeachment of President George Chester Greene."

"Motherfucker," said Theodore.

"You can say that again," snapped Greene, flipping off the TV.

29

American embassy, Hanoi

Zeus ran his hand over the stubble on his chin, tracing the boundary of the wound across his neck. The nurse who cleaned it was so appalled by the dirt and ooze that she had wanted to put him out, fearful of the pain. But Zeus thought an anesthetic would put him out for weeks, not hours, and that was simply too much time to lose.

The cloth and gauze she daubed so lightly against his skin felt like an ax at first. Now, though, it felt slightly warm and even pleasant, as if it were a hot rag a barber applied after a close, bracing shave.

"Major Murphy, I was looking for you."

Zeus rose as Juliet Greig came into the room. She looked prettier than he remembered, but a little shorter, too. She walked over to the desk where Zeus was being treated.

"I've been looking into that matter you asked about," Greig told him. Her voice had a distinctly businesslike tone—the sort of voice someone would use if they thought they were being monitored.

The nurse left. But Greig remained uncomfortable, stiffer than she had been the other day. Much more formal.

Was he being watched? Is that why they'd taken him to the office rather than some other room? Why hadn't Perry come down to see him yet?

Their eyes met. Greig held his glance for a long moment before let-ting her gaze fall to the floor.

"We're not in a position to do anything about your request," said Greig.

"You know where she is?" Zeus asked.

Greig shook her head slightly.

"Is she in Hanoi?"

"It's an internal matter."

Greig raised her head. Zeus looked into her face, trying to understand what else it was that she was saying. Because she *was* saying something else.

"There's nothing we can do?" Zeus asked.

"Nothing."

As Greig turned, her hand brushed into the stack of white steno pads that had been stacked on the corner of the desk. Flustered, she bent and scooped them up, then walked briskly from the room.

Zeus watched her silently, perplexed by their exchange. He got up and began pacing, flexing his tired muscles.

She'd left a piece of paper between the steno books. It was barely visible, poking out from the edge.

Zeus paced some more. There must be a video camera that he wasn't aware of.

So now his own people were spying on him. But maybe they always had.

He went behind the desk and sat down. As idly as he could, he pretended to play with the notebooks, then let them slip to the floor. When he scooped them up, he grabbed the paper as nonchalantly as he could, putting it into his pocket.

"Zeus."

He looked up and saw General Perry, standing in the doorway.

"General."

"Follow me, Major."

Zeus trailed the general as he led him upstairs to the ambassador's office. It was empty. Perry sat behind Behrens's desk.

"I've arranged for your flight home," said Perry. "Your mission here is complete."

"Sir?"

"You've done more than enough," said Perry.

"General—"

Perry shook his head. "The Vietnamese are very appreciative. You've accomplished far more than anyone could have hoped, or even wished for. You were almost killed, or worse, captured. Several times. Your mission is complete."

"General, I did nothing wrong."

Perry stared at him. "Were you ordered to help the Vietnamese use the weapons?"

"I wasn't ordered not to."

Perry scowled, shaking his head ever so slightly before continuing.

"I'm sure it will all come out very agreeably for you, Major," he said. "Now get yourself ready to go home. A car will take you back to your hotel. I'll call you once I have the arrangements for your return."

"I lost my sat phone, sir."

"We'll get a new one over to you."

Zeus saw no point in arguing. He left the room and walked to the stairway, descending slowly.

In the car, he reached into his pocket and pulled out the crumpled note Greig had left.

Cao Dien Army prison

That was where Anna must be. Greig was telling him she couldn't help. Maybe no one could.

No. One person could. And he owed Zeus.

He definitely owed him.

―――――

General Perry sat in the ambassador's chair for several minutes after Zeus left. He'd been utterly unfair to the young man.

True, he was acting in not only the country's best interests, but in Zeus's as well. Yet that was hardly a consolation. There was something about being unfair that bothered Perry on a very basic level. It was a transgression that could not be entirely expunged by the fact that he was simply doing his duty.

And yet he was doing his duty. The U.S. absolutely must not get any more deeply involved in the war.

Greene's policy was taking them there. Inevitably. Inextricably.

And Zeus was helping. It was a miracle he hadn't been killed. Given enough time, he surely would be.

Harland Perry couldn't be responsible for that. More important, he couldn't be responsible for any more Americans getting killed here. What had happened to Christian was already bad enough.

It was wrong, and it was unjust. The country could not be allowed to drag itself piecemeal into this war. If they weren't going to fight it right, there was no sense fighting at all. It was the wrong war at the wrong time in the wrong place.

There was only one honorable thing for Harland Perry to do.

The general picked up the phone.

"I need to talk to the White House," he said. "To the President. It's urgent, and it's personal."

———

When he reached the hotel, Zeus went up to his room. Unsure whether or not he was being followed—he guessed that Perry might have someone watching—he went and started a shower. Then he took out his shaving kit.

"No damn shaving cream," he said aloud, just in case the room had been bugged.

He pulled a shirt and his boots back on. The clothes Chaū had gotten him when they got back—Vietnamese army pants and a civilian sweatshirt—were a little loose, but the shoes were nearly two sizes too small now that his feet had swollen up.

He stuffed his toes inside anyway.

Zeus took one of the towels with him, wrapped over his shoulder.

"I wonder if you have any shaving cream," he asked the desk clerk downstairs.

The man ducked inside the office, and for a moment Zeus worried that he would need to use his backup plan. But the man quickly returned.

"No. Very sorry. No shave. Very, very sorry."

"It's okay," Zeus told him. "I think I know where I can get some." He took off his towel. "Can I just leave this here?"

Outside, Zeus walked to the street and turned the corner. He was going to go to the next hotel and take a cab there, but saw a vehicle approaching from the opposite direction and raised his hand. The driver immediately stopped.

"I need you to take me to a special place," Zeus said after getting in. He dropped five American twenty-dollar bills on the front seat. "You won't get in trouble. But you have to keep your mouth shut. You will tell no one."

"Where?" said the man, reaching for the money.

———

The guards knew who Zeus was and what he had done, and that made it all considerably easier. Still, he expected it would be more difficult than it proved to get to see Trung. Instead of being questioned about what he wanted, or even made to wait, he was shown immediately to his office.

"It is an honor to congratulate you personally for your service," said Trung, bowing his head as Zeus came into his small office. "The Vietnamese people are deeply grateful."

"You're welcome," said Zeus.

"You have heard of our plans?" asked Trung.

"I—"

"I have accepted your proposal for a counterstrike," said Trung. "We are gathering our forces now."

Caught off guard, Zeus could only nod.

"I have decided to lead the battle myself," said Trung. "We lack only one thing: a tactician to assist in the strategy."

"You want me to help," said Zeus.

"It would be most agreeable."

"I will. On one condition."

Trung's face remained emotionless.

"There is a woman, a doctor who treated me a few days ago, when I was brought back to Hanoi from behind the enemy lines. She's been arrested on false charges of treason. You will release her, and then I will help you."

Trung said nothing.

"Her name is Anna Anway," said Zeus. "She's in Cao Dien Army prison."

General Trung remained silent, an unmoving stone.

"You'll also probably have to convince my commander. General Perry has ordered me to return home."

Zeus looked into Trung's eyes. The two men locked stares.

"It will be done," said Trung finally. "Major Chaū will see to your needs."

An explosive new military thriller from
New York Times bestselling author

LARRY BOND
EXIT PLAN

Embark with aviator turned submariner Jerry Mitchell.

Jerry Mitchell is on exercises off the coast of Pakistan when his submarine is ordered to a rendezvous off the Iranian coast. Once there, disembarked SEALs, experts in seaborne commando operations, are to extract two Iranian nationals who have sensitive information on Iran's nuclear weapons program.

But while en route, the minisub suffers a battery fire, forcing the survivors to scuttle their disabled craft and swim for shore. There they find the two Iranians waiting for them, and their attempts at returning to the sub are thwarted by heavy Iranian patrol boat activity. And when they find themselves surrounded by Iranian Revolutionary Guard Corps troops, they create a bold plan to escape by sea. It's a desperate gamble, but it's the only way to get the proof of the Iranian plot to the United States...and prevent a devastating new war.

"Fans of military thrillers, especially those by Clancy and his ilk, should devour this one."
—*Booklist* on *Cold Choices*

"A superb storyteller."
—*Publishers Weekly*
on *Dangerous Ground*

In hardcover and eBook

tor-forge.com